Spindrift

Tamara McKinley was born in Tasmania, but now lives in Sussex and writes full time. She also writes *Sunday Times* top-ten bestselling novels under the name Ellie Dean.

Also by Tamara McKinley

Echoes From Afar
Savannah Winds
Ocean Child
Firestorm
Matilda's Last Waltz
Jacaranda Vines
Windflowers
Summer Lightning
Dreamscapes

Tamara
McKinley

Spindrift

Quercus

First published in Great Britain in 2017

This edition published in 2017 by

Quercus Editions Ltd
Carmelite House
50 Victoria Embankment
London EC4Y 0DZ

An Hachette UK company

A CIP catalogue record for this book is available
from the British Library

PB ISBN 978 1 78648 000 2
EBOOK ISBN 978 1 78429 263 8

10 9 8 7 6 5 4 3 2 1

Typeset by Jouve (UK), Milton Keynes

Printed and bound in Great Britain by Clays Ltd, St Ives plc

Cover design by Debbie Clement

AUTHOR NOTE

The Isle of Skye – *an t-Eilean Sgiathanach* in Gaelic – takes its name from the Old Norse, *sky-a*, meaning 'cloud island', a Viking reference to the mist-enshrouded Cuillin Hills that dominate the island. *Spindrift* is my dedication to the crofters whose lives were devastated by the potato famine, and who then faced eviction and an uncertain future through the Highland clearances – *Fuadach nan Gaidheal* – the eviction of the Gael, which took place during the eighteenth and nineteenth centuries. But for the crumbling remains of the crofts and a few well-preserved field walls, there are scant reminders of what happened, but in the still of a Highland day, when the clouds veil the Cuillin Hills and deserted glens, the atmosphere tells its own story.

Please note that the settlements of MacInnes Bay and Gilleasbuig do not exist, but I have used real instances of what happened during the clearances on the island.

The sheltered harbour in the Tamar estuary of Tasmania was

named Port Dalrymple in 1798, and in 1804 George Town was settled on the port. A year later, Paterson founded another settlement further upstream, which he called Patersonia – it was renamed Launceston in 1907 in honour of Governor Philip King, who came from Launceston in Cornwall, England.

PROLOGUE

Bellerive, Tasmania

It was almost the last day of 1904, and Christy was sitting in her late husband's favourite chair by the French windows, which gave her a view of Storm Bay and the Tasman Peninsula. The summer heat was tempered by a cool breeze coming off the water that carried the scent of eucalyptus and pine into the room, and although she was usually soothed by the sound of the bellbirds chiming in the nearby trees and the panorama before her, she was rigid with tension as she awaited her family's reaction to her announcement.

Family gatherings were rare now her children were scattered across Australia, but they'd come to Hobart to attend their father's funeral, which had been held two weeks before. As they were due to leave the following day, Christy had organised the special luncheon to lighten the mood and celebrate her granddaughter's acceptance into Sydney University to study history. Christy was inordinately proud of Kathryn, for it was no mean feat for a girl to achieve such a thing in this day and age.

However, once the champagne had been drunk and the sumptuous luncheon had been eaten, she'd let her bombshell drop into the ensuing silence and the atmosphere had become charged in quite a different way.

Her eldest son, Hamish, and his wife, Beryl, had travelled all the way from the family's cattle station in outback Queensland. Big, bluff and hearty most of the time, he was inclined to shout and throw his weight about when things didn't go his way, and Christy had seen the rising colour in his face and the spark of challenge in his blue eyes that didn't bode well.

James, younger by two years, was a different kettle of fish entirely. He was in charge of Yarrabinda, the family vineyard in the Barossa Valley, and was a thoughtful man in his late thirties who hated conflict. He'd recently married the shy and rather bookish Clarice, who sat beside him looking daunted by the sudden change in mood. Christy had had great hopes James would be on her side, for they'd always understood one another, but going by his deep frown, there was no guarantee he'd agree to this particular scheme.

Christy shifted in her chair as she looked at Anne, her firstborn, and once again felt the familiar pang of regret that they'd grown apart and could no longer find a way to repair the broken threads that had once bound them so closely. She knew the reason behind it, but there was nothing more she could do to try and heal the breach until Anne had learned to forgive her.

Christy noted Anne's fetching hat and buttoned high-heeled boots, and the fashionable ankle-length skirt and tight jacket, which must have been unbearably restrictive in the heat. There was nothing matronly about Anne, who was now in her early forties, married to Harold Ross, and the mother of eighteen-year-old Kathryn, but her frequently sour expression marred her dark-eyed beauty, and today its glare was fully focused on Christy – a warning of the storm to come.

Christy clasped her hands tightly on her lap as guilt washed over her. She hadn't meant to cause trouble on this special day, but the urgency to reveal her plans had proved too great, and she had hoped that, having been mellowed by champagne and a lavish lunch, her family might have been more amenable, ready to listen and understand how very much she needed to fulfil her dreams. Yet it seemed that wish was not to be.

'Don't be ridiculous,' Hamish blustered, his weathered face flushing to the very roots of his light auburn hair. 'You're still grieving for Father and not thinking straight.'

Christy eyed her eldest son, who was looking more like her own father every day, and knew she had a long way to go to convince him that her plans were quite sensible and well thought out. 'Of course I'm grieving,' she replied calmly, 'but that doesn't mean I'm not fully in control of my faculties.'

'I agree with Hamish,' said Anne. 'It isn't seemly for a woman of your age to travel so far unaccompanied. What if you were taken ill – or, God forbid, died?'

'I might be sixty-five,' Christy had retorted, 'but I'm not yet in my dotage, and have absolutely no intention of dropping dead until I'm good and ready.'

'You won't have much say in the matter when your time comes,' retorted Anne.

'It's sheer lunacy,' spluttered Hamish. 'And I absolutely forbid it.'

'Your father forbade me nothing,' Christy reminded him calmly, 'and I will not be dictated to by my children.' She edged forward in the chair to make her point. 'You all seem to forget that I'm well versed in travelling on my own, and if it wasn't for that sense of adventure and determination, there would be none of what you have today.'

'You were young, and things were different,' said Anne dismissively. 'Besides, you had Father by your side most of the time, so you shouldn't take all the credit.'

Her smug expression was enough to set Christy's teeth on edge and she found it hard not to retort sharply.

'What you're proposing is utter madness,' Anne continued blithely, 'and I'm sure I can count on the others to back me up on this.' Her gaze swept the room imperiously, taking in her brothers, their wives, her daughter and husband, almost daring them to disagree.

'I think we should respect Mother's wishes,' said James quietly into the ensuing silence. 'After all, she's done so much for us over the years, and it's always been her dream to go back to her birthplace.'

'Then she should have done it when Father was alive,' barked Hamish, wresting his arm from his wife's restraining hand. 'A journey like that is hardly an overnight crossing of the Bass Strait – and I will *not* have Ma endangering her life for some silly whim.'

'It's not a whim,' Christy hotly protested. 'It's a long-held ambition, and you know very well that your father would never have contemplated such a sea voyage – not after what he'd experienced as a boy.'

The images this statement evoked were almost unbearable, and she had to stiffen her resolve before she could carry on. 'But sadly he's no longer here; you children have your own lives and now it's my time to do as I please.'

'That's a very selfish attitude,' said Anne with a sniff. 'You have responsibilities here, and can't just abandon us and your grandchildren.'

'Apart from Kathryn, I hardly see my grandchildren,' Christy reminded her. 'They live too far away. As for responsibilities, I have a solicitor and an accountant to see to them, a neighbour to tend my horses, and three sons who are perfectly capable of managing the family businesses without me.' She glanced across at Harold to include him in this statement, for she did indeed regard him as such.

'Instead of going ahead with this hare-brained scheme, perhaps you should use the free time you have now to come and visit us and get to know our children,' rumbled Hamish crossly.

'I'll do that when I come back,' she replied. 'For now, cards and letters will have to continue to suffice.'

'You seem very determined, Mother,' said James, swirling the deep red Yarrabinda Shiraz in his glass. 'But are you sure it's wise? It's a long way to travel on your own.'

'The whole thing's utterly ridiculous,' Hamish snorted, pouring himself another glass of wine. 'Of course it isn't wise to travel – let alone all that way, unaccompanied.'

'Hamish is right, Christy,' said his wife, Beryl, earnestly. 'It's a dangerous journey for a woman of any age, and you'll be stopping off in all sorts of unsavoury places.'

Clarice glanced across at James before speaking. 'I do agree,' she said, blinking owlishly behind her spectacles. 'You could fall victim to white-slave traders, or the awful diseases that are so prevalent in foreign parts. James and I do understand why you want to go, but it really isn't wise, Christy.'

'Perhaps if one of us went with her, we'd all feel easier,' piped up Kathryn, who until this moment had remained silent.

'I can't abandon Yarrabinda for that length of time. Vines are notoriously difficult, even in the good weather; I need to watch them like a hawk.' James glanced across at his glowering brother. 'I doubt Hamish can leave his cattle either, not with the drought still causing havoc in Queensland.'

He shot Christy an understanding smile which warmed her heart. 'Although it sounds as if we'll all be missing out on a grand adventure.'

Kathryn sat forward, her face alight with excitement. 'But I could go,' she breathed. 'I don't have to start at the university until next October, and the experience would be worth far more than anything I could learn in a library.'

As the chorus of protest went round the room, Christy's heart swelled with love for her granddaughter. There was a gentleness about her which hid a core of her mother's steel, but it manifested itself very differently, for, unlike Anne, Kathryn understood the power of speaking out only when she'd considered her words and could make the best use of them to get her way.

'You will do no such thing,' snapped Anne. 'You're far too young to be in sole charge of Mother, and she can't be relied upon to keep out of mischief for more than five minutes. Remember what happened when she insisted on taking part in the horse-and-buggy racing last summer? She ended up with concussion and a broken wrist.'

'Good on her for giving it a go,' Kathryn replied stoutly. 'I can't see why she shouldn't do all the things she wants whilst she still can.'

'Hear, hear,' said James, winking at his niece. 'Mother's hardly got one foot in the grave. In fact, she's probably got more energy than all of us put together. I think it's a bonzer idea, Kathryn, and will certainly put my mind to rest.'

Christy smiled, for she could think of nothing better than having her granddaughter's company throughout the long journey.

But then Anne leaned across Kathryn and dug her silent husband in the ribs. 'Speak up for once, Harold,' she snapped, 'and back me up on this.'

Christy watched keenly as Harold Ross cleared his throat, shifting in the chair, clearly uncomfortable at having been drawn into this family argument. He was a wealthy, clever man when it came to running his export empire, but rather ineffectual when he had to deal with his overbearing wife, rarely opposing her on domestic matters – and certainly never in company.

'It seems to me that your mother's mind is set, and experience has proven that nothing any of us can say will change that,' he began carefully. 'However,' he continued, studiously evading his wife's furious glare, 'I do think it would be unwise for her to travel so far unaccompanied.'

Anne's sour expression turned to momentary satisfaction until Harold continued, 'If the university has no objection to Kathryn travelling, thereby perhaps missing her induction period, then I give my permission for her to accompany Christy on her journey.'

Silence followed this statement and they all waited with bated breath for Anne's reaction.

Anne stared at him in shock and the tension rose as she gathered her wits sufficiently to find a reply. 'Our daughter is barely eighteen,' she managed finally, 'and still a child. Have you *completely* lost your senses?'

Harold flushed – with anger or embarrassment, Christy couldn't tell – and then, as Kathryn's hand crept into his, he sat straighter, clasping his daughter's fingers, his gaze unwavering as it met Anne's glare.

'Travel broadens the mind,' he said firmly, 'and as our daughter has never been abroad, I reckon she'd benefit greatly from the experience.'

Christy silently applauded him, immensely grateful for his support – but Anne was still clearly furious. 'I don't ask much of you,' she said flatly, 'and goodness knows you usually leave all the really important decisions to me. But just for once, I would have liked you to take some responsibility regarding our daughter.'

His mouth became set, his green eyes glinting. 'That's exactly what I am doing,' he said coolly. 'And I have made up my mind on this. If Kathryn wants to go with Christy, then she has my blessing.'

As Kathryn squeezed his hand and smiled back at him, and Anne struggled to regain her composure, there was a general embarrassed throat-clearing and shuffling amongst the others.

It was Christy who broke the awkward silence, for she hadn't meant to cause strife between her daughter and son-in-law – and yet she couldn't deny that having Kathryn with her on the journey was the perfect solution to her family's concerns.

'I'm sorry, Anne, but as Harold has given his consent, and Kathryn seems eager to come with me, I really can't see why you continue to object.' She avoided her daughter's furious glare and smiled at Kathryn. 'I'd be only too delighted to accept your offer, my dear.'

Kathryn's green eyes, so like her father's, sparkled with excitement. 'We'll have a real adventure, Grandma,' she breathed. 'I can hardly wait.'

'I cannot and *will* not sanction this,' Anne stormed.

'It doesn't look as if you've any other choice.' James's eyes held a mischievous twinkle. 'Game, set and match to Harold, I think.'

Anne's glare would have stopped a charging bull at several paces, but it didn't faze James, who, as the youngest of the three siblings, had become all too familiar with it over the years, and he raised his glass in salute to his brother-in-law, who winked back.

'I think the whole idea is utter madness,' Hamish had growled, his initial fury somewhat lessened by Harold's declaration. He glanced round the room and then gave an impatient snort. 'But as Harold has given his consent, perhaps we should accept that some things aren't for the winning.'

Anne shot a venomous glance at Harold and sat up even straighter. 'In that case, I have no other choice but to fulfil my motherly duties and accompany my daughter.'

Gasps and mutters drifted through the room like rustling autumn leaves, and as Kathryn looked at her mother in horror, Christy had to battle to contain her own alarm.

'There's really no need, Anne,' she said hastily. 'Kathryn and I will manage perfectly well without inconveniencing you.'

'It is an inconvenience, certainly, especially with so many social functions already arranged in my diary for the coming year. But my daughter's welfare and reputation is far more important, and it wouldn't be seemly for her to travel so far unchaperoned.'

'She'll have me,' said Christy, still reeling from the thought of her overbearing and hostile daughter taking over all her carefully laid plans and making life impossible.

Anne dismissed Christy's protest with a wave of her hand. 'You're far too unreliable,' she retorted. 'You could get ill, or decide to go off on some wild goose chase which could endanger you both. You know how you're always letting your inquisitiveness get the better of you, and it can cause no end of trouble.'

Stung by her rudeness and lack of feeling, Christy had nevertheless been sharply reminded of the time she'd gone into the bush with five-year-old Kathryn to hunt for a rare bird that had been spotted by the men working on the Gordon River. She'd thought it would be an adventure for the child, but had got them hopelessly lost, and it was more through luck than judgement that she'd eventually found the way back home to her distraught husband and daughter.

'I see you remember that day,' said Anne darkly. 'And that wasn't the only occasion you caused this family a great deal of anxiety through your thoughtlessness.'

Christy suddenly became aware that the others were watching with avid interest as they waited to see how she would reply, and realised then that this whole thing was turning into a circus, and it was time to bring it to an end. She smoothed her linen skirt, adjusted the sash at her narrow waist and took a deep breath before making use of every inch of her not very great height to stand and face her daughter.

'You wouldn't have dared speak to me that way if your father was alive, and I will *not* put up with it any longer,' she said firmly. 'If you insist upon coming, then you must respect the fact that I am your mother, and treat me accordingly. This journey is very personal, and I will *not* have you spoil it. Is that understood?'

Anne's cheeks reddened, but she remained defiant as she held her mother's gaze. 'Oh, I understand all too clearly,' she said, 'but respect has to be – '

Christy realised her daughter was about to say something she'd come to bitterly regret and interrupted her quickly. 'I know you have Kathryn's welfare at heart – and that sometimes you say things without thinking how hurtful they might be. I just hope that by the time we return to Tasmania you will have learned a little humility and understanding for others.'

Hamish snorted. 'Humility? Anne? That I have to see.'

There was a nervous tittering from the others and Christy eyed them sternly before ordering James to open another bottle of Yarrabinda wine so they could drink a toast.

She and her son exchanged smiles of deep affection once the glasses were charged. 'To what or whom are we toasting?' he asked.

'We're raising our glasses to the Isle of Skye, and my long-awaited homecoming,' she replied with a determined smile that masked her sudden misgivings over what the coming months and the long journey might reveal – not only about herself, but about her relationship with her only daughter.

1

Inverness

June 1905

They had arrived from London by steamship and gone straight
to the old coaching inn that stood by the banks of the Moray Firth
in Inverness. Following a leisurely stroll round the town of church
spires, stone bridges and elegant granite buildings, Christy had
suggested they have an early supper and retire for the night to
prepare for the following day. She'd used the excuse of the long
onward journey to seek her own rest without causing concern,
for, uncharacteristically, Christy was feeling every one of her
sixty-five years.

As the ancient timbers of the hotel creaked and groaned, the
salty air drifted in from the Moray Firth and the sound of horses
and carts rumbled up from the cobbled street below her open
window, Christy sat at the dressing table and thoughtfully
brushed out her dark hair. She'd kept it long, despite the fact it
was thinner than before and was now streaked with silver, for
her late husband had loved to run his fingers through it, and she
was loath to cut it – it would feel as if she was severing herself

from all they'd shared, leaving only a terrible void she was not yet ready to acknowledge.

She gave a sigh and stared at her reflection in the mirror, noting that her brown eyes were shadowed with her loss, the passing years etched in her face. She looked away, unwilling to accept that the girl she'd once been lived only in her mind and spirit, and that the world – and her family – saw only an old woman.

Slipping off her dressing gown, she closed the window, turned off the gas lamp and clambered into the high four-poster bed. The heavy drapes were musty with dust, damp and age, but the sheets were clean, the blankets comforting against the chill night, and Christy nestled into the pillows, longing for sleep. Yet despite her weariness, the excitement for what lay ahead bubbled inside her and her mind refused to be still.

This journey had been dreamed about for fifty years, and she could hardly believe that at last she was almost home. And yet the freedom to achieve this long-held dream had come at a price and been hard won, for not only had the opportunity arisen through the loss of her darling husband, but the strong initial opposition from her family had rocked her resolve.

She stared into the darkness as the sounds drifted up from the street and the gulls mewled above the nearby quays where the ships' rigging played discordant tunes in the brisk east wind. Yet as her memories of that confrontation faded, she imagined she could smell the sharp tang of seaweed on a rocky shore, could hear the mournful cries of the curlews as they floated above the Cuillin Hills, and feel the spiky heather in the glens beneath her bare feet.

Christy's eyelids drooped. How could her family have really understood the deep-seated meaning of this pilgrimage? For she'd told her children as little as possible about the experiences and hardships she'd had to face in those early years. The unvarnished reality of them had remained locked inside her, revealed only to her husband in the knowledge that he too had suffered at the hands of others – and that the memories of that time were too stark to share, too dark to overshadow the life they'd made in the new land of sunshine and opportunity.

Yet the need to unlock those memories had become increasingly urgent as they'd travelled nearer to their journey's end, and as sleep finally claimed her, Christy knew that the time was fast approaching when she could begin to tell her story and finally be rewarded with real peace.

*

Kathryn lay in the narrow bed, her riot of autumnal hair spread across the pillow as she stared into the darkness of the heavily beamed and panelled room she'd been forced to share with her mother. She was far from sleep, restless with excitement for the coming day and what it might bring.

She turned over and hugged the pillow, the images of all she'd so far experienced running vividly through her head. She'd realised the minute her grandmother had announced her intentions of returning to Skye that this was a once-in-a-lifetime opportunity not to be missed, and despite her mother's constant complaints and unnecessary fussing, she hadn't been disappointed.

The SS *Celtic* had proved to be very grand, with large first-class staterooms, an elegant dining room, a well-stocked library, a canvas swimming pool on the foredeck and even a marvellous ballroom, where the white-coated ship's officers made sure that every single woman, whatever her age, was partnered in the dancing. Her mother had been very frosty about the whole thing, but Gran had told her firmly not to be a spoilsport and had encouraged Kathryn to fill her dance card every evening.

The crossing had thankfully been very smooth – even when rounding the notorious Cape Horn – so none of them had suffered from seasickness and Kathryn had found the whole experience terribly romantic. She'd crept into bed each night quite starry-eyed from all the attention she'd received, and had written long letters to her friends back in Melbourne extolling the virtues of a sea cruise, and describing a particularly handsome first officer with whom she'd shared a few quite thrilling kisses on the moonlit deck.

She grinned into the pillow, remembering those stolen moments, but accepting them for what they were – a bit of light-hearted fun to match the romance of sailing across a sea glowing with phosphorescence beneath a star-filled sky – and she suspected his attentions had already turned to a different girl on another crossing.

There had also been the exotic sights, scents and sounds of their days ashore, which she'd recounted in her journal so she'd never forget the smallest detail. They'd visited the stunningly beautiful palm-fringed islands of Vanuatu and Fiji before steaming on to Tonga and the western coast of Chile. Rounding the Cape, they'd stopped in Montevideo and bustling, noisy Rio de Janeiro before heading for the African coast and calling into the exotic ports of Senegal and Morocco.

Their day in the Moroccan port of Safi had contrasted greatly with all the other places they'd visited, for they were assailed not only by the unbearable heat, but by the dirt and squalor. They'd discovered the city was overcrowded and stank of spices, burning rubbish and animal dung, which she'd found unsettling. Yet, despite the ever-watchful, insolent dark eyes of the robed men and the whining voices of the beggars, she'd marvelled at the ancient ruins and the seemingly endless desert which stretched beyond the fortress walls bounding the city and was home to the nomads with their trains of camels and brightly dressed women and children.

Her mother had been overbearing and unduly fussy ever since they'd left Melbourne – finding fault, being sharp with Christy over every little thing and souring their pleasure in the trip – but the short visit to Safi had brought things to a head, and Kathryn had been shocked by her mother's animosity towards Christy.

Christy, whose curiosity had proved to be insatiable, had kept them waiting as she'd abandoned their guide and wandered around the ruins of the Portuguese fortress, surrounded by a horde of Arab beggars and merchants. They'd had a terrible job keeping up with her as she'd dived into the souk to haggle with the stallholders or push her way through the jostling crush of humanity in the narrow labyrinth of streets that ran like veins through the city. But then they'd lost sight of her.

The two younger women had searched in rising panic for almost an hour, only to find her happily squatting in the dirt amid a group of veiled women and holding an animated one-sided conversation with them as they washed their babies in tin bowls outside their adobe hovels.

Kathryn had almost wept with relief, but before she could embrace her grandmother, Anne had grabbed Christy's arm and was roughly pulling her through the throng towards the ship.

Horrified, Kathryn had tried to intervene, but Christy soon managed to free herself from her daughter's grip, and had stood, grim-faced, as Anne's harangue caused people to stop and stare. Fearful that her mother might actually use physical force on Christy to vent her anger, Kathryn was about to step between them when her grandmother shrugged off the tirade, smiled sweetly and unapologetically, and then hurried up the gangway with her many purchases, in search of afternoon tea.

Kathryn had tried to defuse her mother's fury by linking arms and coaxing her to board the ship and join Christy on deck to make up with her. But Anne had refused to be mollified, going to their stateroom in high dudgeon, and remaining there until morning.

As Kathryn nestled deeper beneath the blankets, she wondered why her mother felt such enmity towards Christy. She knew it had not always been so, for she remembered the very early days of her childhood when there had been great affection between them.

She could only conclude that something must have happened to bring about this change, and she had hoped the long trip might heal the breach. But for all her gentle persuasion, both women had remained tight-lipped and as distant as ever. Now she wondered if she'd ever discover what lay between them.

2

They'd left Inverness at dawn after a hasty breakfast of delicious porridge and cups of strong coffee. The long journey by horse and carriage to the western point of the Kyle of Lochalsh had taken the entire day, and after a night spent in a small, run-down inn, they'd boarded the island ferry, SS *Pioneer*, for the final leg of their journey.

The weather had deteriorated overnight, and as the *Pioneer* ploughed determinedly through the choppy waters off the southern coast of Skye, Christy stood alone on the rain-soaked deck and blinked back her tears. Time and distance had not played false with her memory, for it was just as she'd last seen it. Heedless of the wind that tugged at her hat and inadequate raincoat, and the sea spray that made her skirt cling to her ankles, she gazed at the towering black cliffs where waterfalls tumbled to the sea and the mist of spindrift became lost in the soft veil of rain.

She planted her feet more firmly on the slippery deck that rolled and dipped beneath her and gripped the railing, her emotions, usually so tightly reined, in turmoil as she breathed in the rich peaty scent of the seemingly barren land that spread out before her. '*An t-Eilean Sgiathanach*,' she whispered in the Gaelic of her childhood. This was her 'cloud island', as the Vikings had called it, and she was glad to be alone to absorb each and every second of the first moments of her homecoming.

As the *Pioneer* slowly headed northwards with her cargo of passengers, mail, essential supplies and livestock, Christy watched the unchanged landscape slowly unfolding before her. It was a strange, unsettling feeling, for it was as if the fifty years of absence had passed in the blink of an eye, and the memories she'd carried with her all that time were now coming thick and fast – as clear and painful today as they'd always been.

Christy finally sought the meagre shelter of the narrow ledge protruding from the roof of the wheelhouse and lovingly caressed the faded tartan shawl that had once belonged to her mother. She drew it more closely about her narrow shoulders and buried her nose in the damp folds, almost believing the scent of the woman she'd adored was still held in the Highland wool. Woven by her grandmother in shades of blue and green, with an occasional narrow line of orange, it was the old tartan of the clan MacInnes, and she treasured it, for it too was redolent with memories, and the only possession she still had of those long-lost days.

'For goodness' sake, Mother. What *do* you think you're doing?'

Christy was startled from her thoughts by Anne's hectoring tone, and it was a moment before she could reply. 'I'm enjoying my homecoming,' she said firmly.

'It'll be your death,' said Anne crossly, clutching at her hat and dipping her head against the windswept spray coming from the ferry's bow.

'I've weathered worse,' she replied shortly, before turning once more to the passing panorama in the faint expectation that Anne would take the hint and go back inside. But it seemed her daughter was determined to continue her vigil.

'I'm sure you have,' Anne retorted, 'but you're older now and not as resilient.'

Christy studiously ignored her. She had harboured the hope that this long journey would bring them a little closer, but despite every effort to appease her, Anne seemed intent on keeping her mother at arm's length – constantly nagging and complaining about everything she said and did – and after so many weeks of enforced closeness, Christy was wearied by the endless battle to keep her patience and not retaliate.

Anne was named after her long-dead Scottish grandmother, but there was no resemblance to the woman who'd faced poverty and hardship with such stoic forbearance, and who'd died tragically and too soon. Christy was saddened to realise that her daughter's unforgiving nature was making her into an unpleasant shrew, in danger of turning everyone against her – even the long-suffering Harold. She'd long suspected their marriage was unhappy, and his standing up to Anne that day in Hobart had been very telling.

Christy dredged up a smile and patted Anne's arm in an attempt to mollify her. 'Please don't fuss about me, dear. I'm perfectly happy out here, and this spring squall will soon pass.'

Anne shivered delicately and pulled her beautiful fur wrap more closely round her neck as she clung to her hat. 'You'd hardly think it was June,' she muttered. 'Does it never stop raining?'

'Of course it does, but you have to remember how far north we are, and the weather is always unpredictable.' She pushed back the tendrils of her silver-streaked hair that had come loose from their pins. 'It's the same in Tasmania, Anne. I can remember many a Christmas spent indoors watching the rain come down.'

Anne dismissed her words with a derisive sniff. 'Whatever the weather, you're far too old to be standing out in it,' she said.

Christy gave an inward sigh, heartily sick of hearing this hurtful phrase from her daughter.

'And what's that disreputable old thing about your shoulders? Where's the fur wrap you bought in London?'

Christy buried her fingers in the shawl and regarded Anne evenly. 'It's safely packed in my trunk,' she replied. 'As for this, it's a family heirloom, and perfectly appropriate for the occasion.'

'It's a disgrace,' said Anne, hastily grabbing the rail as the boat suddenly lurched and she had to battle to keep her balance. 'You can be very difficult at times,' she grumbled. 'What will people think if they see you in that?'

Christy chuckled. 'I really don't care. And I doubt people will even look at me, seeing as I'm old and decrepit. But in these parts they'll recognise the MacInnes tartan and know that I'm proud to wear it no matter how shabby it's become.'

She saw her daughter was shivering. 'Go inside, Anne,' she said softly, 'and leave me to my memories.'

'You always were stubborn,' said Anne, blithely ignoring the fact of her own recalcitrance. 'This whole journey has been one long trial, and I don't know why I let you force me into it.'

That was a bit rich seeing as Anne had insisted on coming

with absolutely no encouragement from either her mother or Kathryn. 'You didn't have to come,' said Christy dryly.

'Of course I did,' she replied bad-temperedly. 'I was not about to let my daughter travel to the other side of the world, knowing how irresponsible you can be. Why, look at you now, standing out here catching your death.'

Christy stifled a deep sigh. 'Go inside, Anne, and I'll join you both once we've docked.'

'It's extremely unpleasant in that cabin, having to sit cheek by jowl with rough people and their smelly animals. I don't know how Kathryn can stand it.'

'Then stay out here and keep quiet,' Christy said sharply. 'You're spoiling my homecoming.'

Anne didn't budge. 'I've been looking at the map I bought, and it seems to me that this awful boat trip was entirely unnecessary – no doubt another of your whims to make our lives difficult. We could have caught the ferry for the short journey to Portree and then hired a carriage, so why didn't we?'

Christy looked away and bit her lip. Portree held memories of dark times and she hadn't felt ready to face them. 'I wanted to see this coastline,' she replied, 'and thought you and Kathryn might find it interesting.'

Anne held her steady gaze. '"Interesting" is not the word I'd use,' she said briskly. 'It's cold, wet and uncomfortable. As for the view,' she glanced in derision at the low clouds capping the hills, 'there's nothing to see.' With that, she turned on her heel and went into the passenger cabin.

Christy was stung by her cruel dismissal of the astonishing

coastline, but relieved to be left alone again. She knew she irritated her daughter, and the feeling was mutual. But there seemed to be no way of putting things right between them, and it really set her on edge when Anne repeatedly treated her like an ancient crone who'd lost her wits. But for all that, Christy loved her, and regretted being sharp with her, for her daughter's appearance on deck had revealed Anne cared enough to be concerned for her mother's well-being. It was just a shame she had such a bossy way of showing it.

She turned back to the railings and realised she could see Ardtrek Point and the narrow peninsula of Ullinish. If the clouds cleared enough, she'd soon have sight of the old wooden lighthouse and the remains of the stone dun – an ancient stone fortress that legend proclaimed was built before the birth of Christ – standing guard on the cliff tops.

And then they would head west again before following the coastline north to round the headland and enter the Loch of Dunvegan, which was their final destination – a place that also held disturbing memories, but ones which were easier to deal with than those in Portree.

She gasped with pleasure as she sighted the seals, sleekly black as they rested on the rocks, and the swirling birds that had nested high in the cliffs where men had once risked their lives to gather them and their eggs so they could feed their families. Yet despite her delight, the constant erosion of her resolve by Anne had begun to take its toll, and she felt suddenly dispirited.

Doubts took hold, picking away at her as she stood there in the wind and rain. Was she being foolish to cross the world at her age, and return to the place where she'd known such sorrow and hardship? Should she have heeded the dire warnings of her friends and Hamish that such a journey was foolhardy in the extreme, and could only end in bitter disappointment? For what did she really expect to achieve by coming back?

Tears threatened again and she determinedly blinked them away. She couldn't allow Anne to spoil everything, not now that her dream was about to be realised. She'd grasped the opportunity, heedless of her family's objections, her age and the rigours that such a journey would inevitably bring, and would see it through.

Christy became aware of footsteps approaching, sniffed back her tears and steeled herself for another argument. Yet when she turned to look at the little figure who'd come to stand silently beside her, she relaxed and smiled.

'So, Kathryn, what do you think of my island?'

The green eyes were concerned above the neat little nose that was lightly dusted with freckles. 'It reminds me of the coastline in Tasmania,' she replied, taking Christy's gloved hand.

Christy nodded. 'They are very similar,' she agreed. 'It's the reason why I feel so settled there.'

'Are you all right, Grandma?'

'I'm fine, whatever your mother might have said. This is an important day, and I think I've earned the right to be a wee bit emotional for once, don't you?'

She gave her a watery smile and continued to hold her hand as they passed breathtaking lines of cliffs and slowly steamed towards Dunvegan Head. They stood close together in companionable silence as they regarded the deserted coves with their black rocks and gritty sand, and the numerous ruins of what once had been stone crofts and farm buildings scattered across glens overshadowed by soaring hills and racing clouds.

Christy had sharp recall of the times she had collected kelp here while her younger brothers had foraged in the rock pools for shellfish. How barren it looked now, the lonely sentinels of the crumbling croft walls standing sharply in focus against the lowering skyline as sheep grazed in the tough grass and frost-blackened heather that had yet to blossom after the winter.

Christy surreptitiously watched her granddaughter's expressive face as she gazed at the scene before her. It was clear the girl was moved by what she saw, and perhaps understood better now why Christy had needed to come on this long and unnecessary ferry trip. Her heart swelled, glad Kathryn was by her side to share this journey, for it would have been very lonely without her.

'Oh, how magnificent,' Kathryn breathed as the ferry followed a curve in the water and they had a clear view of Dunvegan Castle at the end of the loch. 'It's like a fairy-tale castle. I can see now why you decided to come this way.' She turned to Christy, her face radiant. 'How does it feel to be home again after all this time?'

Christy felt the tears prick again and gathered the shawl closer, her gaze avoiding the hated castle and all it stood for, yet aware of the bubble of excitement rising within her for their imminent arrival. 'I don't know whether to laugh or cry,' she confessed, dabbing her eyes. 'I've seen so many changes already that I'm almost frightened of what I'll find when I reach MacInnes Bay.'

Kathryn put her arm about her shoulders. 'I'll be with you, Grandma, and if you feel like crying, then you go ahead – there's no shame in it.'

'Bless you, child.' Christy patted her cheek. 'You have no idea how grateful I am to have you with me.'

Kathryn smiled. 'I wouldn't have missed this for anything. The chance to be with you and learn more about the family history; to see where you lived and to listen to your stories . . . It will be something I can carry with me for the rest of my life, and a wonderful experience to pass on to my own children when the time comes.'

'Not all the stories are happy ones,' Christy warned, 'but it is time you and your mother heard them. This place, the people who once lived here and that awful castle are part of our family history.'

Kathryn frowned at her sudden harsh tone, and Christy turned away, afraid of revealing the rage in her eyes. The story of how the MacDonalds and their factors had changed her life forever would be told soon enough.

To distract herself from these dark thoughts, she looked up as the wind shredded the clouds, allowing a shaft of sunlight to pierce through and illuminate the soaring cliffs and the mellow stones of the castle that still stood guard imperiously over the loch. It had stopped raining.

Wordlessly, she pointed to the perfect rainbow forming above them. Each colour was clearly defined as it arched across the wild, empty landscape like a gift from Heaven to welcome her home.

As Kathryn gazed in awe at the sight, Christy shivered and dug her fingers deep into the tartan shawl. There had been no rainbow to wish her farewell as she'd left the island on that final day, just a bleak wind tearing in beneath scudding, rain-filled clouds, and a sense of profound helplessness and despair.

Christy lifted her chin, determined to keep her emotions under control so she could enjoy this moment. The story of her life, and of those who'd once lived here, would be told – but not today. Today was to give thanks for still being alive and able to return.

*

Anne had tucked herself firmly into a corner, well away from the stack of boxed fish and the two hobbled goats that seemed to be watching her with their devil eyes as they dropped their mess all over the floor. She felt quite nauseous from the stink of smoked herring and unwashed bodies and the heave and roll of the ferry, but she was absolutely determined to keep her breakfast down. The last thing she wanted was to make a show of herself in front of these people who didn't even seem to be able to speak the King's English.

She turned her shoulder to them all, smeared the condensation from the salt-caked glass of the porthole and jealously watched her mother and daughter standing companionably at the rails. There had been a close bond between them from the moment Kathryn had been born, and try as she might, Anne couldn't help but resent the fact.

She looked away, studiously ignored the open curiosity of the other passengers and pulled out her powder compact. Eyeing her reflection in the small mirror, she realised her dark hair was damply bedraggled where it had been torn loose from its pins by the wind, and that her lovely hat was close to being ruined.

She did the best she could with her hair, knowing that the minute she stepped off this awful vessel it would be mussed again by the appalling weather. Her complexion would also suffer if she wasn't careful, she thought, dabbing a little powder across her nose and cheeks. The elements she'd encountered over the last few months were playing havoc with her beauty routine, and goodness only knows what her smart friends would think if they could see her now.

She snapped the gold compact closed and dropped it in her leather handbag before shaking the rain from her fur and replacing it about her shoulders. Her neat gabardine skirt and jacket were damp, the frills on her white blouse drooping after she'd been forced to wear it for a second day due to her trunk being stored in the dockside warehouse overnight. She could only hope that tonight's accommodation would prove to be more amenable than the previous night's, for she hadn't slept a wink on that lumpy and highly suspect mattress, and was looking forward to having a long bath and changing into something warmer.

Another glance out of the window confirmed that her mother and daughter were still out there, but at least the sky had cleared, and there was a magnificent rainbow shimmering over an imposing castle, which actually seemed to be in one piece, unlike the many others she'd seen on this torturous journey.

Aware that she was being observed with quite insolent curiosity by the other passengers and unwilling to be drawn into any kind of conversation – unlike her mother, who talked to everyone – Anne straightened her back and watched the two people on deck.

As a child, she'd adored her mother and admired her energy, sense of fun and adventure, believing she was wise and truthful and that the bond between them would never break. But that trust had been shattered, and now Anne couldn't find it in her heart to forgive her. The coldness between them was uncomfortable, especially when they were with the rest of the family – who thankfully knew nothing of Christy's devastating confession – and as she'd let time slip away, the hurt had festered until it was all-consuming.

Now she wondered if there could ever be any reconciliation on her part – and if she actually wanted it. It wasn't that she no longer loved her mother – of course she did, deep down, withered beneath the bitterness and pain – but the lie she'd been told had been too shocking, turning her world upside down and destroying everything she'd held dear.

Her mother had tried to explain, had shed tears of remorse and pleaded with her to understand, but Anne's faith in her had been irreparably damaged, and without that faith it was impossible to return to how they'd once been.

Anne sighed, for she'd done her best to be pleasant to her mother during this trip, for her daughter's sake, but was all too aware that her well-intentioned concern for Christy's well-being had come across as rather abrupt and bossy, thereby alienating her further.

She tucked the fur more firmly around her neck to ward off the draught coming through the ill-fitting door, as she silently justified her manner to herself. Having been left to make the most of the important domestic and social decisions during her marriage to Harold, she'd fallen into the habit of giving orders and chivvying people about. It was her way of getting things done and she had no intention of changing.

She shivered as she saw Kathryn embrace Christy, their heads together, laughing over something. She couldn't remember the last time she'd laughed with Kathryn like that, or shared such an intimate moment, and she experienced a stab of raw envy which caught her breath. Kathryn was her only child, the one good thing that had come out of her disappointing marriage to Harold, and all she'd wanted for her was the best – to have the things she herself had been denied as a child – to grow closer as the years passed, and to find the right sort of husband for her, who would take charge of things, cherish and spoil her as she deserved.

But Kathryn had proved to be as stubborn as her grandmother, refusing to contemplate a coming-out season, determined to progress with her studies and enter university. Anne, who'd had only the most basic education like her mother before her, couldn't understand where this thirst for learning came from. Harold was a self-made man who'd spent his formative years grubbing in the dirt of the opal fields with his widowed father, and although he had a sharp business brain, he'd had to take lessons from his wife in how to read and write. She'd found that endearing to begin with, but the novelty soon wore off once the first flush of the honeymoon days was over and she became involved in the social whirl.

Anne bit her lip as she watched her daughter, so lovely, even though she'd become bedraggled by the elements. She didn't considerate it entirely seemly for such a carefully raised girl to become a 'bluestocking', for she'd met some of Kathryn's like-minded friends, whom she considered odd and rather suspect with their cropped hair and unflattering, almost mannish clothing, and could only hope that her lovely daughter wouldn't follow suit.

She felt a sharp stab of resentment as her gaze fell on Christy. Mother, of course, had encouraged her, and Harold had gone along with it, so she'd had little choice but to stand back and watch Kathryn set out on a path so very different from the one she'd spent years planning. Now here they were, miles from civilisation in a grubby old ferry which wallowed like an ungainly sow through the icy water while the two of them stood out there with seemingly not a care in the world.

The condensation had misted the glass again, but she didn't bother to clear it. She'd seen enough. Pulling her gloves more firmly over her hands to ward off any germs that were no doubt lurking in every nook and cranny of this filthy tub, she reached for the journal she'd been keeping throughout the voyage.

They'd left Melbourne on the SS *Celtic* – chosen specifically for its name by her mother, who was clearly getting over-sentimental in her old age. Harold had been there to represent the rest of the family and wave them off, and as the band played and streamers were tossed between ship and quay, she'd looked down at him and wondered if he shared the same sense of relief she felt at that moment, for the atmosphere between them had become stifling of late.

The book remained unopened in her lap as she thought of her husband. Harold was a good man, there was no denying it. Handsome too, with rich brown hair bleached by the sun, a strong face, and all the charm in the world when he was in pursuit of something he wanted. And he'd wanted Anne from the moment of their first meeting. She'd been flattered by his attentions, his obvious wealth, and the easy way he mixed with Melbourne society. She'd fallen in love – or what she thought was love – and despite her mother's warnings that she should wait, had rushed headlong into marriage.

The hopes and dreams had slowly disintegrated over the years through mutual disappointment and a growing detachment – a careless disregard for one another's feelings and opinions that had led to their living virtually separate lives. The situation had been exacerbated by the fact that Kathryn would soon leave home for her new life in Sydney and they'd be left with only each other.

Anne firmly pushed back the awful thought as she turned the pages of her journal. She hadn't really wanted to come on this ghastly journey, but she'd realised it would be a chance to escape for a while, to catch her breath and think carefully about what the future held for her once Kathryn went to Sydney. What she hadn't expected was this feeling of liberation that had been brought on by all she'd experienced.

She scanned a page, reliving the beauty of the tranquil Pacific Islands that were in marked contrast to the colourful, noisy throngs in Rio and the crowded, stinking souks of Morocco. Standing on the deck the morning after her confrontation with Christy in Morocco, she'd stared out at the desert, which stretched beyond the city walls, and then watched the small boys diving into the murky water to retrieve the coins some of the passengers were throwing down to them.

Mother, of course, had joined in this madness by tossing overboard all the fruit from her stateroom, as well as every last bit of change in her pocket – seemingly unrepentant that she'd ruined their time ashore by getting lost. Anne shuddered at the memory of how distraught she'd been, and how dangerously close she'd come to actually hitting her mother, and swiftly turned the page.

Their onward journey to Portugal had gone without incident, and she'd finally begun to relax and really enjoy herself. Lisbon had proved to be a wonderfully ordered city, with parks and broad tree-lined avenues of elegant buildings that reminded her a little of Melbourne. Mother had behaved herself, and once they'd reached London, had been an informative and interesting guide, even though she'd never set foot in the city before and had gleaned her knowledge from the many guidebooks she'd bought.

Anne snapped the journal shut and tucked it into her handbag upon hearing shouts from the quay and the running footsteps of the boatmen on deck. They'd reached their destination at last. She could only hope her mother wasn't planning on staying too long, for Scotland had proved empty enough, but this place was positively devoid of anything but a few sheep and old ruins.

3

Christy took a deep breath as she looked up at Dunvegan Castle, for the stone battlements that cast long shadows over the tiny harbour were a reminder of the power and cruelty of the Mac-Donalds' factors. She had hoped the years would have left their mark, that the MacDonalds' self-inflicted poverty and fall from grace would show in crumbling walls and toppled towers – but it stood imposingly on the hill, unchanged.

As the ferry slowly chugged towards the landing stage, the castle was lost from view and Christy could now shrug off her dark thoughts and watch the crew prepare for landing.

'This is your special moment, Gran,' said Kathryn. 'I'll go and help Mother so you can step ashore on your own.'

Christy nodded, thankful for the girl's understanding. This was indeed her moment, and she didn't want to share it with anyone. She smiled and exchanged a few words in Gaelic with the other passengers as they left the ferry, and once they'd all gone ashore, she stepped towards the ramp leading to the wooden quay.

'*Beannachd leat*,' said the ferry captain in the Gaelic farewell.

Christy responded in the time-honoured way: '*Mar sin leat*.'

His eyes were very blue in his weathered old face as he took in the faded MacInnes tartan and handed her on to the ramp. It was as if he knew why she was here, and understood she didn't need his help any further, for he stood back and sketched a brief salute. '*Sealbh math dhuit!*'

She acknowledged his good luck wish with a broad smile, and thanked him. '*Tapadh leat.*' And then she was walking down the ramp, along the wooden quay to the roughly hewn stone jetty.

As her feet touched firm ground, she paused for a heartbeat and then swiftly headed for the sweep of heather and tough grass that grew on the other side of the dirt track which followed the southern curve of the loch.

Heedless of the fact that the ferry captain and his crew were watching her, along with the young man tending his cart, and that the ground was sodden, she plumped down on the grass and wrestled to unlace her boots. Flinging them to one side, she got to her feet and planted them firmly in the grass and scratchy heather, glad she'd had the foresight not to wear stockings today.

She closed her eyes as she felt the rich wet soil seep between her toes and up to her ankles. She could hear the seabirds calling as she breathed in the clean Skye air, and could smell the long-remembered scent of smoke from a distant peat fire. She was a child again, barefoot and ragged in her mother's shawl – but as one with the land she loved. Now she could truly believe she was home.

*

Kathryn had kept her mother occupied by gathering up her things and fussing over whether she was warm enough. Now there were no excuses left to linger, for a glance through the porthole showed that their luggage had been unloaded from the boat on to a large wagon by a sturdy young man in a tweed jacket and scarlet tartan kilt. There was no sign of the other passengers, or Christy, and the crew were busily swabbing the decks.

'Where's Mother?' demanded Anne.

'She's waiting for us on shore. I think she wanted to be alone for a little while to take everything in.'

'Hmph. The way she's been carrying on, *we* might as well not be here at all.' They reached the ramp and Ann peered short-sightedly towards the jetty. 'I hope she hasn't wandered off again. I'm far too tired for any more nonsense.'

Kathryn saw Christy immediately and was thankful for once that her mother was too vain to wear her glasses. Her grand-mother had discarded her boots and was standing as if in a trance amid the hummocks of grass and heather, arms outstretched, head flung back so her face was lit by the sun and her hat threat-ened to fall.

'She's just across the way,' she said quietly. 'Come on, Mother. Mind your step down the ramp.'

Anne allowed her daughter to take her arm as she tottered down the ramp in her high-heeled boots and narrow skirt. As they reached firmer ground, she looked round and gasped in horror. 'Good grief. What *is* she doing?'

'Leave her, Mother,' said Kathryn as Anne made to rush over. 'This is a very private moment and she won't appreciate you interrupting.'

'I don't care if she appreciates it or not,' snapped Anne. 'She'll end up with pneumonia, and who'll have to take care of her then? Me, that's who, because I doubt very much there's even a nurse in this godforsaken place, let alone a decent doctor.'

She wrenched her arm from Kathryn's staying hand and carefully navigated her way across the rutted track. 'Stop this at once and pull yourself together,' she hissed furiously. 'You're making a show of yourself.'

Christy, torn from her memories and the sensual delight of feeling the good earth of Skye beneath her feet again, opened her eyes and stared uncomprehendingly at her daughter.

'Why are you so angry all the time, Anne?'

'Because you would try the patience of a saint,' she retorted. She grabbed the discarded boots and held them out. 'Put these on and try to show some decorum for once. Anyone would think you'd lost your mind, behaving like this.'

Christy sighed, taking the boots but making no move to put them on as she remained where she was. 'I wanted to remember how it felt,' she said softly. 'You see, I only wore boots on Sundays for kirk, and as they'd be my older brother's, they were horribly uncomfortable.' She grinned mischievously. 'It's a wonderful feeling, sinking your toes in the wet peat. You should try it, Anne.'

'Grandma, stop teasing,' said Kathryn quickly before her mother's sharp tongue could cause further trouble. 'It's getting late, and we really should be on our way to the hotel before it gets dark.'

Christy clutched the muddy boots to her chest, adjusted the tartan shawl over her shoulder and looked west. 'It'll be light for hours yet,' she said dreamily. 'Darkness comes late at this time of year, so far north.'

'Well, we can't stay any longer,' said Anne briskly. 'You need to get out of those wet, filthy clothes, and I need a bath and something decent to eat. Did you remember to book the carriage to take us to the hotel?'

There was a glint in Christy's eyes that forewarned Kathryn of mischief ahead, and she waited with some amusement to see what her grandmother was up to now.

'Oh, yes, I've booked our transport,' said Christy lightly. 'It's over there.'

Kathryn and Anne turned to regard the all but deserted jetty and rutted track. 'All I can see is that cart and horse which is carrying our luggage,' said Anne in exasperation. 'Where's our carriage?'

'You really should wear your glasses, dear,' Christy admonished her softly. 'I fear you're quite blind without them.' She adjusted her hat, leaving it askew over one eye, shoved the boots under her arm and stepped, still barefoot, on to the muddy track.

Kathryn saw her mother's horrified expression and had to clamp her lips together to smother her giggles. Grandma was being very naughty, but it was a bit unfair on poor Mother to expect her to ride in a rough cart.

'I'm not going in that,' protested Anne.

Christy didn't reply, but walked across the mud and puddles to engage the young carter in animated conversation.

'It looks like we don't have much choice,' murmured

Kathryn. 'Please don't make a fuss and spoil Grandma's special day, Mother.'

'So it's perfectly fine for my day to be spoiled, so long as she can behave like a half-witted brat?' Anne glared at the muddy path and the woman standing by the cart. 'She did this on purpose. I just know she did.'

Kathryn took her arm to help her tiptoe through the ruts and puddles. 'I doubt that,' she replied. 'This is a very small island, and they probably don't have such things as carriages.'

'It's all so uncivilised,' shuddered Anne. 'Don't they realise it's the twentieth century?'

Kathryn knew there was little point in replying, and although she felt sorry for her mother, she could see the funny side of the situation, and was intrigued as to how she could be persuaded to ride on that cart.

Christy turned with a deceptively innocent smile as they approached. 'This is Gregor MacGregor, and it turns out that he's a very distant cousin.' She beamed with delight. 'The clans MacInnes and MacGregor have always been linked, you see.'

Kathryn shook his rough hand, all too aware of the flecks of gold in his hazel eyes, the amused smile on his rugged face and the strength in his grip.

Anne met his outstretched hand with the tips of her gloved fingers and an almost imperceptible nod of her head.

'Gregor will be our driver and guide all the while we're on Skye,' said Christy. 'He's even promised we can meet his family. Isn't that wonderful?'

Anne's face drained of all colour. 'You mean we'll have to use that . . . that *thing* every time we want to go anywhere?'

'Aye, that's about right,' Gregor replied, his hazel eyes regarding Anne with some curiosity. 'I ken you don't approve.'

'I'm used to more comfortable transport,' she said coldly, her disdainful gaze taking in the cart and workmanlike horse. 'I have my own carriage and very finely bred pair in Melbourne.'

He cocked his head, his weathered face creasing attractively as he smiled. He slapped the sturdy neck of his patient horse. 'Well, now, old Jock here is getting a bit long in the tooth, and although he's no breeding to speak of, he doesn't take too kindly to criticism. But seeing as what a grand lady ye are, I'm sure he'll forgive you.'

Kathryn bit her lip as she caught her grandmother's eye. It seemed Gregor MacGregor was not at all daunted by Anne's manner, which could make things very interesting over the coming days.

'Just how far is this wretched hotel?' asked Anne stiffly.

'I ken it's about three wee miles down the track once we're the other side of the watter,' he replied.

Anne peered along the length of the track. 'Then I'll walk,' she said. 'The exercise will do me good after being thrown about in that nasty little boat.'

Kathryn and Christy looked at her aghast. Anne never walked anywhere.

Gregor shoved back his cap and ruffled his thick brown hair until it stood on end. 'Aye, well you could, but I ken ye'd ruin those fine wee boots.'

Anne dithered, clearly torn between having to climb up on to the wooden plank that served as a seat, or ruin her very expensive footwear.

'Come on, Anne,' said Christy impatiently. 'I know it's not what you're used to, but you must think of it as an adventure – a new experience.'

Anne's face was set in angry lines. 'How *dare* you make light of this,' she hissed, aware of Gregor enjoying listening in as he leaned against the cart. 'You did this on purpose, just to humiliate me.'

'Oh, Anne, I would never be so cruel,' gasped Christy. 'It's not my fault there was no other transport, and if I'd thought for one minute that you'd be so upset, I would have hired riding horses.' Her expression was crestfallen. 'In fact, I did enquire, but unfortunately *they're* in short supply here too,' she tailed off.

Anne held her mother's gaze and then gave a sharp little sigh. 'It seems I have little choice,' she conceded. 'But I'm not in the habit of clambering up things, and don't know how you expect me to get all the way up there.'

'Gregor will help you, won't you, Gregor?'

The corners of his lips twitched. 'Aye, nay problem. She's only a wee lassie.'

Anne blushed to the roots of her hair at his impertinence. 'I couldn't possibly let . . . I mean . . . I'm sure I can find a way quite well without any assistance.'

'I'll show you how,' said Christy. She handed her boots to Gregor, hitched up her skirt to her knees and placed one bare, muddy foot on the metal rung that acted as a step. Grabbing the side of the cart, she hauled herself up until she reached the driver's bench.

She laughed down at them in delight. 'Come on, Kathryn. If I can do it, so can you.'

Kathryn clambered swiftly up and they both looked expectantly down at Anne. 'Come on, Mother. Your turn.'

Anne dithered and shuffled from one foot to another, and then ordered Gregor to turn his back so she could hitch up her skirt.

He grinned broadly but did as ordered, his arms folded as he leaned casually against his cob's broad flank and muttered something in Gaelic into the animal's twitching ear.

Anne tentatively hitched up her narrow skirt, clung tightly to the muddy wheel to keep her balance and raised one dainty foot towards the makeshift step. But her skirt was too tight, her arms weren't strong enough to pull herself up, and her daughter's outstretched hand remained out of reach.

She gritted her teeth, hitched her skirt daringly higher to reveal the edge of her knee-length corsetry, tried again – and failed. 'It's no good. I simply can't do it,' she panted, her face red with exertion. 'Perhaps it would be best for me to walk.'

'Och, you'll no be wanting to do that, wee lassie,' boomed Gregor. 'And we're wasting the day. Jock is in need of his supper.' He eyed Anne momentarily and without warning, swung her into his arms and deposited her rather too firmly next to Kathryn.

'There now,' he said as he leaped up beside Christy and took the reins, 'that wasn't too bad, was it?'

His laughing, scornful eyes and broad grin only made Anne's

face burn with humiliation, and she didn't know where to look as the horse plodded slowly along the track.

'It's all right, Mother,' said Kathryn softly, taking her hand. 'It's like Grandma said – it's an adventure – and as such we must do our best to enjoy it.' She giggled. 'After all, it isn't every day that a handsome young man swings you up into his arms, is it?'

'Your father is getting rather too old for such carryings on,' she replied stiffly. 'And I strongly object to being manhandled in that uncouth manner.' She fumbled in her bag and fanned her hot face with her scented handkerchief.

Anne was grateful for her daughter's kind words, but her heart was racing at the thought that unless she discovered a more dignified way of getting on and off this thing, Gregor would have to lift her in and out every time they ventured from their hotel.

She dabbed her face with the handkerchief, struggling for calm. Gregor reminded her too much of the youthful Harold, all muscular strength, knowing eyes and winning smiles. And as Gregor had lifted her in his strong arms, she'd caught the same scents of horse and hay and the outdoors, mixed with the tang of pipe smoke and good tweed Harold had once carried with him. It was all most disconcerting.

*

Kathryn felt sorry for her mother's embarrassment, but she really only had herself to blame. Grandmother had warned them that they should dress appropriately for their journey, which would involve getting on and off boats and ramps, and although she'd heeded the advice, her mother had, as usual, ignored it.

She cast a surreptitious glance across her grandmother to the young man holding the reins as they rumbled along. Gregor MacGregor looked to be in his late twenties and was very handsome in a rugged sort of way, reminding her a bit of her uncles. He had the same sun-darkened skin, the fine lines already beginning to cobweb from the corners of his eyes, and the rough hands of a man who lived and worked out of doors.

Her gaze drifted to the sturdy brown knees showing between the kilt and the long woollen socks. Not many men could get away with such attire, but it suited him somehow and went with his surroundings and the attractive burr of his voice.

Gregor caught her eye and grinned as if he could read her thoughts. Kathryn looked away hastily and took an inordinate interest in their surroundings as the wooden wheels turned and the cart swayed from side to side, jolting occasionally when it hit a stone or a particularly deep rut.

The shaggy brown-and-white cob continued to plod along the winding track that followed the shores of the loch, and the rhythm of it made Kathryn feel quite sleepy. The sun was now very low in the sky, but at least it wasn't raining and the wind had dropped.

She was soon entranced by the scenery, for the hills on the other side of the water had lost their veil of clouds, and she could see the folds and slopes quite clearly, and make out the yellow grass and black heather. Grandma had explained why it had yet to turn purple, but she was nonetheless rather disappointed, for after her grandmother's vivid descriptions of it, she'd been looking forward to seeing it in great swathes across the glens.

She turned from the view and looked over the cob's broad back and pricked ears to the track ahead. It was still rutted and muddy, but a little further on it had been laid with large flat stones, and now she could see the occasional rooftop and a church spire. Glancing across at her mother, who was clutching the side of the cart as if her life depended on it, she patted her arm. 'It looks like we're nearly there,' she said encouragingly.

Anne merely nodded, her expression grim.

Kathryn left her to it and tuned into the conversation on her other side. Grandma had told her she'd once only spoken the Gaelic, for it was the language of the islands, but Kathryn was surprised at how fluent she still was after all the years she'd spent in Australia. It was quite musical to the ear, but horribly tongue-twisting, and she wished she could understand what they were saying. Whatever it was, it seemed to cause them both amusement, for Gregor's deep chuckle was accompanied by her grandmother's hearty laughter.

Kathryn smiled. She was glad her grandmother was happy again, for the loss of Grandpa had come as a terrible blow, and she knew how hard Christy had taken it. Theirs had been a true love match, and Kathryn hoped that one day she might be fortunate enough to find her own – but not until she'd gained her degree and established her teaching career.

*

Christy sat beside Gregor, the cart jolting her repeatedly against him, bringing back memories of the years she'd spent in the outback, and the man who'd ridden beside her in a very similar wagon.

'It must feel strange, coming back after all these years,' said Gregor quietly as they reached the paved lane.

'Yes,' she replied in Gaelic. 'It does feel strange, but rather wonderful.' She looked up at him and smiled. 'I'm glad I still have family here, and that you'll be with us all the while.'

He grinned. 'I don't think your daughter approves of me, and I'm sorry if I acted hastily and embarrassed her.'

Christy smiled back at him. 'My daughter needs taking down a peg or three, and should learn to relax. She's become too grand for her own good lately, but will soon discover things are done differently here. But I'd appreciate it if you could go easy on her.' She giggled. 'She's not used to being swept up like that.'

They shared an amused look and then he slapped the reins on Jock's broad back to make him speed up. 'The Dunvegan Hotel's down there at the watter's edge,' he said, pointing a meaty finger at the whitewashed building with a slate roof and a wooden veranda running across the front.

Christy read the weathered sign hanging above the door. 'I suppose the MacDonalds own it?'

'Aye, they used to, just as they once owned everything on this island. But most of their land had to be sold to pay off debts, and some rich businessman from Inverness bought it last year and put in a manager. Mungo MacGregor's another distant cousin, and he and his wife, Betsy, will look after you well.'

'Do the MacGregors run everything in this town?' she asked lightly.

He chuckled. 'Not quite, but we're working on it.' He drew the cart to a halt outside the hotel, lashed the reins to the bench, jumped down, and held his hand up to help Christy alight.

'You might need these,' he said, handing over her boots. 'Or are you planning on walking everywhere without them?'

She returned his teasing smile, took the boots and stuffed her filthy feet into them. 'I'm sorely tempted,' she admitted, hastily tying the laces, 'but I think it's time to behave myself, don't you?'

'Aye. But don't make a habit of it, Christy MacInnes. You'd be no fun at all if you were prim and proper.' He tipped her a cheeky wink, turned to discover that Kathryn had managed to alight on her own, and held out his hand to Anne.

'I'm sure I can manage,' Anne blustered, clutching the sides of the cart as she turned her back and tentatively lowered one foot in search of the step.

Gregor looked across at Christy to see if he should help, but she shook her head, and the three of them waited with bated breath as Anne's foot wavered back and forth high above the step, and her grip on the cart began to loosen.

Gregor caught her as she fell backwards, losing her handbag and her fur wrap in the process. 'It's all right; I've got you,' he said, holding her to his chest for rather longer than necessary.

'Thank you,' she said, her face flushing as she avoided his laughing eyes. 'You may put me down now.'

He set her on her feet very carefully while Kathryn hurriedly rescued the fur and the leather handbag from the wet ground.

Anne took back her belongings and turned to regard the hotel with some disfavour as Gregor began to unload their luggage from the cart. 'Is this the only hotel?' At Christy's nod, she gave an exasperated sigh. 'Then I suppose it will have to do.'

Christy and Kathryn exchanged glances and followed in her wake as she swept through the front door.

4

Melbourne

Harold was not a man who could lie in bed past daybreak, so he was dressed and breakfasted by the time the dining-room clock chimed eight. It was a bleak winter's morning, with the wind coming up from the frozen wastelands of the south, the sky overcast and threatening more rain.

The weather matched his mood, for although he'd rather looked forward to having the house to himself, and not having Anne's constant nagging ringing in his ears, he'd come to miss her – which was ridiculous really, considering they'd grown into the habit of virtually ignoring each other.

He missed his daughter too, for she brought light and youthful energy into the house, and it had been a delight to meet her friends and listen to their silly prattling as they slowly blossomed into lovely young women. He was incredibly proud of her, and although it had caused no end of trouble with Anne, he still firmly believed that the trip abroad would be a huge benefit to her, preparing her for living away from home when she moved to Sydney.

It was preparing him too, he thought, as he lit his pipe and stared into the fire in the hearth. These past months had made him realise he was lost without her and her mother – that the excitement of a new business deal couldn't compare to what he really treasured.

It had been rather liberating at first to be able to dine with his friends until all hours, go to the races without Anne fussing about how much he drank or gambled, or to simply pack up a swag of essentials and ride his horse out into the bush to camp for a few days. Anne could never understand these forays, but Melbourne society stifled him at times, and he needed to escape, to be alone and free to wander in the bush, reacquainting himself with who he was and where he'd come from. It was easy to forget his roots and the years of hardship now he lived in a grand house in the best part of Melbourne, with a flourishing trade in transporting cattle and sheep and exporting wool, sugar and beef, and more than enough money to do as he pleased.

Yet, as the weeks slowly passed, the novelty had worn off, and he'd become all too aware of the echoing rooms and the silence of a house empty but for the servants. He puffed on his pipe and looked at the photographs on the mantelpiece. They were stiffly posed studio shots of Anne and Kathryn, taken before they'd sailed, and as he looked at Anne's haughty face, he wondered how they'd let their initial happiness slip away from them. What had happened to the laughing girl he'd once swung up into his arms, and who'd looked at him with such love and trust? What had happened to the young man who'd had so many dreams for their life together?

Impatient with his thoughts and saddened by the realisation that his dreams had withered and died as he'd struggled to build his empire, and the laughing girl had become sour and ill tempered, he left the fire and strode over to the large windows that overlooked Phillip Bay. The rain splattered against the glass, the far shore lost in the low clouds, and as he stood there he felt the slow trickle of a tear run down his cheek.

The light tap on the door startled him and he hastily brushed away the tear. 'Yes? What is it?'

'You have a visitor, sir.'

He pulled out his pocket watch and then turned to look at the little maid nervously standing in the doorway. 'It's too early for visitors,' he said brusquely. 'Send them away.'

'It's Mr Baker, sir. He says he must see you as a matter of urgency.'

A stab of alarm shot through him, and he hastened to find the family's portly legal advisor, who was waiting impatiently in the reception hall. 'What's so urgent it can't wait until business hours?'

'I'm sorry, Harold, but this came by special courier to my home. I thought you should see it as soon as possible.'

Harold took the bulky brown envelope, ordered the maid to bring tea, and ushered Baker into his office. Sitting at his desk, he slid out the contents of the envelope, which proved to be many folded sheets of legal documents, accompanied by a letter from some solicitor in Adelaide. Scanning the letter, he felt the colour drain from his face.

'I'm sorry to be the bearer of such bad tidings, Harold,'

muttered Baker once the maid had delivered the tea and left the room. 'But this has to be dealt with as a matter of urgency.'

'You're damned right it does,' Harold stormed, flinging the papers on to his desk. 'Where do you suggest we begin?'

'We could refute the claim, and counter-sue.'

'I don't want this going to court. The newspaper sharks would have a feeding frenzy, and lives as well as reputations would be ruined.'

Harold gnawed at his thumbnail, his mind racing over the snatch of conversation he'd heard some years before, down in Bellerive, Tasmania. The words hadn't made much sense then, and as he had quite innocently overheard them as he'd been passing the open window, he hadn't thought it wise to ask questions about what was clearly a very private and personal exchange. Now those words were coming back to haunt him, and he felt a chill of foreboding.

'We have to find a way to stop this before it goes any further,' he muttered. Unable to contain his anger and growing dread any longer, he pushed back from the desk and began to pace.

'I could hire someone to look into the law firm handling this,' said Baker. 'For all we know, they could be a bunch of unqualified crooks on a fishing expedition.'

'The papers seem valid enough,' said Harold, eyeing the seals and bits of ribbon.

Baker snorted. 'You only need to have worked as a clerk in a solicitor's office to know how to put such things together.'

'That might be so, but Thomasina Brown is clearly out to make trouble. What if, God forbid, this claim is genuine?'

'Then we'll have to proceed very carefully,' Baker rumbled. He eyed Harold from beneath his brows. 'Is there a possibility that there is some truth in their claim?'

'I really don't know,' Harold admitted, 'but whoever this woman is, she seems to know a great deal about our business.' He continued to pace, feeling trapped and helpless until he realised there was something he could do rather than remain here stewing. He turned to Baker, suddenly impatient to get this meeting over.

'Get someone to investigate this law firm as well as the Brown woman. And have them dig deep, Baker. We need to know exactly who and what we're dealing with before we go any further.'

'I'll see to it today, and dig out the deeds for the family properties,' Baker said, struggling to his feet. 'If I hear anything, I'll let you know immediately.'

'Then you'd better get word to me by telegraph. I won't be here.'

Baker looked startled. 'This is hardly the time – '

'I shall be with my brothers-in-law,' he said briskly. 'Hamish and James may be able to shed light on this, and help prove this claim is spurious. So I'll be leaving for the Barossa Valley today.'

*

Skye

The hotel proved to be surprisingly comfortable, with large rooms overlooking the loch, and a tastefully furnished public area in which blazed a very welcoming fire. They'd been greeted by their friendly hosts, who were delighted to meet yet more members of their widespread family, and while Gregor brought in their trunks and suitcases, Christy and the others warmed themselves by the fire with cups of tea before they were shown to their rooms.

Christy was relieved to note that not even Anne could find something to complain about, but she'd wondered if her daughter was merely tired and the griping would start again in the morning. She rather hoped not, for she had plans for tomorrow and didn't want them spoiled.

Once the maid had brought up the jugs of hot water to fill the small tub that had been placed next to the cheerful bedroom fire, Christy sank into it with a sigh of pleasure. She did feel tired and very grubby, and could still feel the chill of that wet peaty grass in her feet and ankles. It had definitely been foolhardy to discard her boots – but she didn't regret it for one minute.

She eyed the scratched soles of her feet and the dirt-encrusted toenails and fleetingly wondered if her emotional reaction to setting foot once again on Skye was indeed the first sign of senility setting in. It had been years since she'd gone without shoes and she could remember how red and swollen her feet had become as a child, tramping over hills and glens, working the narrow strip of croft land, and foraging for kelp and shellfish on the sharp rocks of the cove. Her feet had been hardened then, the soles becoming like leather throughout her childhood – but they'd cracked from the cold and wet and made her whimper with the pain, even though her mother had smoothed her special herbal balm on them.

She grabbed the nail brush and began to scrub at the embedded dirt until her toenails were clean, and then gently washed her feet with a soapy sponge. She'd clearly become too soft over the years, and would have to use her hand cream on them tonight. She slid down in the water to let it lap beneath her chin as she relaxed and let the day's aches and pains be soothed by the warmth.

Dinner was a hearty meal of haggis, neeps and tatties, which Anne had poked at suspiciously before clearing her plate. Christy hadn't upset Anne's sensibilities by revealing how the haggis had been prepared, but had educated both her companions in the fact that neeps were nothing to do with parsnips, but could be either turnip or swede mixed with creamy mashed potato.

Amongst the other guests were two retired but energetic and rather hearty schoolmistresses. They'd come to Skye on a walking tour, and liked nothing better than a game of bridge after dinner; when they asked if Christy or the others might be interested in joining them for a rubber or two, Christy had declined. She'd never seen the attraction of the game. She waited until Anne and Kathryn were settled at the card table, and slipped out to fetch her coat and shawl.

Wrapping her mother's tartan shawl around her neck, she walked slowly beside the loch, watching the moon's reflection in the still water. The sky was clear, the air soft with the promise of summer, and the only sound was that of her boot heels crunching on the pebbled path.

She came to a halt and stood for a while, letting the essence of Skye reawaken in her, and then she turned back towards the hotel to prepare for the following day.

Anne was quiet during breakfast and, as this was unusual, Christy wondered what was upsetting her now. 'I had the most marvellous night's sleep,' she said cheerfully in an effort to pull her daughter out of her doldrums.

'So did I,' enthused Kathryn, spreading yellow butter on the thick slab of home-made bread and adding home-made bramble jelly. 'It must be all that fresh air we've had.'

'What about you, Anne?'

'The bed was comfortable enough,' she said grudgingly, 'but I didn't sleep well. I think I might be coming down with a cold.' She gave a delicate sniff and dabbed at her nose to prove the point.

'Oh, no, Mother. You can't be ill. Grandma's taking us to where she was born today so she can start telling us her stories.'

'I don't think I could bear another ride in that wagon,' Anne replied. 'My constitution has always been delicate, and being open to the elements all day is bound to take its toll. I think I'll stay here and nurse my cold.'

'But you can't,' gasped Kathryn. 'It's so important you come with us.'

'I'm sure that if you wrap up warmly you'll be fine,' said Christy, who'd never known her daughter to possess a delicate constitution unless it suited her. 'I've asked Mungo's wife to make up a picnic basket, and she's also providing extra blankets.'

Anne glanced out of the window at the clear blue sky. 'If it rains, we'll be soaked,' she muttered.

'Then we'll take our umbrellas and raincoats as a precaution,' said Christy firmly. She eyed the thin blouse beneath Anne's light-weight skirt and jacket. 'And I would advise you to wear the tweeds we bought in Inverness, and the woollen underwear I sent you from Hobart. And I hope you remembered to pack stout boots, as I suggested. We'll be doing some rough walking today.'

'But they're so ugly,' Anne protested. 'As for that awful under-wear, it makes my skin prickle, so I left it at home.'

Christy bit back an impatient retort. 'Then I'll lend you some of mine,' she said.

'Can't you see I have no interest in coming with you?' hissed Anne across the table. 'I want to stay here in the warm. Not be thrown about in an open cart, listening to your silly stories – which I suspect are as fanciful as the tales you told me as a child.'

'Mother!' gasped Kathryn.

Christy was hurt to the core by her daughter's words and the barely veiled meaning behind them, but she patted Kathryn's hand and forced a smile. 'It's a pity your mother won't accompany us, but you and I will have our own adventure,' she said. 'Now eat up. Gregor will be here soon.'

She waited until the girl had finished her breakfast and gone upstairs to fetch her coat and gloves before she faced a sullen Anne across the table. 'I know what this is about,' she said quietly, aware of the other diners around them. 'And I will not have you using it to punish Kathryn.'

'I'm not punishing her,' she replied.

'Yes, you are. You're spoiling this trip with your rudeness and constant sniping. You forced yourself on us – and I warned you I would not tolerate this sort of behaviour.'

'I don't feel well,' Anne replied with a whine of self-pity. 'My chest is always affected in bad weather.'

Christy threw the table napkin down and leaned towards her. 'You might fool Harold and Kathryn with this act, but I'm not impressed. You've always had the constitution of an ox, and a cold has never stopped you doing anything you wanted to do. Don't play games with me, Anne. They are dangerous.'

They held one another's gaze across the table, and it was Anne who broke the tense silence. 'Then perhaps you shouldn't have played games with the truth,' she said flatly. 'You can tell all the stories you want, but I'll never believe you again.'

Christy sat back in the chair and sighed. 'I'm sorrier about that than anything,' she said, her voice breaking with emotion. 'And I do realise that once trust has gone, things can never be the same. But there comes a point, Anne, when both of us have to find a way of accepting and understanding that what happened is in the past, and there's nothing either of us can do to change that. For the sake of everyone in this family, we must try to resolve this and move on.'

She reached for her daughter's hand, but Anne snatched it away.

'I'll never stop loving you, Anne,' she said earnestly, 'and I'm prepared to wait for your forgiveness for as long as it takes.'

Anne's lips were a thin line and a small muscle moved in her jaw as she gritted her teeth and refused to meet her mother's gaze.

'I'm asking you to come today because it's important,' continued Christy. 'It's time you knew where we all spring from – how we've become the people we are. Please, Anne, if not for my sake, for Kathryn's.'

'That's emotional blackmail,' Anne said bitterly.

'It's the only weapon I have.'

Anne pushed back from the table and was about to leave the dining room when Gregor came through the door.

'Are ye ready for your day out, ladies?' he enquired, shooting them a broad grin.

'We just have to fetch our coats and stouter footwear,' said Christy. 'Unfortunately, my daughter has decided not to accompany us.'

'Och, that's a shame, because I have a special treat for Mrs Ross.'

Anne went pink and couldn't quite hide the fact he'd tweaked her curiosity. But she lifted her chin and looked at him haughtily. 'I doubt you could provide anything I might find either special or a treat.'

He raised an eyebrow, his gaze suddenly challenging. 'Well, why don't you come and see? And, if it's not to your liking, we'll leave you be.'

Anne suddenly realised that the other guests were watching this exchange with avid interest. She kept her chin high, meeting his challenge. 'I suppose I'll have to see whatever it is if I'm to be left in peace,' she muttered crossly. 'Where is it?'

'Outside,' he replied shortly. He stepped back so she could leave the dining room and then glanced at Christy and winked.

Intrigued, Christy followed them into the large reception hall and out on to the veranda. The sight that met her eyes made her chuckle in delight.

Jock had been groomed until his dusty coat gleamed against the shining harness, and he stood proudly between the shafts of an old-fashioned but highly polished covered carriage.

'I thought you said there were no carriages on the island,' said Anne accusingly.

'Mungo remembered there was one stored away in the back of the stables,' said Gregor, pointing to the ramshackle buildings beside the hotel. 'It was a bit dirty, and one of the wheels needed attention, but nothing so bad that a lick of paint and some elbow grease couldn't put right.'

Anne stepped down from the veranda to cast a critical eye over the carriage. 'The leather seating is in very poor condition,' she said, 'which will make it most uncomfortable.'

Christy saw how Gregor's brows had lowered, and broke in quickly: 'Well, I think it's a marvellous find, Gregor. You must have been up half the night restoring it.'

'Och, it didn't take too long. Mungo and Betsy helped.' He turned to Anne. 'I'm afraid I couldn't do much with the leather seats, but with a few of Betsy's thick blankets over them, you won't suffer any discomfort.'

Christy watched her daughter's face as she struggled to think up a valid reason for not accompanying them.

'Then I hope the springs are sound,' Anne said. 'I have no wish to be jolted about.'

Gregor's smile didn't reach his hazel eyes, but his voice held no hint of any impatience. 'They've been thoroughly oiled and tested, Mrs Ross. You'll no find yourself being jolted.'

'I will need to change into more appropriate clothing,' she said, avoiding her mother's amused gaze. 'You'll have to wait until I'm ready.'

Christy and Gregor exchanged glances. This day out could prove to be very trying.

*

Kathryn was about to run down the stairs when she met her mother on the landing. 'Please say you'll come with us,' she pleaded. 'It wouldn't be the same without you.'

'I have already agreed,' replied Anne. 'But only because you seemed so set on me coming, and now MacGregor has provided a carriage of sorts, it appears I have no choice in the matter.'

'A carriage?' breathed Kathryn. 'But how marvellous.'

'It isn't in the least marvellous,' retorted Anne. 'But it will suffice.'

Kathryn stifled a giggle at her mother's snootiness and ran down the stairs, eager to see what Gregor had brought them. When she saw Jock looking so handsome, with his carefully groomed mane and white feathered feet, and the shining old-fashioned carriage, she clapped her hands in delight.

'How lovely,' she breathed, giving Jock's neck a pat before she inspected the inside of the carriage. 'My goodness, Mr MacGregor, you are clever to have found it.'

She saw the flush in his cheeks, realised she'd embarrassed him with her enthusiasm, and hastily turned to help Mungo's wife, Betsy, who'd appeared with an enormous picnic basket and an armful of blankets.

Once the blankets had been spread over the weathered leather, and the picnic basket was stowed beneath the seat, Kathryn and Christy climbed into the carriage and waited for Anne.

They had a tiresome wait, in which Jock grew bored and Gregor became restless. Kathryn was on the point of going back inside to find out what was taking her mother so long, when she appeared in the doorway.

Kathryn could see she was disgruntled at having to discard her fashionable clothes for the tweed jacket and skirt and stout walking boots she clearly disliked. There was a swathe of fur about her neck, she carried a raincoat and umbrella in her gloved hands, and her hair had been tightly twisted into a bun beneath the unflattering felt hat.

Kathryn gave an inward sigh of disappointment as her mother coolly acknowledged Gregor and permitted him to hand her up the step into the coach, where she accepted his offer of a blanket for her knees. If her mother was going to keep up this attitude all day, it would ruin everything.

Gregor disappeared from view and the carriage swayed as he climbed up into the high driving seat and Jock eagerly set off down the village street.

The cob's hooves rang on the cobbles as the wheels rumbled and the oiled coach springs absorbed the jolts. They passed the empty slipway into the loch where the fishing boats had been moored the previous evening and continued on through the tiny village that was provided with an old wooden kirk, a general store and a blacksmith's forge. The houses were mostly one-storey stone cottages, huddled into the hill and whitewashed, their sturdy shutters flung open to the sunshine.

'How far is MacInnes Bay, Grandma?' Kathryn asked as they left the village behind and began the long hill-climb, which afforded a breathtaking view of the loch.

'It's a way yet,' she replied. 'So you might as well relax and enjoy the scenery.'

Kathryn settled back as the coach rocked over the rutted track that seemed to meander across the hillside as if it couldn't make up its mind where it was going. She looked out over the almost deserted landscape at the grazing sheep and the few isolated cottages that appeared now and again in the far distance, and wondered what her father would have made of all this. She'd heard his stories about his boyhood, and knew he liked to relive those days by going off with just a horse and his swag into the bush – but this was so open, without a tree in sight, or even the sound of birdsong to disturb the soughing of the wind in the grass.

She thought about her Uncle Hamish's cattle station in the heart of the Queensland outback. That was just as isolated, but stands of eucalyptus – stringybark and red gum – provided some protection from the fierce and unrelenting heat. Swarms of budgies, parakeets and sulphur-crested cockatoos roosted in the branches, their bright colours contrasting with the deep red of the earth, their squawking breaking the great silence of a land unchanged since the beginning of time.

Kathryn still had vivid memories of that one and only visit to

Wallangarra Station, and although she'd found it too isolated and hot after the temperate climate in Melbourne, she'd nonetheless appreciated its grandeur and raw beauty.

Looking now at the blackened heather and the empty miles of pale grass and dark hills, she wondered how her grandmother had fared in a landscape so different from the one she was used to – but she supposed she would soon learn about that once Christy began to tell the story of her life.

5

Christy saw that Anne had become bored with the scenery and was resting back with her eyes closed, but Kathryn seemed to be absorbing her surroundings, even though there was, in truth, very little to see in the unchanging landscape.

She took this quiet moment to admire her granddaughter. Kathryn was wearing the lovely lavender speckled tweed jacket and loose skirt she'd bought in Inverness, and her abundant mop of copper-and-gold hair had been loosely gathered at her nape by a matching ribbon. She'd set the deep lilac woollen beret at a rakish angle over one brow, and her youthful skin glowed with good health. She was growing into a very pretty young woman, with a great sense of style.

Christy turned her attention back to the view. The track was levelling out, and in the distance she could now see a glimmer of the sea loch and the small islands dotted on the horizon. Her heart began to beat faster and her mouth dried as the coach swayed down the hill, towards the path which ran through the glen, towards the broad bay where her earliest memories had been forged. The images flooded back, as vivid as if she'd experienced them only yesterday, and she had to dig deep to find the strength to deal with them.

Gregor brought the carriage to a halt, clambered down and opened the door. 'I can't get any closer,' he said apologetically. 'The wheels will sink and we'll be stuck.'

Christy had eyes only for the bay as she stepped down. 'This will be fine,' she murmured, already moving away from him towards the rough ground that stretched between the scattered boulders and pinnacles of rock which jutted from the sand within the sheltering arms of the towering black cliffs at either end of the bay.

Without waiting for the others, she tramped across the hummocks of grass, which were laced with rivulets of dark water, her gaze fixed on the far side of the bay and the remains of the cottage that had once stood there. And as she finally reached it, she heard the mournful cry of a curlew, which sent a shiver down her spine. The ancient ones believed the curlew's cry was a harbinger of death – and there had been death here – many deaths.

Christy shivered, not from the cold but from the memories and the ghostly voices that seemed to be carried to her on the wind. She dug her fingers into her mother's shawl, took a deep, restorative breath and began to pick her way through the tumbled boulders and scree until she reached the remains of what had once been her home.

Her grandfather had built the croft from the rocks he'd taken from the cliffs to provide shelter for his family. It sat above the high watermark on a flat outcrop, and Christy remembered how safe she'd felt within those thick walls, with the warmth of the peat fire bringing a soft glow into the darkness as the wind stirred up the sea and howled across the bay. Now only the sentinel of the fireplace and chimney, and a few scattered stones remained.

Christy touched the smoke-blackened stone, which had weathered in the wind and rain but had fallen to the hands of man. It was as if these few remnants still held the essence of those who'd once lived here, and she could almost hear their voices and smell the peaty smoke of the fire.

'Are you all right, Grandma?'

Christy nodded, her hand still flattened against the stones that sang to her. Her mind was full of the past, her eyes seeing things no one else could see – things that no child should ever have to witness.

Christy drew back from those sights and sounds and realised Anne and Gregor had come to join them. 'This was once my home,' she said quietly. 'It was built by my grandfather, Alasdair MacInnes, shortly before his marriage to Morag MacGregor.' She glanced across at Gregor with a faint smile. 'Their youngest son, Angus, was my father, and when he married my mother, Anne MacInnes, a distant cousin, they moved in here.'

'It must have been very crowded,' said Kathryn, taking in the ragged outline of what had once been the footprint of the tiny cottage.

'I suppose it was, but I didn't notice. Every croft was the same, you see.'

'What did it look like, Grandma? And was it the only one in this bay?'

Christy moved away from the wall and faced the sweep of the now deserted glen, where only a few rough stones marked what had once been the strips of croft land. She could hear the curlew again, and the sound made her shiver.

'There was a fairly large community here – what we called a *baile* – and there were other cottages scattered across the glen.' She regarded the now empty glen and deserted beach. 'We each had a strip of land to grow crops, although the soil wasn't good – too wet and salty. There were a few cattle and sheep and most of the crofters had chickens. My grandfather had been a fisherman, and when he died my father took over the boat, but he was a farmer at heart, and would often leave us in the summer to go and work for the laird during the harvest so that we had money to pay the rent and see us fed through the winter.'

She stepped beyond the traces of the stone footings and began to clamber further up the slope behind the house until she reached the flat ledge beneath an overhang of rock. 'This was my favourite place to sit and wait for sight of my father's boat,' she explained, as Kathryn joined her and Gregor helped Anne up the slope.

She waited as Gregor spread the blankets over the cold slab, and once everyone was settled, Christy took a deep breath and began her story.

'You asked me what our cottage looked like,' she said to Kathryn. 'Well, it was thatched with the reeds we cut from the river banks, and the floor was a flattened mixture of earth and crushed stone which we sprinkled with straw and wild herbs to keep it sweet-smelling. The two windows and the door were deeply set in the thick walls and faced away from the shore to the glen, to protect us from the winter winds. Consequently, it was very dark inside, lit only by an oil lamp and the glow from the fire.'

She hugged her knees, her chin buried in the folds of the shawl. 'We didn't possess such things as beds and mattresses, so we slept on straw-filled sacks set on the floor close to the fire. But we were rich in love and the sense of belonging.'

As she continued talking, the present faded and she was once again a child of ten, running barefoot through the purple heather of that late-August twilight to her mother, who was tilling the poor soil.

'I've brought you some bread and cheese,' she panted. 'Widow Cameron exchanged the cheese for two of our eggs.'

Her mother leaned on the hoe, easing her back before caressing the mound of her swollen belly. 'That was kind of her,' she said, her dark hair ruffled by the wind, her brown eyes glancing across at the distant cottage. 'I hope you helped with the milking this morning; she finds it a trial now she's so crippled.'

'Aye, of course I did,' Christy replied, slightly hurt that her mother should think she'd forgotten such an important task. 'And Uncle Fergus promised he'd be back in time to do it tonight.'

Anne MacInnes nodded and sat down on a dry hummock of grass to take the hunk of bread and slab of cheese. 'Where are your brothers?'

'Jamie has gone down to the beach with wee Callum to look for shellfish in the rock pools.' She sat beside her mother and watched her tear into the bread, her mouth watering at the thought of that lovely tangy cheese – but she didn't begrudge her mother, for she needed it more, with the bairn growing inside her.

Her mother tore off some bread and a corner of cheese and passed them to her. 'Here, Christy, you need something to keep you going until supper.'

Unable to resist, and encouraged by her mother's insistent nod, she took the scraps and savoured them slowly.

'Granny's finished weaving your shawl,' she said eventually. 'And she's promised to give me another lesson so that one day I can make things just as well.'

Anne MacInnes smiled. 'So, apart from milking Widow Cameron's cow and watching your grandmother weave, what actual work have you done today?'

'I collected kelp once it was low tide, and laid it out to dry just as you taught me, and me and Jamie carried the already-prepared kelp to the kiln, so that Iain MacGregor can burn it, ready to be taken to the factory.'

Anne MacInnes cupped Christy's little face with a work-roughened hand. 'You're growing into a bonny wee lassie,' she said tenderly. 'I don't know how I'd manage without you.' She ran her hand over her belly, her expression suddenly sad. 'We'll soon have another wee mouth to feed,' she murmured, regarding the blighted potatoes she'd dug up. 'If the crop fails again . . .'

Christy was all too aware of how harsh winter would be, for they'd barely survived the previous two without potatoes to eke out the seaweed porridge and nettle stews, and she could remember how hungry she'd been. She saw her mother's worry and took her hand. 'We'll manage, Mum,' she said stoutly. 'Daddy will catch lots of herring, and once it's salted and in barrels, they'll see us through.'

Anne MacInnes gave her a bright smile that didn't quite hide the worry in her eyes. 'Of course he will,' she said, getting to her feet and reaching for the hoe. 'Now, you'd better go and check on the bairns and Granny while I finish up here. Your father and Finlay will be back soon, eager for their supper.'

Christy scampered away, her bare feet splashing through the small streams of water that laced the glen. She raced over the strip of pebbles that met the hard wet sand, and once she saw her brothers were engrossed in their rock-pool hunt, ran as fast as she could towards home. Sketching a wave to her grand-mother, who was sitting outside the cottage, still at her small loom, she scrabbled up the hill, gained the flat stone beneath the overhanging rock, and searched the horizon for a glimmer of sail.

She adored her father, for he was big and handsome, with fiery red curly hair and beard, and a deep voice she loved listening to. Her favourite moments were when he gathered her and her younger brothers on to his sturdy knees, holding them safe and warm in his strong arms as he told stories of the Vikings who'd come from the north in their magnificent ships to change the lives of the islanders.

Her older brother, Finlay, was like his father in looks, but he had yet to grow a beard and he was not as tall or broad. Neither was he as patient with her, and so Christy wasn't sure she liked him as much as perhaps she should.

Christy finally glimpsed the sail far out beyond the headland, and realised the boys had seen it too, for they'd left their hunt in the pools and were now standing in the shallows of the incoming tide, waving eagerly. She was about to rush down to the beach when she heard something that froze her.

She looked towards the sound, and what she saw stopped her breath. Men on horseback – men on foot – dogs straining at leashes, baying for blood. All advancing on the *baile*. The laird's brutal factor and his army of equally brutal Sassenachs from the lowlands had come to evict them.

Christy couldn't move or breathe as she watched her mother running awkwardly from the field, her warning yells almost lost in the terrible shouts and screams coming from behind her. Jamie and Callum stood hand in hand, wide-eyed in terror on the shore, Granny was trembling and white-faced – and her father's boat was still beyond the reef in deep, rough water.

Christy's own terror made her clumsy and she almost fell as she came down the hill. Her mother was already at the cottage, her arm round Granny's shoulders as she helped her out of the chair. 'Get to your brothers and hide in the rocks over there,' she ordered. 'Stay there until we fetch you.'

'But what about you and Granny?'

'She's too frail to go far, and I doubt even the factor's men will harm someone so old and helpless,' she said grimly. 'Run, Christy, and don't argue.'

Despite her fear for her mother and grandmother, Christy ran, her bare feet lightly skimming across the rough stones, her tears blinding her as she raced for the sand. 'Run and hide,' she yelled to her brothers. 'In the rocks, over there.'

As they began to run, she glanced out to sea. The boat was nearer, but still had to navigate the narrow entrance to the bay through the reef. She could see the figures of her father and brother standing at the bow, but they were still too far away for her to make out their faces. A glance over her shoulder revealed the orange flames and thick pall of black smoke rising from the more distant cottages that had already been set alight.

Jamie and Callum were wee, skinny bairns of eight and five, and with Callum's withered foot hampering him, they couldn't run very fast, so Christy scooped them up and tucked them under her arms as she raced for the shelter of the rocks on the far side of the bay.

Her heart was racing and she could barely breathe as she finally reached the rocks and set them on their feet. 'We have to hide,' she panted to the terrified boys. 'Quick, get in there and stay as low as you can.'

Jamie was fighting his tears as he and the sobbing Callum crept into the deep crevice that ran the height of the cliff. Christy wedged herself in with them and gathered them close. 'Hush now,' she whispered. 'We have to be very quiet. Daddy and Finlay will be here soon, and they'll see no harm comes to us.'

'Where's Mama?' whimpered Callum. 'I want Mama.'

'She's with Grandma, and she knows that you and Jamie are big brave boys and will do as she asked by keeping quiet and out of sight.'

'But who are those bad men? Why have they come?' he persisted through his tears.

'They don't want us here,' said Jamie gruffly, his tear-filled eyes glinting with adult hatred as he balled his small fists.

'But why?'

Jamie roughly drew him close. 'Because they hate us,' he said, his expression grim. 'Hush, Cal. You're not a baby anymore, and you wouldn't want Daddy to see you blubbering, would you?'

This seemed to calm Callum, and Christy shot Jamie a look of gratitude. Yet as they huddled within the clutches of the crevice, with its sharp barnacles and stinking wet seaweed, the terrifying sounds of screams and shouts and barking dogs were carried to them on the sea wind. Unable to contain her curiosity any longer, Christy dared to take a peek round the razor-sharp edge of the crevice.

The men had yet to reach their home, and her mother was swiftly collecting their belongings from the cottage and piling them into an untidy heap as Granny sat clutching the newly made shawl, clearly too frail and frightened to move. Her father's boat had come through the narrow reef entrance, and he was pulling hard on the tiller to catch every breath of wind into the sails to speed them to shore.

'Daddy's almost here,' she muttered, before being drawn back to the awful sounds coming from the glen.

Smoke billowed from the burning cottages, filled the glen and darkened the sky. Bodies lay still in the heather as women and children screamed, and riders fought to calm their rearing horses. The men and dogs were now surrounding Widow Cameron's cottage.

A sob of distress and horror escaped from Christy as she saw the frail old woman being dragged from her cottage and thrown to the ground. The men had clubbed Fergus MacInnes, who'd tried to protect her, leaving him broken and battered amid his rotting potato crop as they turned their threats on the helpless woman at their feet. They bellowed and waved their clubs at her while their dogs snarled and strained from their leashes and the spooked horses threatened to trample her with their flaying hooves.

Christy didn't want to see any more, but she was incapable of looking away as the widow tried to crawl to safety. And then one of the men's heavy boots thudded into her frail body and she was still. Blazing torches made short work of her thatched cottage and meagre belongings.

Christy was trembling so badly her legs folded beneath her and she dropped back into her hiding place, unaware of the sharp rock scraping her arms as those images replayed over and over in her head. Terror for her mother and grandmother rose within her like the slice from a sharp blade as hot tears ran down her face and shivers wracked her ice-cold body.

'What is it, Christy? What did you see?' Jamie had grabbed her arms, shaking her roughly until she came out of her stupor.

She shook her head, unable to answer him until she realised she was terrifying both of them and had to find a way to blot out what she'd seen and reassure them. 'I just got some sand in my eyes,' she said tremulously.

Jamie looked at her sharply. He clearly didn't believe her, but as Callum clung to him and sobbed he remained silent, his unwavering gaze fixed on Christy.

The shout from the beach broke the moment and they all looked up to see their father's ashen face. 'Stay there!' he ordered, before turning away and disappearing from sight.

Christy gave her brothers a watery smile and tried to quell her own trembling. 'See? Daddy and Finlay are here now, and they'll look after Mum and Gran.'

The boys clung to her, their grubby faces streaked with tears of fear and some relief, and Christy held them tightly, praying fervently that her father and Finlay would come to no harm. Yet she'd seen the hatred in the brutal men who could club an old woman to the ground and kick her until she could move no more; had seen the way they'd set upon her Uncle Fergus and anyone who defied them. Was God really watching? Could he put a stop to this slaughter?

As the shouts grew louder and the smoke blotted out the setting sun, Christy ordered the boys to stay low, and tentatively peeked over the rocks again.

She gasped as she saw the glen was now a mass of flames, the factor's men advancing swiftly on her home. Her father had lifted his mother into his arms as Finlay shielded Anne and they all edged away from the snapping, snarling dogs and the men with their threatening clubs.

Christy could see her father was trying to reason with the men as he held his mother high in his arms and tried to fend off the dogs with his heavy boots.

But the men kept advancing, their dogs sensing his fear. Backed hard against the rocky hill, and unable to defend himself, her father was clubbed about the head until he fell to his knees, his mother toppling from his arms to thud heavily to the rocky ground.

Christy cried out, transfixed by the horror as the dogs leaped towards the helpless figure on the ground, but Finlay was kicking out at them, his fishing knife held tightly in his hand as he stood over his grandmother and slashed it back and forth. But he was no match for ten men, and the knife was swiftly knocked from his hand and the clubs rained down on him until he too was still.

Anne MacInnes dropped to her knees beside her fallen family, her face contorted with emotion as she screamed and begged the men for mercy. The boot caught her squarely beneath the chin, cutting off the screams and knocking her back against the cliff wall like a rag doll.

'Mummy!' Jamie and Callum had crept from the hideaway and seen it all.

Christy, trembling so badly she could barely move, managed to draw them close and hide their eyes in her skirts as she heard the cruel laughter of the men and saw the torches set fire to the cottage. She began to sob, and as the full horror of what had happened finally broke through she began to scream, the sound of new anguish mingling with the screams in the glen – becoming lost in the baying of dogs, the high whinny of the horses and the shouting of men.

Christy slowly emerged from those dark memories, surprised it was still daylight and that the glen lay peaceful in the sunlight. Yet she could still hear those screams and smell the smoke, could still feel the weight of the awful silence that had fallen on the *baile* after the men had left.

'Once the men had gone, we plucked up the courage to creep out of our hiding place. It was dark by then, the glen glowing from the fires, the rising moon shadowed by swirling black smoke. There was blood in our father's hair and beard as he held our mother in his arms and covered our grandmother in the length of tartan he wore about his shoulders. Finlay was still *glaikit* – muddle-headed – from his beating, and our mother was folded into herself, gasping with pain.'

She regarded her daughter and Kathryn, noted how deeply they'd been affected by her story, and saw the anger spark in Gregor's eyes. 'The woman who attended births across the glen had been killed, so, with mother's instructions, I helped deliver her baby. But she'd come too soon, and before the night was out my tiny sister was dead.'

Tears sprang to her eyes and she didn't bother to wipe them away. 'There were a dozen cottages in the glen before those men came, and as the sky glowed from the fires throughout that night, our community lost eight souls, including the widow Cameron and two bairns. Four of the men who'd resisted the attackers were taken away to the prison at Portree, my Uncle Fergus among them. We never saw any of them again.'

A heavy silence fell on all of them, and it was a while before Christy could continue. 'The survivors gathered up their few belongings and we all found shelter in the caves. It was a night of mourning. We'd lost loved ones; our homes were gone, our beasts scattered, the crops trampled and burned in the fields.'

She took a shallow, trembling breath. 'As the sun rose, the curlews began their mournful cries. It was as if the souls of the dead were calling to us, and even now that sound sends a shiver right through me.'

She twisted her hands in the shawl, her gaze drifting across the glen. 'We buried our dead that day, and one by one the others began to leave – some in search of work and shelter on the mainland, others for the ships that would take them to Canada. There was nothing here for them, and they feared the return of the factor and his men.'

'So what did you do?' breathed Kathryn.

'We eked out an existence in the cave until Mother recovered enough to make the long journey west to her family in the *baile* of Gilleasbuig.'

Anne's face was ashen. 'I didn't realise . . . Why didn't you tell us any of this before now?'

'It's too dark a story to tell a child,' said Christy.

'Oh, Gran,' breathed Kathryn through her tears. 'You were only a child yourself when you had to live through that. No wonder it still haunts you.'

Christy nodded. 'Aye, it does, but there are many others from these islands who witnessed the horrors of the clearances, so I'm not alone.' She looked at Gregor, and knew from his expression that his family had suffered too, and that he'd heard similar stories before this.

She got to her feet and brushed down her thick woollen skirt, suddenly wanting to be gone from this place that still echoed with what had happened there.

As if he'd read her mind, Gregor helped Anne up and began to fold the blanket. 'If ye've a mind to it,' he said, 'I ken there's a bonny wee place an hour away from here, just right for a picnic.'

'I don't think I could possibly eat anything after such a story,' said Anne with a shudder. 'Mother told it so graphically that I imagined I could see it all – and will probably have nightmares for weeks.'

Christy had been living with those nightmares all her life, so made no comment, but turned to Gregor. 'That sounds like a splendid idea,' she said with false brightness. 'It's too fine a day to let the past darken it – and I suspect Betsy has provided us with a sumptuous picnic, which it would be a terrible shame to waste.'

She touched his arm and looked up into his face. 'But first I'd like to visit the kirk and pay my respects.'

At his nod, she determinedly went down the hill and away from the ruined house she would never see again, to the patient Jock who was snuffling in his nosebag. The truth was graphic and cruel – especially when told in such a place – but by returning here and reliving those terrifying hours, she was being forced to face her demons and thereby learning to finally come to terms with them.

The wooden kirk and pastor's house were gone, their place marked only by the crumbling stone walls of the neglected grave-yard. Lonely in its isolation, miles from anywhere, the grass was long, the entangling weeds and brambles threaded through the tufts of heather. A few headstones were visible still, but the words etched so carefully into the slabs of granite had been worn away by the elements.

The grass brushed against her skirt as Christy made her way through the forgotten cemetery where the name MacInnes was etched into so many of the headstones, and eventually managed to find the place where her grandmother and tiny sister had been buried together all those years ago. Brambles had clambered over the roughly hewn headstone, their spiny thorns clinging with determination to the grass against the winds that would blow across the long, broad valley that sat between steep-sided hills.

Christy tried to clear the brambles, but they were too firmly embedded and her gloves were no match for the thorns. She stood and looked around her, remembering the awful weeping and wailing of the women who, through Scottish custom, had not been permitted to follow the men who carried their dead to the burial ceremony. Unable to stand the heart-wrenching noise, she'd defied convention and slipped away to hide behind an outcrop of rock to watch from a distance as the surviving men and boys had clung together and the pastor none of them trusted had moved from one grave to the next to intone his prayers.

'We thought our pastor would protect us,' she said as the others joined her. 'He'd assured us that he'd consulted with the laird and the factors and had secured a promise from them that no harm would come to us as long as we paid our rents and obeyed their orders.'

'As a man of God, that was his duty,' said Anne.

Christy shook her head. 'He might have given that impression, but he turned out to have feet of clay, and proved he couldn't be trusted.' She gave a sigh as she regarded the abandoned cemetery. 'He told us repeatedly he'd stand by us and act as mediator with the laird to ensure we could remain in our homes despite the notice to quit the land, which the factor had nailed to the kirk door. There was no date on that notice, so we trusted the pastor, thinking we'd be safe.'

She took a shallow, wavering breath. 'The pastor must have known far more than us, for there was no sign of him or his family that day the men came. We discovered later that he was looking after his own welfare by siding with the MacDonalds' trustees, and once the *baile* had been cleared, he was given a much richer parish on the mainland.'

Kathryn frowned. 'But why did the laird break his promise not to force you out?'

Christy shrugged. 'My father told me they were never certain that he'd made such a promise – or was even capable of doing so,' she said. 'You see, the laird was bankrupt, and his estates were taken over by trustees who were determined to clear the debts by bringing in sheep, planting trees and encouraging wealthy southerners to come here to hunt deer.' She bit her lip. 'And to do that the land had to be cleared of crofters and cottars.'

A heavy silence fell among them before Christy continued. 'But there was one promise the laird did keep. It was the promise that if we went of our own volition, we'd get free passage and be granted parcels of the land he owned in Canada.'

'But why didn't your father take up that offer?' asked Kathryn. 'Surely it would have been better than staying in Skye? I've read about that time, and the threat of clearance hung over the islands for many more years after what happened here.'

'My father was a proud man – a true Gael of Skye, who could trace his ancestors back to the Vikings who settled here. No man was going to force him to leave.'

'He must have changed his mind eventually,' said Anne, 'otherwise how did you end up in Tasmania? And why there, if the laird was willing to give you land and free passage to Canada?'

'That's a story for another day,' said Christy. She touched the weathered headstone lightly, sent up a silent prayer that those lying here were now at peace, and then headed back to the carriage.

*

Kathryn watched that small, upright figure leave the churchyard, and was filled with overwhelming admiration for her strength of character and her indefatigable determination to live life to the full, despite the horrors of her childhood. Perhaps it was because of what had happened to her then that she was so strong; perhaps those early trials were the force that had spurred her drive and ambition and made her the wealthy, independent woman she was today. For surely the success she'd made of her life was her way of showing those who'd betrayed and exiled her that she would not be defeated – that she was worth far more than their flocks of sheep and could flourish anywhere.

Kathryn's gaze swept the valley. The sun was overhead now and the folds and ridges of the surrounding hills were in sharp focus as the light wind whispered through the grass. Christy's story had affected her deeply; the images she'd evoked were still etched in her mind. They matched those she'd seen after reading the published memoirs of other Scottish migrants to Australia, and fleshed out the brief references she'd found in the history books before making this journey. It seemed that, like the slaughter of the Aboriginals and the American Indians by the early settlers, the crofters of Skye had been victims of a great injustice that had been glossed over to the point where history was altered, and the following generations would never know the truth.

She shivered as she heard the plaintive mewl of the curlews. In this place, and with Christy's tale still vivid in her mind, it was easy to accept the old belief that they were indeed the spirits of lost souls.

Kathryn turned away, and realised her mother was already by the carriage, but that Gregor was still standing at her side, his gaze distant and sad.

'Do you mind if I ask you something?' she said hesitantly.

He withdrew from whatever thoughts had been troubling him and looked down at her. 'Ye can ask, bonny lass, but I'll no be promising to answer.'

'When Grandma was talking about her childhood, I got the feeling you knew and understood exactly what she was describing. Did the same thing happen to your family?'

He was silent for a long moment, and Kathryn was about to apologise for asking such a personal thing when he finally took a deep breath and looked into her eyes.

'Aye, it did. But having seen his croft destroyed and members of his family killed, my grandfather took up the offer of land in Canada and rebuilt his life.'

'I'm guessing he was a farmer.'

Gregor shrugged. 'He could have been one, like those who'd travelled with him, but he staked out a plot none of them wanted. It was high in the hills, thick with trees and scrub, and there was a fast-flowing river running right through it.'

'But surely it was of no use?'

Gregor's smile was wry. 'It was a great deal of use to a man like my grandfather, for he had vision, Miss Ross, and was not a fool.' At her frown, he continued. 'At that time, Canada's population was growing rapidly, the pioneer towns spreading out from the coast, and he realised that those trees would provide the timber for all the building that was going on. He used the river to transport the logs straight into the heart of Chesterfield, on the Hudson Bay, where he also established a sawmill and fur trading post.'

'Gosh,' she breathed. 'How clever of him.'

'Aye, he was that, so my father tells me. He bought more land, sold more timber and fur, built more sawmills, and became a very rich and highly respected man. Unfortunately, I never got to meet him.'

'Why? What happened to him?'

Gregor chuckled. 'He's a grand old man in his nineties now, living with his third – and much younger – wife in Alberta.'

Kathryn smiled. 'And you? How come you aren't in Canada?'

'My father did what your grandmother is doing,' he said. 'He came back to see the places his parents had told him about. He met a wee Scots lassie in Inverness, they got married, and after a short visit to Canada settled here.' His grin broadened. 'And that's why I'm here, back where it all began.'

'Your grandfather must have been disappointed that your father didn't take over the business.'

'Dad was one of six boys and so he wasn't short of heirs to his empire. Dad had never wanted to be a part of it anyway, and had qualified as a doctor after seeing so many accidents among the lumberjacks. He much prefers running his practice in Portree and working hard at his golf handicap to wading through thirty feet of snow to get to his patients and having to protect his animals from marauding brown bears and timber wolves.'

The idea of wolves, brown bears and snow so deep it would cover the roof of a house conjured up exciting images for Kathryn, but she realised it would be naïve of her to share these thoughts.

'What about you, Gregor? What are your ambitions?' she asked instead.

He chuckled as he ran his fingers through his windswept hair. 'Well now, it seems to me that I'm content with life the way it is. I have a roof over my head, food enough to eat, and good company when I want it.'

Without thinking, Kathryn blurted out, 'But surely you must need a proper income?' She felt the heat rise in her face and couldn't meet his amused gaze. 'Sorry, that was rude of me,' she muttered.

'Aye, well, I'll no tack offence, lassie.' He looked over at the carriage, where Anne was signalling impatiently. 'I have income enough,' he murmured, 'but we'll continue this conversation at another time. I think your mother wants you.'

Thankful for the opportunity to flee, Kathryn hurried towards the carriage, her face still warm with embarrassment.

'What *do* you think you're doing, Kathryn?' hissed Anne, glancing across at Gregor, who was ambling towards them.

'We were just having a conversation, Mother.'

'It isn't seemly to engage in such an intimate way with the hired help. He's a young working-class man and your behaviour could give him entirely the wrong impression.'

Kathryn sighed inwardly and climbed into the carriage to be greeted by her grandmother's understanding smile and consoling pat on the shoulder. Thank goodness for Grandma, she thought, returning the smile. If it wasn't for her, Mother's constant nagging would be impossible to bear.

6

Australia

Harold had gone to the telegraph office in Melbourne as soon as Baker had left the house. He was restricted in what he could tell the brothers, for his message would be relayed down the line in Morse and decoded at the nearest point to the addressee. From there, it would be relayed by two-way radio.

The open airwaves had become a lifeline for those living in the far-flung and isolated country communities, but they also provided a wealth of information to be gossiped about and picked over. Harold's message had therefore been brief, assuring them the travellers were safe and well, but he had an urgent matter to discuss and would meet both of them at Yarrabinda.

He'd at first considered going by train to Adelaide, where he could then catch the goods train on the private line, which would take him into the heart of the Barossa Valley. However, travelling by rail was unreliable and frustratingly slow and disjointed, for despite the government's determination to regulate the railway system, most of the lines between Melbourne and Adelaide were still owned by different companies, each with their own gauge of rail. This meant long delays switching trains, or hanging about at isolated stops in the middle of nowhere for a train that might not even show.

Realising it would be less frustrating to make his own way there, he'd ordered his grooms to prepare his strongest and most reliable horse, for it was a long journey. Now he sat with the reins loose in his hands as the chestnut gelding kept up a steady trot through the trees that grew by the side of sprawling pastures, where sleek fat cattle stood knee-high in the good grass.

He'd pulled the brim of his bush hat low over his eyes against the teeming rain, and could hear the water dripping from the brim on to the shoulders of his long, weatherproofed drover's coat as the horse splashed through the mud. He'd been travelling for two days now, with frequent stops to spell the horse and snatch some tucker and a bit of sleep. Harold knew he was making good time, and that by tomorrow afternoon he should have his first glimpse of the town of Tanunda and the great green valley of endless rows of vines that surrounded Yarrabinda.

His eyes felt gritty from lack of decent sleep and his coat and boots were liberally splattered with mud. Yet despite the cold and wet, a stiff neck and aching back, his mind was clear and purposeful. The papers were tucked safely in a breast pocket beneath his drover's coat, their devastating intent burning through to his very soul. He had to find a way to fight this thing, to protect those he held most dear and keep it from the outside world. He could only pray that Hamish had got his telegram and was also on his way to Yarrabinda, and that the three of them could resolve this quickly and without too much pain.

He slowed the horse to a walk and allowed his thoughts to wander as they began the long climb up the range of rolling hills. Baker was a reliable man, with a vast number of contacts throughout Australia, which included several private investigators. If his man in Adelaide could uncover proof that the law firm was shady and the claimant some toerag out to blackmail one of the wealthiest families in Australia, then this journey would prove to be unnecessary.

He sincerely hoped that would be the case – but he feared it was wishful thinking and was prepared for the worst. For how had the claimant gathered such a devastating amount of information about the family secret? And it had clearly been a deeply hidden secret, one that the keeper would never have revealed for fear of what the consequences would be.

Yet that snatch of conversation he'd overhead some eight years ago made terrible sense now in the light of that claim – and it also explained the events that had followed. Nevertheless, it was clear that someone else had learned the truth and was now threatening to use it to destroy them.

Harold let the horse find its own way down the steep hill to the valley, thick with bush. As they reached the edge of the treeline, he made a concerted effort to ease the tension stiffening his shoulders. Nothing could be resolved until he'd heard from Baker and talked to the brothers, and as the gloomy day turned darker still, he decided it was time to make camp and rest.

He brought the horse to a standstill beneath a thick canopy of trees which gave good shelter from the rain, and climbed down. Easing his back and hips, he gave a wry smile. He was only forty-two, and had considered himself to be in his prime, but the long ride had taken its toll on a body softened through the years of good living.

With a sigh of regret for the passing years and the proof that he was no longer as young and strong as his mind had led him to believe, he unsaddled the horse, rubbed him down with the rough blanket, and left him hobbled to crop the patch of nearby grass.

He opened the drawstring on the oiled canvas bag containing his swag, spread the larger of the two sheets of tarpaulin over some of the low-hanging branches to form a makeshift tent and arranged the second as a groundsheet. Once he'd gathered some dry kindling, he dug a pit and sat on a log to wait for the fire to blaze, and then placed the billycan over it to boil water for tea.

The rain eased off as he munched his way through the thick damper bread and cold mutton, and washed it down with strong billy tea, flavoured with a eucalyptus leaf. Sated and very weary, he wrapped his long coat about him, rested his head on the saddle, and drew the blanket up to his chin.

He looked up past the tarpaulin shelter and through the trees to see that the sky was clearing and the stars slowly emerging. Soon they would blaze in vast swathes against the black canopy, and in the great silence the night creatures would stir in the silvery light, hunting for prey across a landscape unchanged since the beginning of time.

Harold gave a sigh of contentment as he drifted towards sleep, for despite the reason for this journey, this was where he truly belonged – following the old tracks, living the way he and his father had lived, and sleeping on a bed of crushed eucalyptus leaves beneath an old horse-blanket as the campfire's glow slowly dwindled.

He was awakened by the sound of kookaburras laughing in the trees above him, and the raucous shrieks of a flock of vividly coloured rosellas, which had taken off with a great clatter of wings from a nearby bush. He ached all over and could have slept for hours, but there was no time for such luxury, so he dragged himself to his feet and briskly rubbed his hands over his face in an effort to scrub away the weariness.

Quickly stoking the ashes of the fire to a blaze with fresh kindling, he ate the last of the damper bread and mutton while the billy boiled. Having slurped down the stewed tea, he packed everything back in his swag, kicked dirt over the fire to ensure it was out, and then saddled his horse. It was dawn, and time he was on his way.

The noon sun blazed down from a clear sky as he arrived at the brow of Mengler Hill and looked down at the wide sweep of valley that had been settled back in the early half of the previous century by Bavarians escaping the religious tyranny that was sweeping through their homeland. Tanunda was an Aboriginal word meaning 'waterhole', and the town was now surrounded by acre upon acre of neat lines of vines, thriving in the well-watered earth and gentle climate of South Australia.

He let the horse crop in the long grass for a few more minutes and then softly nudged his flank with his heels to encourage him down the hill towards the rooftops and storage towers of Yarrabinda that he could see in the distance.

As he reached the whitewashed stone wall and imposing wrought-iron gates that fronted the property, he nodded with approval. James clearly knew how to impress his visitors, for the whole place was as neat as a pin, the many rows of vines stretching away behind the house and up the gently sloping hills in the distance. The wine press and storage tanks were situated behind a stand of pepper trees; the machine sheds, forge and assorted barns huddled together well away from the house.

The gates stood open, so he rode down the long cinder path that cut through velvety green lawns and flowerbeds blazing with colour, which were being tended by several gardeners. There was an ornate fountain set in the centre of the turning circle in front of the house, and the sprays of water caught the sun and sparkled with miniature rainbows, the sound of it splashing into the white marble bowl pleasing on such an unseasonably warm day.

The house itself had been built back in 1842 by one of the first Bavarian settlers, who'd brought the precious vines across the world to the Barossa Valley to begin a new life, and had come into the family when Christy and her husband had bought it many years later. It was a graceful two-storey building of mellowed stone beneath a red-tiled roof. The shutters over the many windows had been painted dark green to blend in with the surrounding acres of vines, and the broad portico above the impressive oak front door provided welcome shade to tubs of bright red geraniums.

To one side of the house, and set back a little behind a stone wall, was the line of sturdy brick stables, tack room and feed store, all fronted by a paved yard. There was no sign of any horses, so Harold had to assume they were being spelled in one of the paddocks.

As he slid from his horse, he realised his arrival had been noted, for a boy was running towards him from the yard. He grabbed his swag, handed over the reins, gave the boy instructions to feed and water his horse before letting him into the paddock, and then brushed down his own coat and prepared to meet his brothers-in-law.

'It looks like you need a bath and a good feed yourself,' said James, who was leaning in the doorway, dressed in his usual white shirt, jodhpurs and long, highly polished tan leather boots. 'Come on in, Harry.'

They shook hands and Harold followed him into the cool reception hall, where a maid was waiting to take his hat and coat. 'Has Hamish arrived yet?'

'He radioed through as soon as he got your message, and left Wallangarra shortly afterwards. What's this all about, Harry? Why the urgency? It's not Mother, is it?'

'As far as I know, they are all perfectly fine. This is about something entirely different.' He looked about the hall. 'Where's Clarice?'

'I sent her off to her mother's for a spell, so she couldn't get agitated. Agitation isn't good for a woman in her condition.'

Harold smiled and clapped him on the shoulder. 'Congratulations, mate. You kept that quiet.'

'It's a bit early to go shouting about it,' he replied gruffly. He shifted from one foot to another. 'Well? Are you going to tell me what this is all about, or do I have to guess?'

'I'm surprised you haven't already been contacted directly, but I really think it's best if we wait for Hamish.'

James's eyes widened. 'Come on, Harry. Hamish could be hours yet and the suspense is killing me. Surely nothing can be that serious to make such a mystery out of it?'

'It is serious, James – very serious, and it could affect us all.' He eased his aching back and couldn't quite smother a yawn as he reached into his breast pocket and held out the brown envelope. 'Read through that while I take a bath. Once I'm clean and fed, I'll be in a better frame of mind to discuss it with you.'

James regarded the envelope, turning it over in his hands as he frowned. 'You know where the guest rooms are, mate,' he murmured distractedly. 'I'll catch you later.'

Harold went up the sweeping staircase and along the wide landing to the suite of rooms in the west wing. He'd visited Yarrabinda on several occasions to discuss business with James, and now he eyed the comfortable bed with longing, for it would probably be many hours before he could sink into that soft mattress and sleep.

'What the *hell* is this all about?'

Startled, Harold snapped his eyes open and saw a red-faced and clearly furious Hamish looming over him, waving the contents of the envelope in his face. He blinked to dispel the dullness of sleep that was fogging his brain, and realised the water in the bathtub had cooled considerably while he'd dozed.

'I'm not discussing anything while I'm sitting bare-arsed in flaming cold water,' he retorted. 'Get out, Hamish, and wait for me downstairs.'

'Then get a flaming move on,' he roared. 'You've got a lot of explaining to do, mate.' He stomped out of the room, banging the door behind him.

Harold sighed as he climbed out of the bath and reached for a towel. Hamish had always been quick to go off like a loose cannon, and was not the easiest person to deal with when so roused. He had every right to be angry, but Harold did wish he wouldn't make so much noise – it was doing his still-befuddled brain no good at all.

Within the half hour, he was dressed and making his way down the stairs to the large drawing room which overlooked the sweep of vineyards and the grazing paddocks. Both brothers leaped to their feet as he entered, and began talking at once.

Harold put up his hands. 'Please. I know you're angry and worried, but I need to eat if we're to discuss this sensibly.'

'There's a covered dish on that table,' muttered James. 'We'll talk while you eat.'

Harold sighed with pleasure as he lifted the lid and smelled the mouth-watering aroma of fried chicken and buttery mashed potato. He quickly tucked into the delicious food, aware of the tension in the room, but once he'd taken the edge off his hunger he looked up from the plate.

Hamish was prowling round the room, still wearing his bush hat, his hands deep in the pockets of his dusty moleskins, his equally dirty boots making tracks on the highly polished floor. James looked calm, but there was a small muscle working in his jaw, which showed an inner tension.

'James, you've had longer to digest what's in those papers, so why don't you tell me what you think?'

'The claims are obviously false,' the younger man replied grimly. 'It's just someone tweaking our tails to get a reaction in the hope we'll pay them off.'

'They're bloody crooks,' stormed Hamish, 'and they won't get a damned penny out of me, I can assure you of that. We should take the bastards to court and sue their backsides off.'

'But that wouldn't be wise, Hamish,' protested James. 'Once in court she can publicly spread her filthy lies and insinuations, and no amount of denial will undo the harm that will cause. We can't afford to be hot-headed about this – not with so much at stake.'

Hamish gave a great snort of impatience and threw himself into a nearby armchair. 'If I had my way, I'd hunt her down and shoot the bitch,' he growled.

'I just thank God Mother and the others aren't here,' said James. 'We must resolve this before they get back.'

As both brothers fell into silent thoughtfulness Harold finished his late lunch, drank down the glass of red wine, and took a moment to fill and light his pipe. He then quietly told them about Baker's investigator.

'It depends on what the man discovers,' he said, 'but we can't be complacent about it and hope it will all just peter out. Crooks or not, these people mean business.'

'Of course they're bloody crooks,' snapped Hamish, 'and if I had my way, I'd string 'em up.'

'I understand why you'd want to,' said James dryly, 'but that would hardly solve anything, if you were hanged for murder.' He began to pace the room, deep in thought. 'What we have to do is prove their claims are false, and that shouldn't be too difficult. All the documents to do with Yarrabinda are stored in a safety deposit box in Adelaide, and Baker has copies.'

'The ones for Wallangarra are about somewhere,' muttered Hamish. 'We had that fire three years ago and a lot of stuff was destroyed. Beryl's been meaning to go through the piles of furniture and junk we managed to rescue, but what with the kids and the stock, she just hasn't had the time.'

Harold and James looked at him in horror. 'But they'll be vital to prove your ownership,' gasped James. 'Why the hell didn't you leave them with our solicitor, or put them in the bank?'

Hamish reddened. 'I've been too busy dealing with the drought and dying cattle to be worrying about bits of bloody paper,' he rumbled. 'They were in an old tin trunk the last I saw them, but when the fire started we just dragged a lot of stuff out of the house and dumped it in the feed-store shed, hoping the corrugated iron would protect it.'

'And did it?' asked Harold.

He shrugged. 'The furniture was a bit singed from the heat, but it survived well enough. As for the rest of the stuff, it's all stacked up waiting for one of us to sort it out.'

James took a deep breath and clenched his fists. 'Then I suggest you get on the two-way tonight and tell Beryl to look for that trunk. We can only pray she finds it, and that everything is in one piece – because without those documents you won't have a leg to stand on in court.'

'I'm not planning on letting this get that far,' he muttered. 'Besides, it's Yarrabinda in the firing line, not my place.'

'You clearly haven't read the documents properly, Hamish,' said Harold crossly. 'If you had, you'd know that both properties have been targeted and it's Wallangarra she's after, with a minor claim on Yarrabinda.'

Hamish snorted and yanked on the brim of his dusty hat. 'Over my dead body,' he muttered.

'What I don't understand is why Thomasina Brown – whoever the hell she is – is doing this all of a sudden,' said James, his frustration showing in his face.

'It is strange,' murmured Harold. 'The name means absolutely nothing to me, even though I've racked my brains and gone right through my old business diaries.'

'Means nothing to me either,' said Hamish. 'But we've all made enemies over the years – it's an unfortunate evil we all have to contend with in business.' He regarded them both from beneath his heavy brows. 'But if this is purely about getting revenge over a lost deal or transport contract, then why those other filthy claims? It doesn't make sense.'

'Maybe they were dreamed up to give more support to her claims,' replied James, 'although it's a disgustingly low way to go about it.'

Harold fidgeted in the chair and fiddled with his pipe. There was something he needed to ask the brothers, but it would be like setting a match to gelignite.

'What's on your mind, Harry?' James was looking at him intently. 'Is there something you haven't told us?'

Harold shifted restlessly in the glare of their attention, and chose his words carefully. 'Have you considered the possibility that those claims were not made to simply shore up their case, but could possibly hold a glimmer of truth?'

'That's a revolting thing to suggest,' roared Hamish, jumping to his feet. 'Take that back, Harold, or God help me, I'll flatten you.'

Harold eyed Hamish, who was taller, broader and fitter than he could ever be, and, not wanting to antagonise the man, remained seated. He wasn't a fighter, and now was not the time to get embroiled in fisticuffs with his overheated brother-in-law.

'Hitting me won't change a thing,' he said as calmly as he could. 'I'm truly sorry if I offended you, but the question had to be asked.'

'Of course it didn't,' said James, who was ashen with fury. 'How dare you even *consider* such a thing – especially in your position?'

Harold struggled to remain calm. 'It's exactly because of my position that I'm questioning the validity of those claims, and if you would only hear me out, you might understand more clearly why that is so.'

'I'm not listening to anything you might say,' muttered Hamish, reaching for the decanter of whisky. 'I thought you were an honourable man, Harold, and I'm shocked by your disloyalty.'

The rising anger brought Harold to his feet. 'I am not, and never have been disloyal. This family means more to me than you'll ever know, Hamish, and I'm as distressed and angry and frustrated as you – but you *will* hear me out; I demand it.'

Hamish raised one fiery eyebrow and glared at him. 'No man orders me around,' he growled, 'least of all you.' He drained the glass of whisky and slammed it hard on to the mantelpiece.

'Do you want to resolve this mess?' Harold demanded, looking him in the eyes.

'Of course I bloody do.'

'Then shut up and let me talk,' stormed Harold.

Hamish threw himself back into the armchair and folded his meaty arms. 'Get on with it then,' he growled. 'But if I don't like what I'm hearing, I'll knock your flaming block off.'

Harold had little doubt of that, but it was vital he got the brothers to listen and fully digest what he had to say. 'Whoever this Thomasina Brown is, she seems to be far too well informed about the family and our business interests. She's even provided documents to back up some of her more damaging claims – and it is those we have to discuss, calmly and with clear heads.'

Hamish glowered at him. 'Documents can be forged; you know that as well as I do. What she's claiming is slanderous, and I will fight it to my last breath.'

Harold glanced at James, who was slumped in a chair, deep in thought. 'What do you think, James? Could they be forged?'

'I hope for everyone's sake they are,' he said fretfully, 'but there is a sense of confidence in those names and dates she's provided that I find deeply worrying, now I've had time to really think about it.'

Harold eyed the brothers. James was gnawing at his thumbnail and Hamish was still frowning , but at least the fires seemed to have gone out of his temper. 'I agree, it is extremely distressing – not to say shocking.' He paused, wary of stoking those fires again. 'But I overheard part of a conversation some years ago, and now I'm wondering . . .'

Hamish sat forward, hands clasped between his thighs. 'Wondering what?' he snapped. 'Spit it out, Harold, before I really lose my temper.'

Harold poured another glass of wine and took a long drink before he told them what he'd overheard while staying in Bellerive. In the heavy silence that followed, he could almost hear their minds working.

He watched as Hamish left the armchair, dug his hands into the pockets of his moleskins and stared out of the window. 'Strewth,' he breathed. 'I can't take all this in.'

'Are you sure you heard correctly?' James sat forward, his body tense, brown eyes almost pleading for his brother-in-law to have misheard.

Harold nodded and poured them both some more wine. He hated what he was doing to these two men, for they'd become friends as well as brothers – but the effect on the rest of the family would be even worse.

Hamish remained at the window for a while and then his chin dropped and his shoulders slumped. 'I reckon I owe you an apology, Harry, mate,' he said, turning back into the room.

'No need for that,' he replied. 'It's a terrible situation, and things are bound to get heated.'

Hamish poured another whisky, drank it down and lit a cheroot. 'There was something you said a minute ago that got me thinking about a strange thing that happened years ago when I was just a little kid,' he said solemnly. 'I thought then it was just part of a dream, but after today, I'm not so sure.'

Harold and James stiffened, their full attention on Hamish, waiting for him to continue and dreading what they might hear.

Hamish puffed on the cheroot, his gaze fixed to a distant time and place. 'It was the hottest part of the day and I was on the back veranda at Wallangarra for my afternoon nap – in a bit of a snit because I wanted to go down to the billabong with Anne and the other kids, and Dad wouldn't let me.'

'How old were you?' asked James.

'Had to be about four or five, I reckon.' His gaze focused once more on the present. 'I know it was a long time ago, and I'd all but forgotten it, but after what Harry told us, it all came back as clear as if it'd happened yesterday.'

The tension was almost tangible between them as Hamish chewed on the cheroot before crushing it out in an ashtray. Taking a deep breath, he told them about that day, and what he'd thought he'd dreamed. When he'd finished there was a long silence, broken eventually by James.

'Strewth,' he breathed, scrubbing his face with his hands. 'That seems to confirm it all right.' He looked from his brother to Harold, the gleam of determination in his brown eyes. 'It looks like we've got one hell of a fight on our hands, so I hope you're both up for it.'

Harold and Hamish nodded, all too aware that it was a fight they couldn't afford to lose if fortunes and reputations were to be preserved. And yet the odds seemed stacked against them, and none of them knew how to even begin their defence.

7

Skye

The last three days had been spent exploring the nearby countryside, travelling through the area of Duirinish, with its rushing streams and great cliffs of rock where waterfalls tumbled down to isolated bays, its flat-topped mountains and legends of battles with giants.

The weather had improved, with clear skies and a bright sun, so they'd picnicked in sheltered coves while Christy told them how she and her mother had once earned money by collecting kelp, which was then burned to release the alkali needed in the manufacture of soap and other cosmetic products. Everyone on the island at that time had relied on the income, but the industry collapsed as a result of raised taxes and the use of the cheaper Spanish variety and this, combined with the failure of the potato crops year after year, meant that whole communities were left starving and poorer than ever.

Christy wanted the others to absorb the essence of her life on Skye, and had described the back-breaking work of digging peat from the bogs and carrying it home in the rush baskets they called '*kishies*', which were strapped to their backs, and how the wet turf had to be stacked carefully so that it could dry out and be used as fuel for their fires. She reminisced about the times her father and uncles had risked their lives by climbing the steep cliff faces to capture birds and their eggs to eat, and became quite animated as she described the great celebrations and feasting on their return, for the birds were considered to be the best and richest food.

Gregor played his part by taking them to see the weathered Celtic crosses with their mysterious carvings that were dotted about the island, and the ancient ruins of churches that had been built by St Columba and which still retained the memorials to the dead; and while Jock grazed contentedly, Gregor helped them explore the remains of a rather eerie dun, which stood high on the cliff tops.

In the quiet moments following their picnic lunch, he told them the legends of the Vikings, who'd brought their skills and their strange language to the northern islands, and they listened, entranced – especially Christy, for it was like being a child again, safe in her father's arms as he told his own stories.

On the fourth day, they enjoyed a wonderful party at the hotel, at which they were introduced to a host of distant relatives, including Gregor's parents and extended family. There had been story-telling over a sumptuous supper, followed by enthusiastic dancing and singing, and the imbibing of a great deal of whisky. Christy and Kathryn had enjoyed it immensely, and even Anne had been caught up in the happy atmosphere and was seen dancing several reels with Gregor's father.

At dawn on the fifth day they said their goodbyes to Mungo and Betsy, and although Christy was sad to be leaving such lovely people, she was looking forward to the next leg of the journey. Their luggage was tied firmly to the carriage, and because of the added weight and the distance involved Gregor brought his second cob, Hector, to help Jock.

Hector proved to be a wayward old cuss, constantly trying to pull to one side, getting out of step with Jock, and giving him a nip now and again to show his displeasure at being strapped into the shafts – which rather reminded Christy of her son, Hamish, who was always cross about something or other.

As the sun rose higher in the sky and the carriage bowled along the broad track which would take them west through the hills to the *baile* of Gilleasbuig, Christy leaned back and regarded the scenery. She would never come this way again, but she felt strangely content. The sense of belonging to this place had never faltered and would remain as strong as ever, and although terrible things had happened here, time and distance had made them feel as if they'd been experienced by someone else – another Christy, in another time, another life.

She thought of the letters she'd written to her sons, describing the places they'd visited and briefly relating the stories she'd told so they would understand why it had been so necessary to come here. What they would make of her story she didn't know, but she hoped they'd learn from it and realise that no matter how trying life became, it was the strength of spirit that would see them through.

That same spirit had been sparked within her at a young age, and throughout her long and eventful life there might have been moments when it had flickered and threatened to leave her, but it soon burned brightly again when it was needed. The loss of her husband had hit the hardest, for it had been so sudden, and even now she still expected him to come into a room, or be lying beside her when she woke in the night. The ache for him was deep; she wished he were here, that she could see him and talk to him just once more.

Christy's reverie was broken by Anne, who'd been sour since the moment she'd come down to their very early breakfast. 'I really don't see why it's necessary to go this way,' she said petulantly. 'Why not just cut straight across to Portree so we can catch an earlier ferry back to the mainland and civilisation?'

'Because I don't want to go to Portree yet,' said Christy firmly. 'We've had this conversation already, Anne, and I'm becoming weary of it.'

'And I'm tired of traipsing all over this blessed island,' she snapped. 'Having talked to Gregor, it seems there's nothing to see where we're going, so what's the point of it?'

'The point is I need to go there and see it for myself,' said Christy with some asperity.

'You should have left me and Kathryn at the hotel and come on your own,' said Anne. 'I'm sure Gregor wouldn't mind returning for us, and then we could all travel down to Portree without having to make this unnecessary detour.'

'Oh, Mother,' sighed Kathryn. 'You know that would have spoiled everything. Grandma needs to retrace her journey so she can tell her story properly, and I for one want to hear what happened.' She took her mother's hand. 'I realise you're suffering a bit after the party and our late night, but do at least try to join in the spirit of this journey.'

Anne swept a hand across her brow, as if to emphasise the fact that she was suffering stoically. 'I'll do my best,' she said tremulously, 'but I just hope Mother's stories don't prove to be too bleak. I feel low enough as it is.'

Knowing that Anne's headache was the result of too much whisky and excitement the previous day, Kathryn and Christy exchanged glances and made no comment as she delicately dabbed her neck and wrists with eau de cologne and gave a martyred sigh.

Christy dug into the hamper Betsy had provided, found the flask of strong coffee, and carefully poured some into the sturdy earthenware mugs. 'Drink this, Anne, and try to relax. I know it must be difficult, but you'll find the scenery will help you enjoy the journey.'

'I don't see how it's possible to enjoy anything,' grumbled Anne. 'The ground is so rough that even the carriage springs can't cope, and all this bouncing about is making me feel nauseous.'

Christy's thoughts turned to the long, exhausting trek she'd made this way all those years ago. 'You should count yourself lucky to be riding in comfort,' she replied. 'When we left Mac-Innes Bay, there was no money for a carriage, or even the possibility of hitching a ride on a passing wagon,' she murmured. 'We had to walk.'

Anne regarded her with some horror. 'Walk?' She glanced out

of the window at the rough terrain and the seemingly endless line of hills through which they were passing. She gave a sniff of dismissal. 'Still, you were young and hardy and probably used to walking such distances.'

'I might have been young, but all of us were starving and very weak,' she said flatly. 'All the while we'd stayed in that cave we lived on shellfish and a thin seaweed broth – hardly enough to keep body and soul together.'

'But your father had his boat; surely he could have gone fishing?'

Christy shook her head. 'In the mayhem and panic to get to Mum and Gran he hadn't anchored it securely enough, and when the sea grew rough it was swept away and foundered on the reef. My father and Finlay swam out to see if they could rescue it, but it was beyond repair.'

'So you really had little choice but to walk,' murmured Kathryn. 'Your poor mother; how did she cope after losing her baby and getting kicked in the face?'

'She recovered well enough to make the walk, but it took a long time and she was never as strong again and had terrible trouble with her broken jaw. It hadn't set straight, you see, so she couldn't eat or talk properly and was in constant pain.'

Christy swallowed hard, determined not to let those memories overwhelm her as the carriage bumped along and the hills they were travelling through blocked the sun and chilled her. 'We set out for Gilleasbuig at the end of September, hoping that the weather would stay fine. But winter came early that year, bringing a sharp northerly wind carrying icy rain, and it wasn't long before we were soaked through and frozen to the bone – which only increased our hunger and weakened our spirits.'

She saw tears gleam in Kathryn's eyes and squeezed her hand. 'But we of the clan MacInnes are made of stern stuff. We found the strength somehow to keep going.'

'You must all have been terribly brave,' murmured Kathryn.

'It wasn't courage that kept us going, but the determination not to be beaten,' Christy replied. 'If we'd perished on that trek we would have let the factors win, and failure in any form was something none of us would contemplate.'

'I know now where Hamish gets his stubborn streak from,' muttered Anne.

Christy smiled at this, for Anne had also inherited that Mac-Innes stubbornness. 'Yes, he's very like my father – even looks like him now he's a man. But my father was a gentle giant who rarely lost his temper and never got embroiled in disputes – unless his family was threatened.'

Silence fell between them as the carriage springs complained and they were jolted over the rough ground of the track leading through the hills, back into the sunlight.

'We didn't have much to carry,' said Christy eventually. 'Our few possessions were put into the sacks we'd used as bedding, and my grandmother's loom was carefully taken apart so it resembled a bunch of sticks, which were strapped to my father's back. Mother and I put our bundles in our *kishies* and, as they were far lighter to carry than the sods of wet peat we were used to, we hardly noticed them.'

Christy had a sharp memory of them traipsing across the

blackened heather and countless rushing streams, heads bowed against the wind and rain, her bare feet becoming as swollen and numb as Jamie's.

'Finlay and Father took it in turns to carry wee Callum on their shoulders – his withered foot would have made walking so far impossible – and Jamie marched along with a bundle slung over his shoulder, his little face set with determination.'

Christy's smile was wry. 'He was only eight but probably the toughest of us all, for it was anger that kept him going – a raging anger against those who'd forced him from his home – and it stayed with him for many years.'

'I've heard you mention him occasionally when talking about the early days in Tasmania,' said Anne. 'Finlay too. How is it we never met either of them?'

'And poor little Callum,' breathed Kathryn. 'What happened to him?'

'That's another story,' she said sadly, 'and one day soon I'll tell you what happened to my brothers. For now, it's enough to know that we all survived that trek – though how we did was a miracle.'

Her voice faltered as the memories came of the bitter nights that followed freezing days, and the constant gnawing hunger. 'We had no food and no proper shelter, and our clothes were little more than rags. We had to rely on abandoned crop fields to grub about for anything that wasn't too rotten to eat, and would bed down for the night under rocky overhangs or beneath the spreading branches of thorn bushes. If we were lucky we found a ruined croft or barn, but it was rare.'

'How long did it take to make this journey?' asked Kathryn.

'In good weather, with decent food inside us, we could have done it easily in two days, but as each hungry day passed and the weather worsened, we got slower, and it took just over a week.'

As the horses slowed and the carriage wheels began to rumble on firmer ground, they all looked out of the windows to discover they were now on a track leading down towards a broad glen where a sheet of water glimmered in the distance.

Christy uttered a soft cry of recognition and leaned danger-ously far out of the window. 'Stop the carriage, Gregor,' she shouted. 'Stop right now.'

He had barely drawn the horses to a halt when Christy opened the door and tumbled out to land with a jarring thud on her bottom. Kathryn raced to her side and Gregor joined her, their faces anxious. 'Are you all right? Did you hurt yourself?'

Christy laughed as she sat there with her skirt and petticoat in disarray. 'I keep forgetting I'm not a girl anymore,' she splut-tered, yanking her clothing over her legs and adjusting her hat. 'It's a good thing it was a soft landing, but – oh, dear – I must look ridiculous.'

'You certainly do,' snapped Anne from the carriage. 'For good-ness' sake, Mother, have some decorum.'

Christy shrugged off the remark and let Gregor and Kathryn help her to her feet. The shock of falling meant that her hands trembled as she brushed down her skirt and tucked loose strands of hair behind her ears. Not wanting them to realise how shaken she was, she smiled brightly. 'No harm done, just a bruised behind and a dented ego,' she declared.

Gregor's eyes twinkled and Kathryn giggled, but Anne gave a disgusted snort and moved to the far side of the carriage to distance herself from her mother's shocking behaviour.

'It's no use you hiding away in there,' said Christy. 'We've got a walk to do before we can eat.'

Anne checked the time on the little watch she'd pinned to her jacket lapel. 'It's already well past lunchtime,' she declared. 'And having had breakfast at such an unearthly hour, I suggest the walk can wait until we've eaten.'

'It won't take long, I promise you,' said Christy, holding on to her impatience. 'Then you can eat to your heart's content.'

Anne glanced out at the sweeping landscape, empty of everything but a scattered flock of shaggy-fleeced sheep. 'Where exactly are you planning for us to walk?'

'Down there.' Christy pointed to the long track that meandered down the hill to the glittering loch in the distance.

'I'm not dressed for walking,' said Anne, sticking out a small foot shod in a dainty boot made of kid leather.

'That's all right,' Christy replied, digging about under the seat. 'I asked the maid to keep your walking boots out when she was packing your trunk last night.' She held them up triumphantly by the laces. 'Hurry up and put them on, Anne. The fresh air and exercise will do you good, and the day is wasting.'

Anne glared at them all before reluctantly taking the boots.

'It's a fair way to walk for someone not used to it,' murmured Gregor. 'D'ye no think I should bring her down to the loch?'

'That's very thoughtful of you, Gregor, but I need my daughter to walk with me, just as I walked with my mother down into that wee glen.'

Anne, now more suitably shod, stepped down from the carriage and walked a little distance away to regard the view and the long hill with disfavour. 'It will take an age to get all the way down there, and I –'

She got no further, for Hector decided he rather liked the look of her straw hat. He clamped his great yellow teeth on the brim and tried to wrest it from her head.

'My hat!' yelped Anne, clutching at it and trying to swipe Hector away at the same time.

Before anyone could do anything to help, it had become a tug of war – a battle quickly lost by Anne as Hector yanked it from her head. 'My hat,' she wailed. 'My lovely expensive hat.'

Hector chewed delightedly on the straw and pretty ribbons, his eyelids fluttering in pleasure.

'You beast,' Anne snapped, giving him a resounding slap on his nose.

Hector dropped the hat and eyed her belligerently.

Before anyone could stop her, Anne made the mistake of bending to retrieve her ruined hat, and with a wicked gleam in his eye Hector gave her bottom a hefty nip.

Anne screamed, dropped the hat and clutched her behind.

Hector whinnied with delight, snatched up the hat and danced on his great feet in triumph.

Anne heard the stifled laughter coming from the others and turned on them furiously. 'It's not funny,' she yelled, thoroughly beside herself with fury and embarrassment. 'That horse is a vicious beast, and should be put down.'

'I ken ye asked for that, Mrs Ross,' drawled Gregor, swallowing his laughter as he drew her away from his horse. 'Hector doesn't like being slapped.'

'And I don't like being bitten,' she stormed. She turned angrily to the others, saw they were still struggling with their giggles, and stamped her foot. 'That hat cost me a fortune,' she wailed, 'and I'm in a great deal of pain. How *dare* you laugh at me!'

'I'm sorry, Anne, but Gregor's right,' spluttered Christy. 'You should never slap a horse in anger, especially one as touchy as Hector – and as for bending down in front of him, knowing how he likes to bite . . .' She broke into giggles again.

Kathryn took her mother's arm, the muscles in her face working hard to stem her own laughter. 'Does it hurt so very much?' she managed.

A gleam of humour lit in Anne's eyes and the corners of her mouth were moving as she nodded and rubbed her bottom. 'It does a bit,' she said, her voice unsteady. 'He's got big teeth, and the shock of it . . .' She collapsed into giggles. 'Oh dear. I'm never going to live this down, am I?' she spluttered.

'Well, it certainly beats me falling out of the carriage,' said Christy. 'I reckon we'll both have sore backsides tonight.'

The three of them sank to the ground in fits of giggles, and when they saw Gregor's look of puzzled disbelief, they collapsed into gales of uncontrollable laughter until the tears ran down their faces.

Gregor shook his head. 'I'll never understand women,' he muttered to Hector, who was making a sterling effort to destroy the hat. He patted both animals and gave a deep sigh. Horses were much easier to deal with, and far more sensible.

Jock lifted his top lip to show huge yellow teeth in a horse laugh, whilst Hector had a knowing gleam in his eye as he continued munching on the delicious hat.

It was decided, after they'd pulled themselves together and could talk properly, that they would have their picnic here at the top of the hill and then amble down to the loch afterwards.

'It's lovely to hear you and Gran laughing together again,' said Kathryn as they made short work of Betsy's delicious meat-and-potato pasties and fresh salad. 'I can't remember the last time I heard you both laugh like that.'

Anne smiled as she tried to bring order to her hair, which had come loose from its pins in the tussle over the hat and was now tumbling over her shoulders. 'It was funny though, wasn't it? And yes, it has been a long time since I laughed like that.' She glanced at Christy and hurriedly looked away.

'When we get back, and I leave for Sydney, you and Daddy should go on a long trip. You've both been so sad lately, and getting away from Melbourne might do you good.'

Anne looked at her daughter sharply. 'Your father is much too busy running his businesses to take a long holiday, and I will have a lot to do getting back into the swing of things for the coming summer season.'

'Daddy's businesses all but run themselves,' said Kathryn firmly, 'and the social round isn't that important. I want you and Daddy to have some fun and enjoy each other's company.'

Anne thought about Harold and the way they'd once been together – and of how much fun she'd had the previous night, dancing those reels with Gregor's father. It had reminded her so vividly of the country dances she and Harold had attended when they were newly-weds, and how his strong arm had held her as he whisked her about the floor, his handsome face looking down at her . . . She withdrew quickly from those unsettling memories. 'I don't know what you mean, Kathryn. Our social calendar is always full, and we have lots of fun together.'

'Do you?' Kathryn's gaze was steady and disconcerting. 'Then why are you both so unhappy?'

Anne prickled with apprehension. 'We're quite content,' she replied. 'Really, Kathryn, you're spoiling the day with all this. Let's have no more of it.'

'I'm not blind, Mother. I can see how distant you are with him, and how he prefers being at his office or out in the bush to staying at home.' Tears sprang in her eyes. 'You do still love him, don't you?'

'Of course I do,' she retorted defensively.

'Then why are you so angry all the time?' Kathryn persisted. 'And why don't you and Daddy laugh together like you used to?'

'As I said before, we have busy lives, and with a large household to run and your father often away on business, I find I get very tired. Life isn't easy, Kathryn, despite the luxuries your father provides, and with you about to leave for Sydney, it's no wonder I'm constantly on edge.'

'Is that why you and Grandma are at odds?'

Anne reddened and didn't dare glance at her mother. 'Not at all,' she said, getting to her feet. She pulled on her jacket and tidied her hair into a rough topknot. 'And I refuse to continue this conversation any further.'

'But —'

'It's time for our walk,' Anne interrupted. 'And I for one will be glad of the exercise after all that pastry.'

'You're right, Anne,' said Christy, before the girl could reply. 'We could all do with some exercise to clear the air, but you should fetch another hat, dear. The sun is still quite strong, and you don't want to ruin your lovely complexion.'

As Anne asked Gregor to retrieve one of her many hatboxes from the roof of the carriage, Christy took Kathryn's arm and drew her out of earshot. 'Darling, I'm sorry you feel that things aren't easy between your parents, but they've been married a long time and will work it out.'

'Do you really think so?' Kathryn's green eyes shone with hope.

'I do,' she replied firmly. 'You see, marriages can get stale after a time, and I suspect your parents are finding that they're missing one another dreadfully. I'm sure that when we get back to Melbourne, they will make a new start and be much happier.'

She patted the girl's cheek. 'And don't fret over me either. I'm more than capable of handling the situation between me and your mother.'

'But why is there a situation between you? What happened?'

Christy evaded answering fully. 'She just has a bee in her bonnet about something and won't let go. I advise you not to ask her about it; it will only make things worse. Leave it to me and Anne – we'll sort it out, never you mind.'

'It's not over me going to university, is it? I know you disagreed on that, and it would be awful if I was the cause of you falling out.'

Christy gave her a hug. 'It's absolutely nothing to do with that,' she said truthfully. 'Your mother has become used to the idea now and is tremendously proud of you – even if she doesn't show it.' She kissed her cheek. 'Let's go for our walk and not spoil this lovely day by being so solemn.'

Anne walked towards them, wearing another straw hat. She eyed them suspiciously as they embraced, and felt a pang of envy that her daughter had turned to Christy for consolation.

However, the deepest regret was for her daughter's realisation that her parents' marriage was far from happy. Tears pricked her eyes as she accepted she was a failure. Her marriage to Harold was a sham, her relationship with her daughter was far from perfect, and she and Christy were growing further apart by the day. Her world was slowly crumbling around her and she didn't have the least idea of how she could put it back together again.

'That's a pretty hat,' said Christy cheerfully. 'Just don't get anywhere near Hector with it – he'll think it's dessert.' She finished clearing up the picnic, stowed the basket back under the seat and turned to Gregor. 'We'll meet you down at the loch.'

Anne determinedly banished her dark mood as they set off. It was a lovely afternoon, with skylarks singing and a bright sun shining down, and because Kathryn seemed much more cheerful, Anne didn't want to spoil it.

They had been walking for about ten minutes when Kathryn ran ahead to inspect what looked like a bird's nest. Anne was deep in thought when she felt Christy taking her hand, and the surprise of it made her footsteps falter.

'I'm sorry, Anne. Sorry that you had to hear all that from Kathryn, and sorry that you haven't felt able to talk to me about you and Harold. But I'm here for you, my dearest girl, and always will be.'

Anne heard the sincerity in her voice, saw the gleam of understanding in her eyes and didn't move her hand from that loving, familiar grasp she'd been missing for so long, but had been too angry and proud to ask for.

A moment of silence fell as they looked into one another's eyes, the unspoken words almost tangible between them. And then Anne remembered how easily her mother had lied to her, had cheated her of everything she'd held dear. She snatched her hand away and hurried to catch up with Kathryn, unable to forgive or forget.

8

For that one fleeting moment, Christy had held out such hope that she and her daughter could bridge the divide. She'd seen the longing in Anne's eyes, the softening of her mouth, had felt the clasp of her hand and willed her to relent. But then her eyes had hardened and her lips had thinned, and she'd snatched her hand away and was gone. Hurt beyond belief, Christy followed them down the hill, blinded by her tears, her feet, usually so sure, stumbling over the tufts of blackened heather.

She paused for a moment to swallow the lump in her throat and still the tremor of emotion that ran through her. There had to be a way to get through to Anne, to convince her that the lie had been told out of love – that she'd done what she did because she'd thought it was for the best – and that in the end none of the things that really mattered had been changed at all. Yet in the light of Anne's determination to set herself apart, Christy had no solution.

Christy realised the others were waiting for her by the ruins of the kirk some way down the hill, so she waved back and slowly set off again, deep in thought.

Anne's bitterness was ruining her life, alienating her from her family and causing damage to her marriage. If Christy didn't find a way to help her, Anne would soon find herself truly alone, and she didn't want that for her daughter.

Christy's thoughts turned to Harold, who she'd come to like and admire very much. He was an attractive, energetic man, who'd slowly grown quiet and withdrawn over recent years, spending hours away from that great echoing mansion and the wife who no longer seemed to love or respect him. Yet he'd shown his old spark of defiance when it had come to Kathryn going to university and accompanying her grandmother on this trip – and Christy wondered just how far that defiance would take him.

Would this long time apart prove to be fatal to their marriage, or bring them to their senses before it was too late? Christy hoped it would be the latter, for she suspected there was still something between them, even if it had become rather lost along the way.

'You're looking thoughtful and rather sad, Grandma,' said Kathryn as she linked arms with her. 'Are the memories of this place very painful?'

Christy pulled her thoughts together and regarded the tumbled-down remains of the kirk, noting that Anne was still studiously examining the ruins, thereby distancing herself from this conversation. Yes, the memories were painful, but she couldn't voice them now – not so soon after Anne's rejection.

'We were footsore and exhausted by the time we got to this point,' she said quietly. 'But seeing the kirk and the loch lifted our spirits, for we knew we'd soon be with our kinfolk.'

Christy's gaze lingered on the ruined kirk and overgrown plot of land that had once been the cemetery. There was no sign of any grave markers now – no memorial to those who'd once lived and died in this isolated glen. She remembered the tragedy of what had happened on her fifteenth birthday, felt the deep sense of loss, but couldn't speak of it.

'We came every Sunday morning to sit on hard wooden benches and listen to the pastor as he berated us and took our meagre offerings before driving off with his horse and buggy to his fine house in the next cove.' She sighed. 'He wasn't a pleasant man,' she continued as they stood there. 'He was rather like the hellfire-and-damnation preachers that visited the mining camps in Australia and passed round their hats for money, which they used to buy women and whisky.'

Kathryn's eyes widened. 'Really?'

Christy chuckled. 'Yes, really. There's no sinner quite as bad as a rotten preacher, and I've met a few in my time, believe me.'

'Gosh – how exciting,' breathed Kathryn.

Christy's smile was wry, for although her time on the goldfields had been exciting, meeting those preachers had been anything but. She linked arms with Kathryn and they began to walk down the narrow track, which had been trodden by generations of folk from Gilleasbuig coming to the kirk, but which was now almost lost in the grass and heather.

'It was a bright day when we first caught sight of our new home, but the wind was chill and brisk, chopping at the waters of the loch until it raised white-capped waves. This is a sea loch, even though, from here, it looks to be surrounded by hills, so it's tidal and very deep, but there was good fishing to be had.'

They walked on in silence, with Anne following slowly behind them. Christy made no attempt to urge her to join them, for she didn't want to suffer another rebuff. Instead she drank in the view, just as she had on that first day.

The green and fertile glen faced the east, the surrounding hills sweeping down to a broad shore of gritty black sand and scattered rocks where plovers and oystercatchers still hunted for food in the shallows. Her Uncle Robert's fishing boat had once lain beached above the high tidemark, the nets strung across the grass to dry, and where there had been strips of croft land covering the lower slopes, there were now only grazing sheep, their thick white fleeces like small, slow-moving clouds against the deep green of the grass.

Sadly she regarded the ruined houses and barns which lay scattered across the glen. They were the only memorial to the thriving community which had lived here all those years ago.

'When we came, there were twenty-one fine cottages and over a hundred people living here,' she said. 'They were mostly crofters and farm labourers, but there were also a couple of women weavers, and that was how I learned to use my grandmother's loom properly.'

She caressed the tartan shawl, which she'd taken to wearing every day, regardless of the weather, and carried on walking until she reached the loch shore. The blue water mirrored the clear sky, and now the sun was slowly moving west, long dark shadows stretched from the shattered walls and chimneys of the cottages, across the abandoned land-holdings, the stone boundaries of which could still faintly be seen amid the long grass.

'We moved into our uncle's cottage, which was over there,' she said, pointing to the sentinel of a crumbling chimney. 'Robert and Morag MacInnes were good people and very welcoming, but their cottage was tiny and they already had four children, so it was a tight squeeze.'

She smiled at the memory of them packed round the fire at night, sleeping like sardines crammed in a barrel on the hard-packed earthen floor. 'But it was warm and dry, and there was always plenty to eat, for other than the blighted potatoes, the rest of the crops flourished here, and there was nearly always fish to be had.'

Christy walked a little further along the shore and then climbed up the gentle slope to the broken wall of one of the abandoned houses. Perching on the warm stone, she waited for the others and saw that Gregor had left the horses to graze and was heading towards her. Once everyone was seated, she carried on with her story.

'My father and the other men set about building us a cottage during that first winter.' She patted the old stone that had been warmed by the sun. 'And this was our home for the next five years,' she said softly.

'Were you happy here?' asked Kathryn.

'Oh, yes,' she replied with a sigh. 'We were surrounded by family and friends, had food to eat and sturdy shelter. We even had a school of sorts, so we children could learn to read and write. It was over there, in Miss Fleming's cottage. She was a bit strict, but not half as bad as the pastor, who liked to use his cane to punish us if we fidgeted or talked through his Bible lessons.'

'So you didn't miss MacInnes Bay?'

'There were times when I longed to see it again, of course, but back then I had other things on my mind.' She chuckled softly, her gaze dreamy. 'I was growing up, you see, and there was this boy . . .'

'What was his name? How did you meet?'

'His name was Fraser, and he worked on my uncle's fishing boat. Don't forget, we were very young and it was a long time ago, so it was all very innocent.' She thought fondly of the fair-haired boy with bright blue eyes and a winning smile. 'I used to sit and watch him as he helped Uncle Robert mend the nets, and I can remember how hard my heart fluttered every time I saw him, and how red I went if he happened to look at me.'

Kathryn laughed. 'I remember feeling exactly the same way about Paul Simmons when I was about thirteen or so. I thought he was the most handsome, the cleverest boy in the world, and would dream about him every night.'

Anne looked at her askance. 'I never knew that.'

'It was my secret passion,' she replied. 'I told no one and was heartbroken when he left Melbourne with his parents to go and live in Adelaide.' She turned back to her grandmother. 'So what happened with you and Fraser?'

'Fraser's family and two others applied to the Highland and Island Emigration Scheme for sponsored resettlement. They were looking for a new life of opportunity, away from the threat of the clearances, which they feared would soon come to this peaceful place.' Christy dipped her chin. 'But they were unlucky because they were allocated berths on the HMS *Aramis*, bound for

Australia, and fever broke out on board. Most of the passengers were dead before the ship reached Ireland – including poor Fraser.'

'Oh, no,' breathed Kathryn. 'How tragic.'

'Yes, it was,' she sighed, 'and because of it, there were no more families willing to risk such a journey. It was said the conditions on board those ships were appalling and they were not even fit to transport animals, let alone men, women and children, so it wasn't long before the Highland and Island Emigration Scheme was closed down.'

'So despite the threat of being evicted, you and your family stayed?'

Christy nodded. 'Like the rest of the people living here, we had nowhere else to go, and my father refused to even contemplate leaving for another country. We naïvely thought we'd been forgotten by the factors because we paid our rents and some of us were actually working as labourers on the laird's farmland.'

Christy regarded the peaceful, silent glen and the still waters of the loch, gathered her mother's shawl about her shoulders and shivered. 'It all changed in the blink of an eye,' she murmured. 'It was my fifteenth birthday, and a day which will live with me forever.'

A deeper silence fell as she began to describe the scenes that had lived in her heart and mind for fifty years.

Christy was sitting outside in the morning sunshine, working on her grandmother's loom. She was making a blanket from the soft, fine strands of fleece she'd gathered from the laird's pastures during the winter, which she'd spun into skeins. She'd found it caught on brambles and heather, or in the niches of walls where the laird's sheep liked to shelter from the weather. The factor would probably accuse her of stealing, but she saw no harm in gathering those drifts of wool that were of little use to the factories in Inverness, who needed whole fleeces for their huge looms.

It was a lovely late-summer's day, with a light, warm breeze blowing in from the sea, the waders pecking in the shallows of the loch while cormorants sat on the rocks with their wings spread and their necks stretched as they sunned themselves. The fishing boat had gone out at dawn and wouldn't be back for two days, in the hope of a good catch. The other women were either working in their vegetable patches or doing their laundry in the communal washtub that was set on the beach, above a roaring fire of peat and seaweed.

Her mother had gone up to earn her weekly wage by scrubbing the floor and cleaning the windows in the kirk to prepare for tomorrow's service, while Jamie, who was now thirteen, had left with Joseph MacInnes, who'd taken him on as an apprentice carpenter, and was at the moment working on repairing the window frames at the pastor's house in the next cove.

As she continued to thread the shuttle back and forth, Chirsty wondered vaguely where Callum could have got to. He was ten years old and small for his age, with skinny arms and legs, and a weak chest that always troubled him during the damp, cold winters.

Callum was a constant worry, for he had a habit of

disappearing, and today he was supposed to be helping Aunt Morag with fetching clean water from the hillside spring. As there was no sign of him, she suspected he'd wandered off to the rock pools. They were his favourite haunt, and he could spend hours watching the tiny creatures that inhabited them.

Christy knew Callum was frustrated at being hampered by his useless foot, but he was willing enough to lend a hand with the meanest of chores, and never lost his sunny disposition. She smiled as she thought of his cheeky grin and bright, enquiring eyes. He was an imp, but everyone adored him.

She returned to her work, her thoughts turning to her father and Finlay. Finlay was seventeen and a strapping, handsome lad who drew admiring glances from the girls. He and their father had left with some of the other men for the mainland, weeks ago, to help with the harvest and earn enough money to pay the rent through the coming winter. They weren't expected back for at least another two or three weeks.

She gave a sigh, for she missed her father, and the cottage didn't feel the same without him. Her mother felt his absence too and disguised her feelings by being constantly busy and keeping up a flood of bright chatter – but Christy knew she found it hard to sleep at night without Angus's arms about her.

Easing her back, she got up from the stool and stretched. She could see by the sun that it was after noon, and her mother was usually home from the kirk by now. Perhaps she'd stopped to gossip with one of the other women, or had gone down to the rocky cove just along the way to have a dip. It was private there, a secret place she went with Christy when it was hot, and they could strip off and immerse themselves in the cool water, away from prying eyes.

The thought of the silky feel of cool water on her skin was tempting, and as it was her birthday, it would be a lovely treat. It wouldn't be long before winter came, and as it was rare to have such a warm day so late in the summer, this might be her last chance.

She carefully covered the loom and the unfinished blanket with a piece of sacking to protect it from the gulls' droppings, and went into the cottage to fetch some bread and smoked herring, which she wrapped in a cloth for their lunch. Her mother would be hungry by now, and they could eat it on the beach after their dip.

She set off up the hill to the kirk, striding out, eager to share some quiet time with her mother. She passed no one on the track, and there was no sign of Anne making her way down the steep path to the next cove, so she had to assume she was still busy cleaning. They'd soon finish it together, she thought happily, and then they could have their swim.

There was no sound of her mother's singing, which was unusual, for Anne loved how her voice sounded in the echoing kirk, with its stone floor and high rafters, and had always maintained that a song made the work go quicker.

Christy pushed at the door. 'Mama? What's taking you so long?' She stepped inside. 'I thought we'd . . .' The words died as she froze in shock.

Anne lay sprawled on the stone floor, the ladder she'd fallen from toppled over her, the bucket of water spilled at her feet.

There was blood – lots of blood – pooling darkly from beneath her head.

'Mama!' Christy raced to her side, tossed away the ladder, fell to her knees and gently cupped her mother's waxen face in her hands. 'Mama?' she whispered. 'Mama, it's all right. I'm here.'

There was no movement in those staring blue eyes, no rise and fall in her narrow chest, nor the sound of breath from her parted lips.

'Mama! Mama!' Christy drew her limp body into her arms and rocked back and forth as the tears streamed down her face and her heart broke. 'You can't leave us, Mama,' she sobbed. 'You mustn't leave us.'

But Anne MacInnes had passed from this world, her eyes now fixed on a distant horizon far from the kirk and the glen and the people who loved her.

Christy wept as she rocked her mother in her arms and the blood slowly congealed on the freshly scrubbed flagstones. She drew her lifeless hands beneath the shawl she'd worn since Granny MacInnes had passed away, and kissed the cool, smooth cheek. 'I love you so much,' she whispered. 'So, so much.'

As her tears slowly dried and the chill of the flagstones rose to meet the chill in her heart, Christy realised she had to go and tell Morag what had happened. But she didn't want to leave her mother alone on the floor.

She gathered Anne to her heart and struggled to her feet, surprised at how heavy her mother was for one so small and slight. It would be impossible to carry her back home, so she gently laid her on a nearby bench in the shaft of sunlight that poured through the window she'd been cleaning.

Tenderly drawing her mother's skirt over her legs, she then closed her eyes, as she'd seen her Aunt Morag do after old Mr Campbell had died, and kissed her cheek. Stroking back her blood-matted hair, she adjusted the shawl over her folded hands, kissed her again and ran, sobbing, from the kirk.

She was halfway down the hill when she heard a shout behind her. Stumbling to a halt, she turned, shielded her tear-filled eyes from the sun and realised it was the carpenter, Joseph MacInnes, and her brother, Jamie. They were running hard, their arms waving as they shouted. It was clear they were warning her of something and that they were scared – but she couldn't make out what they were saying.

And then Joseph's booming voice reached her. 'They're coming. They're coming. Run, Christy! Run and warn the others!'

She hesitated, torn between running and staying with her mother – but then she heard the sound of baying dogs and the thunder of hooves. She turned and fled towards the glen, yelling a warning to the women on the beach and screaming for Callum.

Joseph and Jamie were now hard on her heels, but she had no breath left to say anything. The fear was all-consuming as she flew down the hill to the cottage in search of Callum.

There was no sign of him and the panic had now spread to the rest of the community, who were dashing about, rescuing their belongings and rounding up their children. She could only pray he was still at the rock pools and therefore out of sight and safe from the factor's men.

Her breath was a sob as she hastily gathered cooking pots, bedding and clothes, and tossed them far from the cottage door. She snatched up the bag of vegetables she'd harvested the previous evening from their croft, and the small sack of oats, carrying them quickly away from the cottage, before lifting up the small loom and taking it down to the beach, the unfinished blanket still dangling from it.

She looked towards the hill. The men were coming. She could see their silhouettes on the brow of the hill, could hear the baying dogs and the clatter of the horses' hooves on the stony track.

All around her was mayhem, with women screaming and children crying as they desperately tried to clear their cottages and help the elderly and sick from their beds. Apart from Joseph, there were only a couple of elderly men and a few young boys to help defend them – for the more able men were labouring on the laird's estate, out fishing, or on the mainland, helping with the harvest.

Christy piled their belongings further away from the cottage, and then ran to Morag to help round up her children and empty her cottage. There was still no sign of Callum, and all she could do was pray that wherever he was, he'd stay there.

Jamie was out of breath as he dumped his bag of carpentry tools by the stack of their belongings. 'We saw them arriving in the other cove,' he gasped as he helped Christy and Morag haul a heavy barrel of salted fish down to the beach. 'The cottages are already alight over there.' He looked round. 'Where are Mum and Callum?'

Christy had no time to reply. The men and horses had arrived in the glen, their voices loud and threatening as the dogs snarled and snapped on straining leashes. Firebrands were thrown into cottages, clubs were wielded and crashed over the heads of those who dared to protest or weren't quick enough to run away, and the horses threatened to trample small children.

The invaders went into old Mrs Kinross's cottage to drag her off her bed, shoved her wailing daughter out of their way and threw the old woman to the ground as if she was a sack of straw. And then, as her daughter struggled to carry her to safety, they laughed as a spark from the blazing thatch caught the old woman's sacking skirt and burst into flames.

With screams of horror the daughter quickly smothered the flames with her shawl, and another woman dashed forward to help carry the poor woman to the shore so they could bathe her scorched legs.

Christy put her arm round Jamie's shoulders as everyone backed away to the water's edge. They knew that to protest would end in a beating, to fight back would lead to arrest – so they watched through their tears as their homes began to burn.

Smoke clouded the blue sky and rose in a pall to overshadow the loch and block out the sun. Flames crackled and devoured the dry thatch roofs and licked through the windows and doorways with voracious appetite, consuming everything in their path and scorching the surrounding grass.

Christy felt the tension in Jamie as he watched, dry-eyed and full of hatred, raging against his inability to do anything to stop the destruction. She held on to him tightly, fearing he would do something rash and end up being clubbed or imprisoned.

The glen was aglow with fire, the smoke darkening the day as the air was rent with the howls of dogs, the screams of women and children, and the harsh voices of the factor's men.

When he was satisfied that all shelter had been destroyed, the factor brought his horse towards the people huddled together on the beach. He was a weasel-faced man from the lowlands, who'd earned the reputation of being utterly ruthless in his determination to rid the glens of the Gael.

He sat tall in the saddle as his spooked horse rolled its eyes and nervously danced on its toes. Unfurling a length of parchment, he bellowed for silence.

Sullen eyes turned to him as children were hushed and terror tightly tamped down.

'By the order of the laird's trustees, you are to clear this glen immediately,' shouted the factor. 'Anyone caught here after today will be thrown into prison – and that includes the women.' He regarded them all through narrowed eyes; then, satisfied they'd got the message, he turned his horse around with a vicious tug on the reins and led his men back up the hill.

Christy could feel Jamie trembling against her and she drew him away from the water to sink on to the dark, gritty sand. Morag was wailing as she gathered her children to her, and her piteous cries were echoed through the glen by the other women. As those desperate cries rose to the surrounding hills, the smoke thickened and the heat from the fires brought stone walls tumbling.

Christy emerged from the past, and was surprised to see that the sun was still shining and there was no sign of smoke across the glen – and yet she thought she could smell it on the wind, could almost hear those pitiful cries of the terrified women and children.

'Callum had heard and seen it all from his hiding place in those rocks.' She pointed to the outcrop below the high hill to the west. 'He was shaking and shivering with fear when Jamie found him, so he had to carry him home.'

Tears blinded her and her voice broke as she described how she'd held her young brothers and told them about their mother. 'They were as heartbroken as I was,' she managed, 'and wanted to go up to the kirk to see her, but our Aunt Morag warned me it would not be wise.'

'They were very young to see such a sight,' murmured Anne, who'd clearly been greatly moved by her mother's story.

'They'd seen worse,' said Christy, 'but that wasn't the reason we didn't take them with us. All the glens along the loch were now ablaze, and we didn't know if the kirk had been torched as well. To see it alight with their mother's body inside would have been too much after what they'd just gone through.'

Christy's hands were trembling as she clutched the shawl. 'The kirk was untouched, so Morag and I fetched water and washed my mother's face and hair, and scrubbed her blood from the floor. We wrapped her in this shawl, and Morag went back down to the glen to send the boys up to me.'

She took a shallow, trembling breath. 'We sat vigil through the night, as the dark skies glowed red from the fires below, and in the morning the pastor came.'

'I suppose he'd made himself scarce throughout the clearance,' said Gregor gruffly. 'Just like they all did.'

Christy nodded. 'But at least he came back to help us bury our dead,' she said softly. 'Old Mrs Kinross didn't survive the night, and one of the children was killed outright when a horse trampled her.'

She caressed the worn tartan and was silent for a moment so that she could control the strong emotions flooding through her. 'I kept Mother's shawl and her boots. They were all I had to remember her by – to remember her and Granny. And when I'm gone the shawl will go to you, Anne, and then on to Kathryn.'

'Oh, Gran, I hope it will be many years before that happens; but I'd be honoured to have such a precious family heirloom.'

'And I promise to keep it safe, especially now I know the story behind it,' said Anne. 'I'm sorry I was so scathing about it – I didn't realise . . .'

'You weren't to know,' Christy replied with a watery smile.

'So, where did you go from here?' asked Gregor quietly.

'We couldn't go far from the glen because we had to wait for my father and Finlay to return from the mainland. But we lived in fear that the factor and his men would come back, so we gathered up our belongings and hid in the hills with Morag and her children.'

'Couldn't you have found shelter in the kirk?' asked Gregor.

Christy shook her head. 'The pastor padlocked the kirk door and nailed wood over the windows to keep us out after the funeral service. It was a deliberate and wicked act to deny us refuge, while he lived in his fine house and continued his ministry for those still working for the laird's trustees.'

'Where did everyone from the glen go?' asked Kathryn.

'Some took up tenancies of crofts in distant villages, some went down to Portree and got on ships for Canada and Australia, and others went to work in the factories and farms of Inverness. When Uncle Robert got back from his two days of fishing, he urged me to sail with him and his family to a fishing village on the mainland. But I couldn't go. Father and Finlay would never have found us over there.'

'How long did you have to wait for their return?' Gregor asked.

'Almost a month. Autumn had set in hard by then, and although we sneaked down into the glen to dig for vegetables, we were all suffering from the cold, especially poor little Callum, who'd never been strong. In desperation, I took the boys to the cove where my mother and I used to swim, and found a cave in the rocks and stayed there.'

'Your father and brother must have been shocked when they got back,' said Anne, regarding the remains of the settlement.

Christy nodded. 'We'd been foraging for vegetables in the crofts and were on our way back to the cave when we heard them calling for us. They were standing in the wreckage of our cottage, their cries growing ever more fearful. I snatched up Callum, perched him on my hip and ran with Jamie over the rocks and into their arms.

'But Daddy demanded to know where our mother was, and when I told them, my father and brother stood there in numbed silence, the tears streaming down their faces. It was the only time I saw either of them cry.'

Christy ran her hand over the stones of what had once been her home and then got to her feet. 'I'll tell you the rest tomorrow, on our way to Portree,' she said quietly. 'For now, I'd like to spend a while on my own.' She looked up at Gregor. 'Perhaps you could take the others back to the carriage? I shan't be too long.'

At his nod, she walked down to the shore and stared out at the loch, remembering the joy of seeing her father and brother again, and the utter despair in their faces when they knelt at Anne's graveside and had to accept that the true heartbeat of their family was gone.

She turned to regard the silent glen and the abandoned ruins, which lay so peacefully in the late afternoon sun. The people of Gilleasbuig were gone too, scattered to the four corners of the earth. Did they still remember what had happened here? Had they told the next generation about the clearances which had torn them from their homeland and cast them into uncertain futures? She suspected they had, for such memories were too deeply ingrained ever to forget.

Christy's boots crunched over the shingle until she rounded the jutting rocks and scrambled over the sharp-edged boulders to reach the tiny cove where she and her mother had shared those precious moments of quiet happiness.

She looked up at the cave, set in the cliff high above the water. They'd stayed two more nights there, mourning for what they'd lost and discussing what they could do next. By sunrise on the third day, they were tramping south across the heather towards Portree harbour.

9

The Barossa Valley

Harold had been staying on Yarrabinda for two days now, and
although he'd slept well and should have felt rested, the lack of
resolution to their problem, and the arguments and worry it was
causing, was mentally exhausting. Doubts clouded every issue,
for Hamish might well have dreamed that childhood scene, and
Harold was now wondering if he'd got the wrong end of the stick
about that overheard conversation. There were too many possi-
bilities and too much that they didn't know for absolute certain,
and the frustration was getting to them all.

Hamish had been prowling about the house like a bear with a
sore head, and had finally taken their advice and gone for a long
ride to help him cool off. James had left the house early to check
on his vines and the fermenting vats, and Harold was left to pace
about the house, his thoughts in turmoil, the frustration of not
being able to do anything growing by the minute.

He dug his hands into his trouser pockets and stared out of the
window to the sweep of vineyard and the distant hills. If only

Baker would send news, it might ease things, but Harold had heard nothing, and he didn't know if that was good or bad. Unable to stand about and do nothing, he went into the hall, picked up his hat and strode out into the warm sunshine. He would follow Hamish's example and go for a ride.

Harold was saddling up his horse when one of the maids came running into the stable yard. 'There's someone on the two-way for you, sir. A Mr Baker from Melbourne.'

Harold raced back to the house and skidded into James's study, where the two-way radio stood next to the large desk. He sat down and pedalled furiously to fire it up, and then reached for the headset and mouthpiece.

'This is Yarrabinda,' he said. 'Harold Ross speaking. Over.'

Baker's voice was distant, fading in and out through the atmospherics, making it difficult to understand. 'I've heard from my man in Adelaide,' he said. 'The company you were enquiring about is legitimate and greatly respected. Over.'

Harold's heart sank. 'Remember this is an open line,' he warned. 'What about their client? Over.'

'Being looked into at present, but everything appears to be above board, so far.'

Harold swore under his breath as the white noise came down the headset and Baker remembered to clear his end of the line. 'Did you find the copies of all our property deeds? Over.'

'I was not permitted to keep some of them, by order of one of the owners,' said Baker carefully. 'But a certain person in Hobart always kept meticulous records and could have persuaded him to use her safe. Over.'

Damn Hamish for not trusting solicitors, thought Harold. 'I'll ask him when he gets back,' he said. 'If that is the case, do you have access to Hobart?'

'Not unless I get written permission from the owner,' said Baker, who was sounding most uncomfortable at the other end of the line. 'And that, of course, would be impossible in the circumstances. But the safe was emptied and all the paperwork gone through for probate. There was no sign of those particular deeds. Surely they must be with the owner?'

'He appears to have mislaid them,' said Harold shortly.

'What?' Baker spluttered at the other end. 'But they'll be vital should it . . . Well, you know,' he ended lamely.

'Yes, I'm all too aware of the fact,' replied Harold.

'And the other matter?' asked Baker, clearing his throat. 'If you have managed to clear that up and can prove it's false, then I can bring the whole thing to a halt today.'

'Unfortunately we can provide no proof to the contrary,' said Harold. 'There's only one person who must have all the answers, and they are out of the country.'

'When are they due to return?'

'Not until the end of August.'

'Should I send a telegraph? Ask them to get in touch?'

'No,' said Harold sharply. 'Not unless it's absolutely necessary. We'll get to the bottom of this, Baker, and sort it out somehow.'

'Then you'd better get a move on,' said Baker. 'The people in Adelaide are already suggesting a date in early August.'

'Then you'll have to stall them,' he said firmly. 'Make it clear we need more time, and that this must – must, I repeat – be kept between the two parties concerned and not go public. Is that understood, Baker?'

'Of course,' he replied with hurt dignity. 'Will you be staying at your present address for much longer?'

Harold thought quickly. 'I'm doing no use here,' he said eventually, 'so I'll be returning to Melbourne and then going down to Hobart. Do you have keys to that safe, Baker?'

'Well, yes, but I don't think – '

Harold broke in by flicking the speaker switch. 'This is an emergency, and if the answer to everything is in that safe then it must be retrieved. She would agree, I'm positive of that.'

'What if you find something that only confirms things?'

'Then we'll have to think of another way to fight this,' he replied. 'I'll speak to you when I get back. Over.'

He flung the headset to one side and let the machine whirr quietly back to sleep as he hurried out of the office and up the stairs to pack his swag.

'You can't go poking about in that safe without Mother's permission,' stormed Hamish as the three of them met for lunch on the back veranda. 'There could be all sorts of personal things in there she might not want you to see.'

'That's what I'm hoping for,' Harold replied bluntly. 'We have to clear up this mess, Hamish, and it's not the time for delicate sensibilities. If there is proof in that safe that all of this is a bunch of vicious lies, then it can be silenced and over with before she and the others get back.'

'But what if you find something damning, Harry?' asked James quietly. 'What do we do then?'

'We bury it and pay the bitch off,' he retorted. 'It's the only way.'

'Blackmailers keep coming back for more,' James said with a frown. 'How can we be sure that would be the end of it?'

'Baker would have to make her sign something to say she's accepted the money in full and final reparation and will have no right to anything further.'

Hamish snorted. 'I wouldn't trust that bitch as far as I could throw her,' he growled. 'And bits of paper mean nothing – she or her relatives could still go to the press and get even more money by airing our dirty linen in public.'

Harold was sick of fighting Hamish at every turn, but he did see his point. 'Then Baker would have to demand complete media silence along with everything else. But we're getting ahead of ourselves,' he said, pushing back from the table.

'I might not find anything, incriminating or otherwise – and you still have to find those deeds to Wallangarra. So, I suggest you go back home and look for them – and when you find them, lodge the bloody things with a good solicitor, or put them in a bank's safety deposit box.'

Hamish's eyes gleamed dangerously; he hated being told what to do; but, knowing he was in the wrong for once, he kept his mouth shut.

Harold finished the glass of beer and got to his feet. 'I'd better be off. The sooner I get going, the sooner I'll be in Hobart.'

'How long before we can expect to hear from you again?' James asked as they stepped down from the veranda and headed for the stables.

'It'll take the best part of three days to get back to Melbourne, and then I'll need a day to meet with Baker and check that my managers are doing their jobs properly, and not robbing me blind. The crossing over the Bass Strait will take another day, and then I have to get down to Hobart.'

He hooked his swag over the pommel, took the reins from the stable lad, shook James's hand and swung into the saddle. 'Give me a week. I should know by then what the situation is.'

'Of course, you realise there might not be anything in that damn safe after all this,' growled Hamish. 'And we'll be no further forward.'

'Then it'll be our word against Mrs Brown's,' said Harold, 'and she's the one who will have to prove her case.' He leaned down from the saddle, shook Hamish's hand and tugged the brim of his hat low to block out the sun. 'Find those deeds, mate. They're vital.'

*

Skye

Anne was silent as the horses strained to pull the heavily loaded carriage up the steep hill. Her mind was full of the images her mother's story had evoked, and there was a part of her that wanted to take Christy in her arms and hold her tightly to ease all the pain she was clearly still suffering.

She stared out of the window, torn between wanting to show

how deeply she'd been affected, and the insidious little voice in her head that reminded her that she couldn't trust her mother. But her story had been too real to be a fantasy, and there was no reason why they should come all this way if it was only to garner pity and bring her closer to Kathryn.

She glanced across, noted that her daughter was holding Christy's hand, and quickly looked away again. Why couldn't she forgive and love openly? What was it that kept her aloof when all she really wanted to do was make peace? And why couldn't she just let go and give in to her feelings, when others seemed to find it so easy?

They were questions that had plagued her since the beginning of this trip – ones that had been easy to ignore when there had been so much distance between them. Now, as the carriage jounced over the rough ground, she had to accept that she didn't like the woman she'd become, didn't admire the way she was treating her mother and her husband – when all they'd wanted from her was love, forgiveness and understanding.

And yet something inside her closed down and made her withdraw, ambushing any hope of reconciliation, and she could only think it was some inner safety mechanism that switched on when she feared rejection or hurt – and she had been hurt, not only by her mother, but by Harold.

Anne thought about her husband and the very real possibility that her long absence might prove fatal to her marriage. Harold was a handsome, wealthy man, and she'd seen the way some of the women looked at him. There had been a particular young widow, Florence Hardwick, who'd caught his eye, and although he'd vehemently denied any wrongdoing, Anne had not been totally convinced. He'd protested too strongly, in her opinion, and Florence suddenly seemed to be at every social function they attended. Anne had watched as they'd gravitated towards each other on every occasion, and had seen the old flash of charm in Harold's eyes and smile as they'd conversed.

She had no proof that anything untoward had gone on – just one of those intuitive feelings. The timing had been right too, for their marriage was already on rocky ground due to Harold's long absences for his business affairs and her inability to cope with her mother's devastating revelation – and then, to top it all, her beloved father had died, leaving her inconsolable.

Anne gave a tremulous sigh and blinked away her tears. She'd never felt so lonely as during that awful time, and yet her pride had not allowed her to turn to either Harold or her mother for consolation. She'd buried the hurt, and now it lay bitter in her heart.

'Are you all right, Anne?' Christy leaned forward and touched her hand.

'I was thinking about Father,' she replied. 'I do so wish I could have seen him once more before . . .'

Christy came to sit next to her. 'I do too,' she murmured. 'But it all happened so suddenly and unexpectedly that none of us got the chance for a last farewell. My only consolation is that he loved us, that he was a good man, and died doing something he loved in a place he adored.'

Anne returned the pressure of her mother's fingers, seeing again in her mind the tall, handsome man, with his shock of silver hair and merry blue eyes, working one of his thoroughbreds in the paddock behind the house, at peace with the world. Her mother had told her how she'd found him sprawled on the ground, his horse nuzzling him in puzzlement. The heart attack had been swift and brutal, taking him from them on that warm summer's day and leaving a huge void in all their lives.

'He remains alive in my memory,' said Christy with a sigh. 'And there are moments when I feel that he's beside me still, watching over us all. The shock of a sudden death is so very hard to bear for those left behind, for there are things we should have said, emotions that should have been shared. And then the opportunity is snatched away, and we must live with our regrets as well as our loss.'

Anne thought of that young girl who'd lost her mother in the kirk, but had somehow found the courage and strength to protect her young brothers until her father and Finlay returned – and then to console them. Now she was mourning the man she'd loved for so many years, and yet still retained that indomitable spirit which had seen her through so many tragic times.

'You're so strong,' she said softly. 'How do you keep going when life has been so cruel to you over the years?'

'Because I have a family,' she replied. 'I find strength in the knowledge that I'm loved and needed – and this is why we've come here, to Skye. My story isn't so very different to many others, and hasn't been told to shock or garner pity, but to show you both that the love and loyalty of family provides that spark of spirit which sees you through, no matter what happens.'

She placed her hand softly on Anne's cheek. 'Loss is part of life, but their memory lives on through the generations if those stories are told. This journey is a way for me to show you how important it is to say the things we need to say – to tell those we love how we feel. Because once they're gone, it's too late.'

Anne bit her lip, determined not to let her mother see how deeply her words had touched her. 'I understand all that,' she said carefully, 'but sometimes family can inflict the most terrible damage on those they love, and it's hard to forgive and forget.'

'I know it is, my dear,' said Christy. 'But I pray that by the end of our journey you will have learned that forgiveness is healing. It lifts the burden from your heart and the veil from your eyes so that you can see what has truly been there all the time.'

Anne looked down at their clasped hands and nodded. 'Perhaps I will,' she conceded, before unlinking their fingers and turning towards the window.

Kathryn had watched and wondered as the two people she loved turned away from one another. There was sadness in both of them, and she couldn't understand why they just couldn't talk to one another and settle their differences. Whatever had happened between them was causing them both pain and regret, and although her grandmother was clearly trying to make amends, it seemed her mother was still struggling to do the same.

As the awkward silence grew in the carriage, Kathryn's patience ran out. 'I don't know what's going on between you,' she said briskly. 'And I don't want to. But I do wish that you'd stop avoiding whatever it is and clear the air. None of us got the chance to talk to Grandpa before he died, and I want you, Mother, to consider how you'd feel if this state of affairs continued and you left it too late to really talk to Gran.'

'What has gone on between your grandmother and I is none of your business, Kathryn,' said Anne.

'It's very much my business,' retorted Kathryn. 'Grandma's just talked about love, loyalty and family, but all I can see is division and unhappiness. Whatever is going on needs to be resolved.'

'That's quite enough,' snapped Anne. 'Your grandmother and I do not need your interference. And I don't appreciate your meddling.'

'It's not meddling, Anne,' murmured Christy. 'Kathryn is simply trying to put things right between us – and we do need to settle this, Anne. It's clearly affecting others and has gone on for too long.'

Anne took a deep breath, and then let it out on a sigh. 'None of this was my fault,' she said. 'I didn't ask to have everything I believed in destroyed by you and your lies. If you want me to forgive you, then it will take more than a few stories about the old days and a lecture on family loyalty.'

She looked coldly at her mother. 'It's ironic that you choose to even use the word "loyalty" when you clearly have very little idea of what that means.'

Christy returned her daughter's steady gaze. 'I'm perfectly aware of what it means,' she said flatly. 'And you can be assured, Anne, that what I did was out of love for you. Neither was I alone in that decision. Your father supported me every step of the way.'

Anne didn't reply, and Kathryn slumped back into the carriage seat, knowing that there would be no resolution that day – and probably not for a long time. Whatever her grandparents had done must have been very bad for her mother to be so adamant in her refusal to forgive. And that made her extremely sad.

A heavy silence fell in the carriage as Kathryn looked out of the window and the horses trotted along a broad track through a pleasant glen and around the edge of a loch. She saw a fine old building sitting amid sweeping grounds that went down to the water's edge, the forest behind it throwing shadows across the red tiled roof and manicured lawns. It looked like a hunting lodge, for there were stables and barns off to one side, and she thought she could hear the baying of hounds as they rattled past.

'This is Glen Bernisdale,' said Christy, 'and that's the hunting lodge where my father asked for work. There wasn't any, of course; we were behind a long line of people who'd come from the clearances looking for employment. But the housekeeper took pity on us, gave us food, and let us sleep in one of the empty barns overnight. We were very grateful to be warm and dry for once.'

'Why did your father decide to come down to Portree?' asked Kathryn.

'He thought that, as it was a busy town, he might stand a chance of getting some sort of work. Also, he was hoping to hear about Robert and Morag. As Robert hadn't told me the name of the fishing village he was going to, and my father didn't know any of his family living on the mainland, it proved impossible to trace them.'

Christy looked out of the window as the carriage bowled along the smooth track through the glen of Skeabost, where stone cottages had been built on the hillsides overlooking the many streams that fed into the loch. She gazed at the passing view as they continued south through Carbost and on to the main road which led to Portree. She'd been barefoot, cold and hungry the last time she'd passed this way, and she'd had little care for the scenery, just the hope that at the journey's end they would be given the chance of employment and shelter.

'There are many more sheep than when last I came this way,' she said. 'But they were already being hefted into the area, even then. None of us had experience of working with sheep, but we were desperate, so we called at every farm along the way, begging for a chance to do something to earn our next meal.'

Her voice faltered. 'There's no place for pride when faced with hunger, and my father must have been despondent as, one by one, his pleas were rejected. Yet he never showed it. He kept up our spirits as we walked by telling us stories about the Vikings, and the legends his grandfather had told him as a boy.'

'Couldn't he have gone back to the farm on the mainland to work?'

Christy shook her head. 'He and Finlay had only been taken on for the harvest season. The farmer already employed enough men to take them through the rest of the year.'

She felt a chill run through her as the carriage bowled along and she realised they were on the outskirts of Portree. 'We arrived here late one winter's afternoon to discover hundreds of people camped in the fields, under bridges and anywhere they could find shelter. Like us, they were the lost, the hungry and the dispossessed.

'We stopped to talk to some, and although he was told time and again that there was no work to be had, my father plodded on with Callum on his shoulders. We arrived in the town and saw the beggars, the children in rags and the mothers with starving babies in their arms – the defeat and hopelessness of their situation hanging like a pall above Portree. It soon became clear that we weren't welcomed there by the townsfolk, or the local constabulary, for, no sooner had we found a spot to settle, we were moved on.'

Glancing through the window, she leaned out and called to Gregor. 'Can you stop here, please?'

The horses were drawn to a halt and Gregor scrambled down from his high driving seat to open the door. 'You're not planning on walking barefoot into town, are you?' he asked with a teasing light in his eyes.

She grinned back at him. 'Well, I hadn't planned on doing so, but now you mention it . . .' She chuckled. 'I think my barefoot days are over, Gregor. I'm still suffering from the last time.'

He helped her down, and, once Kathryn and Anne were standing on the pavement by the stone wall, he looked at Christy. 'Are the memories very bad?' he asked softly.

Christy nodded and looked down on the loch, far below, where boats were moored at the quay and the ferry was steaming out to the mainland. The row of terraced houses lining the quay had been painted in pastel shades, and white-sailed yachts were skimming over the water as fishermen hauled in their nets and tourists returned from their day trips up and down the loch.

'It looks much more respectable than before,' she said. 'I

remember the old wooden warehouses that stood by the quay, and the rough hotel which rang with the raucous, drunken sound of men who worked hard and drank even harder. And those little houses hadn't been painted pretty colours, either. As for the yachts and tourist boats, they are a new thing – and I'm glad. Portree needs to move with the times.'

She turned away from the view and began to walk along the cobbles until she reached the town square. 'When we came, there were whole families gathered here,' she said, as she took in the fine old grey stone buildings, the little shops, and the two hotels. 'That building over there was run by one of the charities that were offering passage to Australia and America, and the queue outside it never seemed to shorten.'

She dipped her chin. 'We were lucky that my father and Finlay had money from their harvesting, so we moved into cheap lodgings, over there.' She pointed to one of the side streets that lead off the cobbled square. 'It was a poor place, ridden with vermin, and we had to share a room with another family, who were waiting to be given passage to Canada.'

Christy had strong memories of that stinking hovel where the noise was continuous, the smell nauseous and the biting fleas a constant irritation. Washing facilities were virtually non-existent, and they'd taken it in turns to use the water pump outside the town hall. At least the water from the well was clean to drink.

'Twelve families shared an outside lavatory, and if you think a dunny in the outback is awful, you'd be shocked by how much worse such a place could be.' She shivered at the memory of rats and the stench of blocked drains.

'Daddy took the boys with him every morning to try and find work, whilst I stayed to look after poor little Callum. He wasn't at all well, struggling to breathe, covered in flea bites and flushed with a fever. The cost of buying medicine soon ate away at our savings, but it didn't seem to do any good, and Callum got worse. In the end, Daddy carried him down to the hospital, where he was admitted immediately.'

Her voice was unsteady as she felt the emotions build. 'The doctor said he had pneumonia as well as asthma, and, being so malnourished, he had little chance of surviving the night.'

The tears streamed down her face as she thought of the little brother she'd loved so much. 'We were allowed to stay with him, but just as it was growing light, he opened his eyes, smiled at us and passed away.'

Kathryn put her arm about her grandmother as Christy tried to stem her tears.

'Callum's death broke my father,' she managed eventually. 'He knew then that he had to accept there was no future on Skye for his family, and so, the day Callum was buried in a pauper's grave, he joined the queue outside the charity office. I don't think he cared where we went, he just wanted his surviving children to be safe.'

She dipped her chin. 'He wasn't to know how appalling the conditions would be on that ship – or that, by the time we docked in Tasmania, our family would have suffered yet another dreadful loss.'

'Oh, no,' breathed Kathryn. 'Who was it?'

Christy shook her head. 'I can't talk about it now,' she

managed, struggling to control the emotions that were tearing through her. 'I'm sorry.'

Silence fell amongst them and Christy managed to pull herself together enough to concentrate on other things. She took a deep breath, wiped away her tears and turned to Gregor. 'We shall all be staying at the Isles Inn tonight, so if you could deliver our luggage there, I'd be grateful. I took the liberty of booking you a room too, but I suspect you'd rather stay with your parents, now we're so close to them.'

He nodded. 'I don't get to see them enough; so, if you don't mind . . .'

'Of course not, but I hope you'll agree to have dinner with us. It will be our last evening here, and, after all the sadness, I think we all need a bit of cheering up.'

'Aye, I'd be honoured to join you, and I ken it'll be a lively evening. The Isles Inn is popular for the music they have most nights.' He grinned. 'The tourists love it.'

She managed a watery smile. 'I'm sure they do,' she murmured. She drew him aside as Kathryn wandered off to join Anne, who was looking in the shop windows. 'I will need you tomorrow morning to help me with something, Gregor,' she said quietly. 'But I have to ask you not to say anything to the others.'

'You have my word,' he said solemnly. 'Can you no give me an idea of what this something might entail?'

'I need to speak to the bank manager and a couple of other people before we leave tomorrow night, and I'd appreciate your company.'

He raised an eyebrow and then grinned. 'I'll be no getting much sleep tonight, I ken,' he said. 'Can you no give me a wee hint of what you're up to?'

She gave a small shrug. 'It's something I need to do for Callum. I'll see you at eight o'clock, for dinner.'

As Christy moved away to join the others, Gregor chuckled. Christy was a feisty, brave woman who'd seen the worst that life could offer and suffered terrible tragedies – but there was a core of steel in that little body, and a strong sense of purpose in the tilt of her chin. Yet she wasn't too proud to cry, or show her emotions. He admired her hugely, and could only hope that her sour-faced daughter would come to realise what a treasure she was.

10

As Gregor wouldn't be staying the night, Kathryn moved into the single room with some relief. It would have been awkward and uncomfortable having to share with her mother, for since their exchange in the carriage, the atmosphere between them had become frosty.

The small room was on the first floor and overlooked the town square. Heavy beams supported the low ceiling, and the lath and plaster walls had been partially panelled in a dark wood that matched the sturdy furniture. The floor creaked at every step and dipped towards the window, and the bed was an ornately carved affair with a deep mattress, white linen and dark green tartan blankets. There was very little light coming through the tiny diamond-paned windows, so the whole room was gloomy, yet it felt snug now the lamps had been lit and a fire blazed in the hearth.

Kathryn thanked the maid for bringing up a jug of hot water and opened her trunk to unpack her nightclothes and select a dress for the evening and something suitable for the next day's ferry trip to the mainland. Having hung everything up in the vast wardrobe that took up most of one wall, she stripped to her underwear, poured the hot water into the china bowl and washed away the dust of the day's journey.

Sitting at the dressing table some time later, she brushed out her hair and carefully coiled it on top of her head into the fashionable loose bun. Tweaking a couple of curls out to frame her face, she noted that the sunshine and fresh air had brought a glow to her cheeks, and that the colour of her eyes was enhanced by the green of her simple dress. She put gold studs in her ears and added the gold locket and chain her father had given her just before they'd left Melbourne. It was enough for an evening in a small hotel.

She smiled, wondering if Gregor would notice how well she looked tonight, and then dismissed the idea. They were from different worlds, and although he'd proved to be a wonderful companion and guide throughout their time here, and she'd enjoyed the mild flirtation between them, she would be leaving tomorrow and heading back home to begin her new and exciting life in Sydney.

As there was still an hour before she had to go down to dinner, she picked up her pen and opened her journal – but where to begin with so many things to record? Her love of history had taken her to the giddy heights of being accepted into university, and she couldn't begin to add up the hours she'd spent in the state library, poring over the many dusty books there. However, those hours spent in the library couldn't compare with what she'd learned over these past days, for her grandmother had brought her history – and that of Skye – to vibrant, heart-breaking life.

The images her stories had evoked were so clear in Kathryn's head that as she gazed down to the town square, she could almost see those poor, wretched souls wandering in hope of finding work, food and shelter, only to be moved on or shipped out.

She became tearful as she thought of little Callum, for he'd sounded such a bright little boy with a happy nature, despite his crippled foot and the terrible things he'd been forced to witness. It was little wonder his death had broken his father, coming so soon after he'd lost his wife, his home – his hope. The proud, patriotic man, with his ancient lineage, had been bloodied and bowed by forces beyond his control, and he must have been devastated by what he could only have seen as his failure to protect and provide for those he loved.

Kathryn blinked back her tears. How very fortunate she was to have a comfortable home, to have never known the pangs of starvation, the loss of hope, or the terror of eviction. This journey had been an eye-opener – a window into another world and another time, where people counted for nothing and could be cast aside without thought or care.

She took a calming breath and thought about how her grandmother had survived and flourished in the new country she'd been forced to embrace. The spirited spark of determination had seen her through it all, and although Fate had dealt her many a cruel blow, it had clearly come right for her in the end. Yet Kathryn wondered if *she* possessed such a spirit – if, faced with things as horrific, she would be able to do as well. She could only pray she would never find herself in such a situation.

As she sat there, the pen still poised above her journal, her thoughts turned to her grandfather. Grandpa had rarely spoken of his childhood, but the few snippets he had told her revealed a time of grinding poverty, followed by terror and near death in one of the ships sailing to Australia. But, like her grandmother, he too had survived to live a happy and prosperous life.

Kathryn thought, too, of her father. She'd heard his stories of his childhood, how his mother had died and his father had taken him to the opal fields, where a boy had to learn fast and become a man too soon. Those years still lived within him, and although life had been harsh, he'd always spoken of them with affection and pride. She wondered where he was and what he was doing, for it would be dawn now in Melbourne. She missed him, and knew he must be missing her – but did he miss her mother?

Kathryn swallowed a sigh. She was far from the naïve young girl that her mother considered her to be, for she'd overheard the furious arguments that had gone on behind her parents' closed bedroom door, and shared her mother's worry over the widowed Florence, who was far too pretty and lively for any red-blooded man to ignore.

She wanted to believe her father's strong denials, but she'd become all too aware of the coolness between her parents, the slow but ever-growing distance they put between themselves, and the increasing frequency of her father's absences. Harold Ross was a man of great energy and charm, and this long journey would mean he'd be left to his own devices – a dangerous thing for a man unhappy in his marriage and alone in that great big house, vulnerable to temptation.

Kathryn put aside her journal and reached for the small leather case which contained paper and envelopes. She would write to him and tell him that her mother was miserable without him, and couldn't wait to get home. She was taking liberties, she knew, but something had to be done to make things better between them.

She paused after she'd written a couple of pages, her thoughts turning back to the chill between the two women she loved so much. If, as her grandmother had said, her grandfather had been party to what her mother called an unforgivable lie, then surely it had been done through love and a need to protect? Her grandparents weren't the sort of people to lie easily about anything – they'd both been exposed to too much tragedy in their lives to lack the courage to face up to reality. So whatever the trouble was, it had to be very serious indeed.

She bit her lip, remembering the conversation in the coach. Her family was being torn apart and because she didn't know why, there seemed to be nothing she could do about it.

Continuing with her letter, she told her father about what had happened to Christy after the second clearance, described the town of Portree that her grandmother had known, and wrote that she was missing him quite dreadfully and looking forward to the journey home.

At the very end of her letter, she told him how sad she was that her mother and grandmother were so at odds, and asked him if he knew why this had come about. Signing off with love, she blotted the wet ink and carefully folded the pages into an envelope. He probably wouldn't get it for at least six or seven weeks, and by that time she'd almost be home.

*

Christy thanked the little maid for bringing hot water and towels and then prepared for the evening. It felt strange to be back in this inn – stranger still to be a guest and not a lowly kitchen maid, forever hungry and cold. Her smile was wry as she wrapped the thick, fluffy towel around her and stepped out of the hip bath, for the landlord had been surprised when she'd asked him for a tour of the kitchens, and quite shocked when she'd told him she'd once worked here as a scullery maid. Yet as he'd escorted her through the busy kitchen, which hadn't changed very much in all the years she'd been away, he'd been happy to introduce her to his staff and expound on his plans for the place. The tourist trade was booming, and he was determined to make a success of his business now he was the proud new owner of the Isles Inn.

The sight of the little scullery maid, with her reddened hands and pinched face, brought back the awful memories of that time, and as Christy left the kitchens for her bedroom they'd crowded in, bringing the horrific sights and sounds with them. She and her family had had a desperate struggle simply to survive, and yet here she was, the grand lady, touring the place as if she owned it.

How far she'd come, she mused, as she dressed her hair and eyed her reflection in the mirror. The skinny, half-starved girl was long gone, living only in her memories now, and in her place was a slender woman with life's experiences etched into her face, the sadness dulling her eyes.

With a sigh, she pinned the cameo brooch to the ruffed collar of her plain black dress. Her beloved husband had given her the brooch on her last birthday, and she touched it softly, remembering his loving kiss and his sweet smile. How she wished he were here – solid, warm and real. He would have known the right words to say to Anne – would have helped heal the breach, which now seemed too wide to cross, and bring the family together again. But, like Callum and the others, he was gone, and she wouldn't see any of them again until it was her time to join them.

Deciding that the town, the inn and her memories were making her morbid, she picked up her book and settled in a chair by the fire to read. There was an hour before dinner, and she needed to be in a far better mood to be able to enjoy it; G. K. Chesterton's comedy novel *The Napoleon of Notting Hill* should do the trick.

*

Anne had attempted to rest for an hour or so, but her troubled thoughts wouldn't allow it. She left the bed and began to prepare for the evening, choosing a plain skirt and lacy blouse, her best high-heeled buttoned boots and a blue silk stole, which she'd bought on board ship. Having dressed her hair to her satisfaction and put on her pearl jewellery, she gathered up her evening bag and headed for her mother's room. It was time to clear the air.

Christy was wearing the tartan shawl over a plain black gown on which she'd pinned a cameo brooch, and Anne was shocked at how old and tired she suddenly looked.

She glanced up from the book she was reading and greeted Anne with a welcoming smile. 'Hello, my dear. This is a lovely surprise.'

'I thought it was time we had a talk,' she said stiffly.

Christy set the book to one side and patted the chair that stood on the other side of the hearth. 'Then let us do that,' she murmured.

Anne settled into the chair, smoothed her skirt and chose her words carefully. 'Firstly, I'd like you to try and understand why I've been so angry and rude to you throughout this trip. It's not in my nature to be so aggressive, but it's been extremely hard to accept what you and Father did, and I'm afraid I've behaved appallingly over it. I can see now that you had the best intentions, even if they were misguided.'

She knotted her hands on her lap, her gaze avoiding her mother as she waited, heart pounding, for her reply.

'Of course I understand,' said Christy softly. 'Something like that can only be profoundly hurtful, and you were lashing out at everyone, which is only natural in the circumstances. I wish with all my heart you'd been spared such pain, but I'm hugely thankful you've accepted the reason behind the subterfuge.'

Anne nodded, clenching her hands together, holding down on the emotions that were building inside. 'This journey has taught me a great deal,' she said tremulously. 'Not only about you, but about myself – and I find I don't like the woman I've become.' She rushed on before her mother could interrupt. 'You were right when you talked about family and how important it is, but I seem to have let things spiral out of control, and now I can't find a way to put them right.'

She looked at her mother finally. 'Can you forgive me?' she whispered through her tears.

Christy went to her and enfolded her in her arms. 'There's nothing to forgive, my precious girl,' she whispered into her hair. 'It is I who must shoulder the blame for all that has happened between us.' She drew back, cupped Anne's face and kissed her forehead. 'Perhaps, together, we can put things right.'

'Oh, Mother,' Anne sobbed. 'I've been so foolish. Kathryn clearly prefers her father to me, and I've pushed him away and ignored him. What if Harold isn't there to meet us in Melbourne? What if he decides to leave me?'

'Shhh,' Christy soothed, holding her close. 'Harold is a steadfast man, and I firmly believe he still loves you and will be overjoyed to see you home again. As for Kathryn, of course she loves you. She loves both of you, and just wants you to be happy together so she won't have to worry about you when she leaves for Sydney.'

Anne drew back, the spark of jealously swiftly igniting. 'I suppose she confided in you, as usual?'

'Not at all,' said Christy firmly, 'but I know my granddaughter, and I can see that she's worried about you both.' She reached for Anne's hands and held them tightly. 'Kathryn is no longer a child, my dear. She's an intelligent young woman who has noticed things aren't right between you and Harold, and it's clearly troubling her.'

'Then what must I do?'

'I think if you confided in her, and let her know how things stand between you and her father, you might find it brings you closer.'

'I can't discuss the intimate details of my marriage with Kathryn,' she gasped. 'It isn't seemly.'

Christy gave her a handkerchief and waited for her to calm down. 'That's not what I meant at all,' she said patiently. 'Talk to her about how you feel, what irritates you about Harold – all men are irritating at times; I know your father was,' she added to lighten the mood – 'and why you fell in love with him. It might even remind *you* too, because I think that somewhere along the line you've both forgotten what you meant to each other in those early years.'

Anne thought of Harold. She hadn't forgotten the passion they'd shared, but over the years it had faded, the love had withered, and she was as guilty as Harold for letting that happen.

Christy broke into her thoughts. 'Discuss with her how you felt when Harold was busy building his empire and left you to cope for weeks on end while he went all over the country to drum up business. Tell her how precious she is, and how proud you are of her achievements, and offer to go shopping with her before she packs for Sydney. But above all, just show her how much you love her and how willing you are to make good your marriage.'

Anne was calmer now, and she could see that her mother was right, as always, for in her disappointment and dread of Kathryn leaving home she'd distanced herself from her – and from Harold. She and her daughter had shared so few intimate moments lately, and she could recall how sharp she'd been with her, how dismissive of her hopes and dreams that clashed with her own. If it hadn't been for Harold, their daughter would not have achieved so much.

'I just hope I haven't left it too late,' she said sadly.

'It's never too late between mother and daughter,' replied Christy, handing her a fresh handkerchief. 'We have a bond, and even when it's stretched to its very limits, it doesn't break. Trust Kathryn, and trust yourself, Anne, and you will see that I'm right.'

'But what of my marriage? I might have left that far too late – especially now we've been apart for so long.'

'That is between you and Harold, but I would suggest you write to him and tell him how much you miss him, and how you hope your homecoming will be the start of something stronger between you.'

'Yes, I'll do that,' she murmured. She looked into her mother's eyes and took her hands. 'I'm sorry, Mother,' she whispered, 'so sorry to have caused you pain when you least deserved it.'

Christy clung to her hands, her own eyes glistening as she kissed her daughter's cheek. 'Pain can be healed,' she murmured, 'and the ties that bind us will become stronger than ever if we put our faith in each other. There will be no more secrets, Anne. I promise you.'

Anne embraced her, the tears flowing once more as she breathed in her mother's scent and felt those loving arms holding her close again. A new strength surged through her, bringing hope for a brighter future in which she and Harold could repair their marriage and Christy was once more the heart of the family.

Perhaps then her daughter would become more secure in the knowledge that the three generations had reached a closer and more loving understanding.

*

Kathryn knocked on her mother's door and receiving no reply, looked in to find she must already have gone downstairs. She hurried along the narrow landing towards her grandmother's room, which was at the top of the stairs, eager to join in the fun, for she could already hear the sound of many voices and the discordant notes of musicians tuning their instruments.

As she reached the stairs, her grandmother's bedroom door opened and Kathryn stared in amazement at the two smiling women who stood there. Her amazement turned to delight as they held their hands out to her and she was swamped in their embrace.

'You've made it up,' she breathed happily, looking from one radiant face to the other.

'We certainly have,' said Christy, putting her arm round Anne's tiny waist. 'And I think we should hurry downstairs and order a bottle of champagne – if this place has such a thing. By the sound of it it will be a lively evening, and I for one am in the mood to celebrate.'

Anne's smile was soft, making the years and her cares fly away and giving her daughter a glimpse of how lovely she'd been as a girl. 'Let's order two bottles,' she said, with a twinkle of mischief in her eyes. 'Now, come on, before we miss all the fun.'

Kathryn was in a happy stupor as they went down the narrow

stairs and pushed open the door into the main room to be met by a wall of sound from the musicians, who'd struck up a lively jig. Her delight in knowing that the feud was over gave her hope that her mother would now try to make peace with her father. All was right with her world, and as she looked across the room and saw Gregor watching them, she felt a little thrill of pleasure. He'd clearly taken his time to prepare for their last evening, for he'd brushed his hair and had a shave. He looked very handsome in his kilt, jacket and white shirt, the fine fur sporran hanging from his slim waist, the length of tartan pinned across his shoulder by a magnificent brooch of yellow quartz surrounded by filigree gold. His sturdy legs were covered to the knee by woollen socks, one of which held a small dagger, and his feet were shod in highly polished brogues.

'My goodness,' breathed Anne. 'He certainly scrubs up well.'

Kathryn was about to reply when she saw that Gregor was not alone – and that he was coming towards them with a girl on his arm. She was very pretty, with black hair and blue eyes and an open, friendly smile, and although Kathryn was rather put out that he'd brought a guest on their last night, she was glad he seemed so happy.

'Good evening,' he said above the loud music. 'This is my wife, Freya.'

Kathryn realised she was staring at them and hastily switched on a smile.

'Well, you kept that under your hat,' laughed Christy as she shook the girl's hand and introduced the others to her. 'How long have you and this rogue been married?'

'Just a year,' she replied in her soft Scottish burr. 'I hope you don't mind me coming tonight, but it's our anniversary, and I've come to be with him for the weekend.'

'That calls for even more champagne,' said Christy in delight. 'Come along, let's find our table and see if the landlord has some decent bottles in his cellar.'

There was only one main room, but their table was on the far side, away from the musicians, and was partially screened from the noise by the enormous and ornate bar. It was not the sort of place Kathryn and her mother would have dreamed of going into, for such places in Australia were the haunts of rough men – but here it didn't seem to matter. Men and women of all ages and class mingled together happily as the band played softer tunes, the delicious food was served and the first bottle of champagne was swiftly despatched.

Kathryn remembered the conversation she'd had with Gregor at the cemetery, and felt horribly embarrassed as she learned that Gregor had met his wife when he'd attended university in Dundee to take a degree in ancient history. Freya had just become qualified as a teacher, and when they married they'd moved to Inverness. Gregor was a lecturer at the university there, while Freya taught the kindergarten class in the local school.

'You're full of surprises,' she teased, to cover her shame. 'But what I don't understand is how you came to be driving a coach around Skye.'

'It's the long break, and when I heard your grandmother needed a guide, I jumped at the chance,' he replied and grinned. 'Mungo put me on to it when she wrote to him to book the hotel.'

'But what about your wife? Surely she must get bored when you go gadding about?'

Gregor laughed. 'I'd hardly call it gadding about – it's been hard work, I'll have you know, what with women walking about in no boots, horses biting backsides, and certain people demanding the impossible.'

'Oh dear,' she sighed. 'Were we really so terrible?'

He shook his head and chuckled. 'It's all been great fun and I've learned a lot from your grandmother. She's a remarkable woman, and I admire her tremendously.' He reached for Freya's hand and kissed her fingers. 'As for Freya, she'll be joining me again once her school breaks up, and we'll spend part of the summer here before we go down to Aberdeen to visit her family.'

Kathryn saw how happy the two of them were and couldn't help but smile. 'It's certainly a night of celebration,' she said as the waiter opened the second bottle of champagne and poured it into glasses. 'Mum and Grandma settled their differences earlier, and they're much happier for it.'

Gregor glanced across at Anne, who was looking quite animated as she chatted to her mother. 'Aye, I can see that, and I'm glad for both of them. I ken it's no been an easy time for either of them, these past days.'

He pushed back from the table and stood to raise his glass. 'I would like to make a toast,' he said, 'to my beautiful wife, and to the new friends I've made; there is an old Scottish verse which I think might be appropriate for the occasion.'

Silence fell in the room as he cleared his throat and began to speak in his rolling brogue:

'"May the best ye've ever seen / Be the worst ye'll ever see. / May a moose ne'er leave yer girnal / Wi' a tear drap in his e'e. / May ye aye keep hale an' herty / Till ye're auld eneuch tae dee. / May ye aye be jist as happy / As we wish ye aye tae be."

'*Slàinte!*'

There was a roar of approval as the toast was echoed around the room, and Gregor sat down looking a little embarrassed.

'Are there moose in Scotland?' asked Anne innocently. 'And what on earth is a girnal?'

Everyone laughed and Christy explained to a baffled Kathryn and Anne that it was a mouse who must never leave the larder or store cupboard with a tear in his eye, for that would mean there was no food in the house.

The musicians struck up again, and very soon chairs were moved, the tables were drawn against the walls and everyone began to dance. As the champagne ran out and the whisky flowed, so the music got louder and faster, and by the end of the evening it was only the very fit and very young who still had the stamina to keep up.

As the clock behind the bar struck eleven and the landlord began to ring his bell, they trooped outside to get some fresh air and say goodbye to Freya and Gregor. Christy, Anne and Kathryn stood for a while after the couple had disappeared down the road in their buggy, looking up at the millions of stars floating against the black canopy of night.

'It reminds me of the night skies in the outback,' said Christy. 'Perhaps when I get back I will go out to Wallangarra and see my grandsons – take them out camping and tell them the old

Aboriginal stories about how the stars were born and why the sun and moon never meet.'

'I doubt Hamish will let you,' laughed Anne. 'You know what he's like when you suggest anything even slightly risky.'

'It's only because he cares,' murmured Christy. 'Perhaps I should persuade him to join us. It's been years since we camped in the bush.'

'Let's get to bed,' said Anne affectionately. 'We've got a long day ahead of us, and I don't know about you, but my feet hurt after all that dancing.'

Christy smiled and linked arms with both of them. 'I've so enjoyed tonight,' she said softly. 'It was the perfect ending to my homecoming, and I shall keep these happy memories for the rest of my life.'

Kathryn came down to the dining room just as Christy was finishing her breakfast. 'Mother's had a tray taken to her room,' she said as she sat down. 'I think all the excitement of last night has left her feeling a little the worse for wear.'

'I don't feel particularly spritely myself,' replied Christy. 'I'm obviously getting too old for such shenanigans.'

'You loved every minute of it,' teased Kathryn, 'and by the look of you, you're raring to go all over again.'

It was the opening Christy had been hoping for. 'Well, I do have several things to do before we leave Portree,' she said casually. 'Gregor is due to meet me in ten minutes to introduce me to the local bank manager, and then I have some purchases to make before hiring a buggy.'

'A buggy? But why? Surely Gregor will be taking us down by coach with our luggage to the ferry?'

'There's somewhere I want you to see later this morning, and a buggy is much more suitable.' She glanced at the little watch she'd pinned to her jacket lapel. 'I should be back by eleven, so please don't stray from here. But encourage Anne to be dressed and ready by then.'

'But that's two hours,' said Kathryn in surprise. 'I thought you were seeing a bank manager, not buying the bank.'

Christy giggled. 'Now, that would be a thing, wouldn't it?' She got to her feet and gathered up her shawl and handbag. 'I'll see you later,' she murmured, before hurrying away so there would be no further questions.

Kathryn watched her go through the double doors that led to the pavement, and through the glass saw Gregor greeting her before they walked away. Her grandmother did love to tease, she thought, as she tucked into the delicious porridge. She was probably only going to the bank to get some money to pay her hotel bill and Gregor, and to purchase a few mementos to take home to her grandchildren. Though, what they'd make of kilts and sporrans, Kathryn wasn't at all sure.

By half past eleven, Kathryn and her mother had finished their morning coffee and were anxiously waiting for Christy to get back.

'She can't have gone far,' said Anne. 'This isn't exactly a city, so it wouldn't be too difficult to track her down. Do you think we ought to go and find her?'

Kathryn shook her head. 'She was most specific that we wait here, and if we leave now, we could miss her.'

Anne gave a fretful sigh. 'This is so typical of Mother. I bet she's gossiping somewhere and has forgotten all about us.' She caught her daughter's eye and relaxed into a smile. 'Still, we have until five this evening before the ferry leaves, and as it's her last day on Skye, I suppose we mustn't begrudge her.'

It was another fifteen minutes before Christy burst through the doors trailing Gregor behind her, who was loaded with packages. 'I'm so sorry I've kept you waiting,' she said breathlessly, 'but I got talking to this fascinating stonemason, and then I was distracted by a lovely woman who weaves her own tartan, and the time simply ran away with me.'

She looked up at Gregor with a beaming smile. 'This poor man has been trying to chivvy me up, and was an absolute godsend when it came to carrying everything. You wouldn't think there'd be much to buy in such a small place, would you? And you should see what I've got the boys and Harold and . . .' She finally ran out of breath and everyone laughed.

'I can see you're on better form than me this morning,' said Anne affectionately. 'Would you like me to order you some coffee so you can catch your breath?'

Christy shook her head. 'We'll run out of time if I do, and the buggy is already outside.' She turned to Gregor. 'Would you ask the landlord to put everything with our trunks and bags? I don't want to carry it all with me.'

Gregor left the room and Christy plumped down into a chair. 'I'm not used to walking on cobbles,' she said, flexing her feet.

'How I ever managed it as a child, I'll never know – and with bare feet too.'

'So, Mother, where are you taking us this morning?'

'To a very special place, which I'm assured has not been left too neglected.' She flexed her feet again and stretched out her legs, and then stood up as Gregor came back into the room. 'Come on then, let's get going.'

They trooped outside to find a sleek chestnut horse between the shafts of a large buggy, which had a folding cover in case the weather turned. The driver was a taciturn man who merely nodded and left Gregor to help them up and into the buggy. It was quite chilly, even though the sun was shining, and they were glad of the thick blankets the driver had supplied.

'Mr McLeod is not a man for idle chit-chat,' explained Christy, as he cracked the whip and they set off. 'Unfortunately, when he does speak, I can barely understand a word he's saying.' She leaned forward and kept her voice low, her eyes bright with laughter. 'He's from Glasgow, you see, and they have their own strange language down there.'

As the buggy clattered over the cobbles and then on to the broad track they'd come down the previous day, Kathryn saw Gregor and her grandmother exchange secret smiles. 'How did the meeting with the bank manager go?' she asked slyly.

'Very well, thank you. He was most helpful.' She giggled. 'I won't keep you in suspense for too long,' she said. 'We just have to get to where we're going and then I'll tell you everything.' With that, she pulled her shawl round her neck and turned to study the view, her expression unreadable.

Anne and Kathryn exchanged glances. They would simply have to be patient and play along with Christy, who was clearly in a strange mood.

It was almost half an hour before they left the broad track and began to climb a gentle hill, passing a farmhouse and barns along the way, until they reached a stile and could go no further.

'Here we are,' said Christy, as the driver brought his horse to a halt. 'Now we just have a short walk and then you'll discover what all this is about.'

'It's a good thing I thought to wear my sturdier boots,' said Anne, as Gregor helped her down and she looked at the rough ground beyond the stile.

'We're not going that way,' said Christy. 'Follow me.' She strode off towards a high bramble hedge and showed them the narrow opening. 'It's just through here.'

Anne and Kathryn carefully avoided the grasping brambles and stepped through to find a wide field where an area of rough grass had been enclosed by a smart new paling fence. Above the five-bar gate was a willow arbour, and someone had cleverly entwined the willow into a crucifix at its apex.

'This is where Callum is buried,' said Christy softly as she opened the gate. 'He's with all those who never made it on to the ships. I would have had him moved to the proper cemetery, but realised this was where he belonged, far from the public eye and with his own kind, in a place of peace.'

She looked beyond the few weathered gravestones to the silent glen and the rushing streams that ran through it towards the sea.

'As you can see, there are very few memorials, for these were the paupers' graves; most of the poor souls here died of a fever that the townsfolk of Portree were in fear of catching. I'm reliably informed that the headstones you see have been placed here by people like me – people who've made the pilgrimage from their homes across the world to remember those of their family who hadn't survived long enough to make the journey to a new life.'

There was the clatter of wagon wheels and the plod of a heavy horse making its way along the track behind the hedge, and Christy turned and smiled at the thickset man who came through the gate some minutes later, hefting a large stone.

'This is Mr Cameron,' she explained, 'master mason and engraver. He has been working on this since Mungo gave me his address, and this morning I was finally able to pay him.'

Gregor had gone to help the man carry the enormous slab of marble, and following a nod from Christy, they planted it just inside the gate, in a narrow trench Anne and Kathryn hadn't noticed before.

Straining and puffing, they finally got it squared up and solidly embedded in the ground, and then stepped back so everyone could admire it.

In loving memory of Callum MacInnes, 1844–1854.
This memorial honours the fallen of the clearances.
Their names may be unknown, but their story is carried
on the wind across the glens. They will not be forgotten.
RIP

'It's lovely,' breathed Kathryn, 'and so fitting. But how will anyone know it's here?'

'Those who lost loved ones will know,' replied Christy, 'and they are the ones who matter.' She regarded the small cemetery, her expression peaceful. 'I've arranged an annuity for the upkeep, and soon the grass will be cut, the hedge trimmed and the opening widened. There will be a sign erected at the bottom of the lane so that people will know where to come, and a wreath will be laid here every November in memory of all those who died.'

'No wonder you took so long this morning,' said Anne.

'There was a lot of paperwork to sign at the bank, and then I had to visit the head of the local council and the pastor. But I think it's worth it, don't you?'

'Oh, yes,' sighed Kathryn.

Christy turned as the mason came through the narrow opening with a wreath. He laid it reverently at the foot of his marble monument, took off his cap and stood with his head bowed as Christy recited the Lord's Prayer.

'Sleep peacefully, my darling Callum,' she murmured at the end, 'and know that I will never forget you.'

She turned away and they all rode back to Portree in solemn silence, each with their own thoughts.

Christy regarded the scenery as they trotted along. She felt calm and peaceful, despite the sad memories of sweet little Callum, for she'd returned to Skye as she'd promised her father all those years ago, had passed on the events they'd lived through and done her best to instil in her daughter and granddaughter the belief that no matter what happened in life, it was how you dealt with adversity that mattered.

As they reached the outskirts of Portree, and she looked once again down to the harbour, she knew it was almost time to begin relating the next chapter of her young life – the pages of which had been written during that final day on Skye and on the terrifying sea voyage to an uncertain future on the other side of the world.

The leaving of Skye was far more painful than she could ever have imagined, and as they stood on the quayside and watched their luggage being stowed into the ferry's hold, Christy really had to battle with her emotions.

It was a very different day from the one when she'd last seen these shores, when the rain had been carried by a chill wind, with scudding clouds and a sense of gloom looming over the huddled mass of defeated humanity waiting on the quay. Today it was cool, the wind slight, the sun glittering on the water, and she liked to imagine that the island wanted to send her on her way back to Australia with happier memories.

She watched Gregor saying goodbye to Anne and Kathryn, glad that she'd come to know him and delighted that he was obviously so happy with sweet Freya. She'd made him promise to stay in touch and to let her know when his first child arrived – after all, he was a member of her family, and family had always been important to her.

'It's been grand to meet you, Christy,' he said as he took her hand. 'I'll no be forgetting you, or your stories, and I wish I could hear more, for I ken there are many still to be told.'

'Indeed there are,' she replied with a smile. 'But being an intelligent man, with a family history much the same, I'm sure you can use your imagination as to what those stories entail. But perhaps I'll write them down one day and send you a copy.'

'Aye, you do that. 'Twill make grand reading, I'm sure.'

She reached into her jacket pocket and handed him an envelope. 'This is what I owe you, Gregor. You've been such a help, and if you should ever want to come to Australia, I can guarantee you'd be very welcome in any of our homes.'

He didn't open the envelope, but slid it into his plain leather sporran before taking her hands in his great paws. 'I'll no be moving far from here,' he said softly. ''Tis in me blood and in me bones. Tack care, bonny lass, and keep everyone guessing about what you'll do next.' He grinned. 'But keep your boots on,' he added mischievously.

'Aye, that I will,' she replied. Standing on tiptoe, she kissed his cheek lightly and then turned away and walked up the gangway and on to the ferry.

As the captain blew two blasts of steam from the funnel and the ropes were tossed from the capstans, Christy stood on the deck, her mother's shawl about her shoulders, her head held high despite the inner turmoil she was battling. She watched the familiar shoreline and the Cuillin hills, so dark and jagged against the sky, become ever more distant, and she blinked back her tears as she whispered her last farewell to the island she loved so much. She would never see Skye again, but she would carry it in her heart until her last breath.

*

Gregor waited until the ferry was almost on the far shore, and then ambled back to the carriage, where Jock had his nose firmly dug into the long grass that grew beside the dockside wall, and Hector was shaking his head in impatience. He leaned against Jock's sturdy side and stroked his neck.

'I ken we'll no see the likes of Christy again,' he murmured thoughtfully. 'That is one grand wee lassie.'

Jock lifted his great head, stamped his foot and nuzzled Gregor's hair.

Giving him a friendly nudge, Gregor clambered up into the high driving seat, gently slapped the reins over the horses' backs, and they set off for his family home on the outskirts of the town.

The horses knew the way, so Gregor left the reins to droop over his knee so he could open the envelope. He wanted to buy Freya a gift before he got home, and he'd seen a lovely silver Celtic cross and chain in the jeweller's window this morning that would be perfect.

As he opened the envelope, he was astonished to see far more money than he'd asked for. He rifled through the notes and gasped when he realised there was over fifty pounds – enough to leave their rented flat in Inverness, buy a house, and probably even furnish it.

He tugged on the reins and drew the horses to a halt on the bridge. His tears almost blinded him as he stood on the seat to try and catch one last glimpse of that tiny figure on the deck of the ferry. But the little boat was already approaching the harbour on the mainland. It was too late.

'*Tapadh leat*, Christy MacInnes,' he whispered. '*Sealbh math dhuit.*'

Having thanked her and wished her luck, Gregor blinked hard against his tears, took up the reins again and headed home to his family, his heart full.

11

Melbourne

Harold had arrived home just after dawn on the third day since leaving Yarrabinda. He'd bathed, changed into fresh clothes and eaten a hearty breakfast of steak and eggs as he quickly scanned through the post that had accumulated during his absence. He then dealt with some business paperwork before leaving the house again.

Riding a fresh horse into the bustling city, his senses were assaulted by the noise after the peace of the outback – and the smell of the new-fangled petrol cars that had suddenly become popular. He checked on his manager in the office and went through the paperwork for the proposed new warehouses he was having built down at Phillip Bay, and then sat in on a board meeting to discuss the planning application. This meeting went on for longer than he'd expected, so he got his secretary to book him on to that night's ferry to Tasmania.

His visit to Baker's office overlooking the tannin-brown Yarra River took up more time, for, despite their conversation over the two-way, Baker was still most reluctant to give him the key to Christy's safe. Harold insisted, they had quite an argument over it and in the end Baker put the key on his desk and left the room, muttering about the dangers of being struck off should Christy find out what he'd done.

Now, with the key safely tucked away in an inner pocket of his jacket, and carrying a swag packed with two changes of clothes, Harold was leading his horse up the ramp and into the vast hold of the *Black Swan* at Port Phillip. The steamship ferry that particular night unfortunately didn't go down to Hobart, but would take him through the night to the northern shores of Tasmania and Port Dalrymple.

Once he'd settled the horse in the partitioned stable area in the hold, which was packed with sheep, cargo and luggage, he headed back to the passenger deck, found his overnight cabin, and collapsed on to the unyielding bunk. He was exhausted after having had such little sleep over the last three days, but soon discovered that his mind was too active to let him rest.

Opening his swag, he drew out the letters from Anne and Kathryn. He'd skimmed through them over breakfast, but now he had the time to read them more thoroughly.

It seemed they were enjoying their journey, and he'd been surprised by the enthusiastic descriptions from Anne about their various ports of call, and her delight in London's grand old buildings, the shops, museums, galleries and theatres. He was pleased that she was having such an exciting time, but saddened that she made no mention of missing him during their long separation – she didn't even bother to ask how he was or what he was doing during her absence.

What was more worrying was the lack of any mention of how she and her mother were getting on after their years of barely speaking to one another – which could only mean that things hadn't changed between them. He could only hope that his little Kathryn hadn't been caught up in the feud and made to take sides – although he doubted if that was Christy's way at all; she was far too sensible and fair-minded. But Anne could be quite daunting at times, and he knew how easy it would be for her to demand loyalty from her daughter, should it come to that. He could only pray that Kathryn kept her own counsel and refused to bend to either of them.

He'd opened Kathryn's letters with some trepidation, but she said nothing about any trouble between them, and they were full of joyous descriptions of everything she'd seen and experienced. He smiled as he read them again, for it was almost as if he could hear her talking to him in that slightly breathless way she had when she was animated.

Folding the letters into their envelopes, he tucked them back into the bottom of his swag and wondered where the women were now. They'd been gone for almost twelve weeks, so they must have been to Skye, and would now be on their way back to London to catch the ship home.

Harold sighed. He was looking forward to seeing them again, for the past weeks had dragged – and yet he didn't want them arriving before he'd cleared up the awful legal mess that had arisen. It would not be a happy homecoming at all if they got caught up in that, for it would fuel the fire between Anne and her mother and also drag his daughter into it.

He glanced at his pocket watch just as he heard the blast from the funnel and felt the gentle roll as the ship eased away from the dock to begin its departure from Phillip Bay into the Bass Strait. It was only eight o'clock and he wouldn't be able to sleep, despite his exhaustion, so he pulled on his hat and coat and went on deck.

The water was calm in the bay, the black sky strewn with stars, and he began to relax as he watched the twinkling lights of Werribee and Geelong slowly fade away on the starboard side. Soon he would see the regular beam flash from the lighthouse on the headland of Sorrento, which signalled a warning of rocks and much rougher waters ahead.

Harold remained on deck long after they'd reached the turbulent waters and the other passengers had gone inside for dinner, for as the cold wind buffeted him and he had to cling to the railings as the ship rolled and heaved through the sleek black waves, he felt the same sense of freedom he experienced in the outback. There was no light to dim the stars, no sound but that of the ship's steam engine and the waves crashing against the bows – and the air was salty and clean and invigorating.

He eventually went in search of dinner, his appetite whetted by the cold and the lack of anything to eat since breakfast. An hour later he checked on his horse, lit his pipe, and took a last stroll around the deck before returning to his cabin. He fell into a deep and unbroken asleep, lulled by the throb of the steam engines and the roll of the ship.

*

Harold was dressed and ready long before the dining room opened, so he packed his swag and went down to check on his horse again, passing the time with the chatty groom until he heard the gong for breakfast.

Returning to the deck after eating his fill of bacon and eggs and downing a pot of good strong coffee, he stood at the railings and watched the island slowly emerge on the horizon. He'd always liked Tasmania, for it was green and sparsely populated, with a cooler climate than the mainland and plenty of room for a man to wander. There were isolated farms and apple orchards, huge lakes to fish in, mountains to climb, hills to trek, bush to explore, long, deserted beaches of white sand, and tiny bays where the sea crashed against the towering black cliffs or exploded through blowholes.

And yet this beautiful island had a dark history of tortured convicts imprisoned in the hellholes of Port Arthur, Puer Island and Sarah Island, of Aborigines being slaughtered or exiled from their native land to islands that couldn't sustain them, and of shipwrecks, piracy and convicts so desperate to escape they risked their lives trying to cross the wild Gordon River and find their way through the thousands of acres of unexplored bush that lay to the west of the island.

Harold considered himself to be a fortunate man, for although he hadn't had things easy in the early years, he'd never felt the cut of a lash or been beholden to anyone, much less imprisoned – although he'd come close to arrest on a couple of occasions in his youth when the drink had led him astray and he'd thought he could fight anyone or anything.

He smiled at this and then lit his pipe. He'd been a bit of a larrikin back then, but the local copper had clipped his ear and taken him back to his dad for an even heftier wallop, and he'd soon learned to drink less and mend his ways.

The island was clearer now, coming out of the morning mist in a soft green haze. He leaned on the railings as black cliffs and tree-lined sandy coves were revealed, and small towns nestled together against a backdrop of green fields and rolling hills. It was a peaceful place since the end of the convict transports half a century ago, settled by respectable, hard-working people who wanted to put those awful times behind them and make the most of the fertile land and temperate climate.

'Harold! Harold Ross.'

Startled from his thoughts, he turned to find himself looking into a pair of all-too-familiar sparkling blue eyes. 'Florence,' he gasped. 'What on earth are you doing here?'

Florence Hardwick pouted prettily and looked up at him through her lashes. 'There's no need to sound quite so cross about it,' she said. 'A girl could take offence, you know.' Then she smiled and two little dimples appeared in her creamy cheeks. 'I'm on my way to visit my grandmother in Hobart. What about you?'

'I have some business to attend to,' he said, feeling the colour rising in his face. Florence was an extremely attractive young woman and knew exactly how to discomfort a man with her teasing, and those eyes, which seemed to see right into his soul, and her pretty mouth . . .

He pulled himself together. 'Surely you're not travelling alone?' he asked.

She smiled impishly. 'My mother's with me, so it's not much fun. Are you going to Hobart by any chance, Harold?'

'Eventually,' he hedged, unable to think straight with her looking at him like that.

'Is Anne with you?' She glanced up and down the deck.

'Not this time,' he admitted unwillingly.

'What a shame.' Florence's dimples showed again and her eyes flashed with mischief. 'We shall be staying in Patersonia overnight, at the Ocean Inn,' she said. 'Perhaps we could have lunch – or dinner, if you'd prefer?'

Harold cleared his throat, avoided her gaze and became businesslike. 'I'm sorry, Florence, but I shall be leaving for Hobart the moment we dock.'

A hint of disappointment lit in her eyes, but it was fleeting and soon replaced by her usual teasing glint. 'Why, Harold Ross, I'm beginning to think you're trying to avoid me.'

'Not at all,' he said firmly. 'It's just that I have important things to attend to in Hobart and time is of the essence.'

'Goodness me,' she breathed. 'That all sounds most exciting. Are you planning to extend your empire?'

It was more a case of saving Christy's, he thought. 'Something like that,' he said, edging away.

'Well, you're to promise to call on me at the Star Hotel while you're in Hobart. Mother always has a snooze in the afternoon and is usually in bed by nine, so . . .' The dimples flashed again as she took a step nearer. 'You must eat, no matter how busy you are, and it's said that the seafood in Tasmania is the very best in the world.'

'I really can't promise anything,' he said, backing even further away. 'I'm sorry, Florence, but we're about to dock and I need to go down to my horse.'

*

Florence experienced a frisson of excitement as she watched him hurry away. He was a good-looking man tied to a sour-faced bitch who didn't deserve him, and she had enough experience of men to know he found her attractive and could be easily tempted, given half the chance. But until today the wife had always been there, scowling in the background, watching him like a hawk, and Florence had never quite managed to lure him away.

She stifled a giggle as the ship slowly approached the quayside of Port Dalrymple. She did so love the start of a liaison. It was a delicious game of cat and mouse, made all the better by Harold Ross playing hard to get, and with his wife out of the picture – and being so far from Melbourne – who knew where it might lead?

Florence would have purred if she'd been a cat, for what had started out as a tiresome trip to visit her grandmother – who was a sharp-tongued harridan at best and a sly old witch at worst – had suddenly become very exciting.

*

Harold was hot under the collar and in a rush to get his horse and leave the ship. He was flattered to be pursued by Florence – what man wouldn't be? But he needed to avoid her at all costs. She was too attractive, too forward and far too dangerous. Anne had

194

already noticed the attraction between them, and had accused him of being unfaithful – something he'd managed to avoid despite the many temptations of women like Florence and the lack of affection at home.

It had been fairly easy to resist her back in Melbourne, for he'd always made sure they were in a crowd and never alone in the same room. However, Florence possessed a stubborn streak when it came to men who took her fancy – and she'd had a few, according to the rumours he'd heard at his gentlemen's club, reeling them in like stunned fish on the end of her gossamer line of unspoken but tacit promises – and it seemed he was her latest prey.

He could imagine the delights that were on offer – indeed, he'd spent many a night thinking about them – but he was looking for more than sexual gratification in a brief fling that could destroy everything. He yearned for the love and stability he'd once had with Anne, and when she returned to Melbourne he was determined to do all he could to reignite that flame. The last thing he wanted in the midst of everything was the complication of Florence Hardwick. Yet he suspected Florence was already plotting something in that mischievous, rather wicked mind, and the thought made him tense.

Fetching his horse, he led it down the gangway to the quay and then swung into the saddle. Catching sight of Florence and her mother, he quickly looked away and spurred his horse into a trot in the opposite direction. It was clear he would have to stay alert during his time in Hobart, but it shouldn't take too long to search through Christy's safe, and then he could head straight back to Melbourne.

As he left the outskirts of George Town behind him and headed south, he nudged the horse into an easy canter. With regular stops to spell the animal, he was fairly confident of arriving at Christy's before nightfall, but what he might find there still worried him.

*

Inverness

Christy hadn't looked back as she'd stepped off the ferry, for her time in Skye was over and she could let it slip back into the past where it belonged. She had been almost silent during the long coach journey back to Inverness, and was grateful that Anne and Kathryn seemed to understand she needed this quiet time to think and come to terms with this feeling of having come to terms with all that had haunted her since childhood, and accept that it was over.

As the coach rattled along the road and finally turned off for the hotel on the outskirts of Inverness, she found it strange to be so calm and accepting that she would never see Skye again. She'd expected her emotions to run away with her, as they had all those years ago, and yet the retelling of her story and the return to the places that had haunted her memories for so long had been a catharsis, easing those pent-up emotions and finally bringing peace.

Having arrived at the Lodge Hotel, they went to their rooms to wash and change their clothes before meeting for a late dinner. The hotel had once been a hunting lodge on the estate of a wealthy family and was built from creamy mellow stone, the turrets and towers making it look like a miniature castle.

It was positioned beside a sea loch, with views of a distant island shore and the bridges and lights of Inverness. Surrounded on three sides by woodland, the grounds were manicured and provided a putting green, shady arbours and a tinkling fountain. But it was the views of the loch from the dining-room windows that held their attention throughout their meal, for the moon was rising, casting a golden glow across the water and the distant hills.

Christy thought the owners had gone a bit overboard with the tartan carpets and curtains, the enormous oil paintings of proud Highlanders and the stags' heads on the walls, but it was obviously popular with foreign visitors, for she could hear several languages being spoken in the dining room.

Dinner was a triumph, and they left the table over an hour later for a stroll around the grounds before Christy led them to a small private sitting room where they were served coffee.

'You've been very quiet, Mother,' said Anne, settling into a deep couch by the roaring fire. 'Are you sure you're not too tired to head back to London tomorrow?'

Christy shook her head. 'Not tired,' she said, 'just thoughtful.'

'That's hardly surprising,' said Anne. 'You've been through the mill this past week and it couldn't have been easy for you to dredge up all those sad memories.'

Christy smiled at her daughter. 'It was easier than I thought it would be, but then those memories have been with me all my life, and although the images are still bright, time and distance have softened the heartache and fear that I experienced as a child.'

Kathryn set down the delicate cup and saucer. 'Would it trouble you if I asked you something, Grandma?'

'That depends entirely on the question,' she replied warily.

'It's just that I wondered . . . I mean, I'm curious . . .' She took a breath and squared her shoulders. 'It's wonderful that you and Mother are friends again, but I'm curious about what happened between you to cause such a breakdown in the first place,' she ended in a rush.

It was the elephant in the room and Christy fleetingly caught Anne's eye before answering. 'I think we should all be grateful that things have settled down,' she said carefully. 'Anne and I have no wish to stir up old troubles, and are content to put them behind us and look forward to a happier future. So we'll say no more about it.'

Kathryn regarded them both from the other side of the low table and nodded before changing the subject. 'When you left Skye as a child, did you come this way?'

Christy silently let go of the breath she'd been holding and poured more coffee. 'The Skye ferry took us to Mallaig, where we boarded the *Mary Elena*. From there we steamed through the Firth of Lorn, past the islands of Jura and Islay and down to Dublin.'

'Oh, so why aren't we doing the same journey?'

'Because once was enough,' she replied.

'Was it so very bad?' Kathryn's voice was soft with concern.

'It was hell on earth,' she replied shortly.

'Then you mustn't tell us any more,' urged Kathryn. 'You've been through enough already.'

Christy shook her head. 'No, it's best I tell you now, while we're still in Scotland, and then, when we're on our ship going home, I can tell you the much happier story of what happened after we arrived in Port Dalrymple, and how I came to have a real adventure in the goldfields of Victoria.'

'Gosh, that sounds exciting,' breathed Kathryn.

'I don't think Kathryn needs to know too much about that time,' said Anne stiffly. 'It's not exactly the sort of thing to share with your young granddaughter.'

There it was again, Christy realised – the subject that couldn't be discussed in the open, but which lay between them like a dark spectre.

'Of course I won't go into too much detail,' she said hurriedly, 'but Kathryn deserves to hear some of it, and I'm sure her father must have had similar experiences in the opal fields which he's told her about.'

Anne's lips thinned. 'Harold's time in the outback couldn't possibly have been anything like yours, and he certainly wouldn't have boasted about it to his daughter if it was. I'd appreciate it if you were mindful of what you say from now on.'

'Oh, Mother, please don't get cross again. Grandma's stories are as fascinating as Daddy's, and I want to hear all of them, not just the bits you think I should hear.'

Christy broke in before Anne could reply. 'I have to confess there are incidents which I'm unwilling to share with you, Kathryn, but you'll just have to forgive me for leaving them out. They'll not make any difference to the stories, I promise you.'

She reached for Anne's hand, noting how stiff she'd become, and how there was no answering squeeze from her fingers. 'You can rely on me not to say anything that might shock Kathryn,' she murmured. 'But for now, may I tell you both what happened in Portree?'

Anne gave a nod, but didn't pull her hand away, which Christy accepted as an apology of sorts for snapping earlier.

She took a shallow, tremulous breath and let the images in her head come alive again as she talked. 'We were still grieving for Callum when our father managed to secure us free passage through the charity called the St Andrew's Emigration Service. But we had to wait in Portree until well into the New Year before we could leave.

'It was 1855,' she continued, 'and we barely survived the particularly harsh winter. Portree was much quieter when everything was covered in a thick blanket of snow, for those who remained in hope of getting a free passage to warmer climes were much fewer in number. Those who hadn't been taken by the fever were dying of the cold and starvation, and the sight of a frozen body in an alleyway or on the street had become commonplace.'

Kathryn paled and Anne's fingers tightened on Christy's hand.

'We managed to survive because Jamie had resisted selling his woodworking tools to buy food, and finally got a job doing repairs in the Isles Hotel. I was taken on as a scullery maid, so we both had one proper meal a day. Between us, we managed to sneak out enough scraps to keep the four of us going.' Her smile was wry. 'I'm sure the cook knew, but she said nothing and often gave us an extra helping, which we hid in Jamie's tool box.'

She gave a deep sigh. 'Finlay kept badgering the men down at the docks for work, and although there was little enough of it, he earned a few pennies now and again and would sometimes come home with a meat pie or a small corner of cheese.

'But our poor father could find no employment and even resorted to begging – tramping from door to door in the hope someone would give him something. He was rarely successful and although he never said anything, I think he felt ashamed that he had to rely on his children for food. As the winter set in even harder, he seemed to shrink and age before our eyes.'

She had a sharp memory of the brawny giant fading and shrivelling, blinked it away and brightened determinedly. 'The only good thing to come from that awful winter was that we were deserted by the fleas and vermin – it was too cold for them, it seemed, and there wasn't a spare crumb of food to be had, so they left for better pickings.'

Christy remembered the empty room with the empty grate, the thin blanket they shared at night to cover their rags, and the sound of a starving baby whimpering in the next room. It was the death of the children that had really affected her, and even now she was overwhelmed by a great sweep of sadness.

'By February, Jamie had come to the end of his repairs with no prospect of getting other work, in spite of tramping from one end of the town to the other in the hope of someone having something to mend. And then I was dismissed by the landlord.'

She looked down at her hands, so soft and white, the nails neatly manicured and polished. 'My hands were raw from being in hot water and lye soap all day, and frozen during the night. When I picked up a stack of dinner plates that cost more than a month's wages, they slipped out of my fingers on to the stone slabs and shattered into a million pieces.' She dipped her chin. 'Even the cook couldn't persuade him to keep me after that, but she did give me some bread and cheese, which we eked out over two days.'

Taking a deep breath, she gazed beyond them into the past. 'Our clothes were rags by then, our bellies constantly clawing with hunger, but Jamie and I knew we couldn't sell either his tools or my grandmother's loom, for they were our only real assets and we'd need them when we got to Tasmania. And yet it got so bad that we were on the point of going to the pawn brokers when we got news that the *Mary Elena* was due to dock that day, and we had to report to the harbour to take the ferry down to meet it.

'We trooped down to the quay with all the others who'd be travelling with us, and we must have looked a pitiful sight, huddled together as the clouds glowered overhead and the wind seared through our rags to our very bones. But we'd heard there would be food on board the *Mary Elena*, and beds and blankets, and we were prepared to wait there all day for the chance of such luxury.'

Christy gave a small grunt of disdain. 'The *Mary Elena* was an old merchant clipper which had been adapted to take human cargo. When we boarded her, we were herded down into the hold to find that hundreds of wooden partitions had been erected where once the ship had carried coal, and that the promised beds turned out to be narrow planks of wood nailed to the partitions and barely long enough for a child to lie upon.

'The men in charge sent the single men to one end, the lone

women and girls to the other, with the families allocated the middle section. It was very dark down there and still stank of the coal dust, which lay over everything. There was a barrel of drinking water, but none to wash in, and steel buckets for lavatories, which we were told had to be emptied each morning over the side.

'The blankets were thin and not much better than rags, and the food was doled out a ladle at a time, on tin plates, from an enormous pot set out on the deck. But at least it was proper food: rich stews and porridge.'

'You make it sound like one of the convict ships,' said Anne.

'We weren't chained, but having heard the stories of those poor convicts, I believe the conditions were similar,' Christy agreed softly. 'And once we set sail and the hatches were closed against the high seas, it was like being entombed. It wasn't long before we all got sick and the stench was horrific, but there was nothing we could do but wait for those few precious moments we were allowed on deck to eat. I remember Finlay helping our father up the ladder and them simply collapsing on the deck, gulping in the cold, clean air.'

'Such conditions must have been a breeding ground for germs,' said Anne with a shudder.

Christy dipped her chin and nodded. 'People were already weak from starvation, and it wasn't long before fever struck. We'd not long left Ireland when they opened the hatch one morning and we realised some had died during the night.'

She lifted her chin and blinked back the tears. 'The fear ran like a wind through all of us, and as the clipper battled through the rough waters off South America we were all very sick, and a lot of the weaker ones didn't survive. But it was worse when we entered calmer waters and the heat below decks made it almost impossible to breathe. We lost many more, especially among the children and the elderly, and they were buried at sea.'

She swallowed hard and took a shuddering breath. 'The captain finally took pity on us and allowed those who hadn't fallen sick to stay on the deck, where the crew doused us in buckets of salty water. He was clearly worried about his crew getting the fever, and the moment any of us looked as if we were ailing, he ordered us below and refused to let us up again until we died or recovered.

'Jamie was the first to get ill, and my father refused to let me care for him, ordering me to stay on deck while he tended to him himself. We were now steaming across the Pacific and the heat, even on deck, was intolerable – what it must have been like in the hold doesn't bear thinking about. Finlay and I were constantly on edge, wanting to go down to help but knowing that if we did, we too might get sick and never come up again.'

'Dear God,' breathed Anne. 'It was inhuman – especially as the ship had been chartered by a Church charity. I'm utterly amazed any of you survived.'

Christy's smile was wan. 'Not many of us did, and it was a close thing for our family, because I too got sick and had to go back into the hold. It was like hell down there – a fiery furnace in which death hovered at every hour. I don't remember much at all; Jamie told me later that I was delirious most of the time and burning up with fever. But like him I pulled through, and by the time we'd reached Polynesia I was allowed to return to the deck.

'My poor, brave, patient father was now ill, and I disobeyed the captain's orders and went down to care for him. But he was too weak already, his spirit defeated utterly by all we'd gone through, and he died in my arms two weeks before we glimpsed our first sight of Australia.'

Christy pulled a handkerchief from her pocket and dabbed at her tears as the memory of that awful day flooded in. 'We buried him at sea,' she managed tearfully. 'It was a short ceremony, with a prayer from the captain and a brisk salute from the sailors as they lowered his body, stitched into his blanket and weighted down with stones, into the water. The sea was so blue and clear, we could see him floating down for a long time before he finally disappeared forever.'

She brushed away fresh tears. 'My poor father had been a strong, vibrant man with a good heart and a deep pride in who he was and where he'd come from. The clearances had robbed him of his spirit and pride – the starvation and fever had finally broken him. As we steamed on across that glassy ocean, I could see the rage once again burning in Jamie's eyes. But this time it also burned in Finlay's, and in my own heart. I knew then that it would be a long time before any of us could forgive those who'd brought us to this point – and perhaps we never would.'

'And have you forgiven them?' asked Anne softly.

'I've learned to, because I couldn't let such hatred colour the rest of my life,' she replied. 'But I'll never forget.'

12

Bellerive, Tasmania

The journey had taken far longer than Harold had expected, for the horse had cast a shoe and he'd had to walk him several miles to find a blacksmith. By the time he'd found one in Richmond, which was one of the first towns to be settled by free migrants on the island almost a century before, it was very late, so he decided to spend the night. There were still twelve miles or so to go, and the horse was as weary as he was.

He rented a room at the Bridge Inn, settled his horse in the stables at the back and, after a hearty dinner, fell into bed and was asleep within minutes.

Harold woke at dawn as usual, ate a quick breakfast and saddled his horse. The day promised to be fair and he was in a hurry to get to Christy's place, do what he had to do, and then see if he could catch the ferry from Hobart. It would mean a longer journey – the boat would call in at Sydney before reaching

Melbourne – but at least it would give him a quick getaway from Hobart and Florence.

Bellerive was a sparsely settled suburb of Hobart on the eastern bank of the River Derwent, which flowed into Storm Bay and eventually out into the Tasman Sea. This south-easterly part of the island was made up of several peninsulas, one of which held the notorious, and thankfully decommissioned, convict prison at Port Arthur. As Harold reached the old fort on top of Kangaroo Bluff, he was afforded a magnificent view of Hobart and its vast harbour against the imposing backdrop of Mount Wellington. Easing the horse down the hill and taking the narrow track which ran alongside the river, he soon caught sight of the roof of Christy's home in the distance.

Skye House was a traditionally built wooden Queenslander that had been given a sturdy tiled roof in place of the more traditional corrugated iron. Built above the ground on concrete blocks to deter termites, it had been extended over the years to provide a comfortable home for Christy's family. It sprawled across the vast plot, its white painted walls gleaming in the sun. The ornate wrought iron decorating the deep veranda which ran round three sides of the house had also been painted white, but was now almost smothered in a tumble of roses and clematis, which would bloom in the spring into a riot of pink and white and purple. There were cane chairs and tables on the shaded veranda, and tubs of winter pansies and ferns added to the sense of comfort and welcome.

A manicured lawn swept down towards the small private bay of white sand and shingle; flowerbeds and pretty specimen trees that would come alive with blossom in the spring were dotted across the lawn, and at the back of the house were the paddocks and stables, and the sandy schooling ring where Christy's late husband had spent his final hours.

The bush encroached on the far boundaries of the property, and as Harold approached the gateway he could hear the kookaburras laughing at him while colourful parakeets shrieked and squabbled, almost drowning out the single clear note of the tiny bellbirds. It was a beautiful place and he always enjoyed coming here, but he wondered if Christy would stay on now she was alone and her children were scattered across the mainland. She'd find herself rattling around in that large house with its many acres of land, and as she got older she would struggle to cope with it all.

He smiled wryly as he took the horse to the empty stable-yard, where once there had been a string of thoroughbreds when his father-in-law had been alive. He let the horse drink from the trough while he rubbed him down, and then set him free in one of the paddocks and took a moment to absorb the beauty and peace. Christy wouldn't appreciate him thinking such thoughts about her aging; she would find them insulting – and quite rightly. To his mind, she would never grow old or lose that feisty spirit, and he doubted she'd ever leave, for even after she'd taken her last breath, her spirit would live on here.

The screech and clatter of a screen door being opened alerted him to the fact that he wasn't alone. Surprised, he turned to face a large woman swathed in a floral apron, who was glaring at him from the kitchen step.

'Can I help you?' she asked, folding her meaty arms beneath her large bosom.

'I'm Christy's son-in-law, Harold Ross,' he said, tipping his hat to her and walking towards her with his hand out.

She eyed the hand and then ignored it. 'I've never seen you before,' she snapped. 'What do you want?'

Harold forced a smile, although it was difficult in the face of such belligerence. 'And I have never seen you before, Mrs . . .?'

'Ryan,' she said. 'Edna Ryan.'

'Well, Mrs Ryan, I've come on behalf of the family solicitor, Mr Archibald Baker,' he said. 'There is something he has asked me to retrieve from her safe.'

Her stare told him she didn't trust him. 'Then he should have come himself,' she said.

'He's unavoidably detained,' said Harold smoothly as he advanced and put one booted foot on the step. 'Whereas I am at a loose end now my wife and daughter are travelling with Christy, so I offered to come in his stead.' He held her gaze and gave her his most winning smile. 'It's a most important document, Mrs Ryan, and time is of the essence.'

'I'm sure it is,' she said with a sniff. 'But I'm under specific instruction to take care of the house and make sure there are no unsavoury visitors.' She eyed him as if he was something rather nasty she'd found on the bottom of her carpet slippers.

'I can assure you that I'm far from unsavoury,' he said, barely keeping his patience as he drew one of his business cards from his waistcoat pocket and hastily scribbled on the back with the stub of pencil he'd found in his jacket. 'If you have any doubts, do feel free to telephone Mr Baker in Melbourne, and he will confirm why I'm here. That's his number.'

She took a while to read the card and suddenly didn't look quite so certain of herself. 'I don't hold with those new-fangled telephonic things,' she said with another sniff. 'Dangerous, I call 'em, and not natural.'

Harold could see she was torn and so kept his impatience in check as she continued to bar the way with her bulk. 'It's been a long ride from George Town,' he cajoled, 'and I was rather hoping I could have a cup of tea?'

She sucked her false teeth while she looked him up and down, and finally relented. 'You'd better come in, I suppose,' she said grudgingly. 'But take those boots off. I've just mopped the kitchen floor.'

Harold toed off his boots and set them on the step before following Mrs Ryan's broad beam into the kitchen. There was a smell of fresh baking in the air, a half-filled coffee cup on the scrubbed pine table and the remains of breakfast. Mrs Ryan was clearly making herself comfortable in Christy's home.

'Are you staying here while Christy's away?' he asked casually.

'I only live down the road,' she replied, slamming the kettle on to the hotplate of the range. 'But I come in each day to check on things, collect the post and do a bit of cleaning.'

She saw him eyeing the remnants of her breakfast and far from being embarrassed, became cross. 'Madam said I could help myself to anything I wanted, and use her stove when mine was playing up – so it's no good you looking at me like that, young man.'

Duly chastened, Harold didn't reply but sat meekly waiting for the kettle to boil and the tea to mash in the pot, not daring to light his pipe. Edna Ryan was clearly not a woman to cross, and he might need her cooperation should he have difficulty in finding what he was looking for, so it was best to try and keep her on his side.

She set the pot down on the table, hastily cleared away her breakfast dishes, and then opened the range to retrieve a tray of small buns and two tins of wonderfully risen sponge cake, which she set on a wire tray to cool. Plumping down at the table, she opened an ornately decorated tin to reveal buttered scones.

'I suppose, like most men, you're hungry,' she said grudgingly. 'I made these cheese scones yesterday, so you might as well have one before they go stale.'

'They look lovely,' he said truthfully as he took one. Biting into it, he closed his eyes in delight, for the scone was the most delicious thing he'd tasted in a long while.

'My goodness, Mrs Ryan, you could win prizes with these. Could I have another?'

She went slightly pink and pushed the tin towards him. 'I've won prizes for my scones six years running at the Hobart fair,' she said proudly. 'You should taste my fruit ones – and my Victoria sponge.'

'I'd love to, but as I'm only here for such a short time, I doubt I'll get the chance,' he said with real regret.

'But you're staying the night, aren't you?'

'Well, I was hoping to.'

'Of course you were,' she replied. 'It wouldn't make any sense to go all the way back to Port Dalrymple after you've only just arrived. I'll make a fresh batch in the morning.'

'I look forward to tasting them,' he murmured.

She selected a scone and bit into it with relish, and Harold was beginning to relax, thinking she'd started to warm to him, when she suddenly dashed his hopes. 'What exactly are you looking for in her safe, then?' she asked, wiping the crumbs from around her mouth, her eyes sharp with suspicion.

'Certain documents that Baker needs rather urgently,' he replied, on his guard again.

'What sort of documents? That safe was cleared out after her old man died.'

'I'm afraid I can't tell you, Mrs Ryan,' he said, shooting her a regretful smile. 'Baker was most insistent that I keep everything confidential.'

She narrowed her eyes, clearly not happy with his answer. 'Well, there isn't any key here for the safe, so I don't know how you plan to get inside it. And even if you did have a key, there's a secret number you have to dial to open the door.'

Harold wondered how she knew. Had she watched Christy opening the safe and taken note of the number, and then searched for the key to satisfy her own curiosity? It wouldn't have surprised him, for the temptation of an empty house would have been far too great for a nosy woman not to pry. He also suspected Edna Ryan had taken the chance to go through cupboards and drawers with Christy being away, and he wondered if his mother-in-law was aware of the dangers of having such a woman look after her home.

'Baker gave me a key,' he said, plucking it from his pocket to show her, 'and I already know the code, so you needn't concern yourself.'

A gleam of something lit her eyes momentarily and then she looked away and selected another scone. 'Well, that's good. Once we've finished our elevenses, I'll take you into her study and show you where the safe's hidden.'

'That's very kind, Mrs Ryan, but I do know where it is.'

She shrugged with studied nonchalance as she munched on the scone, and Harold became increasingly concerned that this woman seemed to know far too much of Christy's business.

He finished the scone, which suddenly didn't taste quite so nice, the suspicion growing that Edna was not only a nosy parker, but probably a gossip. He was just thankful the woman wasn't living here during Christy's absence, for it would hamper his search enormously.

'I shall be here until lunchtime,' she said as she closed the tin and cleared the table. 'So if you want me to help with anything, you'd better ask me now. I know where everything is, you see.'

I just bet you do, he thought darkly as he forced a smile. 'Thank you, but I'm sure I'll find my way about, Mrs Ryan. I don't want to keep you from your duties.'

She eyed him thoughtfully for a moment, and then turned away to begin on the washing up. 'You'll have to fend for yourself once I've gone,' she said. 'But there's plenty of food in the larder. I like to keep it stocked in case visitors call.'

Harold doubted she'd have visitors, unless it was her cronies. He carried his swag into the comfortable room he and Anne always shared when they visited Christy, and having used the bathroom, made his way into the large drawing room at the front of the house. It was a pleasant, light-filled room, furnished with comfortable chairs, colourful rugs and low tables, Christy's grandmother's loom taking pride of place beside the marble mantelpiece.

He stood at the French windows which opened on to the veranda, and gazed out at the spits of land that protruded into Storm Bay, and the few yachts that were already taking advantage of the brisk breeze. It really was a magnificent view – but he was wasting time.

Striding away from the window, he went through the dining room to the small office. Firmly closing the door behind him, he drew back the curtains, which had been pulled to block out the sunlight, and surveyed the room. He'd only been in here a few times, but it was redolent with the old man's favourite cigars and there was still some whisky in the cut-glass decanter that stood on the desk.

The large leather-topped desk was placed by the window, with a comfortable leather chair tucked into the kneehole. Two of the walls were shelved to hold the many books Christy's husband had collected over the years – mostly to do with the breeding of thoroughbred horses – and the last wall was occupied by rows of files and business documents pertaining to the vineyard, the cattle station and the many properties he and Christy had invested in over the years.

The safe was tucked away beneath the bookshelves, hidden behind one in a line of cupboard doors. Feeling like an intruder,

Harold opened the door, turned the dial on the squat metal safe, and then slotted in the key. Pulling the heavy door open, he eyed the contents with sharp disappointment. Apart from a couple of jewellery boxes, there was very little in there.

Determined to check everything thoroughly, he dragged it all out and spread it on the desk. The jewellery consisted of a magnificent set of necklace, earrings and a bracelet, set with black opals that gleamed with fire and turquoise. There was a three-stone diamond ring, another of purple amethyst, and a gold bracelet set with diamonds and rubies.

He was about to return them to the safe when he remembered how he'd hidden his most precious opals beneath layers of sweet-meats to carry them safely from Lightning Ridge to the buyer's office in Moree. Christy might very well have hidden something in much the same way – although it obviously couldn't be as large as a document or deed – but one never knew.

He gently eased the velvet padding from the leather boxes and smiled, for indeed there was something hidden there – but unfor-tunately it was only a tarnished, misshapen ring and a small key.

Harold plucked them out, set the key aside and regarded the cheap ring thoughtfully. It was a strange thing to hide, and why keep it at all? What significance did it hold? Yet it had to mean something to Christy, but what on earth could that be? He held it up to the light to search for a silver mark, but as he'd suspected, there was none. Looking more closely, he saw there was some-thing crudely scratched on the inside.

Digging about in the desk drawer he found a magnifying glass, and after much deliberation concluded that the barely visible marks showing through the tarnish were capital letters. He squinted and moved the glass about, trying to decipher them; he held the ring closer to the window so he had more light, and then a chill of foreboding ran through him and he sank back into the chair. He now realised what terrible significance that cheap little ring might have.

'But what to do with it?' he muttered. 'What the hell do I do now?'

He sat for a long moment, staring at it as it lay in the palm of his hand, and then came to a decision. Hastily returning it to its hiding place, he put the padding back into all the jewellery boxes and stuffed them into the safe. It would have been better not to have found it at all – but now he had, it was vital to ensure it never saw light of day again.

Feeling slightly nauseous he plumped back into the chair, and after gathering his scattered thoughts began to go through the other things he'd found. There were letters tied in ribbon, which turned out to be ones written to Christy during her courting days, and he quickly set them aside. There were deeds to this house and the others in Tasmania, which Christy rented out, a few childish drawings from her grandchildren, along with their school report cards, and a copy of her will. But there was nothing pertaining to Yarrabinda or Wallangarra, and no birth, death or marriage certificates either.

He dumped them back into the safe, slammed the door and spun the dial, before locking it and closing the cupboard. Returning to the desk, he examined the small key more closely. It looked like the ones Anne had for her fancy trinket boxes, but again the question was why had it been hidden away? There had been no little boxes in the safe, and there was nothing in this office that the key might fit.

Harold wondered if perhaps the answer was in Christy's bedroom, and although he was loath to go prying in there, he knew he'd have to if he didn't find what he was searching for in here. But any further search through the house would have to wait until the Ryan woman was off the premises.

He tucked the tiny key into the top pocket of his waistcoat and turned his attention to the desk drawers. They mostly contained household account books, very old bank statements, receipts for purchases and bills, old cheque book stubs, writing paper and envelopes. In growing exasperation he took the drawers out to see if anything had been hidden beneath them, but found nothing. When he tried opening the bottom drawer, however, he discovered it was locked.

A thrill of excitement coursed through him, for surely a locked drawer must hold something of importance? He searched the other drawers again, but there was no sign of a key.

He was giving it a series of hard tugs when Mrs Ryan came into the room without knocking. 'You won't open that,' she said. 'There's no key, you see.'

Harold eyed the keyhole in the sturdy oak. 'There must be,' he replied, giving the handle a forceful yank.

She shook her head. 'It's one of them secret drawers, what don't need a key. And it's no good you asking me how to get in there; Madam never told me.'

'How very frustrating,' said Harold.

Mrs Ryan nodded, the sarcasm going right over her head. 'And don't even think about trying to break into it,' she warned. 'Madam's very fond of that desk. Her brother made it.'

'I wouldn't dream of such a thing,' he replied coolly.

'Mind you clear up after yourself,' she said, her gaze flitting over the drawers on the floor. 'I have enough to do.' She sniffed and turned away. 'See you in the morning.'

He waited until he'd heard the screen door slam behind her and then got down on his hands and knees and closely examined every inch of the drawer and the desk for some clue as to how to get into it.

An hour later he was still flummoxed, and he plumped back into the chair, thoroughly frustrated. The locked drawer had become a challenge, and even if there was nothing in there, he was determined to find a way of getting into it.

Despite the Ryan woman's warning, he was tempted to go to one of the sheds to find a crowbar or something to prise it open, but the desk was such a fine piece of craftsmanship, he was very reluctant to damage it. Retrieving the small key from his waistcoat, he jammed it into the lock and wriggled it about, but of course that did no good at all and merely bent the key out of shape. Stuffing it back in his pocket, he swore mightily as he kicked the bottom corner of the blasted drawer with the heel of his stockinged foot.

There was a sharp click, and the drawer slid silently open.

Harold delved into it eagerly, his fingers searching every inch, only to find yet another flaming key. It was larger than the other and reminded him of a key he'd seen before, but couldn't remember where. He tried it in the lock on the drawer but it didn't fit, and comparing it to the one that opened the safe, he saw it was cut completely differently.

Frustrated beyond belief, he slumped into the chair and stared long and hard at the key as if it would reveal what the hell it was for. He'd seen one very similar, but where? When? Why? The memory eluded him, and on hearing the clock chime the hour in the hall he stuffed the damned thing in his trouser pocket and went in search of some lunch.

The contents of the larder were quite surprising considering the fact that Christy was away for so long. There was half a loaf of bread, some sliced ham, eggs and a slab of cheese, as well as butter on the marble slab. Edna Ryan had certainly ensured she didn't go hungry, but was she using Christy's generous house-keeping to feather her own nest as well?

'I wouldn't mind betting her larder's even better stocked than this,' he muttered, putting the kettle on to boil again as he made a stack of cheese and ham sandwiches. 'Christy needs to be warned about that awful woman.'

Feeling in need of fresh air, he went out on to the veranda to eat his lunch. The wind was quite chill, even though the sun was shining, so he didn't linger over his meal. Once he'd finished the sandwiches and tea he lit his pipe and walked along the veranda to the back of the house, where it was more sheltered. His horse was grazing happily, the birds were making a racket in the trees, where the sunlight was casting dapples across the white-railed paddocks, and he could hear the distant murmur of the river.

Feeling much calmer now, he returned his china to the kitchen.

He locked the back door, in case Mrs Ryan decided to return, and secured the French windows again, steeling himself to go into Christy's bedroom.

The blinds had been drawn to protect the highly polished furniture from the harmful rays of the sun, and he pulled them up just enough so he could take a good long look about the room. He'd never been in here before, so it was interesting to see this private haven Christy had shared with her late husband for so many years.

It was a large, feminine room, with a wide bed placed so she had a perfect view of the bay through the windows. The curtains, bedcover and dressing-table stool's padding had been sewn from the same floral chintz, and the lovely old oak furniture gleamed in the pale shaft of light. The rugs were deep and soft underfoot, and a range of silver-framed sepia photographs stood on top of a chest of drawers, but there was no sign of a trinket box.

He regarded the single oil painting depicting a Scottish loch and mountains that had been hung on the wall over the bed, and wondered if it was Skye. If so, then it was quite majestic, if not a little barren. Peering at the signature daubed at the bottom, he noted the artist had a Scottish name, but, not knowing much about paintings, it meant nothing to him.

He walked towards the large wardrobe and, after a momentary pause, opened the doors. It was much like his wife's wardrobe, stuffed full of clothes, with neat lines of shoes beneath them and drawers filled with sweaters and nightwear at the bottom.

He prickled with unease, and almost looked over his shoulder before he drew the hanging clothes to one side in search of another safe, a box, or anything which might give him a clue as to what those keys he'd found fitted. He even pressed against the back and sides of the wardrobe to see if there were other secret compartments – but, if there were, they remained hidden.

He gingerly opened drawers and, becoming more uneasy by the minute, delicately dug beneath Christy's most personal attire. He hated this, and just wished he'd never come, for Christy had been good to him over the years and he felt he was betraying her trust.

Having given the dressing-table drawers a cursory rifle through, he slammed them shut and gave an impatient sigh before he spotted the hatboxes on top of the wardrobe. It was worth giving them the once-over, he decided, for you never knew where women thought to hide things.

He reached up and carefully pulled them down, but found nothing, and had to stand on the dressing-table stool to put them all back again. But as he was about to replace the largest box on top of the wardrobe, he saw something tucked into the far corner. He had to stand on tiptoe to reach it, for the wardrobe was not only high, but also very deep.

His pulse began to race as he finally caught hold of it and carefully climbed down. Running his finger over the accumulated dust, he saw it was a fairly large rosewood box, inlaid with ivory and mother-of-pearl, with brass hinges and keyhole. He fumbled the small key from his waistcoat pocket and held his breath as he slotted it in. It fitted perfectly.

With rising excitement, he eased back the lid, only to give a soft cry of sharp disappointment. The box was all but empty, holding only a large nugget of unrefined gold, a hessian draw-string purse containing old silver coins dating back to the 1860s, and a scrap of paper.

It wasn't yellowed or brittle, which meant it must have been hidden here fairly recently, but he took great care when he unfolded it. The numbers 4462 had been carefully written in faded blue ink. He swiftly turned the paper over, but there was no other writing – no clue as to what those numbers meant.

He scrubbed his face hard in an effort to clear his head and think straight, realised his hands were filthy with dust and reached into his pocket for his handkerchief. His fingers brushed over the key he'd found in the secret drawer and, as he held it up next to the paper, it all suddenly made sense.

'That's it,' he breathed. He jumped off the bed and ran back to the office. Grabbing one of the drawers he'd left on the floor, he tipped the contents out on to the desk. Forcing himself to stay calm and work methodically, he began to go through each and every one of those bits of paper again. The clue he needed would be there. He just had to find it.

13

Port of London

Christy stood rather tensely on the promenade deck of the SS *Southern Cross* alongside Anne as they slowly steamed away from the dockside. Kathryn had gone to explore the ship with Lucy, a girl she'd become friendly with during their second short stay in London, and this was the first time Christy and Anne had been alone since that awkward conversation in Scotland about her time in the goldfields.

There had been a thick fog earlier – what the Londoners called a 'pea-souper' – and although it had cleared somewhat, there was still a sepia haze over everything, which simply made the scene before her even more depressing. The many warehouses and quays of the enormous port were the same murky grey as the water, and even the great variety of boats which used the port lacked colour.

She wrinkled her nose at the smell of coal and smoke and something indefinable which seemed to be held within the torpid air, and watched the small tugs dart back and forth, the great barges loaded with wood and coal lumbering past the elegant ocean-going ships, and the busy ferries that chugged from quay to quay, leaving a trail of acrid black smoke in their wake.

Christy's gaze trawled over the many cranes which lined the docks and were hauling cargo in and out of the holds of the merchant ships, and the brawny dockers who were pulling loaded carts of goods from warehouses, and she gave a sigh, for it wasn't an attractive sight.

'It's at times like these that I really miss Hobart,' she said. 'It's so lovely and clean compared to this dirty old place.'

'I hardly think you can make the comparison,' said Anne. 'This is one of the largest ports in the world, whereas Hobart is merely a provincial little harbour that very few people even bother to visit unless they have to.'

Christy was stung by the dismissal of the magnificent harbour at home, but was disinclined to voice her thoughts. Anne had shown her old frostiness with her ever since leaving Scotland, and she was reluctant to say anything which might damage the fragile armistice they'd reached.

'Perhaps I'm just feeling homesick for the clean air and sunshine of Bellerive,' she murmured, looking up at sulphur-coloured clouds through which the sun had yet to break – and probably wouldn't, now the day was almost over. 'It's hard to believe it's summer.'

Anne looked at her in surprise. 'Well, you've certainly changed your tune,' she said. 'It wasn't long ago that you were feeling the same way about Skye.'

'Yes, I know I was,' she replied in a reasonable tone. 'But, having been to Skye and done all the things I'd planned for so long, I realise I am a stranger there after all the years I've been away, and the things I've experienced – and no longer know the way of things or how to fit in.'

She gazed out at the murky scene without really seeing it. 'Skye will always be in my heart, of course, but Australia is where I've put down roots and lived the majority of my life. It's become my home, and I'm missing it.'

Anne rolled her eyes and shook her head. 'Well, it's been an expensive way of discovering where you belong,' she said. 'I hope you feel it was worth it.'

Christy smiled. 'Oh, yes, it was worth every penny,' she replied. 'And I'm sure Kathryn has benefited hugely from the experience.' She glanced along the deck. 'I wonder where she and Lucy have got to. They've been gone for ages.'

'They've probably discovered the shops on board,' Anne replied dryly.

Christy smiled. 'One would have thought they'd shopped enough, going by the bags and packages they turned up with last night. I'm sure Kathryn bought up half of London yesterday.'

She regarded Anne's unsmiling face. 'And what about you, dear? Have you enjoyed this trip?'

'In parts,' she said grudgingly. 'I'm still disappointed we didn't see any of the royal family as I'd expected when we went to look at the palace – and I can't get over how old everything is in London, and how grand the theatres and shops are. The city has such a sense of antiquity and stability that can't be found any-where in Australia.' She gave a wry smile. 'Even our oldest buildings can only be traced back to the early eighteen hundreds, and most of them are falling to bits.'

'That's because they were built of wood and corrugated iron,' said Christy. 'But Melbourne and Sydney have some fine old stone buildings still.' She hesitated momentarily. 'And what did you think of Scotland?'

Anne pursed her lips. 'Scotland was different from anywhere I'd ever been. But empty glens and looming mountains don't really excite me. If it hadn't been for you and Gregor telling us the history of the place, I would have found it utterly tedious.'

'Oh dear,' sighed Christy.

'Well, I'm sorry,' said Anne shortly, 'but you did ask.'

Christy eyed her daughter thoughtfully. 'You seem rather down in the dumps today. Aren't you looking forward to going home?'

She didn't reply for a while, and then turned her gaze from the view of the now-distant port and looked at her mother. 'I have to confess, I'm feeling rather nervous about seeing Harold again.'

'But why, dear? Surely he'll be delighted to welcome you home?'

'I don't know how he'll be,' she admitted. 'I did as you suggested and wrote him a long letter telling him how much I wanted to start again and see if we could make our marriage work the way it once had, but of course the mail takes weeks, so I haven't heard back.'

'I'm sure that, once he receives it, he'll send a telegraph to the ship confirming that he feels the same way,' she said comfortingly.

Anne fell silent for a while, gripping the railings as the ship began to head into choppier waters. 'I should never have come,' she said finally. 'Harold has been left to his own devices for too long, and with women like Florence Hardwick forever lurking . . .'

Christy frowned. 'Who's Florence Hardwick?'

'A predatory tart who's had her beady eye on my husband this past year,' she replied sharply. 'And Harold might swear there's been nothing between them, but I've seen the way he looks at her.'

'Oh, Anne. I'm sure Harold is merely flattered and wouldn't dream of going astray like that.'

'Florence has earned the reputation of a coquette who always gets the man she's chasing, and Harold is far from being a saint,' she replied. 'We've become distant over the past few years – mainly because of what happened between us – and this long separation could do inestimable damage.'

'I don't understand how our falling out could possibly have anything to do with the state of your marriage,' Christy protested.

'Of course it did,' said Anne flatly. 'I couldn't talk to him about it, and began to distance myself from him through the shame of it all. I felt betrayed – not only by you, but by him.'

'I accept my guilt for that, but he's denied being unfaithful.'

'Constant denial is the oldest defence, Mother. And, like all men, Harold is very good at it.'

'I'm so sorry, Anne,' said Christy softly. 'I never realised that our rift would go deep enough to affect your marriage.'

'Toss a pebble into a pool and the ripples spread wide,' said Anne darkly. 'Throw in a boulder and you'll get a tidal wave.' She blinked rapidly and kept her gaze firmly on the receding shore-line. 'Add into the mix someone like Florence Hardwick and the damage is cataclysmic.'

Christy had never heard her daughter be so eloquent, but it was clear she was deeply hurt by what she thought of as betrayal, and Christy could only hope that Harold proved to be as honest and loyal as she'd always thought. As to the part she had played in this tragedy, it was yet another added burden to her heavy heart.

Anne lifted her chin and finally faced her. 'Actually, Mother, it's not just the uncertainty of what I might find when I get home that has made me edgy these past few days – it's also the fact that I'm finding it very difficult to be at ease with you.'

Christy knew where this was going, for she too had found it hard to ignore the omnipresent subject that could never be broached. 'We are both finding it hard,' she said softly, 'but given time, I'm sure we can overcome it.'

'I'm not so convinced of that,' Anne replied. 'The things you told me back home will always be between us, and although I'm willing to forgive you for what you did, I'm finding it impossible to forget.'

Christy felt a twist of pain at the thought of how she'd made her daughter suffer. 'I do understand,' she replied. 'It's how I feel about those who were responsible for the clearances. But I can't change what happened, Anne. And although it's hard, neither of us must allow my actions of the past to sour things between us – not now that we've found each other again.'

'But that's just it, don't you see?' she hissed urgently. 'Every time you mention the goldfields and those early years, I'm on tenterhooks wondering what you'll come out with.' She carried on quickly before her mother could defend herself. 'Now you're planning to tell Kathryn about those times, and I can't see how you can possibly avoid telling her things I really don't want her to know.'

Christy took her hands. 'I've already promised to say nothing that you'll find distressing or hurtful. Please have faith in me, Anne.'

'It would only take a slip of the tongue,' she muttered, pulling her hands from her mother's grasp, 'and you're inclined to get carried away with your stories.'

Christy saw how her lips had thinned and her gaze had become challenging, and knew then that her daughter would not be mollified. 'If I told Kathryn the whole story, it wouldn't exactly show me in a very flattering light either,' she said. 'This isn't all about you, Anne. There are others who could be hurt deeply if it all came out.'

Anne was silent, and Christy asked the question that had been troubling her for some time. 'Have you confided in anyone?'

'Of course not,' she snapped. She lifted her chin defiantly. 'I haven't told a soul, so if it ever gets out, I'll know exactly who to blame.'

Christy refused to be cowed. 'The only way it will get out is if someone follows your example and goes poking about in my personal papers,' she said briskly.

A flush of colour rose in Anne's cheeks and she looked away. 'As I told you before, I was merely looking for your opals to wear to the summer ball,' she muttered.

'You had no right to go in that safe without my permission,' said Christy. 'And as for rifling through my private papers . . . Your prying has led us to this, Anne, so don't try and justify what you did.'

Anne's eyes widened. 'How *dare* you try and put the blame on me,' she rasped. 'It was you who kept secrets for years and even had the arrogance to keep the evidence in that damned safe. Why didn't you burn those papers? You must have known what trouble they'd cause if they were found.'

'I assumed they were secure in my safe and would remain hidden there until my death.'

Anne's lips thinned further. 'So, when you die, the truth will be revealed, and I'll have to go through the humiliation of having to admit I knew your dirty little secret all along. That's not what I'd call the action of a loving mother.'

Christy managed to keep hold of her impatience. 'I have made arrangements in my will to have those papers destroyed,' she replied.

'You should have destroyed them years ago.'

Christy shook her head. 'I have my reasons for not doing so – and should you take it into your head to destroy them, you won't find them in that safe. They've been moved to a very secure place, and I'm the only one who knows how to get them.'

'Then how will they be destroyed on your death?'

'There's a letter with someone, which is guaranteed not to be opened until that time.'

'But why do you need them at all?' protested Anne. 'What possible purpose could they have other than to bring me humiliation?'

Christy couldn't explain to her that those documents were her security against any trouble which might befall the family – not that she expected there to be, but then caution had always been her watchword.

'I have my reasons for keeping them, which really don't concern you, Anne.'

Anne frowned. 'It's not logical to keep something so inflammatory.'

'Maybe not,' she said smoothly. 'But perhaps you should just accept my rather eccentric wishes and put them down to an old woman's fickleness.'

Anne eyed her with suspicion. 'Eccentric, maybe,' she muttered, 'but you've never been fickle when it comes to family business. What's the real reason you've kept them?'

Christy thought about the papers Anne hadn't found in the safe that day and how, put together, those documents would secure the family's fortune should the very worst happen and it was contested. But she said nothing of this to Anne, for she wanted the conversation to come to an end.

'I learned very early on that bits of paper are important – even if they don't seem to be at the time. So I keep everything, just in case I might need it.' She smiled and gently touched Anne's arm. 'I'd be grateful if you'd humour me on this, Anne.'

'As long as you can promise me they'll never see light of day again.'

'You have my promise.'

'Then I suppose I must. But I still think you should burn everything and have done with it.'

'I'll think about it,' Christy said, with absolutely no intention of doing so.

'And I'll try not to,' said Anne stiffly. 'But you have to understand that it's far from easy for me to feel as close to you as I once did. It will take time and a great deal more openness on your part before I'll feel able to really trust you again.'

Christy could have wept, for she'd thought they'd gone beyond that stage following their reconciliation back in Scotland. 'I'm heartily sorry to hear that,' she murmured, 'but let's not continue this now. I see the girls are coming back.'

*

Bellerive, Tasmania

Harold was dreaming he was in the depths of an opal mine in Lightning Ridge. The vertical walls descended from the square opening he'd made at the top, and he somehow knew it had taken him many months to get down this far. He was chipping away at the base when he thought he could hear shouts and banging coming from above ground. Thinking it was probably yet another fight breaking out among the other miners, he carried on carefully digging away at the silica with the pick.

As the banging became more insistent and the shouts grew louder, he began to wonder if he should go up the ladder to see what all the noise was about. But, at that moment, his small pick knocked a gold nugget to the ground, and this was followed by a small hessian drawstring bag.

Ignoring the rumpus overhead, he squatted down, examined

the nugget in the light of his kerosene lantern and put it quickly in his pocket before reaching for the hessian bag. Spilling the coins into the palm of his hand, he began to count them, not thinking it was at all strange to find such things in the depths of an opal mine.

'Mr Ross! Mr Ross, if you don't open the door immediately I shall have to call the police.'

Harold recognised the voice, but couldn't think why Edna Ryan should be anywhere near the opal fields. As for calling the police . . . He'd done nothing wrong . . . but how to explain the silver coins?

'Mr Ross, I can see you,' shouted Edna furiously. 'Wake up! Wake up!'

The deep opal mine faded away and Harold reluctantly opened his heavy-lidded eyes to find he was sprawled over the desk, his head all but buried beneath the mound of paper that was scattered across it. He blinked and slowly drew himself back into the chair to be met by the unedifying sight of Edna Ryan's furious glare on the other side of the window.

'I've been calling you for half an hour,' she yelled. 'Open the door immediately.'

Harold quickly came to his senses – Mrs Ryan was better than any alarm – and hurried into the kitchen to unlock the back door.

He'd only just turned the key when the door was thrust open and Edna barged in – a fury in floral apron and headscarf. 'How dare you lock me out,' she snapped. 'What have you been up to?'

'Nothing,' he retorted. 'I always lock doors at night.'

'We only lock doors here if the house is empty or we don't want folk to see what we're up to,' she retorted. 'And we certainly don't leave keys in so people can't use their own,' she added, pushing past him on her way to the office.

Harold quickly followed, not wanting her to see the paperwork on the desk. But as he entered the room, she was already walking towards it. He dodged round her and stood with his back to the desk. 'I realise what this must look like,' he said hastily, 'but I can assure you it is entirely necessary.'

Her gaze darted over the desk, down to the discarded drawers on the floor, and finally to the secret drawer, which now lay open. A gleam of excitement lit in her pale blue eyes. 'How did you get that open?' she breathed.

'More by luck than anything,' he replied, 'and, before you ask, there was nothing in it, which was most disappointing.'

She eyed him suspiciously and then ran her fingers inside the drawer as if to check that he hadn't missed something. 'How do I know you aren't lying to me?' she demanded, arms folded. 'Madam wouldn't have left a secret drawer empty.'

Harold shrugged. 'Well, I'm afraid she did, which is most frustrating.' He saw her gaze trawling over the mess on the desk and floor. 'I'm sorry about all this,' he said, 'but there was nothing helpful in the safe, either, so I've had to resort to going through everything in the desk.'

'What are you looking for exactly?' Her eyes narrowed.

Harold wondered for an instant if he should tell her, and then dismissed the idea. The woman was unreliable, and no doubt his night's escapade would be recounted to her cronies before the day was out. 'As I said before, Mrs Ryan, I'm looking for a specific document that Mr Baker asked me to deliver.'

Her jaw worked as she held her temper and her curiosity. 'You'd better get on with it then,' she said shortly. 'And make sure you clear all this up when you've finished. Madam doesn't pay me to run about after other people.'

She stalked out into the dining room and, as he heard her footsteps going into the drawing room, Harold quickly darted into the hall. He'd suddenly remembered he'd left the rosewood box open on Christy's bed.

Her footsteps were coming down the hall as he swiftly buried the box beneath the mound of pillows and bent to pick up one of the hatboxes.

'What on earth?' Edna stormed into the room, glowering. 'How *dare* you come in here – and what are *they* doing all over the floor?'

'I was hoping there was another secret compartment in the wardrobe,' he said blithely. He climbed on to the stool, which still stood within the open doors of the large piece of furniture. 'If you'd care to hand them up to me, I'll tidy them away.'

Her stormy expression mirrored her dire thoughts, and Harold held his breath as she tweaked one of the pillows into place and smoothed the counterpane. But it seemed she was satisfied, for she then started to hand up the boxes.

'So, did you find any secret compartments?' she said, once the hat boxes had been restored, the stool returned to the dressing table and the wardrobe doors closed.

'Unfortunately, no,' he replied, taking her arm and gently steering her towards the kitchen before she noticed the corner of the rosewood box poking out from behind the pillow. 'Let me make you a cup of coffee and see to breakfast,' he cajoled. 'It's the least I can do after causing you so much trouble this morning.'

She gave a sniff as she sat at the table. 'Well, I could do with a cup of tea, certainly. And, if you've a mind to it, there's some bacon and eggs in the larder.'

As Harold laid the table and made himself busy at the range, Mrs Ryan sat in silence, clearly still stewing over the fact that he'd told her nothing. 'It must be a very important document for you to turn the house upside down looking for it,' she said eventually.

'It is,' he said, turning the sizzling bacon in the pan. 'So important, in fact, that it appears my mother-in-law has taken very great care to hide it.' He placed the pot of tea on the table and poured himself a cup of coffee from the percolator.

'Well, as far as I know, there aren't any other hiding places in the house,' she muttered, 'so she must have lodged it with her bank.'

Baker had already confirmed to him that Christy had nothing lodged at her bank, and so far he'd found nothing to prove otherwise. 'Maybe,' he murmured, setting a heaped plate of bacon, egg and fried bread in front of her.

'It's a bit of a mystery, isn't it?' she said, picking up her knife and fork and greedily eyeing the feast, before tucking in.

Harold brought his own plate to the table and sat down. They ate in silence, and he could see that her mind was working on the problem – which was a good thing, because it meant she was becoming less hostile.

'So what is it you're looking for through all those old bills and receipts?' she asked.

'I have a feeling there might be some clue in them as to where she hid that document,' he said carefully. 'But it could take time to trawl through it all, so I'm afraid you'll have to put up with me for a while longer.'

She mopped the last of her breakfast up with a doorstep of bread and poured another cup of tea. 'I could always help you, if you know what it is you're looking for,' she said all too casually.

He felt a stab of alarm. 'That's very kind of you,' he said carefully, 'but as I don't really know what I'm looking for, I think you could best help by keeping up a regular supply of coffee and some of your delicious scones to the office.'

Her disappointment was clear, but she shrugged anyway. 'Well, all right, if that's the way you want it.'

'Thank you, Mrs Ryan – you're a star.'

She tried to look disgruntled, but failed. 'Yes, well, I'd better get on. I can't sit here chatting to you if you want scones.'

Harold left her to the washing up and hurried back to the office to lock the door against her snooping, and then he left the house to see to his horse. When he'd reassured himself that no harm had come to him through the night and that he had plenty of food and water to see him through the day, he went back to the office and began to trawl through the years of old bank statements.

Mrs Ryan appeared at eleven with warm scones and a fresh pot of coffee, and he thanked her profusely before continuing to work through the rest of the morning. He was about to start on the statements for 1897 when he heard someone knocking on the front door. He didn't think much of it and was continuing to sift through the statements when Mrs Ryan came stomping into the room.

'You got a visitor,' she said.

Harold was immediately on his guard. 'Did they give a name?'

'Hello, Harold. I thought you must be here.'

Harold couldn't disguise his shock at seeing Florence Hardwick, and was momentarily rendered speechless.

'I told you to stay outside,' Edna said crossly.

Florence waved away her objection and fluttered her eyelashes at Harold. 'Harold and I are old friends,' she simpered, 'and he wouldn't want me left on the doorstep, would you?'

'Of course not,' he blustered, 'but it isn't really a convenient moment, Florence. I'm very busy.'

She pouted prettily and eyed the detritus of his night's search. 'Goodness me, so you are.' The dimples flickered in her cheeks. 'All work and no play makes Harold a very dull boy,' she teased. 'Why don't we have some coffee and chat about where we'll have dinner tonight?'

Harold could see Edna was simmering behind Florence, and the last thing he needed was for word to get out that he'd been entertaining a woman in Christy's house without the presence of his wife. 'Florence,' he said carefully, 'I really am far too busy for social calls; as for dinner . . . I might not even be in Hobart tonight.'

Florence advanced on him and brushed a speck of dust from

his jacket collar. 'Oh, I'm sure you can find time for little old me, Harold,' she purred. 'Why don't we make ourselves comfortable in the drawing room and send the maid to rustle up something?'

Edna bristled and shot daggers at Florence's back, and Harold knew trouble was brewing, for he suspected Edna spoke as she found. 'Mrs Ryan is not the maid,' he said firmly, 'and I'm sure she'd like to join us for some coffee and cake.'

'That's very irregular,' said Florence with a frown.

Harold looked at the glowering Edna. 'Would you care to join us in the drawing room, Mrs Ryan? I'm sure we could both do with a short break before Mrs Hardwick has to leave.' With that, he took Florence's arm and steered her rather firmly past Edna towards the drawing room.

'Goodness me,' Florence breathed, 'aren't you the forceful one? Do you treat all your visitors with such vigour?' She giggled and sat down on the couch, smoothed her navy linen skirt and eased off her kid gloves. 'I do so admire a man who can take charge,' she said, her eyes flashing a challenge as she patted the couch. 'Come, sit beside me and let me tell you all the plans I have for us this evening.'

Harold remained standing by the hearth, well away from the couch, and pointedly drew out his pocket watch and checked the time. 'I'm sorry, Florence,' he said without a hint of regret, 'but any plans you may have will not concern me. I'm here on important business and I simply don't have the time for—'

'Coffee,' said Edna, entering the room with a laden tray, which she placed with rather too much force on the low table. She plumped herself on to the couch next to Florence, shot her a withering look and handed her a cup and saucer. 'Milk?'

Florence's blue eyes lost their twinkle and were suddenly arctic. 'No, thank you.'

'Perhaps you'd prefer a saucer of cream?'

'It's fine the way it is,' Florence said stiffly.

'Good, because we haven't got any.'

Edna turned to Harold and, as she handed him his cup of coffee, he noted there was a gleam of something in her eyes that didn't bode well. He sipped the coffee, desperately trying to think of how he could get rid of Florence before the two women really fell out. 'How are you enjoying your stay in Hobart?' he asked.

Florence put her untouched cup of coffee on the table with a grimace. 'It's a duty visit,' she said flatly. 'Hardly exciting.'

She ignored Edna, who had made herself comfortable in the cushions beside her and was deliberately slurping her coffee with relish. 'I have a table booked at the Ocean Child fish restaurant for this evening. I know Mother would love to see you, and I'd be delighted to have some lively company after being incarcerated with my grandmother all day.'

'Thank you for the invitation,' he said, 'but I shall be otherwise engaged this evening.' He drained his cup and returned it to the tray. 'Was there anything else you wanted, Florence? Only, I have work to do.'

Her lips thinned and her eyes sparked with anger. 'As you've made it patently clear that I'm not wanted, I'll take my leave,' she said with all the dignity she could muster. 'Perhaps, when you return to Melbourne, you will remember your manners.'

Harold took her hand and helped her to her feet. 'And perhaps it would be better if you didn't call unannounced,' he countered. 'I'm happily married, Florence, and although you are delightful company, it would be better if you didn't visit me unchaperoned.'

Florence eyed him coolly as she pulled on her gloves. 'You're a fool to cross me, Harold Ross,' she said, almost matter-of-factly. 'There are some, back in Melbourne, who would be most interested to know that you've come to Hobart, and will be otherwise engaged this evening.'

'I don't take notice of silly gossip,' he replied. 'And if this is your way of spiting me, then I'm glad I had more sense than to fall for your dubious charms.' He strode to the French windows and opened them. 'Goodbye, Mrs Hardwick.'

'I'll make you the laughing stock of Melbourne,' she hissed. 'And by the time I've finished, your bitch of a wife will really have something to be sour about.'

He caught her arm as she was about to walk away. 'Do that, and you'll be sorry,' he snapped. 'And if you call my wife ugly names again, I'll take my horsewhip to your backside.'

'Did you hear that?' she barked at Edna. 'He's threatening me with violence.'

'I didn't hear a thing,' said Edna, 'but it's time you slung your hook, miss, and took that dirty mouth elsewhere.'

'Are you going to let her talk to me like that?'

'Just leave, Florence,' said Harold, 'while you've still got some pride.'

Florence glared at them both, spun on her heel and flounced

off across the veranda and down the steps to the carriage waiting in the driveway.

'Good riddance to bad rubbish,' muttered Edna as the carriage bowled away. 'Common as muck, that one, despite the powder and paint and those fancy clothes.'

'I think you're being a little harsh, Mrs Ryan,' he said carefully. 'But thank you for supporting me. It would have been most inappropriate to entertain her alone.'

She raised an eyebrow and regarded him with open curiosity. 'Have you and her . . .?'

'Good heavens, no,' he said sharply. 'Florence Hardwick is merely an acquaintance.'

Edna sniffed. 'It's a funny way for acquaintances to behave, calling unannounced and pawing all over you.'

'Florence Hardwick is a widow who has caused several unpleasant scandals and means only trouble to me, Mrs Ryan,' he said earnestly. 'I am happily married to Anne, and have made it quite clear to the woman on several occasions that I have absolutely no intention of getting involved with her.'

Mrs Ryan smiled for the first time since they'd met. 'Well, you certainly made that clear today,' she said. 'She's nothing but a trollop, and you're well out of it, if you ask me.' She began to put the china back on to the tray. 'But I'd watch out, if I were you. She's got a vicious tongue, and a woman scorned can be very dangerous.'

'I'll keep that in mind, Mrs Ryan,' he said, taking the tray from her and shooting her a smile. 'The saucer of cream was a stroke of genius,' he murmured.

'Yeah, well, that particular cat is well fed enough.'

Harold was still smiling as he unloaded the tray. Florence had certainly met her match this time.

Edna looked at the kitchen clock and became businesslike. 'I have to go, but I've made you a plate of sandwiches and there's the rest of the scones, and there're a couple of pork chops in the larder for your tea.'

She looked up at him with a glint of humour in her eyes. 'I'm assuming you haven't really got an engagement tonight and that you'll still be here in the morning?'

'There's no engagement, Mrs Ryan, and unless I find what I'm looking for this afternoon, it's highly likely you'll be stuck with me for another day at least.'

'Right. Well, try to sleep in a bed tonight and, if you have to leave before I get here, write me a note so I know what's what.'

Harold took her work-roughened hand and kissed the air above it. 'Thank you, Mrs Ryan. I don't know what I'd have done without you.'

Her plump cheeks reddened. 'Go on with you,' she softly protested. 'I haven't had such a good time in ages.'

'I'm glad my discomfort amused you,' he teased.

She laughed. 'There's nothing like seeing a man squirm to brighten my day, Mr Ross.' She shook his hand and then gathered up her things. 'Good luck with the search,' she said, pushing through the screen door.

He watched her waddle down the driveway and grinned. The old dragon might breathe fire, but she had a good heart and he was glad they would part as friends.

He returned to the office, eyed the stack of paper still waiting for him and decided he needed some fresh air and exercise to restore his mood before he tackled it. Leaving the house, he lit his pipe and, instead of saddling his horse and going for a ride, he strode off up the hill towards the bushland at the back of the property, where he knew he'd find sanctuary.

He'd returned to the house over an hour later to make more coffee and, as the clock ticked away the time in the hall, resumed his trawl through the bank statements.

It was almost midnight when he began to feel a growing sense of excitement. He set aside the cooling plate of chops and mashed potato, and hurriedly checked back through the statements he'd been reading. There was a particular debit from her account which appeared regularly every six months after the August of 1897, and as he quickly rifled through the later statements, it became clear that it was still ongoing.

Snatching up the chequebook stubs, he impatiently searched for the corresponding entries. And there they were – made out to Smithson and Son. He could only guess at what sort of company they were, and he was proved right when he went through the great jumble of receipts to find their letter heading.

He sat for a long while in the flickering light of the oil lamps, thinking about what he should do next. If Christy had been so determined to keep something hidden from everyone, then it had to be very important. But someone else must know of her hiding place, otherwise, what would happen to that secret after her death?

He opened the safe and drew out the copy of her will. Spreading it open on the desk, he read swiftly through it, and at the end found the codicil:

I charge that upon my death, and not before, Mr Charles Smithson of Smithson and Son, or his heirs, must adhere to the instructions in the letter that I have lodged with their bank. In recognition of this, I leave one hundred pounds in full and final payment of my account to that company.

Harold read the date beneath the signature, and realised that it coincided with the date of her first payment – which was also around the time he'd overheard that strange conversation between Christy and Anne. It was all beginning to make terrible and rather daunting sense.

He folded the will back into the envelope and returned it to the safe. It was now very late and, although he was elated that he'd finally unravelled at least a part of the mystery, he was extremely troubled by what he might find at the end of it. The lengths to which Christy had gone to keep everything hidden didn't bode well at all – and if things turned out as he most dreaded, then he and Christy's sons had a huge moral dilemma ahead.

He cleared away his barely touched supper and all the papers he no longer needed, put the drawers back into the desk and closed the secret compartment. Placing the account books, receipt stubs and chequebooks in a large envelope, he added the key he'd found in the desk, and the slip of paper from the rosewood box.

He turned down the wicks on the lamps and headed into Christy's bedroom to return the little box to the top of the wardrobe, and once he'd placed the envelope of evidence in his swag, he dropped in the safe key and carried the canvas bag back to the office.

Draping a blanket over his shoulders, he settled into the deep leather armchair to catnap through what remained of his last night in Hobart. The ferry would be leaving in less than six hours, and it was imperative he didn't miss it.

14

Aboard the SS Southern Cross

The ship had docked at Lisbon, and Christy had decided to stay on board while Anne accompanied Kathryn and the others for an excursion on shore. As she'd explained to a concerned Kathryn, she didn't really want to visit the capital of Portugal again and was looking forward to sitting on deck with a book to enjoy the warm sunshine after the chill of London.

In reality, she was glad to have some time alone, for she was exhausted from the endless rollercoaster of emotions she'd been on since this journey began, and needed these quiet moments to rest and recover. In the warmth of the sunshine and the peace of an almost deserted ship, the book lay unread in her lap as she sipped from a glass of champagne and began to relax.

Settling back in the well-padded steamer-chair that a steward had thoughtfully placed for her beneath a parasol, she closed her eyes and gave a wry smile. The luxury and comfort of this journey was so very different from the one she'd made as a young girl, and she could hardly believe how far she had come since those days.

Life was full of surprises, she thought, for that ragged, bewildered girl who'd stepped off the *Mary Elena* at Port Dalrymple had never even begun to imagine how drastically her fortunes would change over the ensuing years.

The sights and sounds of that day crowded in, and Christy was once more on the brink of her sixteenth birthday, walking down the gangway with her brothers, the heartache of losing their father still raw within them all.

'Stick close to me,' muttered Finlay as they reached the quayside and discovered their balance had been affected by the ninety-two days they'd been at sea.

Christy clung to her older brother's arm as the quay seemed to buck and sway beneath her feet, and Jamie staggered and almost dropped his precious box of tools.

Shivering with the early-morning cold, she wrapped her mother's shawl about her shoulders. 'What will happen to us now, Finlay?' she asked in Gaelic.

'I know as much as you,' he replied in the same language, 'but it looks as if that man over there's in charge. Perhaps he'll tell us.'

Christy maintained her clutch on his arm as they slowly approached the man who was now surrounded by the other migrants. They were a ragged, dirty group, blackened by the coal dust and weak from their ordeal, and Christy realised that the people watching them from the far end of the quay must have thought they were the dregs of the earth.

As she stood waiting for the surviving migrants to join them, she regarded the well-fed, warmly clothed people and wondered if it was merely curiosity that had brought them here, or if they had come for a particular purpose – either way, she didn't like being watched.

Her attention was drawn back to the sturdy man, who was now standing on an upturned wooden crate so he could be seen and heard by everyone, and calling for order.

Silence fell immediately. 'Welcome to Tasmania,' he boomed. 'I know most of you understand English, so that is the language I will speak to you from now on.'

He waited for the muttering to die down and then continued, 'If you wish to do well here, then English is the language you must speak. That's not to say you can't use the Gaelic, for you'll soon discover that there are many other Scots living here, but most employers are not familiar with it, so be warned that, if he cannot understand you, he probably won't hire you.'

There was further mumbling, and Christy felt Finlay shuffling his feet at her side, his expression grim. 'So, we're to be English now,' he mumbled. 'Nothing's changed, then.'

Christy's low spirits tumbled further. It seemed they'd crossed the world to yet another land ruled by the enemies their ancestors had fought during the Jacobite war.

'The St Andrew's Emigration Society has selected you for free passage as you fulfil the requirements of this colony for a superior class of labour, which means you can all read and write, and are healthy in mind, body and spirit.'

There was another general muttering and a few sniggers, which he chose to ignore, for surely he knew that almost seventy souls had been lost, and couldn't help but see how weak and defeated the survivors were. 'Unfortunately,' he continued, 'the charity cannot provide you with free land as others have done in Canada.'

He held up his hand for silence until the rumble of protest died down. 'But there is plenty of work to be had on the island, and the charity has arranged for local business people to come today to offer you employment.'

Christy looked across at the gathering by the large shed, noted the numbers had swollen greatly in the past few minutes, and finally felt a spark of hope.

'There are procedures to go through first,' said the man, 'and once they are completed you will be approached and interviewed by the good people over there. The St Andrew's charity has also provided clothes donated by the generous citizens of George Town and Patersonia, and there are washing facilities at the back of that warehouse.'

'What if no one takes us on?' shouted Finlay.

'Then you'll be given a bed in the local mission hostel for a week. After that, it will be up to you to find work,' the man replied. 'Now, if you'll follow me, we'll get the processing started.'

As he stepped off the crate and marched towards the sheds, they followed him like obedient, bedraggled sheep, finding comfort in their numbers and the familiar faces surrounding them. On drawing nearer to the men and women congregated by the sheds, Christy was not the only one to regard them with some trepidation, for the new arrivals were being eyed by these people in the same manner as the stock for sale at market might be scrutinised by farmers.

'Hurry up, Christy,' hissed Finlay. 'We need to get to the front of the queue so we have a better chance of getting a good job.'

Christy kept hold of his arm as the three of them pushed and elbowed their way forward. It became a bit of a scrum, as everyone had the same idea, but they eventually found themselves close enough to the front to be able to hear the questions being asked and the instructions of what they had to do after their initial process.

Christy waited impatiently as the mass of people slowly shuffled forward. She watched as those ahead of her left the long line of tables and went through a door at the back for the promised wash and fresh clothes, and she wondered what sort of thing she'd end up with. She'd never had anything that hadn't been handed down or made by her mother, and she could hardly wait to get out of the stinking rags she'd been wearing since leaving Gilleasbuig Cove. She looked down at her feet. She was wearing her mother's boots, and although they were tight and the leather was very worn, she was determined to keep them regardless of what the good citizens of this place might provide.

They reached the table and stood in line before the man, who had a large book and a stack of papers in front of him.

As Finlay was the eldest, Christy and Jamie let him do the talking. Their names were ticked off on the long register, their skills noted beside them. Then it was time to sign their names on a formal-looking document.

Finlay read carefully through it, gave a deep sigh and then reluctantly signed it. Turning to his brother and sister, he explained, 'This is to make us free citizens of Australia. We have no choice but to sign it, so be quick about it so we can get out of here.'

The man behind the desk added his own signature to each document and then dripped a blob of wax on it, which he stamped with a seal. Handing the documents back to them, he gave a broad smile. 'You are now legal citizens of Australia,' he drawled. 'G'day to you, and good luck.'

Finlay took charge of the documents and the bundle of Christy's loom before they hurried away and went through the far door to find two men waiting for them in white coats, who turned out to be medics. They were poked and prodded, their eyes, ears and mouths checked over, and their heads examined for lice. They were each given a cake of lye soap and then sent to different parts of the long, narrow building.

Christy felt utterly ashamed that she'd been brought so low and couldn't wait to be clean again and free of the lice that itched in her hair, and the fleas that bit her relentlessly. As she entered the women's section, she was greeted by clouds of steam coming from the enclosed cubicles and the sight of great stacks of clothing and shoes.

One of the women in charge eyed her up and down, and then plucked out a plain dress of pale blue wool, some much-laundered underwear, thick stockings and a tweed jacket that had seen better days, but was far superior to anything Christy had owned before. She held them up against Christy to see if they would fit and then handed them over. Eyeing Christy's boots with dis-favour, she plucked out a pair that was only slightly less disreputable.

'If none of it fits, come back after you've washed,' she said, dumping a thin towel on top of the pile in Christy's arms. 'Leave your own things in the chest you'll find in the cubicle. They'll have to be burned.'

'I'm keeping the shawl and boots,' she said firmly. 'They were my mother's.'

'Then you'd better wash that shawl thoroughly,' she replied. 'We don't want your vermin spreading.'

Duly chastened and utterly belittled, Christy went into the cubicle. The floor was a slab of concrete with a drain hole at the centre, a large metal basin had been fixed to one wall, a small scrubbing brush, still damp from previous users, was next to the tap and there were hooks on the back of the door for her new clothes.

Stripping off, she dumped the rags into the battered old tea chest and carefully hung her mother's boots by the laces on a peg with the shawl. She turned on the tap, sighed with pleasure to find the water was almost too hot to bear, and began to vigorously scrub away the dirt and vermin of many months.

The combination of hot water, lye soap and the unforgiving bristles of the scrubbing brush brought a glow to her skin and made her tingle from head to toe. She quickly dried herself with the scrap of clean towel and wrapped her hair in it whilst she washed her mother's shawl and wrung it out.

Carefully hanging it over the basin to drip, she pulled on her fresh clothes. The dress was too big, but it was warm; the underwear felt strange after not wearing any for so long – her own had disintegrated before they'd even boarded the ship – and the jacket fitted so well it could have been made for her.

She tried on the boots and was surprised at how comfortable they were, so she kept them on and hung her mother's around her neck by the laces. She was just rubbing her hair dry when a sharp rap on the door was followed by a brisk warning that her time was up.

She quickly folded up the wet shawl, gathered the soap and towel and unlatched the door.

'Well, you certainly look better,' said the woman, giving her a smile for the first time. 'And I see the clothes fit quite well too.' She took the soap and towel and then pointed to the far door. 'Go out that way, dear, and you'll find people waiting to see you. Good luck.'

Christy went through the door to find her brothers impatiently waiting for her, and as Finlay grabbed her arm and hurried her across the quay to the waiting group, she had to run to keep up with him.

'What have they done to your hair?' she managed.

Both Finlay and Jamie ruefully ran their hands over their shaven heads. 'Lice,' said Jamie shortly. 'You're lucky you didn't get the same treatment.'

Christy was deeply thankful it hadn't happened to her, and didn't pause to wonder why the girls hadn't been treated the same as their menfolk. 'But you look very smart,' she said, taking in the moleskin trousers, sturdy boots, thick shirts and oversized jackets, which had been woven from a mixture of wool and flax. Each was now sporting a broad-brimmed hat of some dark, hard-wearing material which bore the stains of sweat and wear from their previous owners.

'Aye, but I never thought I'd be wearing another man's clothes,' muttered Jamie.

'Better that than the rags we had before,' countered Finlay. 'Now, look lively and smile. We need to show these people we aren't afraid of hard work – but that we still have pride enough to be paid properly for it.'

Christy opened her eyes and returned to the present to find her glass had been topped up and the parasol shifted to counteract the westward path of the sun. She sipped the champagne and then left the steamer-chair to take a circuit round the deck before returning to stand at the railings.

Looking down at the bustling quay and out over the many warehouses and storage sheds to the distant city that shimmered in the heat haze, she was reminded of Port Dalrymple and all the ports she'd visited since.

She recalled something one of the French whores she'd befriended on the goldfields had said to her many years ago: '*Plus ça change, plus c'est la même chose*' – which means everything changes, but remains the same.

Christy thought of Nadine, and how that phrase encapsulated everything about the sad life her friend had lived, for Nadine hadn't wanted to be a whore, but circumstances had forced her down that path, and it had ultimately led to her death.

Not wanting to dwell on such sad memories, Christy returned to the steamer-chair, finished her glass of champagne and let her mind wander back to those first bewildering hours in Tasmania.

Finlay had been a tower of strength that day, and Christy realised how very much he'd become like their father – taking
responsibility and making sure they were all treated fairly.

The day had passed in a haze of new sights, smells and sounds.
She found it quite difficult, at first, to understand the strange
accent of the people who lived there, for their English was
drawling and certain words were emphasised in different ways,
which confused her.

She'd felt as if she was being closely judged as she was eyed
up and down and asked questions about her health, her background and her skills. And she noted that some of the men were
looking at her with more than a little unsettling interest; she
sensed they were after her for very different reasons, and stuck
close to Finlay and Jamie – which was how they were all taken
on by a group of people who'd travelled up from Hobart looking
for workers.

Finlay was taken on by a Mr Jackson, who had what he called
a large sheep station just outside Hobart, where Finlay would be
given bed and board as part of his pay, and a promised bonus
once the wool-clip cheque was cleared.

Jamie was hired as a junior carpenter by a Mr Williams, who
owned a thriving building company, which had just won the
tender for new housing in the heart of the city. The pay was generous, but he'd have to find his own board and lodgings.

Christy had wanted to be within reach of her brothers, so she'd
reluctantly agreed to work as a scullery maid in the hotel owned
by a couple called Keller. The money was as poor as she'd earned
back in Portree, but at least she'd be fed and housed – and, by the

look of things, she could always find work more to her liking once she'd settled in and found her way round Hobart.

They were not the only ones to be hired that day, and there were fifteen people sitting in the wagon that was taking them south. The long journey had been an eye-opener to them all, for the landscape in the heart of the island reminded them of the Highlands. Mountains soared above vast tracts of moorland dotted with wild flowers and heather; huge lakes, too numerous to count, shimmered as brightly as any loch, and the undulating hills dipped into broad, river-fed glens that seemed to go on for ever.

Christy could remember that wagon ride very clearly, for they'd followed their employers, who were riding in carriages or on horseback, and it had taken them the best part of two days to reach their destination. They'd stopped overnight at an inn, and although they'd been generously fed, there was no room for them, so they'd had to sleep in the hay barn, next to the stables. But it had been warm and sweet-smelling, and far more comfortable than what they'd become inured to – and they slept deeply.

It was as they approached the southern end of the island that Christy began to embrace this new country. They were greeted by fertile farmland which stretched for mile upon mile and was thickly planted with vegetables and winter wheat; she saw acres of apple orchards and great stretches of lush pastures that were being grazed by woolly sheep, fat cattle and sleek horses. It was still winter in this southern corner of the world, although it was late May, but the sky was clear, the air crisp and clean, and she realised she could easily feel at home here.

Christy smiled at the memory, picked up her unread book and left the deck in search of lunch. That young girl had been at the very start of a great adventure, and, although she'd experienced love, heartache and betrayal along the way, she'd come good in the end – found her place in the world – and was content.

*

Sydney

Harold had been a last-minute passenger, so he was unable to get a cabin. Not that it was any great problem; he could sleep anywhere. He'd settled his horse in the bowels of the *Empress* and found a bench in a sheltered corner of the top deck. Stretching out along it, he'd pulled the brim of his hat over his face and was asleep before the ferry had left Hobart.

Sydney was not a city he was familiar with, for, on the rare occasions he'd been here, it was on business and, once that had been completed, he'd left immediately. Now he was riding his horse along the city streets that were noisy with motorcars, horse-drawn delivery wagons and carriages of all shapes and sizes.

The pavements beneath the awnings and overhanging balconies of the tall buildings were awash with a crush of people as they strolled past the shop windows or hurried importantly along. Harold decided he'd never call Melbourne busy again after this, and, like his horse, he found the whole thing most confusing and unsettling.

He noted there was a hotel on nearly every corner, many with horses tied to tethering posts within reach of stone water-troughs donated by the city council. Deciding that he would feel more at home in such a place, he tethered his horse to a hitching post outside the Victoria Hotel in Pitt Street and went inside.

The building was typical of most hotels throughout Australia, built of brick, with stained-glass windows and ornately tiled walls, each storey finished off with a broad veranda decorated with wrought-iron lace. The inside was gloomy, but the red floor-tiles had been scrubbed, the furniture dusted and the runner of carpet up the stairs looked as if it had been recently brushed clean, the brass rods polished.

He got a room on the first floor which opened on to a broad veranda that looked over the busy street, and managed to persuade the landlord it wasn't too early for a long cold beer. Having settled his horse in the stables at the back, he tested the springs on the iron bedstead, the comfort of the mattress, and checked the cleanliness of the linen – all of which passed muster – and then took his beer out to the veranda and sat in one of the creaking raffia chairs to study the map he'd bought on board the ferry.

As the noise of the busy street drifted up to him, he searched for and found the street he needed. Checking his watch, he swiftly downed the last of his beer, took the envelope from his swag and placed it deep in an inside pocket of his drover's coat. Grabbing his hat, he locked the door and ran down the stairs.

He had to check the map several times as he walked, for he was getting confused by the mass of humanity that was jostling him on the pavement. Crossing through Hyde Park, he left William Street and turned into a narrow side street called Rum Lane.

The offices of Smithson and Son occupied a four-storey terraced building, which was in good order compared to some in the lane, and he walked up the few steps and through the double doors into a small, square lobby.

He pushed the second door open and entered a long, narrow hallway lit by a large gas lantern, which hung from the ceiling. The walls were panelled, the paintwork fresh cream and the floor was highly polished boards of oak. There was a hatchway set into the wall on his left, which clearly served as a reception desk, so he rang the bell and waited.

A man long past retirement age emerged through a door at the back, his pale face evidence of a life spent indoors. He was dressed conservatively in a dark suit, white shirt with a starched collar and a bow tie. 'Good morning, sir. How may I help you?' he asked in the rich, plummy tones of an English butler.

Harold drew the envelope from his pocket and placed the receipt and key on the polished counter. 'Mr Charles Smithson?'

The head was bowed momentarily. 'At your service, sir.'

'I am Harold Ross, and this lady's son-in-law, and I wish to open this deposit box,' he said firmly.

Long, pale fingers plucked up the receipt and, after a moment of silence, the piece of paper was pushed back to Harold. 'I'm sorry, sir, but this particular client has left strict instructions that only she may open that box.'

'I realise that,' said Harold. 'But she's abroad with my wife and daughter, and not expected back for some time. As this is a matter of urgency, I'm sure she would agree to me opening the box.'

'Do you have a letter from her giving you permission?'

Harold knew it was vital to appear calm and in charge of the situation, even though he was becoming impatient. 'No, unfortunately. The crisis arose after she'd left for England, but, as I said, the papers in that box are needed urgently.'

The man's expression became even more mournful, but there was a glint of something in his eyes that Harold realised was dark suspicion. 'I'm sorry, sir, but I don't know you, and the lady was most specific with her instructions.'

He was about to turn away, and Harold knew he had to act swiftly. 'Mr Smithson, I would like to confide in you so you fully understand why it's so urgent I collect those papers.'

The man raised an eyebrow as he regarded Harold. 'It seems you are very persistent, Mr Ross, and, as I find myself presently unoccupied, I should be delighted for you to enlighten me.'

'Not here,' said Harold, darting a gaze towards the many doors in the corridor. 'What I'm about to tell you is highly confidential.'

'I find myself intrigued,' he said with the ghost of a smile. 'Wait there and I'll escort you to one of our private consultation rooms.'

Harold impatiently shifted from foot to foot until Smithson emerged from a doorway further along the hall. He hurried towards him and was led into a room which had the aura of a funeral director's parlour.

Smithson sat down in one of the deep leather chairs. 'We use this to consult with clients who have suffered a loss,' he said, as if he'd read Harold's thoughts. 'My company began as a law practice and, over the years, my son and I have branched out into the embalming and funeral business.'

Harold didn't need to know the history of the place, but he was interested in how Christy had come across it. 'Have you ever met my mother-in-law?' he asked.

The pale face lit up in a smile. 'Oh, yes. Christy and I are well acquainted. In fact, we have known each other for over forty years, if my memory serves me correctly.'

Harold frowned. 'But she has always used Baker, in Melbourne, as her solicitor.'

He gave a small nod. 'I know that, but sometimes it's necessary to get certain advice from a trusted friend who has a more intimate knowledge of one's circumstance.'

'So she has confided in you?'

'Of course. All my clients confide in me, Mr Ross. It's my job.'

'If you've been in Australia for over forty years, how come you still sound so English?' Harold asked bluntly.

Smithson didn't seem to take offence at this. 'I doubt, if I was to return to London, it would pass muster any more, but my clients seem to find the accent reassuring and it has served me well over the years.'

'So, how did you meet Christy?'

Smithson lit a cheroot and dropped the spent match in a glass ashtray. 'I came out from England shortly after I qualified as a solicitor and headed for the Victorian goldfields – which is where we met. It's a long-standing friendship based on trust, Mr Ross, and your story would have to be very convincing for me to break that confidence.'

'Do you have any inkling as to what's in that safety deposit box?'

His expression was unreadable as he regarded Harold steadily.

'Why don't you tell me what you think is in there and why you should have access to it?'

Smithson settled back in his chair and, as Harold began to speak, watched him with narrowed eyes through the curling smoke of his cheroot, his expression still giving nothing away.

When Harold came to the end of his story, there was a long silence in which the cheroot was carefully ground out in the ashtray as the steady gaze remained on Harold. 'It is certainly a serious dilemma,' Smithson murmured thoughtfully. 'But, in all conscience, I cannot allow you access to that box without her permission.'

'Can you honestly tell me you have no idea of what is in there?'

'I can give you no such undertaking, for either way it would be breaking a client's confidentiality.' The eyes narrowed again. 'And should you contemplate getting access illegally, I should warn you we have an excellent alarm system here.'

Harold had certainly thought of it as a backup plan, but as he wouldn't know where to start looking for a safebreaker in Sydney, the idea had been swiftly dismissed.

He slumped back into the chair. 'If her sons and I lose this case, then not only will reputations be ruined, but the family business too.'

Smithson pulled at his bottom lip, deep in thought. 'A telegraph to the ship would cause her great concern,' he murmured. 'It's bad enough that this case has been brought at all, but being so far away and unable to do anything about it will surely be deeply distressing.' He looked at Harold finally. 'What was the name of the claimant?'

Harold told him and waited anxiously for some sign that Smithson was beginning to soften.

'And has this individual been investigated?'

'Baker's on to it, and so far it seems to be a genuine claim.'

Smithson rose from the chair. 'Christy is lucky to have you on her side,' he said, 'and I wish I could do more to help you, but –'

'But you can,' snapped Harold. 'Open that damned box and look at the papers yourself. If they are what I suspect, then you too can help Christy and her family to beat this thing.'

Smithson gave a deep sigh. 'I admire your determination, Mr Ross. But what you ask is against everything I've ever stood for.' He hung his head for a moment, sighed again and then met Harold's gaze. 'I do not pretend to have the wisdom of Solomon, but I will ponder over this with great care before we meet again.'

Harold felt a spark of hope. 'You mean you will consider opening it yourself?'

'I said I will consider the dilemma before I decide what to do.'

'And how long will that take?'

'As long as necessary,' he said ponderously. 'Come back on Friday and I might have an answer for you.'

'But that's five days away and –'

'Friday, Mr Ross.'

Harold bit down on his impatience as he gathered up the key and the slip of paper and tucked the envelope back into his coat pocket. He shook the man's hand. 'If you come to a decision before then, I can be found at the Victoria Hotel on Pitt Street.'

*

Charles Smithson watched him walk away and then returned to his office, which overlooked the small square of garden at the back of the building. Sitting down in his leather chair, he stared out of the window, not seeing the paved patch between the high brick walls that blocked out the sun, but the harsh landscape of outback Australia, and the girl who'd stolen his heart all those years ago. It had been an unrequited love, but one that had turned into a deep and lasting friendship.

He reached for the decanter and poured two fingers of whisky into a glass. He savoured the taste, his thoughts centred on the contents of that box. He'd always known what they were and, like Christy, had hoped they would never come to light. Now he had a decision to make – and he dreaded it.

15

Aboard the SS Southern Cross

As the ship sailed south to Cape Town, the heat increased and the scent of dry, dusty earth mingled with the salty tang of the restless Atlantic. A great many of the passengers went down with *mal de mer* and sought refuge in their cabins, but Christy was made of sterner stuff, having survived far rougher conditions in that awful clipper. To combat the heat, she took to sitting outside her state room long into the night, watching the stars and the phosphorescence glimmering on the water as she enjoyed the peace and let her mind wander.

The *Southern Cross* was making good time, and the captain was hopeful of breaking the record for the journey and sighting the western coast of Australia by the end of the month. Christy cradled the cup of tea a steward had brought her and looked out at the stars, finding Orion and remembering how she'd been so puzzled when she'd discovered it was upside down in the endless skies above Australia.

Her thoughts drifted back to those early days. She'd had so

much to learn – not only in what was expected of her, but in the countless unfamiliar scents, sights and sounds of her new country. Her smile was soft as she remembered how she'd spent the few hours she had off work exploring Hobart, with its endless coves and waterways, the busy port and the confusing narrow streets of warehouses and dwellings. She remembered hearing the bell-birds for the first time and the laughing kookaburras, and going with Jamie into the bush, where the scent of eucalyptus, pine and golden wattle filled the air, and she remembered discovering the suburb of Bellerive on a tourist ferry-boat ride.

She'd known, even then, that she would live there one day, and as the years had passed, her thoughts would constantly stray back to what she considered to be her Eden. There had been times when she'd thought her dream would never be fulfilled, for life had proved to be far harder than even she could have imagined – taking her to places many thousands of miles from that sheltered bay, and into situations she had to dredge up every ounce of courage to escape – but the dream had sustained her through it all and had finally become reality.

The sudden, heart-rending loss of her darling husband had overshadowed everything, but she'd never felt alone in Skye House, for his spirit lived on in every corner, and she knew he was watching over her.

She let the memories of him soothe her and ease the ache of loss, which always seemed to linger, and then turned her mean-dering thoughts back to the earlier years and the Tasman Hotel.

It still stood in the heart of Hobart town, and hadn't changed very much over the years, although there were new owners now and the clientele was less salubrious. Built of sturdy red brick, there were deep verandas jutting out from the top two floors that were laced with white wrought iron and furnished with comfortable cane chairs. In Christy's day, there had been a bar, an elegant dining room and a large area lined with cabinets of books and furnished with deep leather couches and chairs. Now, there were three bars and the rooms upstairs were usually filled with sailors or shearers and jackaroos, who came into the town to drink their wages.

The kitchen was still at the back of the hotel, which overlooked a vegetable garden, beyond which was scrubland and the wooden shacks which once provided accommodation for some of the female staff. They'd long been turned into storage units.

Christy remembered the long hours she'd worked there, cleaning and scrubbing, carrying up wood and coal for the guest-room fires, washing dishes and preparing vegetables for the cook. In the heat of summer, the kitchen and scullery became unbearable, and she'd sweltered in the simple woollen dress and heavy linen apron, her hair sticking to her head beneath the white linen cap she had to wear as part of her uniform.

She'd had very few hours to herself, and in the early days had fallen into bed at night so tired, she wasn't even woken by the drunken shouts and singing coming from a nearby pub. But she'd been well fed, the other girls were good company, and the cook had even shared some of her recipes with her and let her take over now and again when her swollen legs troubled her.

Christy had gradually given up the idea of looking for other work, as she felt comfortable where she was, was learning new skills and, despite Mrs Keller being a hard and demanding taskmistress, enjoyed the camaraderie amongst the servants and had been swept off her feet by Peter Keller, the owner's nephew.

She smiled at the memory, for Peter had been tall and fair, with dark blue eyes, an infectious laugh and the ability to make friends with everyone. He was eighteen when he returned from his Sydney boarding school for a holiday before going back to the city to attend college. The attraction between them had been instant.

Mrs Keller had not been at all pleased that her nephew was courting the scullery maid, but Peter always managed to slip away to see her, and together they would sneak from the hotel and go walking in the soft, velvety nights. They shared their dreams and talked for hours about all the things they wanted to do once they had the money and opportunity to do them, slowly falling deeper in love as the summer waned and the time fast approached when he would be returning to Sydney.

Christy closed her eyes as she remembered how they'd gone on the ferry boat to Bellerive to wander the plot of land down by the water on their last night – and the kisses they'd shared, their tears mingling as they held one another close and made a vow that one day they would marry and build a fine house there. He'd promised to write every week, for he wouldn't be coming home until the following summer, and she had promised to wait for him.

Christy gazed into the past, remembering her hurt and confusion when no letters had come – and the slow-dawning realisation that he must have used her as an amusing distraction during that long, hot summer, and his promises had meant nothing. Her heart had been broken, leaving her feeling empty and isolated, for she'd been so sure of him, so certain that they were meant to be together to fulfil all those dreams they'd shared. But when Mrs Keller let slip that he'd recently got engaged to a Sydney girl, Christy had to accept it had all been lies, and had cried into her pillow, vowing she'd never trust a man again – let alone fall in love with one.

Christy's smile was wry, for of course she'd trusted again, fallen in love again and been hurt again. It was the circle of life's experiences and everyone went through it.

But she'd been so young and innocent back then, hiding her anguish in hard work, crying into her pillow at night and spending most of her free time with Jamie, who was lodging in a nearby boarding house.

Finlay would come into town about once a month to check up on them both, hand over some of his wages to her and then spend the rest in the bar. He'd changed since working on the sheep station and preferred the company of the hard-drinking men to that of his younger siblings, and the two of them accepted that he was growing away from them.

Christy shivered as she remembered the late-autumn evening when Finlay had turned up unexpectedly with a determined expression and a heavy canvas swag hoisted over his shoulder. They'd been in Tasmania for just over a year, and his recent visits had made her anxious, for he was clearly becoming restless.

'I'm going to the goldfields,' he declared, as the three of them sat on the veranda outside Jamie's lodgings. 'I've had it with sheep, and that bastard, Jackson,' he growled. 'He cheated me out of my proper share of the wool cheque, I'm certain of it.'

'But you can't just go,' Christy protested. 'What about us?'

'Jamie's old enough to take responsibility for you,' he replied gruffly. 'I can't live my life tied to your apron strings, Christy. I need to go and find my fortune.' His face lit up with excitement as he continued, 'It's there to be found, just under the ground. There's money to be made and, when I'm rich, I'll send you a share, and Jamie can build that house you're always talking about at Bellerive.'

Christy and Jamie both realised then that their older brother had caught the gold fever that was so rife all over Australia, and that nothing they could say or do would make him change his mind. 'Then we'll come with you,' said Jamie.

Finlay shook his head. 'It's no place for girls,' he said dismissively. 'And you have a good job, Jamie. Dad would have wanted you to finish your apprenticeship and look after your sister.'

Christy and Jamie bridled at this, for she was quite capable of looking after herself, and Jamie didn't really want the responsibility of her welfare, seeing as she was older than him. And yet they could both see that Finlay had a point about Jamie's work, for, within the next few years, he'd be qualified enough to earn more money and perhaps even start his own little business.

However, they still had reason for concern. Finlay was family, and the three of them were all that was left, and they'd promised to stick together. The thought that he was going so far away and they might not see him again was sobering and distressing.

They spent the rest of the night arguing about it, but he was adamant, and, when the dawn ferry left the harbour, Finlay was on it.

*

Christy felt chilled, despite the heat. They'd received a few letters at first, which had been filled with descriptions of his journey through Victoria to the goldfields, the people he'd met there and the excitement of finding his first tiny nugget of gold.

However, it seemed that, after that initial small find, the rich lode he was after was proving elusive, and his letters had tailed off as he moved from field to field in pursuit of the riches he was certain he would soon uncover. Christy had wondered then if he would ever return to them.

As the months passed and there was no news from him, Christy tried her best to keep her dread at bay by working hard at her new position of assistant to the cook. In fact, the cook's bad health meant she was all but in charge of the kitchen, as well as the menus and the ordering of supplies. Consequently, her pay was higher, but the hours were even longer than before and Mrs Keller more demanding.

It was almost a year after Finlay had sailed away when Christy received a letter from a lawyer called Charles Smithson, who gave his address as First Floor, General Store, Sturt Street, Ballarat. He was writing on behalf of Joseph O'Driscoll, who was a gold prospector and friend of Finlay's.

Christy could still remember the conflicting emotions she'd felt as she read that letter. Finlay had at last found gold, but he'd been badly injured in an accident and was living in much-reduced circumstances, since his cache of gold had been stolen. It was not Finlay's wish for his family to be told, but Smithson and O'Driscoll agreed that it was only right they should be informed.

Christy had immediately taken the letter to the building site where Jamie was working, and, by dawn the next day, they were watching Hobart disappear into the distance as they stood on the deck of the ferry that would take them across the Bass Strait to Melbourne. They had no idea then how radically their lives would be changed.

Following her night of disjointed thoughts and troubled dreams, Christy had slept late and ordered breakfast to be served in her stateroom. She was sitting by the doors that opened on to her private area of deck, enjoying the hazy view of the west coast of southern Africa as she ate, when there was a sharp rap on the door.

Christy frowned and was about to go and see who it could be, when a clearly furious Anne barged in, waving a piece of paper in her hand.

'What on earth's the matter, Anne?' she asked in alarm.

'You may well ask,' she stormed. 'This disgusting thing was delivered to my cabin a minute ago.' She slammed the paper on to the table so hard the china rattled, and then stood breathing heavily, arms folded, expression furious.

Christy reached for what she could now see was a telegraph that had been sent from Hobart via Perth, in Western Australia, to Cape Town.

Delighted to see Harold in Bellerive * Skye House a delight * Bon voyage * Florence Hardwick *

She read the telegraph twice, realised it was not the pleasant message it first appeared to be, and fully understood why Anne was so upset and angry.

'Did you ask Harold to go down to the house?' demanded Anne.

'Why would I? Edna Ryan is perfectly capable of looking after it, and the horses are being stabled over at Eric Patterson's place.'

'Then what's he doing down there?'

'I really have no idea,' said Christy, with a puzzled frown. 'Perhaps he had some business to attend to and decided to stay at Skye House – which, of course, he's very welcome to do.'

'His businesses are all on the mainland,' Anne snapped.

Christy was well aware of that, but couldn't believe this telegraph was anything more than a vicious bit of troublemaking. She'd always found Harold to be an honourable man who doted on his little family, and she doubted he'd ever risk that by getting involved with a woman like Florence. Then again, men were easily led – especially when left to their own devices for too long – and Anne had had her suspicions about his relationship with Florence even before this journey began.

'Maybe he felt like a change of scenery and decided to go down to check the house and have a bit of a holiday,' she said, hearing the lameness of this excuse even as she spoke. 'But, whatever the reason, Anne, you must not allow this nasty piece of spite to upset you. Florence Hardwick is clearly out to make trouble.'

Anne simmered as she clenched her fists and began to pace the stateroom. 'Oh, that she certainly is,' she snarled. 'I doubt Florence had even heard of Bellerive and Skye House before, but mentioning them both is a clear message that she and Harold have met there.'

Christy's thoughts were in a whirl as she tried to find a logical explanation for Harold being in Bellerive, and Anne wasn't helping by continuing to pace the floor.

'Do sit still, Anne, and try to calm down,' she pleaded. 'I can't think straight with you going back and forth.'

'Calm down?' she raged. 'How do you expect me to calm down all the while my husband and that . . . that . . . *trollop* are carrying on – and in your home, I might add?'

'But you only have Florence's word for that,' pointed out Christy with more calm than she felt.

'Then why bother to send that telegraph, if she and Harold haven't met there?'

Anne was distraught and not thinking clearly, and, in an effort to assuage her, Christy kept her tone low and reasonable. 'You don't know for certain that Harold is anywhere near Bellerive,' she said. 'And what would a woman like Florence be doing down in Tasmania? I thought she was a Melbourne socialite?'

'She has a grandmother in Hobart,' muttered Anne, plumping into a chair and glaring out towards the sea. 'No doubt she used her as an excuse to meet Harold.'

'But did she, Anne? She may very well have gone to visit her grandmother, but a few enquiries in Hobart would have quickly told her where I live, and I suspect she's using that knowledge to stir up trouble.'

'I wouldn't put anything past her,' said Anne, her eyes bright with tears. 'But what if Harold has gone down there – and they did meet? Surely it's too much of a coincidence they should both be in Hobart at the same time?'

Christy really didn't have an answer to that, but it seemed she had more faith in Harold than Anne did, and that truly worried her, for, without trust, their marriage was doomed.

A silence fell as she read the telegraph again. Florence was certainly a sly and dangerous cat, for she'd worded it in such a way, there could be no different interpretation. And on accepting this, her thoughts cleared and she was able to see everything in a very different light.

'I shall send a telegraph home to Harold,' said Anne, making to rise from her chair. 'If there is no reply within the next twenty-four hours, I shall know for sure that he's not at home.'

Christy grabbed her hand and stilled her. 'Before you do that, Anne, take a moment to consider this message more carefully,' she advised.

'It's about as plain as it could be,' retorted Anne bitterly.

Christy kept hold of her hand, her heart aching for her distraught daughter. 'I agree, it is plain, and designed to cause you the deepest anguish – but there's an old saying, Anne, and I think you should heed it.'

Anne frowned as she looked at her mother through her tears. 'I hardly think this is the time for homilies,' she muttered.

'Ah, but this one is very apt, and if you read that again in a different frame of mind, you will see that "hell hath no fury like a woman scorned".'

There was a long silence as Anne stared at that spiteful message, then she screwed the telegraph up and dropped it back on to the breakfast table. 'I do see what you mean,' she said finally. 'But if Harold has spurned her, it must have been very recently for her to send that from Hobart.'

'Then surely it's time to have faith in Harold, and put this spiteful act behind you? She wants you to be hurt and angry – and to put a wedge between you – and she'll succeed, if you let her.'

'I accept Florence is out to make trouble,' she said grimly, 'but, for my own peace of mind, I need to know exactly where Harold is.'

'He could genuinely be away on business or visiting your brothers,' Christy said evenly. 'Don't condemn him before you have any real proof that he's playing false, Anne.'

'You always did have a soft spot for Harold,' she said in exasperation. 'But I know my husband far better, and I've seen the way he looks at Florence.' She bustled purposefully out of the stateroom, banging the door behind her.

Christy gave a sigh of distress. Sending telegraphs across such a vast expanse of the world took time, and Harold could be anywhere – from Wallangarra to Yarrabinda, Melbourne to Adelaide, or even Sydney. His empire was spread across the south-eastern quarter of Australia, and it could be days before Anne heard back.

She stared, unseeing, towards the swell of the sea, her thoughts troubled. There was always the possibility that Harold *had* gone down to Bellerive, perhaps even bumped into the Hardwick woman – but what possible reason could he have for being there, if it wasn't for the express purpose of meeting her? Had she misjudged her son-in-law, after all?

Despite the growing doubts, she refused to countenance them as she left her half-eaten breakfast and went to get dressed. It was time to send a telegraph of her own. Baker would know Harold's movements far better than anyone.

The following days were tense for all of them. Anne was still fretful, her moods swinging from hope to despair, her temper shortened each day there was no reply from Harold. Kathryn became concerned about her mother and, because neither Anne nor Christy could truthfully explain their concerns over her father, they decided to use the heat and terrible storms they were encountering as they rounded the Cape of Good Hope as an excuse for Anne's odd behaviour.

Christy didn't think Kathryn was fully convinced by their explanation, and noted that the girl was keeping at her mother's side much more than before. But Christy was also feeling the tension, her worry increasing as each day passed and there was no word from either man. Were they in cahoots? Was Baker trying to get hold of Harold to warn him before he replied?

It seemed that Anne's fears and doubts were contagious, and Christy had even begun to wonder if she should telegraph Edna Ryan and ask her if Harold was there. This idea was swiftly quashed, for Edna was almost illiterate and was frightened of using the telephone, and Christy suspected she wouldn't have the nerve to go into the telegraph office to send a message back.

Christy began to feel imprisoned on this luxury ship that was now sailing serenely towards Madagascar. She was restricted from doing anything to ease the situation – they were too far from home – communication was unreliable and took far too long, and making a telephone call to Melbourne was impossible. Frustrated and unable to do anything about it, she took to walking endlessly round the decks, taking part in games of quoits and deck tennis, and spending sleepless nights outside her stateroom.

Three days had passed and she was alone as she made her usual afternoon visit to the purser's office to see if she had any mail. He smiled and handed her two letters and a telegraph, and she could barely breathe as she ripped open the brown envelope.

Harold on business Sydney * Expected return soon * Contact Victoria Hotel Pitt Street if urgent * Baker *

With a deep sigh of relief that her faith in Harold had not been misjudged, she thanked the purser gratefully and hurried off in search of Anne.

She eventually found her on the top rear deck, sitting in the shade of a deep awning, while Kathryn and the other girls splashed about in the large canvas pool. 'This should put a smile on your face,' she said, handing over the telegraph.

'Thank God,' breathed Anne. She read the few words again and carefully folded the telegraph back into the torn envelope. 'I was having the most awful doubts, you know – and when I didn't hear . . .'

'I do understand, dear, and I have to confess that even I was beginning to wonder what was going on. But it's all explained now, so we can stop worrying and enjoy the rest of the trip.'

Anne's face was radiant with renewed hope. 'How clever of you to think of contacting Mr Baker.'

Christy shrugged. 'He and Harold work closely together and it seemed logical to contact him – after all, he never strays far from

Melbourne, and can always be reached one way or another.' She patted Anne's hand. 'I'm sure Harold will reply to your telegraph the minute he gets home.'

'This calls for a celebration,' Anne said. 'I think a bottle of icy champagne should do the trick, don't you?'

'Champagne always works for me,' she replied with a loving smile. 'It's so good to see you happy again, Anne.'

Anne chuckled. 'It's good to be relieved and hopeful again,' she admitted. 'Thank you for believing in Harold when I'd begun to lose faith in him. I hope he realises what a very special mother-in-law you are.'

'Oh, I doubt he gives it much thought,' she replied, watching the girls in their bathing dresses of dark-blue wool with white-and-blue striped sailor collars and matching bands around the weighted hems. 'That looks great fun,' she said brightly. 'I think I might join them.'

Anne looked at her aghast. 'But you can't,' she gasped. 'It isn't seemly and you're far too old to be gadding about half naked.'

'I'll show you who's too old,' muttered Christy without rancour. She shot her an impish grin before she left to see if she could purchase a bathing costume from the on-board shop.

*

Sydney

Harold was beginning to feel trapped in this city which never seemed to sleep, for Smithson had twice postponed their meeting and now he'd been in Sydney for almost a week.

He'd spent some of that time visiting the warehouses he owned down at Darling Harbour, and had called in to his Sydney manager to check on the books and discuss the new orders that had come in. It seemed they were now one of the main exporters of wool, and with the vineyards of the Hunter Valley as well as the Barossa really starting to come into their own, and his new tobacco plantation bringing in a bonanza profit, business was flourishing.

Now, he was restless and yearning to go home, but until Smithson contacted him, he was forced to remain here. What on earth was the man doing? he'd asked himself repeatedly. Surely it was a case of opening that damned box, finding out if it would help his case and reporting back? A conscience was all very well, but, at times, one had to do the right thing, even if it was judged to be wrong.

He was brooding over a beer in the bar when the landlord came in. Leaning over the bar, he said quietly, 'Phone call for you, mate. Hope it's the one you've been waiting for.'

'So do I,' he replied earnestly. He hurried into the reception hall and picked up the receiver. 'Hello? Smithson?'

'It's me, Baker.'

'Oh, hello, Baker.'

'There's no need to sound quite so despondent about it,' he replied dryly.

'Sorry. I was hoping to hear from Smithson.'

'No word from him yet? Is that why you're still in Sydney?'

'As I told you in our previous call, he's reluctant to cooperate and so I just have to wait it out. Do you have any further news about the case? Have you managed to stall them?'

'They've refused a delay in the court date and are still insisting their claim is valid. I've had my contacts go through all the records, and unfortunately we can find no proof to the contrary – in fact, they've unearthed several things which could have an adverse effect on certain people.'

'Don't say anything now,' Harold warned. 'I'm not sure about the security of this telephone line.' He gave a deep sigh. 'Do you have any good news for me?'

'Hamish has found the documents and I'm reliably informed by a law firm in Dubbo that they have been copied, and the original is now secure in their safety deposit box.'

'That's not the only thing in a blasted safety box,' said Harold. 'And, if it wasn't for an old man's conscience, we might at least have a chance of putting this puzzle together and calling a halt to it all.'

Baker was silent for a while and Harold thought they'd been cut off, but then he cleared his throat and Harold tensed. 'We don't have much time, Harold,' the other man said down the line. 'Can Smithson be relied upon not to get in touch with his client for advice?'

'They go back a very long way,' he hedged, 'and I can't be certain about anything at the moment. I just have to be patient – but all this hanging about is killing me.'

'I can understand that, but there is something else I must tell you, Harold, and, because of it, you will have to tread very carefully from now on.'

'Now what?'

'Nothing to do with the case,' Baker said quickly, 'but, since our last telephone conversation, I have received a telegraph from a certain person at the heart of the dispute, asking after your whereabouts.'

'What did you tell her?'

'Because you'd returned from Hobart by the time it had arrived, I was able to answer truthfully that you're in Sydney on business and are expected back in Melbourne soon.'

Harold was about to sigh with relief when Baker continued. 'But there was another communication from your lady wife, which is of far deeper concern. It was delivered to your home a week ago, and has only just been passed on to me. She asks that you reply immediately.'

Harold felt a prickle of unease. 'What does it say?'

'Rumour of you in Hobart, stop. Confirm whereabouts, stop.'

Harold swore and clenched his fist. 'How the *hell* did she hear that?'

'I haven't the faintest idea,' said Baker. 'You and I are the only ones who know you went there – other than Mrs Ryan.' He cleared his throat. 'Her mother would have got my reply by now, so that should mollify her, but it might be a good idea to send one of your own. You know what women are like.'

'Don't I just,' he muttered, as a chill of foreboding ran through him. Harold thanked Baker, disconnected the call and stood in the reception hall for some minutes, deep in thought.

Edna would undoubtedly gossip about her visitors to Skye House, but her tittle-tattle would certainly not be widespread enough to reach the ears of the well-heeled in Hobart, let alone a ship in the middle of the ocean. But Florence Hardwick was quite a different kettle of fish, and certainly had a sharp axe to grind after he all but threw her out of the house. He remembered her threats and was in no doubt that she'd been the one to inform Anne, to get her revenge.

'Bloody women,' he muttered, pulling his bush hat low over his eyes and stomping out of the hotel. He had enough on his plate already, without Florence bloody Hardwick stirring up trouble.

He marched along the pavement in a fury and then ran up the steps to the telegraph office, where he spent a fortune on a telegraph to Anne, assuring her of his whereabouts, his faithful devotion and his longing for her to come home. That done, he returned to the Victoria Hotel and got very drunk.

16

Aboard the SS Southern Cross

They were refuelling with coal and supplies at the old port of Fort Dauphin, in Madagascar, but because there was local unrest against the French rulers of the island, the captain had advised his passengers not to disembark. There had been discontented muttering and loud complaints, followed by some of the more adventurous men disobeying the order and going ashore.

Christy and the other women were tired of being restricted to the ship, and had stood along the decks, looking with longing at the beautiful sandy bay curving beyond Le Fort, the turquoise water lapping at the shore and the lush green of the rainforest, which seemed to cover the island. There didn't appear to be any unrest, for they could see no sign of rioting on the quay, nor hear the sound of gunfire.

'It's not fair,' grumbled Kathryn, watching the jolly boat taking a party of men to the bay. 'Why is it always the men who have the fun?'

'Why don't you and Lucy have a swim in the pool?' suggested

Christy, who was sweltering in her corset, petticoats and the tight bodice of her dress.

'It's far too hot to do anything,' said Anne. 'I'm going for a sleep under the ceiling fan in my stateroom.'

'That sounds like a marvellous idea,' said Christy. 'I think I might do the same and have a swim later, when it's a bit cooler.'

'Well, Lucy and I will go for a swim now,' said Kathryn. 'If either of you change your mind, you'll know where to find us.'

As the girls rushed off, Christy made her way back to her stateroom and quickly stripped off the layers of clothes which were deemed appropriate for polite society on board ship, but which were unbearably restricting in this torpid heat. As a girl, she'd possessed very little clothing and had worn the same thing whatever the season, but by the time she left on that boat for Melbourne, her employer was insisting she wear a corset, petticoat, thick bloomers and stockings, for she was then almost eighteen and her figure was maturing.

When she arrived in Ballarat it was the height of summer, and she'd almost fainted from the heat and the layers of restricting clothes until the English wife of a hotel owner had advised her to discard all of it and had given her some dresses of thin cotton to wear.

Now, Christy ran a cool bath and sponged away the perspiration before pulling on a wafer-light muslin nightgown. The blinds had been drawn over the double doors, which had been left open to garner the slightest breath of air, and the overhead fans whirred pleasantly as she poured some iced water from the crystal jug her steward had left on the side table. She then stretched out on the chaise longue. It would have been fun to go ashore and explore the island, for it looked rather exotic, but, in truth, she didn't really think she had enough energy to go anywhere.

'You're getting old,' she muttered. 'Old and lazy.'

She gave a wry smile, drank the water and decided she was nothing of the sort. The heat of Madagascar was damp and drained the energy – rather like that in northern Queensland – but, although she now lived in the cool, almost Scottish climate of Tasmania, she felt at home still in the harsh dry heat of the outback's miles of emptiness surrounding Wallangarra.

Closing her eyes, she drifted back to those far-off days, when she'd been young and full of energy.

The coach had set off from Flinders Street at five o'clock on the evening they arrived in Melbourne, and as they finally left the city limits, the six horses picked up their pace. The coach springs complained as the yellow painted wheels ran over the rough ground, and the passengers, already squeezed tightly inside and on the top of the coach with all the baggage, were jolted against one another.

Christy kept her bundle firmly gripped on her knees, thankful that she'd been early enough to grab a seat by the door so she could look out of the window and garner a bit of air to counteract the smell of tightly packed, unwashed bodies and dirty clothing. The heat was stifling in the crush, and she could feel the sweat soaking her hair and through to her underwear. They had seventy miles to go to Ballarat, according to the coachman, and he expected to arrive there early the following morning. She could only hope the temperature would drop during the night and make the journey more bearable.

Wedged into the corner of the coach, the leather seat became uncomfortably warm, and she rather envied the Chinamen who were perched on the roof, for at least they'd got room to breathe. She tried to settle, but, unlike Jamie, she was too excited by all that she'd seen in Melbourne, and the thought that she'd soon be with Finlay again and experience what it was really like on the goldfields she'd heard so much about.

As they travelled through the miles of empty, fertile grazing country, she turned her thoughts back to their short time in Melbourne. They'd managed to hitch a ride on a bullock cart from the port into the city and, although it had saved them from walking or paying for the tram, the sixteen oxen had lumbered along at a snail's pace, pulling an enormous dray loaded high with vast sacks of supplies.

Melbourne had been a revelation, and the people were so finely dressed that Christy was quickly made aware of how countrified and shabby she must look in her plain woollen dress and second-hand boots and jacket, but she soon forgot her appearance as she took in the sheer beauty of the bustling town.

Melbourne was far bigger and grander than Hobart, and had a prosperous, settled air about it, even though it had only been founded two decades before. The buildings were of fine creamy-coloured sandstone, decorated with finials, towers and statuary. There were hotels on every corner, restaurants and cafes, and large shops displaying everything anyone could possibly want lined streets that were broad enough to cater for the many bullock teams that hauled their massive wagons of wool and supplies.

She and Jamie had marvelled at the elegant bridges over the brown River Yarra, and people picnicking on the grassy banks that were as smooth and green as cloth, or strolling in the dappled shade of eucalyptus, pine and wattle trees. Exotic flowers grew in the parks, where ornate fountains stood at the crossways of neat gravel paths, and stalking, long-legged ibises pecked at the manicured lawns or circled the orangery tea houses in the hope of stealing a titbit.

They'd wandered in awe along Collins Street, staring at the Melbourne Club building, the Goode House and the Olderfleet building, before entering the hushed atmosphere of the recently completed St James's Cathedral, which had been built of bluestone and sandstone. Then, in Bourke Street, they'd stood and watched the builders hard at work on what would soon be the very grand Houses of Parliament.

She glanced across at Jamie, who'd fallen asleep, arms folded, chin to his chest, his toolbox and her loom tucked beneath his feet. He'd wanted to stay in Melbourne because he could see there was plenty of work for a carpenter, but Christy was impatient to get to Ballarat before their money ran out. Melbourne was beautiful, but she'd soon discovered it was very expensive. Jamie had become moody at the idea of leaving, and as she hadn't been able to cajole him into a better temper, she'd left him to sulk while she'd booked their passage on the coach and found them something to eat.

The man who'd sold her the tickets had warned her of the

rough types she would encounter, and as she surreptitiously examined her fellow passengers, she could see what he meant. They were mainly grizzled men of indeterminate age, with horny hands and clothes that would withstand the hardest wear. Each wore a broad-brimmed hat stained with sweat and dirt, and their sturdy boots were covered in the dust and scars of long use. They were a taciturn lot too, for they said very little, merely acknowledging her with a tug of their hat brims before they settled down to snore and mutter in their sleep.

As the journey progressed and swift darkness descended, Christy could no longer see the view through the window, and was lulled to sleep by the cooling breeze and the dip and sway of the coach.

It seemed only a minute later that she heard the shout of the coachman, realised the horses had come to a halt, it was daylight again, and that the other passengers were hurrying to alight. She quickly gathered up her bundle and followed Jamie as he jumped down from the coach.

The Chinamen were scrambling down from the roof, loaded with bags and spades and pickaxes, their long pigtails swinging from beneath their strange conical hats. She couldn't help but stare, for she'd never seen their like before and was fascinated by their almond-shaped eyes and golden skin.

She was distracted by a sharp dig in the ribs from Jamie's elbow. 'Let's find something to eat,' he said through a vast yawn. 'I'm starving.'

Christy hitched her bundle more comfortably in her arms and

regarded the town which Finlay had made his home. They'd come to a halt in front of a large hotel, with verandas that gave shade to a wooden walkway that seemed to follow the line of similar buildings down the broad, dusty street. The other side of the street had awnings above another boardwalk, and the buildings were a hotchpotch of different styles, sizes and heights.

The sun was rising and the sky was a pearlescent peach and grey above the rusted corrugated-iron roofs, but, despite the early hour, it was already warm and there were men and mules, horses and overloaded wagons in the street, and the blacksmith was busy in his forge. All the stores were open to sell everything from a toothpick to giant sieves, and great piles of spades and pickaxes were set up outside, along with barrows stacked with tins of flour, sugar and rice.

She could see some substantial buildings further down the street and, as they stretched their legs and tried to relax their stiff muscles by ambling along the boardwalk, she realised they were not grand houses, but the post office and the town hall.

They stopped by the general store, where a neat wooden shingle hung over a side door, proclaiming this to be the office of *C. Smithson, Esquire, Commissioner of Oaths and Attorney at Law*. The door was locked and a notice told them Smithson didn't open until nine, so they had plenty of time to get their bearings and find something to eat.

Following the scent of cooking, they found a man working over a brazier of sizzling meat, cobs of corn and a pan of frying onions. Jamie paid for two small steaks with onions, which were buried in a hunk of bread, and a cob of corn dripping in butter, then they went and sat on one of the benches beneath the shady veranda to eat their fill.

Christy was fascinated by the people of Ballarat, for there didn't seem to be any women or children, and the men all looked alike in their rough clothes, wide-brimmed hats and thick, tangled beards, some of which flowed to their waists. Many of them wore just trousers over their long combinations, with braces or bits of twine to hold them up, and it looked as if none of them had had a bath in months, let alone done any laundry.

There were also a great many Chinese, chattering away in their strange language as they hurried along, and some exotic, dark-eyed men in flowing robes and headwear, who were in charge of strings of camels, the like of which she'd never seen before, except in the battered old picture books at school. The animals seemed placid enough as they plodded down the street with their huge loads of tools and machinery, but their pelts looked as if they were peeling beneath the brightly coloured fringed blankets, and they made strange rumbling noises as if protesting their lot.

She finished her food, washed her hands and face in the horse trough and quickly brushed out her hair before tying it back into a topknot. Leaving Jamie with their belongings and a bottle of beer, she set off to explore further.

She discovered that the town sat in a broad valley between gently rolling hills, which were thickly covered in trees. There were signs everywhere that gold had brought prosperity to the little town, for even the smallest building had fresh paint and clean windows, the shops were well stocked and there was even a small park of manicured grass, shady trees, benches and flow-erbeds blazing with colour.

Reaching the outskirts, she looked out to acres of lush green pastures and copses of shimmering eucalyptus, beyond which lay a city of canvas – and she guessed it must be where the prospectors had set up home.

She shielded her eyes against the sun, which had now breached the highest hill, and wondered if Finlay was in one of those tents or had been brought into town so his injuries could be tended. There had been so little information in Smithson's letter that she didn't really know what to expect, and she could only pray that he'd recovered enough for her to persuade him to return with her to Tasmania.

Christy ambled back to find Jamie in deep conversation with a big, tough-looking man, who had a weathered face and arms as big as hams. At her approach, they shook hands and the man went through the swing doors into the saloon bar.

'That was Fred Harris,' said Jamie, who was looking much brighter. 'He's the landlord of this place and has asked me to do some work for him while we're here.' He grinned. 'I warned him we wouldn't be staying too long, but he's got windows to ease, floors to repair and bits of furniture that need sorting out, and is offering a fair wage.'

Christy smiled at his enthusiasm, glad that he was no longer out of sorts. 'That's marvellous,' she said, just as the town hall clock struck the hour. 'When do you start?'

'Now,' he replied, picking up his box of tools and hitching his swag over his shoulder. 'You don't need me to come with you to see Smithson, and I might as well earn a bit of money whilst I can.'

Christy didn't really want to see the lawyer on her own, but as Jamie was so cheerful, she was reluctant to argue. 'That's fine. I'll come and find you when I know how and where Finlay is.'

Jamie hurried into the saloon bar and Christy smoothed back her hair, ran her fingers down her dress and then picked up her bundle and loom. The heat was rising with the sun, and she felt quite light-headed in the woollen dress and tight corset, but until she'd found Finlay and had somewhere to stay, she could do nothing about it.

She approached the freshly painted door, found it had been unlocked and stepped into the small, square hallway to be confronted by a steep flight of highly polished stairs. She hoisted her heavy bundle into her arms and slowly climbed, hearing her footfalls echo in the silence. She reached the landing, where another flight of stairs led to the upper floor, saw a glazed door with Smithson's name on it and tentatively knocked.

She had imagined Smithson to be elderly and fat, with a balding head – but he was actually in his early thirties, she guessed, and very tall and lean. He had a long, pale face, kind brown eyes and a welcoming smile, which made her feel immediately at ease.

'I'm Christy MacInnes,' she said, still breathless from lugging her belongings up that long staircase. 'You wrote to me about my brother, Finlay.'

'How very nice to meet you,' he replied in the plummy tones of an Englishman as he shook her hand. 'Please, let me carry that; it looks heavy.'

Christy was immediately on her guard again as he took her bundle, for she hadn't expected to have dealings with an Englishman, and he sounded like some of the men who'd worked for the laird and his factor.

She hesitantly followed him into the office, which was barely furnished with a desk, two chairs and three large cabinets. The sunlight was diffused by the blinds that had been partly pulled over the row of open windows overlooking the street, and an oil lamp hung from the centre of the ceiling.

'You look hot and thirsty, Miss MacInnes. May I offer you some refreshment?' He waved his rather elegant, long-fingered hand towards a jug of water and a bottle of cordial, which stood on one of the scarred cabinets.

She opted for water, as she felt quite light-headed in the heat. She'd drunk down two full glasses before he'd fully settled into his battered leather chair, behind his equally ancient desk. As she drank, she noted the framed certificates proclaiming his qualifications, the large clock on the wall and the lines of shelves holding thick law books and a jumble of rolled documents tied with pink ribbon. There was nothing personal to provide any other information about him.

'How badly injured is my brother?' she asked, sitting on the edge of the only other chair. 'And where is he? I need to go to him.'

'He was found at the bottom of a mineshaft,' said Smithson. 'It appears that one of the rungs of his ladder was rotten and broke beneath his weight.' He regarded her solemnly. 'He sustained several broken bones and was concussed, so his friend,

Joseph O'Driscoll, brought him into town on his wagon and paid the wife of one of our hotel owners to look after him.'

'Which hotel?'

'The Ballarat Hotel, across the street,' he replied.

'Then I must go to him,' she said, making to rise.

'He's no longer there, Miss MacInnes, and it seems no one knows where he's got to.'

She slumped back into the chair. 'But if he was badly injured, he couldn't have gone far,' she protested. 'And this isn't a big place; he can't have simply disappeared.'

'People come and go all the time,' he said solemnly. 'And Mrs Harris tells me he was well on the mend the night before he left, for he and Joe were drinking together up in his room. He could easily have decided to move on to another field. I understand Finlay was not inclined to remain too long anywhere.'

'But surely you told him you'd written to me?'

'I certainly did, but he ordered me to write again and tell you not to come under any circumstances.' He gave a sigh. 'That letter is probably waiting for you in Tasmania.'

Christy frowned as her thoughts raced. 'I don't understand,' she murmured. 'He knows me too well to expect me to ignore such a letter, and must have realised I'd come, so why did he leave in such a hurry?'

Smithson poured her another glass of water. 'I'm sorry, Miss MacInnes, I cannot help you by speculating on that.'

Christy sipped the water, deep in thought. 'You said in your letter that his gold had been stolen. Was that before or after his accident?'

'His friend, Joseph, told me he had it the morning of his accident, and was planning to bank it later that day,' he replied, his brown eyes not quite meeting hers.

'So, it might not have been an accident at all,' she mused. 'A broken rung on a ladder, a man falling to possible death in a deep shaft and a missing cache of gold all add up to skulduggery, if you ask me.'

'That had crossed my mind,' he admitted, 'and it wouldn't be the first mysterious accident to happen in these parts. Rivalries and jealousies flare up quickly, and when the drink is involved, things can get out of hand.' He sighed. 'But Joseph told me your brother was a popular man at the diggings, that he didn't boast about his finds or get aggressive when he was drunk. I've also heard from others that he often helped them when they fell on hard times or were ill.'

'But I've also heard the stories in Hobart, Mr Smithson, and gold makes men greedy,' muttered Christy. He made no reply, so she hurried on: 'I need to talk to Joseph O'Driscoll. Where can I find him?'

'At the diggings by the Eureka Stockade,' he said reluctantly. 'But it's no place for a young girl like you, and –'

'I'm almost eighteen,' she said firmly, 'and hardly a child. Joseph and the other miners might have some inkling as to where Finlay could have gone; I have to speak to them.'

'Then I shall send a message asking Joseph to come here,' he replied, equally firmly.

She shifted impatiently. 'That will take too long. How far away are these diggings?'

'You can see some of the miners' tents from here, but I would earnestly advise you not to go there alone.'

'It can't be that dangerous, surely?'

'The men are coarse and uncouth, and not used to a decent woman's company, Miss MacInnes.' He regarded her kindly and then gave a sigh of defeat. 'But, as you're so insistent, I will accompany you.'

Christy opened her eyes as she felt a welcoming breath of cool air wash through the open doors. The sun had sunk lower in the sky, which was darkening, and she could hear the low rumble of the ship's engines and feel the gentle roll of her ploughing through the glassy sea as they left Madagascar behind. And yet her mind was still entangled in the memories of that first day in Ballarat.

Charles Smithson had been so kind, despite her prickliness. He'd asked about her younger brother, and their life before they'd come to Australia, and, upon discovering they had nowhere to sleep, offered them the upper-floor rooms for as long as they wanted, in return for her cooking him a meal each evening. Christy had been suspicious of his motives at first, but the rooms proved to be clean and furnished, and as her brother would be with her, Smithson seemed very respectable and it wasn't costing a penny to stay there, she'd eventually agreed.

Christy moved from the chaise longue, fetching a robe to put over her sheer nightdress before pulling up the blinds and stepping on to her private section of deck.

Her time in Ballarat and Bendigo had changed her life, for not only had she learned a harsh lesson in the vagaries of love and all its nuances, she'd had to go through the agonies of betrayal and heartbreak again – and the dire consequences of being naïve and very foolish.

She gave a deep sigh as she revelled in the cool air, for, despite her age and all she'd been through, she still felt the same old pangs of deep regret and sorrow. Deciding she was getting maudlin, she thought a swim might put her in a happier mood, and was just about to go inside to change into her costume when there was a tap on the door, followed by the discreet slide of a brown envelope beneath it.

Regarding it with some trepidation, she picked up the telegraph and held it for a moment before nervously opening it.

Harold has key * Advise urgently * Smithson *

Christy staggered and almost fell into a nearby chair. Her heart was hammering, her thoughts in such a whirl she could barely withstand the full impact of that stark message. She read those few devastating words repeatedly until they blurred.

Closing her eyes, she felt the thud of her heart and the throb of her pulse in her head. Harold *had* been in Bellerive – not on a secret tryst with Florence, but to search through Christy's most secret of things. How he'd discovered the key and the box number and then linked them to Charles's office in Sydney, she had no idea, for she'd thought she'd buried all that information so deep, the connections would never be made.

But she'd been wrong – so very wrong – and now Harold had put poor Charles in the most terrible position.

She found she was trembling, not from the chill of the cool breeze coming off the sea, but from the realisation that something very serious must have happened for Harold to be forced into doing such a thing. Was Baker involved too? Had his telegraph been a ruse to shield Harold's secret journey to her home? And what of Hamish and James? Were they at this very moment facing a dilemma they couldn't solve without Harold's help?

It was clear from their lack of communication that the three of them had decided not to tell her anything – and although she could understand that they were only trying to protect her, she felt a flare of anger that she'd been kept in the dark. It was an unreasonable reaction, she knew, for what could she have done, being so far away? Yet the thought of Harold being so underhand rankled, and she wondered what else he'd found during that search.

She read the telegraph again, wondering how long it had taken Charles to make the decision to contact her. He knew what was in that box, knew how it would affect not only her, but the very fabric of her family. The poor man must have been frantic with worry to have sent this – which meant she had no choice but to trust that he would do the right thing, regardless of the consequences.

As the sky darkened further, she wrapped the robe more firmly about her and thought how Charles had advised her so wisely all those years ago, and had drawn up those papers, which she'd hoped would give her the freedom to move on with her life – and the security she so badly needed for her loved ones.

But the sins of the past were catching up with her, and although she had no real idea who might be threatening to destroy her family, she could hazard a guess. It was time to face up to what she'd done and vigorously defend everything she held dear.

17

Sydney

Harold was at the end of his patience when he stormed into Smithson's office building; he was confronted by a middle-aged man behind the reception desk, who, going by his appearance, could only be Charles's son.

'I need to see Charles Smithson,' he demanded.

'I'm sorry, but my father is not in the office today,' the man replied smoothly.

'Where is he? I have to speak to him urgently.'

The other man regarded him with cool appraisal. 'Are you Harold Ross?'

'Yes, I am, and I'm sick of waiting about in Sydney for your father to make up his mind. The matter is urgent and I've wasted almost two weeks in this damned city already.'

The man's smile didn't quite reach his eyes. 'My father is a busy man, despite his age,' he said, 'and I'm sure that, if your business is as urgent, as you say, he will contact you when he feels it's necessary.'

Harold tamped down on his frustration and decided he had no choice but to go for plan B. He pulled the thick envelope from his inside pocket. 'If I'm to be stuck here, then I'll need a safety deposit box for this,' he snapped.

'Certainly, sir.' He slid the appropriate form across the desk and waited for Harold to fill it in. 'If you would like to come this way,' he said, once he'd taken the fee, and he locked the office door behind him.

Harold followed him along the corridor to a flight of stairs which led down to a thick steel door. Smithson's son shielded the alarm system as he spun the wheel at the centre of the door and then unlocked the door with two keys to reveal an enormous basement, lined with deposit boxes. The light was dim and the lines of boxes stretched far into the gloom, making it impossible to see the numbers and gauge where Christy's might be.

The man opened a nearby box; Harold slid the precious envelope inside and locked it in, noting the number was sixty-three, and realising it had to be a long way from Christy's, which was in the four thousands. He placed the key into his waistcoat pocket and gave a sigh of relief, for it had been a constant worry, and the longer he was forced to stay in the city, the more he'd fretted it might be stolen.

He followed Smithson's son out of the basement and back up the stairs and, without another word, left the building. He was still burning with frustration as he headed back to the hotel to fetch his horse. It had now been proved to him that the security arrangements for those boxes would defeat the most talented of burglars, so there was little point in going to the slum area of Sydney to try and find one.

Saddling his horse, he decided that, as Smithson wouldn't be around for the rest of the day, he might as well get out of the city and breathe good clean air. There seemed to be numerous cars and delivery vans spewing out fumes and making a constant racket, and he yearned for peace, far from the jostling crowds.

His horse didn't like the noise either and constantly skittered and shook his head as cars backfired and people dodged across the road in too much of a hurry to wait for a proper gap in the traffic.

Harold kept a firm hand on the reins, trying to soothe him with soft encouragement as they headed away from the centre of the city for the hills he could see in the distance. The morning rain had eased off, leaving everything glistening and fresh, and as he climbed further away from the smog and noise, the air became cleaner and easier to breathe.

He soon discovered that the suburb of Surrey Hills offered peace and quiet. The houses were terraced dwellings in quiet tree-lined streets that wound steeply away from the bustling city and, with no traffic and only an occasional pedestrian on the pavements, he felt the horse ease up and could begin to relax his grip on the reins.

However, his frustration was still churning, while his thoughts raced. His long, difficult two-way telephone conversations with James and Hamish had ended with them arguing, and, as it had been vital to be careful what they said on the open lines, the angry exchanges had been most unsatisfactory.

The calls had ended with both brothers declaring that they'd be coming to Sydney immediately to have a full and frank discussion about what he'd found and was planning to do – and it was a meeting he definitely wasn't looking forward to.

Smithson was proving to be a thorn in his side by shilly-shallying, and although Harold realised the man had a difficult decision to make, he did wish he'd show a bit of gumption by opening that blasted box. After all, Harold had told him everything and, should the right papers be in there, Christy would surely approve of using them to stop the lawsuit dead in its tracks. He was rapidly growing sick and tired of the whole thing, for he'd done his best, and was beginning to feel isolated by the family he was trying so hard to help. Without cooperation from anyone, his task was proving impossible.

His thoughts were shattered by the sound of a fast-approaching engine and, before he could react, the motor car roared over the brow of the hill at speed.

The horse propped and skittered in the middle of the road as Harold fought to get him under control and away from the rapidly advancing car.

The driver slammed on his brakes, making the tyres screech on the damp road surface, and the car backfired as it swerved out of control and headed straight for Harold and his horse.

The animal reared up with a whinny of pure terror and pawed the air.

The car skidded and rocked on two wheels, missing the flailing hooves by inches.

Harold had a glimpse of the driver's ashen face as he wrestled with the steering wheel, the brakes screeching and the narrow tyres slithering over the fine sheet of water which lay on the crushed stone.

Harold clung on grimly as the horse reared and bucked and corkscrewed beneath him.

The car screeched to a halt and the driver leaned on his horn, shouting abuse and waving his arms, before revving the engine and roaring away with a series of very loud backfires.

The horse reared again, thudding back down with such force, Harold was almost propelled over his head. But, before he could regain his balance, the animal snorted and took to the air with a corkscrewing buck, which sent Harold flying.

Harold felt the bone-jarring thud of his body hitting the unforgiving ground and taking away his breath, but as the sound of his fleeing horse faded, his head cracked against the kerb, and he knew no more.

*

Charles Smithson was tired, for it had been a long, distressing day and he was left wondering if, at seventy-nine, he really should think about retiring. His client's will was being fought over by her grasping, greedy relatives, and he'd spent the past few hours trying to discourage them from contesting it. Yet it seemed the threat of losing a large proportion of their inheritance through solicitor and court fees was not enough to quell the family rivalries, and the whole process would be dragged through the law courts.

He'd left the meeting and gone to the cemetery to lay some flowers on his wife's grave and talk it over with her, just as he'd always discussed the things that bothered him throughout their marriage, for she was very wise in her gentle, unassuming way. Sadly, she could no longer provide the answers, but merely talking about his troubles usually led to some sort of conclusion, and he always felt the better for it.

The interlude in the peaceful graveyard had restored his spirits somewhat, but he was still fretting over Christy and the telegraph his conscience had forced him to send. He could only imagine the distress it must have caused her, and wished that he'd been able to come to a decision without the need to consult her, but that would have broken the vow he'd made all those years ago never to reveal what was in that box – and their close friendship demanded absolute honesty on both sides.

He slowly climbed the steps to his office building and found he didn't need his keys, so pushed through the two sets of doors into the hallway to find his son busy behind the reception desk with the funeral-business accounts. 'It's after six, John, and time you went home to your wife and children,' he said wearily.

John regarded him with affectionate concern. 'It looks as if you've had a tiresome day,' he replied, closing the account book. 'Problems with the Jackson will?'

Charles sighed. 'Where there's a will, there's always a relative,' he said wryly. 'And poor old Mrs Jackson must be turning in her grave.' He dumped his briefcase on the counter and scrubbed his face with his hands. 'Anything I need to know before I go up to my rooms?'

'You had a visit from an irate Mr Ross, who's taken out a deposit box for some papers.'

Charles raised an eyebrow. 'Did he now?' he muttered, retrieving his briefcase from the counter as John pulled down the steel shutter and fastened the latch.

'I got the feeling he was checking out our security system,' John replied, closing the office door behind him and pocketing the large bunch of keys. He regarded his father with a frown. 'I do wish you'd slow down, Dad. You look very tired this evening. Why don't you come home with me for supper? Margaret always cooks enough to feed an army, and you know you'd be welcome.'

Charles patted his shoulder, thankful and proud that he was such a good and caring man. 'As much as I enjoy your wife's cooking and my grandchildren's company, I have a lot to think about, and need some quiet time to myself. But thank you, John. Perhaps tomorrow.'

John was about to open the main door when he stopped and felt in his jacket pocket. 'I nearly forgot,' he said apologetically. 'A telegraph arrived for you this morning. Is it the one you've been waiting for?'

Charles glanced at it, nodded, wished his son a good night and, instead of going upstairs to his suite of rooms on the third floor, went into his office. Lighting the gas lamps against the gathering gloom, and the fire to combat the late-July chill, he hung up his hat and coat, poured a large whisky and sat down in his favourite chair.

He swallowed a healthy slug of the whisky, carefully set the glass back on the side table and, after a momentary hesitation, opened the telegraph.

If Ballarat connection open * Help Harold fight * If not * More detail first * Christy *

Charles let the telegraph flutter to the table and sat in deep thought as night fell and the gas hissed and popped, the light from the lamps flickering in a draught coming from beneath the door. Christy had known immediately what must have happened – it was something they'd both feared all those years ago. And yet, as time had gone on, it seemed the threat had lessened and they'd all but forgotten about it.

For it to have reared its ugly head now had come as a terrible blow to him, but how much worse must it be for Christy? He ached at the thought of her having to bear the burden of it on her own, and wished he could be at her side to offer the comfort and advice she would now need.

It was at times like this that Christy must miss the support of her husband, he thought sadly. He'd been such a wise counsellor and had loved her so deeply, and because he'd been there during the worst of Christy's troubles, he would have understood and been a staunch supporter through the minefield of what was coming.

He sat wondering what was going through her mind and how she was managing, not only with the undoubted frustration of being so far away and not fully informed, but with the realisation that she would now have to reveal things – very personal and private things – to her daughter and granddaughter. Anne already knew some of it, which was why those papers had been added to the others eight years ago, but how much Christy had revealed to her, he had no idea.

Now her hand was being forced by Thomasina Brown, Christy would have to prepare her family for the worst by telling them everything, and his soft heart ached as he realised she would find it very hard to rake over it all again. But Christy had always been a little battler, from the moment she'd appeared in his office at Ballarat, and all through the turmoil of what had happened after he'd taken her out to the Eureka diggings in search of her brother.

He still blamed himself for that. He should have warned her to be on her guard, kept a closer eye on her and called a halt to things sooner. After all, he reasoned, he had considered himself to be her guardian – and had failed miserably at the very moment she'd needed him the most.

Charles finished the whisky and unlocked the desk drawer. He'd placed the safety deposit key there after he'd battled with his conscience and sent the telegraph to Christy. Now it was time to reacquaint himself with the papers that would hopefully bring Thomasina Brown's lawsuit to an end.

Returning to his office some time later, he wearily plumped down in his chair and spread the papers out on his desk. With his reading spectacles perched on the end of his nose, he went through each document carefully, checking back and forth to make sure they tallied and would prove Mrs Brown's claims on Wallangarra to be unsubstantiated, despite her so-called proof to the contrary – and where on earth she'd found that, he couldn't begin to guess.

Yet, as he gathered the documents together again and slid them back into the thick buff envelope, there was a niggling sense that he'd missed something – and that it might be important. He paused for a moment, struggling to think what on earth it could be, and then decided he was too tired to concentrate on anything. If he had missed something, then no doubt he'd remember it after a well-earned night's sleep.

He placed the envelope in the desk drawer, pocketed the key and took off his glasses. Pressing the bridge of his nose between his fingers to try and relieve the dull thud of a blossoming head-ache, he rubbed his eyes and poured another whisky. He didn't really need it, but it was a way of putting off the moment when he'd have to face Harold again. His reluctance to share the con-tents of those papers was growing, for he'd been their custodian for more years than he cared to count, and they had become his personal responsibility.

It really was a Pandora's box Christy had asked him to open, and yet she was trusting him to keep it out of court and away from the press, who'd have a field day if they got wind of any of it. But he could no longer hide anything from Harold, and he could only hope the man proved up to the task of using the infor-mation wisely – and very discreetly.

He drew a sheet of paper on to his blotter and made several attempts to draft a reply to Christy. Once satisfied, he copied it out and slipped it into his pocket. The telegraph office was open all hours, so he would send it tonight.

Charles was almost staggering from weariness, and his chest felt tight as he reached for his hat and coat and left the building, to discover it was raining again. He pulled down his hat brim and plodded through the streets, which were still busy, despite the hour and the weather, but at least the air was a bit fresher now and it had eased his breathing.

He sent the telegraph and, upon reaching the Victoria Hotel, slowly made his way up the stairs to the first floor and rapped on Harold's door. There was no reply, so he tried the handle only to find the door was locked. He rapped again, waited, and then gave up. In a way, he was relieved, for it meant not having to face him until tomorrow; but, on the other hand, he wanted things to be resolved quickly, and Harold would play an important part in that.

He went back downstairs and was about to go home again when he had a thought and headed for the broad entrance to the stable yard, where several horses poked out their heads to watch a man who was sweeping the cobbles.

'Is Mr Ross's horse here?'

Narrow eyes regarded him from a weathered face lined by years of hardship. 'Nah, sorry, mate,' he replied in broad Cockney. 'Went out this morning and ain't back yet.'

'When he does return, would you give him this? Ask him to contact me, whatever the hour.' Charles slid a business card and a sixpenny piece into the dirty palm of the man's hand. 'It's very important,' he said firmly.

The man tugged at his worn cap. 'Right y'are, guv'nor. You can rely on me.'

Charles slowly walked home. There was nothing more he could do today, and his bed was calling him. Yet, as he closed the inner door behind him, he suddenly realised what had been niggling at the back of his mind, and instead of climbing the stairs, he returned to his office to search through those papers again.

The mantel clock struck midnight as he finally returned the papers to their envelope and locked them away. His worst fears had been realised, for a vital document was missing – and, without it, Christy could lose Wallangarra as well as her reputation.

His fingers were clumsy and he almost dropped the crystal decanter, slopping the whisky on to the desk as he tried to fill the glass. He gave up on the idea, for his headache was getting worse and whisky was not the answer. He needed to take a powder and go to sleep so he could think things through and try to work out what Christy had done with that vital document.

Hauling himself out of the chair, he turned off the gas fire and the lamps and opened the office door. He was about to tackle the long flight of stairs to his top-floor rooms when he staggered from an overwhelming wave of giddiness. Clutching at the newel post, he tried to fight it, but his legs gave way as darkness filled his head, and he'd passed out before he hit the floor.

*

Harold was incandescent with rage as he stomped through the dark, deserted streets of the Sydney suburbs in the teeming rain. Not only had he been robbed of his wallet and pocket watch whilst being out cold in the middle of the flaming road, but his head throbbed, he was soaked to the skin and his bloody horse had shot through, leaving him miles from anywhere. It felt as if every bone in his body had been bruised and he cursed the driver of that car, vowing that, if he saw him again, he'd punch him so hard he wouldn't know what day it was.

His boot heels rang on the pavement as he reached the outskirts of the city and tramped along the badly lit streets. He ignored the dubious pleasures offered by the prostitutes, and kept a wary eye open for anyone who might think he was a soft target for another robbery. He pitied anyone who tried, he thought grimly, because they'd find he was just itching for a fight.

The rain was dripping off his hat, on to his drover's coat and down beneath the collar of his jacket, the cold wind scythed through his wet shirt and he was trembling with cold and anger and the shock of his horse dumping him. He finally reached the Victoria Hotel as a church clock struck two, and went straight into the stable yard, concerned that his horse might not have found his way back.

The animal whickered from the stall in greeting, and although Harold was in a foul temper, he was hugely relieved to see the damned thing.

'It wasn't your fault, mate,' he muttered as he opened the stall and ran his hands over the animal to check that he was all right. He'd lost a shoe, but apart from that he'd come through without a scratch – which was more than could be said for Harold.

Stroking the horse's nose, he then slapped him on the neck and fastened the stable door, just as he heard footsteps behind him. Turning swiftly, ready to defend himself, he came face to face with the old stable-hand.

'Whoah, there, mate,' the old man said, raising his hands. 'I mean no 'arm.'

Harold uncurled his fists. 'You startled me,' he said, 'and I'm in no mood for people coming up behind me tonight.'

'The 'orse come back two hours ago,' he replied, his faded eyes taking in Harold's bedraggled appearance. 'Looks like you've 'ad a rough night.'

'Rough enough. Thanks for looking after him.' He dug in his pockets for a sixpence, but the thieves had taken his last penny.

'I got a message for yer,' said the other man, handing over Charles's business card. 'He said it were urgent and to call him, no matter what the hour.'

A stab of expectation raised Harold's spirits immediately. 'Thanks, mate. I'll see you right in the morning,' he said, before limping out of the yard and hurrying as fast as he could towards Smithson's office.

Rum Lane was in the deepest darkness and he had to feel his way down it to the front door. It was almost three in the morning now, but Smithson had left a clear message to contact him whatever the time, so he had no compunction about banging on the door and ringing the bell.

He stood waiting in the rain as a nearby gutter overflowed and splashed on to the cobbles. There were no lights in any of the windows, the moon was hidden behind the roofs and the darkness was profound. He listened hard for any sound of footsteps approaching, but was met with only silence.

Rapping heavily on the door with his fists, he opened the letter box and peered into the dark lobby. He could see nothing in the all-pervading gloom, and there wasn't a murmur of sound coming from anywhere. Harold tried the door, but of course it was locked – the Smithsons seemed to have a fanatical habit of locking everything – so he kept his finger on the bell.

Smithson was an old man, so it could take him some time to get down the stairs, he reasoned. But surely, even the heaviest sleeper would have heard the racket he was making.

As if to prove the point, a window on the building opposite was thrown up and an angry voice shouted, 'Shut yer bloody racket and let decent people sleep, ya flaming mongrel!'

'I'm trying to get hold of Smithson. It's urgent,' Harold called up.

'He's probably asleep,' shouted the man. 'Just as I should be.' With that, he slammed the window shut.

Harold took a step back and looked up at Smithson's three-storey building in the hope of seeing a light come on, but all was silent and still, the house closed against the night, the windows dark.

He tugged at his hat and turned away. Smithson must sleep like the dead, but a ringing telephone would surely waken him? With that thought, he hurried as best he could back to the hotel.

A low gaslight was flickering in the hallway as he unlocked the door and tiptoed inside. The only sound was water gurgling in the pipes and the usual soft creaks and groans of a building settling into its foundations. He reached for the telephone, asked the operator for Smithson's number and let it ring for several minutes before the woman came back on the line to tell him there was obviously no one there to answer.

He told her sharply that he knew for a fact there was, but, although he let it ring for many more minutes, it seemed the operator was right. Smithson was out.

He went up to his room, not noticing the telegraph fluttering away from beneath the door to land under the bed, and gingerly dragged off his sodden clothes, which made him wince, for every movement sent rivers of agony flooding through him. He eyed the bruises that covered his torso and marvelled at the fact he hadn't broken any bones in the fall, before traipsing out to the bathroom to have a hot bath.

Wrapping himself in a large towel, he returned to his room some time later and crawled beneath the blankets, still shivering with pain and shock. Unable to sleep, despite his exhaustion, he lay there staring at the ceiling, utterly confused as to why Smithson had left that message and then gone out.

He must have dozed off at some point, for when he next opened his eyes, he realised the sun was up and it was almost nine o'clock. Gasping with pain as he moved too quickly off the bed, he gritted his teeth as he dressed, and discovered that it was even painful to walk down the stairs. Stiff and aching, he ignored the tempting aroma of coffee and bacon and headed straight for Smithson's office.

The son was just approaching from the other end of the street and they acknowledged one another with a curt nod. 'Your father left a message for me to call him urgently,' said Harold, as the other man slotted a key into the main door. 'But he seems to have gone out.'

John Smithson frowned as he opened the door. 'My father was very tired last night,' he said. 'I doubt he was anywhere but in his bed.'

Harold followed him into the square lobby and waited

impatiently for him to unlock the inner door. 'I wish I could sleep as soundly,' he muttered.

John stepped into the hall and, with a gasp of horror, hurried to where his father was lying, ashen faced and frighteningly still at the bottom of the stairs.

'Call an ambulance,' he ordered sharply, tossing his bunch of keys at Harold. 'The telephone is in the office.'

Harold fumbled through the keys and finally managed to find the right one and got the door open. Within moments, he'd called for help, and then he hurried back to the bottom of the stairs. Smithson was now cradled in his son's arms and seemed to be coming round. He looked ghastly and Harold feared the worst.

'Fetch a glass of water,' John said. 'There's a tap in the back room.'

Harold found the tiny kitchen and hurried back with the water just as the strident sound of a clanging bell alerted them to the arrival of help. He opened the front door and stood aside as two men carrying a stretcher rushed in with a medic, then he waited anxiously alongside John as Smithson was examined.

The old man had come round, but he was clearly confused, and his speech was slurred. He was quickly placed on the stretcher and carried outside to the horse-drawn waggonette waiting at the entrance to Rum Lane, where he was carefully loaded through the wide back doors.

John hustled Harold out of the building and locked the doors, before clambering in next to his father. The driver flicked the whip and the horse trotted off, the bell jangling to clear a path through the traffic to the Sydney General.

Harold went back to the hotel, fetched his horse and headed

straight for the hospital, every muscle and sinew complaining at each jolt of his horse's hooves on the cobbles.

He found Smithson's son anxiously pacing the floor outside the ward. 'Any news?'

He shook his head, his eyes almost blank with fear in his ashen face. 'I told him to slow down,' he muttered. 'He's almost eighty, and already has a weak heart. All this worry over Christy has been too much.' He stopped pacing and looked at Harold. 'My name's John, by the way. Thanks for your help, but there's no need for you to be here.'

'There's every need,' Harold replied. 'He left a message saying he wanted to speak to me urgently – and I have to know why.'

'It was probably something to do with the telegraph he got yesterday.' John dug his hands into his pockets, his worried gaze fixed on the closed curtains around the bed where the medics were working on his father.

'Telegraph? What telegraph?'

'It was sent from the SS *Southern Cross*.'

Harold was overcome with fury that the old fool had ignored everything he'd said and brought Christy into this mess – no doubt causing her unimaginable distress. 'Do you know what it said?'

He shook his head. 'I didn't open it, so I have no idea.'

'I have to see it. It could be our only hope of clearing up this mess.'

'Well, I'm not leaving here until I know how Dad is, and there's no way I'm letting you loose on your own in his office. You'll just have to be patient.'

Harold took a shallow, wavering breath as he tamped down on his rising frustration. 'I've been patient for two weeks,' he retorted. 'And if that telegraph is giving him permission to open that deposit box, then I need to get to the papers inside it.'

'I'll be the judge of that,' John replied grimly. 'Just go, Mr Ross, and let me concentrate on my father.'

Harold fumed in silence as he plumped down on a nearby chair and folded his arms. He wasn't leaving the man's side until he knew what was in that telegraph.

18

Aboard the SS Southern Cross

The ship had stopped for a few hours on the island of Mauritius, and Christy was thankful that Anne had finally received a loving and contrite telegraph from Harold, which had cheered her up and brought her renewed hope that her homecoming would be the fresh start she so wanted for their marriage.

They were now full steam ahead for the western coast of Australia. The Indian Ocean was like blue glass, the heat a dazzling, dancing haze on the horizon, which Christy would have enjoyed, if she hadn't been so worried about what might be happening in Sydney.

Since sending Charles the telegraph, and firing off another to Harold and the family solicitor, Baker, she'd become almost reclusive, taking refuge in her stateroom, incapable of being sociable while her thoughts were fully occupied with the awful situation she'd been forced into. There were decisions to be made that could have far-reaching consequences, and she could no longer bear this burden alone, but, with Anne happy at last, it was imperative she keep her wits about her and tread carefully around her daughter's delicate sensibilities.

Yet tread on them she must, as this burden had to be shared if they were to see this thing through, and as they drew nearer to Australia with no reply to her telegraphs, she knew the time had come to confide in Anne – and she dreaded her reaction.

She was half-heartedly picking at her afternoon tea when the tap on her stateroom door startled her from her troubled thoughts. 'Who is it?' she called out irritably.

'It's me, Grandma. Can I come in?'

Christy realised that if she told Kathryn to go away it would cause her concern and make life even more complicated. 'Yes, dear,' she replied, forcing a smile into her voice.

Kathryn looked lovely in a green day dress that enhanced her deep copper hair and startling eyes, but her bright smile disappeared the moment she saw Christy, and she dashed across the room. 'What's the matter, Grandma? Are you ill?'

Christy dredged up a smile. 'Oh dear,' she said, on a shaky laugh. 'Do I look that bad?'

Kathryn squatted beside her chair and took her hand. 'You look really crook, Grandma. Should I fetch the ship's doctor?'

'Of course not,' she retorted. 'I'm feeling the heat, that's all. Please don't make a fuss, Kathryn.'

Kathryn glanced around the stateroom at the scattered clothes, the unmade bed and the crumpled dress Christy had thrown on carelessly that morning. 'Mother and I are very concerned about you,' she said earnestly. 'You've been avoiding us these past two days, and it's not like you to hide away like this.' She looked at the barely touched tea tray. 'And you don't seem to be eating enough, either,' she added.

'Of course I'm eating,' she said distractedly. 'But my appetite has never been up to much in such heat. I'm quite all right, really.'

'I'm going to get Mother,' Kathryn said purposefully, and before Christy could stop her, she was out of the door.

'Oh, God,' she groaned, slumping back into the chair. 'I can't do this – really, I can't.' She closed her eyes, willing the image of her beloved husband to come to her. She longed to be able to hear his voice and be led by his wisdom, for he was her *darach* – her oak – and she needed him now more than ever.

As she listened to the soft rumble of the ship's engines and the silky slither of the sea against the great steel hull, it seemed to hold a whisper: *Be strong, Christy. I'm with you.*

She smiled and her pulse stopped racing as the fear subsided and she realised he would always be guiding her, just as he had in life. The knowledge gave her strength and she quickly left the table to tidy her hair and change into a clean dress before Anne and Kathryn came back.

Regarding her reflection as she drew her hair up into a loose topknot, she understood why Kathryn had been so concerned. Her face was quite gaunt, there were shadows beneath her dull eyes and a pulse ticked in her jaw. She looked and felt positively ancient.

They came in without knocking and startled her as she was dabbing powder on her face. 'You see,' she said defiantly, 'there's nothing wrong with me but this awful heat.'

'You look dreadful,' said Anne flatly. 'I'm going to get the doctor.'

Christy stayed her by grabbing her arm. 'No, Anne. I don't need a doctor. What I need is for you to stop worrying about me.'

'I can't help but worry,' she replied. 'Are you planning on hiding in here for the rest of the voyage?'

'I plan to finish my tea and just sit here enjoying the cooling fan while I admire that gorgeous blue sea.' As if to underline the point, she popped one of the tiny cucumber sandwiches in her mouth.

'It's not like you to keep to yourself and take no part in things,' Anne said fretfully. 'We've hardly seen you since we left Madagascar; you've been eating in here, and you didn't even come ashore with us on Mauritius.'

'I'm hot and tired after our long journey, and simply need some time on my own,' she said carefully. She gave her daughter a wan smile. 'But why don't you come back later and keep me company?' She wetted her dry lips, suddenly nervous. 'There is something rather important that I have to discuss with you before we reach Melbourne.'

Anne's eyes narrowed suspiciously. 'What is it? You're not dying of something ghastly, are you?'

'Nothing like that,' she said firmly, 'but if I was, then I'd find your lack of concern deeply worrying.'

Anne went scarlet. 'Of course I'm concerned, and I certainly didn't mean it to come out like that. But you've been behaving strangely, and really don't look well – and you have an awful habit of not telling us anything, and then shocking us with some awful revelation.' She frowned. 'It's as if you take pleasure in it.'

Christy silently acknowledged that her habit of keeping things to herself must be infuriating for her family, but it was a long-held habit and she couldn't change now.

'I'm sorry if my ways are disconcerting, and I certainly don't get any pleasure out of keeping you in the dark,' she said. 'But there are things I prefer to keep to myself until it's absolutely necessary to divulge them.' She lifted her chin and met her daughter's puzzled gaze. 'But there is something I need to discuss with you, Anne, and it's important we do it today.'

'Go on, then.'

'No, it's better if we talk alone, after you've had your afternoon tea.'

Kathryn frowned. 'But why can't you just tell us now?'

'Because I'm not ready yet, and I have to think things through.'

'Goodness. That sounds serious.'

'It is, rather,' Christy murmured, 'but nothing to worry your pretty head about.' Crossing the room, she opened the door to encourage them to leave.

Kathryn folded her arms. 'Don't patronise me, Grandma,' she said flatly. 'I know you well enough to realise something is very wrong, and if you've got anything to say, then I think I should hear it too.'

Christy tamped down on a stab of impatience. 'I'm sorry, Kathryn, I didn't mean to be patronising, but what I have to discuss with your mother really doesn't concern you, and I'd appreciate it if you'd just accept that and not be difficult.'

Christy caught Anne's gaze in an attempt to make her realise she didn't want Kathryn hearing what she had to say – and the message seemed to have got through, for Anne gave a deep sigh and took her daughter's arm.

'Let's just go, Kathryn,' she said. 'Your grandmother is simply being dramatic, as usual. I'll come back after tea whilst you and Lucy are having your ballroom dancing lessons, and catch up with you when she's done.'

Kathryn was clearly reluctant, but Anne bustled her out before shooting a worried glance at Christy and closing the door behind her.

Christy let out the breath she'd been holding, relieved that she had some time to prepare for what would no doubt be a very difficult exchange. She tidied away her clothes, placed her barely touched tray outside her room and went to stand at the railings to garner the lightest breeze that came from the turquoise sea.

Closing her eyes and lifting her face to the sun, she could almost feel him beside her, tall and straight and reliable – her rock, her best friend: her husband. He would help see her through the gathering storm – just as he'd done all those years ago, in Queensland.

*

Sydney

Harold had stayed with John Smithson throughout the long morning, watching the comings and goings of doctors and nurses and getting ever more anxious, as no one came to tell them what had happened to Charles.

It was almost noon when a doctor finally came to tell them

that Charles had had a minor apoplectic attack, and although his speech was somewhat impaired and his right hand was weak, the prognosis was good and it was hoped he'd make a full recovery.

'Can I see him?' asked a frantic John.

'For just a few minutes,' the doctor replied solemnly. 'He needs absolute rest and will be taken up to the medical ward very soon.'

Harold had been refused permission to go behind those curtains, so he dug his hands in his trouser pockets and began to pace the floor. His patience had been stretched to breaking point; the frustration of knowing that somewhere in Smithson's office was the answer to all the questions that were plaguing him burned in every aching muscle.

The curtain flicked back and John appeared. 'He's agitated,' he said, 'and although it's difficult to understand what he's saying, I think he's asking for you.'

Harold quickly followed him to the bedside, shocked to see how old and frail Smithson looked. His face had sunk in on itself and seemed to be drooping to one side, and there was a blue tinge to his top lip. 'I'm here, Mr Smithson,' he said softly.

'Ross?' The word slurred on the old man's tongue.

'Yes, Mr Smithson. It's Harold Ross.'

'Key,' he managed, lifting his good hand from the white sheet to point to the jacket hanging over a nearby chair.

Harold waited for John to find it, then grasped it firmly and bent closer to the bed. 'Are you giving me permission to look at those papers?' he asked.

'Yes,' he slurred, a line of drool running down his chin. 'In desk.' The pale hand gripped the sleeve of Harold's jacket.

'Missing,' he faltered, his eyes boring into Harold with urgent intensity. 'Something missing.'

Harold and John leaned nearer. 'What's missing?'

Charles closed his eyes and sank further into the pillows, as if exhausted by the exchange, his next words coming in a whisper so soft Harold couldn't catch it.

'What was that?' He put his ear close to the old man's mouth, but all he heard was the sibilant hiss of his breath on a word he didn't know. He looked at John. 'Did you understand that?' he demanded.

He shook his head. 'We didn't understand, Dad,' he said, his ear almost touching the old man's crooked lips. 'What's missing?'

They could see he was struggling, his lips trying to form the word around his uncooperative tongue. 'Afff . . . d,' he managed.

John frowned. 'An affidavit?' he asked. 'Is there an affidavit missing?'

But Charles's eyes were closed, his mouth had fallen open and both hands now lay limp on the bedclothes.

'We'll get nothing more out of him today, poor old chap,' said Harold. He straightened and regarded John, who'd suddenly aged with all the worry. 'I'm sorry this has happened, mate, but you did hear him say I could look at those papers?'

John held his father's hand and nodded reluctantly. 'Yes.'

'Come on, then; there's nothing we can do here.'

'I'm staying until he's taken up to the ward. I'll meet you back at the office after I've informed my family about what's happened.'

'And how long will that take?'

'At least a couple of hours.'

Harold felt for his pocket watch, remembered it had been stolen along with his wallet and gave a grunt of impatience. 'I'll meet you at two, then.'

He didn't wait for his reply, but pushed through the curtains and strode away. He needed to get some money from the bank, and have at least a whole pot of coffee and something to eat before he found a replacement for his watch and prepared himself for what he might find amongst Christy's papers.

It was almost an hour later that he returned to his hotel room and found Christy's telegraph on the bed. Tearing it open, he read the short message.

Relying on you * Charles and Baker have answers * Christy *

*

Aboard the SS Southern Cross

Christy tore open the telegraph which had just arrived from Charles and her spirits plummeted further, for now she knew without doubt what the panic was about. She tucked it away in her pocket and waited nervously for Anne to arrive.

Anne's demeanour was cool as she entered the stateroom an hour later. 'What's this all about, Mother?'

Christy took a deep breath, praying for the strength she'd require to get through this, and then reached for her daughter's hand.

'I need your understanding and support, Anne,' she began softly, 'because a situation has arisen and we must discuss the promise I made you, back in London.'

Anne paled visibly, her expression immediately wary. 'What situation?'

Christy kept a tight hold of her hand. 'I'm sorry, my darling, I'll explain everything in a minute, but I wanted to warn you that I might be forced into breaking that promise.'

Anne went ashen and clung to Christy's hand to steady herself. 'But why?' she breathed. 'What's happened?'

Christy drew her down to the chaise longue and sat beside her. 'I fear that someone has discovered our secret and is threatening the family with it.'

Anne shook her head, her eyes glistening with angry tears. 'You told me no one else but Daddy knew,' she rasped. 'You promised you had those papers so well hidden that they'd never be found.'

'And I truly believed it at the time I made that promise,' she replied earnestly. 'And I can guarantee that those papers you found eight years ago are not the ones being used to threaten us now. Someone, somehow, must have found something – perhaps another document, or a letter of which I have no knowledge.'

Anne snatched her hand away and got to her feet. 'Who is this person?' she demanded, her voice rising, her fists clenched at her sides. 'And how are they threatening us?'

Christy struggled to find the right words, for she was as much in the dark as Anne and knew that anything she said would only hurt her daughter. 'I know very little,' she admitted, 'and can only suspect that the person responsible is questioning the ownership of Wallangarra – perhaps even Yarrabinda.'

Anne frowned. 'But why? Those properties have been in our family for years.'

'Because the person causing trouble is, I suspect, distantly related to your father.'

'Daddy?' she asked tremulously. 'But how so?'

'Not your daddy,' she said gently, 'but the man who fathered you.'

'Oh my God,' Anne gasped, sinking back on to the seat.

Christy could almost see her daughter's thoughts racing and braced herself for the storm to break.

'But what has this person to do with our family properties – and how did they find out about you and him? You told me he was dead, and that your sordid little secret had died with him.' Her face was angular with rage, her eyes brittle. 'Or was that just another one of your many, *many* lies?'

Christy shook her head. 'He's long since dead and buried, I can assure you.'

'Then how did our secret get out?'

Christy bit her lip, for the question had plagued her from the moment she'd received Charles's telegraph. 'I have absolutely no idea,' she admitted. 'And I'm not even going to try and speculate.'

'I suppose this person is using that information to blackmail the family,' Anne muttered darkly, 'but I still don't see how Yarrabinda and Wallangarra come into it all.'

'It's far too complicated to go into now, Anne, especially as I have no knowledge of what sort of threat we're facing,' she replied. 'Whatever the facts, it's best to be prepared for what might be awaiting us back in Melbourne – and, to do that, I might have to confide in Kathryn.'

'Over my dead body,' Anne rasped. 'She doesn't need to know about your disgusting behaviour, and I forbid you to tell her anything.'

'Anne, I understand and respect your need to protect Kathryn, and hope with all my heart that it isn't necessary to tell her anything. But if this person's threat cannot be quashed, then we'll all be forced to face the glare of the public scrutiny that a court case engenders – and to do that you must both know the whole story of what happened all those years ago.'

'What do you mean by that? I thought you'd already told me everything.'

'I told you what you wanted to hear,' she said. 'And as you didn't seem to be overly curious about the man who fathered you, or the circumstances surrounding your conception, I glossed over things.'

Anne's eyes narrowed. 'You *glossed over things*?' she hissed furiously. 'Why not just tell the bloody truth and have done with it?'

Christy flinched at her bad language, but, under the fraught circumstances, could forgive her. 'The truth is ugly, Anne, and you were in no mood to hear it then.'

Anne regarded her coldly. 'He couldn't have been all that bad for you to have slept with him,' she snapped.

Christy realised her daughter wanted to believe that there was some good in her father and, to avoid causing her any more pain, decided to highlight his better side and keep his true nature to herself.

'I was young and foolish, still in the throes of a broken heart, and he dazzled me, made me feel special. For all his faults – and they were numerous – he had great charm and was all too easy to fall in love with.'

Anne seemed satisfied by this and sat for some moments, deep in thought. 'How long have you known about this threat?' she asked finally.

'For two days,' Christy admitted, her gaze flitting momentarily to the brown envelope on the bedside chest. 'I received a telegraph from Sydney. It was sent by a man I have trusted all my adult life, and concerns the key to one of his safety deposit boxes.'

Anne frowned. 'But if this man sent you a telegraph, then he must also know our secret.' She jumped to her feet, her fists curled, her eyes glinting in her furious face. 'Just how many people *have* you told, Mother?'

'Charles was there when it all happened,' said Christy, warily eyeing those fists, for Anne was so angry she might even resort to violence. 'I have no secrets from him.'

'It seems you have no secrets at all,' she retorted bitterly. 'I'm surprised you didn't put an advertisement in the newspaper and tell the whole of Australia whilst you were at it.'

Christy didn't respond – there was no point.

Anne buried her face in her hands with a howl of despair. 'If this gets out, then everyone will know and we'll be the laughing stock of Australia.' Her head snapped up and her tear-filled eyes flashed dangerously. 'It will not only ruin Kathryn's reputation and probably get her barred from university, but what about Harold? He won't want to have anything to do with me when he discovers what I am. You've ruined my life,' she stormed. 'And I hate you.'

Christy tried to tell her that Harold probably already knew and, rather than turn his back on her, was doing his utmost to protect her.

'I'm not listening to anything you say,' yelled Anne. 'You're a liar, and I wish I'd never been born.'

Christy realised there was nothing she could say or do to calm her daughter, who was behaving like a recalcitrant toddler, and so she bit back on a retort and waited impatiently for the squall of tears and temper to blow itself out.

Yet she ached with shame for her youthful indiscretion that had caused her child such pain and burdened her with the stigma of illegitimacy that might now overshadow the next generation. She could only pray that Charles acted swiftly on her reply to his first telegraph, and worked closely with Harold and Baker so that disaster was averted.

She burned with frustration that she was so far from home, that there was absolutely nothing she could do and that she had to rely on others to fight her corner. But, as she watched her daughter struggle to come to terms with things, she realised she had her own battle to fight right here.

Once Anne had gained a bit more control of her emotions, Christy neither reached for her hand, nor offered soft words – Anne would only spurn them, and frankly, she didn't blame her. 'Harold probably knows everything by now,' she said quietly, handing over Charles's initial telegraph. 'In fact, he must have known before he sent that telegraph to you, and it clearly hasn't changed the way he feels about you.'

'You don't know that,' she growled. 'You're just saying it to keep me quiet.'

'I do know, actually,' said Christy. 'If you read that message, you'll see that it was Harold who found the key, made the connection and took it to my friend, Charles.'

Anne read the telegraph and then regarded her mother sullenly. 'I don't understand,' she muttered. 'What's so important about a key?'

'It opens a safety deposit box Charles has been keeping for me over the past forty years. That box holds the papers I've retained as security against something like this happening,' she replied.

'Then I don't see why you have to tell Kathryn anything,' said Anne, sniffing back her tears and dabbing her eyes with a sodden handkerchief. 'If this friend of yours can clear up the threat by using those papers, then Kathryn need never know the shameful thing you did back then.'

'He may not be able to,' said Christy, with a sigh. 'The person attacking us might very well pursue their claim through the courts regardless of the evidence we can put before them.'

'But why would they do that?'

Christy shrugged. 'Greed. The chance to claim something they think they have a right to. The opportunity to demand a hefty payment to keep quiet. It's all about money, Anne, and some people will do anything to get their hands on it.'

Anne plumped back on to the chaise longue, her tear-streaked face solemn with her thoughts. 'If this person is taking action against the whole family, then Hamish and James must know too.' She turned reddened eyes to Christy, her face gaunt with distress, before breaking into noisy tears again. 'I can't bear the shame,' she wailed. 'I simply can't bear it.'

'Pull yourself together, Anne,' she said firmly. 'The shame is all mine and I will deal with it. You'll make yourself ill, if you go on like this.'

'I have never hated anyone as much as I hate you,' she snarled. 'You've brought me nothing but disgrace – and I have no doubt the rest of the family feels the same.'

Christy felt a pang of deep remorse that was tinged with fear. 'I can only hope that they love me enough to forgive my youthful indiscretion and bad judgement,' she replied sadly. 'But I have faith in Harold. He went all the way to Hobart to find that key and is working his hardest to protect us all – which is why he's in Sydney now with my friend, Charles.'

Anne stared at her. 'He *was* in Hobart, then – and you knew about it?'

'Not at the time of Florence's telegraph, no,' she said firmly. 'But I can assure you, Anne, he wasn't there to meet that woman, but to try and do all he could to help the family fight this thing.

'As for your brothers –' she allowed herself a flicker of a smile – 'I suspect Hamish is raging about like a bull in a china shop, and James is quietly working with Harold and Charles to resolve things before we get back home. They might be shocked, but I have to believe our family ties are strong enough to help them beat this – whatever form the threat might be taking.'

'But it's all so shaming,' Anne sobbed. 'I don't think I could ever look them in the eye again.'

'It's a shame we'll both have to bear when we see them all again,' said Christy sadly. 'But, regardless of how they might feel about what I did, your brothers won't desert you, and Harold is a good, honest man, who would never turn his back on you because of something which you couldn't possibly be blamed for.'

'But society will,' she snuffled. 'I'll always be tainted by the shame of what I am.'

Christy realised they were going round in circles, but she handed Anne a clean handkerchief and waited for the storm of tears to abate before she spoke again.

'I'm waiting to hear back from Baker and Harold,' she said eventually. 'Depending on their answers to my many questions, we might have to tell Kathryn. And if that's the case, then I'll need you to keep calm and clear-headed and forget about how you feel, so you can give her your support.'

'It will turn her against me,' sniffed Anne. 'I'll have no part in it and forbid you to say a word.'

'Have you learned nothing from all the stories I've told over the past months?' she asked wearily. 'This is not about you, Anne, but about our family coming together to stand against this attack. Kathryn won't forgive either of us if this blows up in our faces and she discovers she's been kept in the dark.'

'Then I'll make sure she never finds out,' snapped Anne. 'And if you breathe one word of this to her, I'll never speak to you again.'

Christy took a breath and tried very hard not to think of her daughter as a blinkered nincompoop. 'That might prove to be impossible, Anne,' she said firmly. 'Kathryn is no fool and you can't keep something like this from her – especially as the rest of the family know all about it and will demand answers the minute we step ashore.'

'They won't if I send them telegraphs warning them not to,' she mumbled.

'Don't be naïve,' said Christy sharply. 'If they can't put a stop to whatever's happening at home, then the press are bound to get hold of it and the scandal will be unavoidable.'

She stilled Anne's nervous hands that were twisting in her lap. 'I promise not to say anything to Kathryn until I've heard from home and know more of what's going on.'

'It's easy for you to make promises you have no intention of keeping,' retorted Anne. 'I will *not* have my daughter dragged into this – and that's final.'

'You might not be given the choice,' replied Christy crisply. 'And should their replies confirm my worst fears, I'll be forced to tell her regardless of how you feel.'

Anne balled the handkerchief in her clenched hands. 'I might have known you'd ignore my feelings,' she said bitterly. 'She's my daughter, and I will decide what is right for her.'

'I'm old enough to make my own decisions,' said an ashen-faced Kathryn as she pushed through the lightweight curtains drifting over the French windows and stepped into the room.

Christy felt the colour drain from her face and noted that Anne had gone a deathly white. 'How long have you been listening?' she managed.

'Long enough to learn what you've both been hiding from me all these years,' she replied, battling to keep her emotions in check and her tears from falling.

'Oh, Kathryn,' sobbed Anne, reaching for her. 'None of this was my fault. Your grandmother . . .'

Kathryn ignored the beseeching hand and regarded both women. 'I'm shocked by the pair of you,' she replied. 'But at least now I understand why you and Grandma fell out.'

'You shouldn't have been eavesdropping,' stormed a distressed Anne.

Kathryn sat stiffly on a nearby chair and smoothed her dress over her knees to play for time and keep her emotions in check. 'I know it was wrong,' she admitted finally, 'but I was worried about Grandma. She's been acting oddly lately, and seemed so determined to get you on your own, I was concerned she might be really ill.' She lifted her chin defiantly. 'I was also worried that you might end up fighting again, and wanted to be on hand to put a stop to it.'

'We don't fight,' protested Anne.

'You've been waging a war of words for years,' she retorted, 'and you're always trying to pick a fight, Mother. So don't try to deny it.'

'You have no idea what torture it's been to have to bear such shame,' Anne sobbed into her handkerchief. 'I've barely been able to look her in the eye, knowing what I do, and now this awful thing is happening and I was just trying to protect you and—'

'That's enough, Mother,' she said sharply. 'Tears and hysterics won't help anything. You've always blamed everyone but yourself

339

when things go wrong, and it's time you took a long hard look at the way you treat people, and borrowed some backbone from Grandma.'

'How *dare* you speak to me like that!' Anne gasped.

'I dare because your selfish, self-centred attitude hasn't let you see how much this will affect the whole family.' She blinked rapidly on the blossoming tears. 'I'm not surprised you feel so bitter – it is a shameful thing Grandma did – and now we must both bear the stigma of your illegitimacy.'

She turned to Christy, who was staring at her with frightened eyes. 'I've always loved you, looked up to you and admired you – but you aren't the woman I thought you were, and I'm finding it hard to believe you kept all that to yourself for so long.'

'I kept that one secret to protect your mother,' Christy managed. 'I'm not a wicked person, Kathryn, and what I did, I did out of love,' she said tremulously. She studied the girl's tear-streaked face. 'I never meant for anyone to find out.'

'But someone did,' replied Kathryn, 'and now my father is doing his best to clear up the mess you've left behind.'

'That isn't fair, Kathryn,' she replied, her throat restricted by tears and pain. 'I have no control over what is going on back home – and if your mother hadn't . . .' She bit her lip and fell silent, ashamed that she'd been so rattled that she'd put the blame on her daughter.

Kathryn turned her icy green gaze on Anne. 'What did you do, Mother?'

Anne squirmed on the seat. 'I found some papers in her safe when I was looking for her opals,' she said. 'I faced her with them and she was forced to confess everything.' She shifted to the edge of the chaise longue, eager to justify her actions. 'Can you begin to imagine what it was like to discover that your father, who you adored, wasn't really your father at all? That your mother had been lying to you for years, and everything you believed in was lost in a moment?'

'After hearing you both today, I know exactly how you felt,' she said. 'If this gets out, I can forget about going to university, and will probably never be given the chance to become a teacher.' She dashed away her tears and fought for calm.

'I'm so sorry, Kathryn,' whispered Christy, tortured by her granddaughter's very real pain. 'I never wished for you to be involved.'

'But I am, aren't I?' She regarded both tearful women and took a shuddering breath. 'Regardless of everything, I still love you both,' she said quietly, 'and Grandma's right, we must stick together as a family and be strong to face this threat – and we can't do that if we continue to argue over who's to blame.'

Anne broke into noisy sobs and dashed across to take her daughter in her arms.

Christy caught Kathryn's gaze and softly blew her a kiss before wiping away her tears. She'd overcome many challenges in her life, but she would have found it impossible to fight this latest one without the love of her granddaughter and a united family.

Christy took a tremulous breath. She would soon have to tell her unedifying story, and although she'd been the hapless victim of one man's cruel deceit, the weight of guilt was heavy in her heart. She'd never intended either of them to know about her shameful past, and if only she'd hidden that birth certificate away with the rest of the documents in Charles's depository, Anne would never have discovered it and she wouldn't now have to rake over all the old hurts.

But I would, she thought, her gaze fixed on the muslin curtains that were drifting out from the French windows in the breeze coming off the ocean. The threat of a court case would still have been brought; the family would still have had to fight – and she would have been forced to confess everything to her unforgiving daughter and shocked granddaughter, perhaps losing them both in the process.

As night fell and the sky filled with stars, calm was slowly restored. Kathryn helped her mother to her feet, and then softly kissed Christy on the cheek. 'I do love you,' she murmured, giving her a hug, 'and I can understand how very brave you must have been to carry that secret for so long.'

'So you forgive me?' she asked.

'Of course.' Kathryn kissed her again and stepped back. 'But there are to be no more secrets from now on, and, in the morning, I would like to hear the full story of what happened to bring about the situation we now find ourselves in. And please don't spare the details. I'm neither naïve nor prim and have a far better understanding of things than either of you give me credit for.'

As Kathryn helped her wilting mother out of the stateroom, Christy moved out on to the deck and took a deep breath. The air was cool in the darkness of night and, as they approached Australia, they would enter the southern hemisphere's winter, which would be a blessing after the heat of the tropics.

Christy felt a tremor run through her – a reaction to the emotional ups and downs she'd been through, and which were still to come. She lifted her chin and squared her shoulders, determined not to crumble or fail the ones she loved.

Kathryn had a right to know everything, but where on earth could she begin? The story she had to tell was of a tangled web of lies, deceit and betrayal, and she was caught at the very heart of it – just as she'd been trapped all those years ago, on the Eureka goldfields.

19

Sydney

Harold was just going down the stairs to make a quick telephone call to Baker, when the front doors crashed open and Hamish stomped in. Dirty and dusty, and clearly in a foul mood, he glared at Harold and headed straight into the bar. 'I need a cold beer,' he rumbled. 'Been eating the dust of a thousand head of bloody beef cattle since leaving Quilpie.'

'Surely it would have been quicker and easier without the cattle?'

'Too right it would, but the cattle needed shifting before they died from the drought, and as I got a good offer from a stock agent, I thought I'd kill two birds with one stone. They're down in the stockyards now, with my drovers.'

He leaned on the bar, propped one booted foot on the low brass railing that ran beneath it and wiped his sweating face with a filthy handkerchief as he watched his beer being pumped. 'James here yet?'

'No, but I booked rooms upstairs for you both,' said Harold, glancing at the large clock above the bar. 'I've got an appointment to see Christy's papers in about ten minutes, so get that down you and we'll be off.'

The frothing pint went down in several vast swallows and was swiftly followed by two fingers of whisky. 'It's about time the old bludger saw sense,' he growled, chucking some money on the bar and yanking at his hat brim. 'We've wasted enough time hanging about and getting nowhere.'

As Hamish hadn't been the one hanging about in Sydney, Harold only just managed to hold his tongue on a sharp retort. He told the landlord where they were going, in case James arrived, and they left the hotel.

He brought Hamish up to date with things as they walked, and braced himself for the outburst he knew would come.

'Flaming old fool,' Hamish spluttered. 'Now Ma knows, she'll be worrying herself sick. D'you reckon she'll have to tell Anne and Kathryn?'

'I doubt she'll be able to avoid it,' he replied. 'If we can't clear this up before they get home, then there'll be no hiding what's going on.'

'I wish I could sit in on that conversation,' muttered Hamish. 'It would clear things up so we aren't working in the flaming dark. Ma could probably solve this straight out.'

'Yes, she probably could,' said Harold on a sigh, as they waited for a gap in the heavy traffic. 'But it's Anne and my daughter I worry about, because, if our suspicions are proved right, they'll be devastated.'

'Ma will handle it. She's good like that,' said Hamish comfortably.

They dashed across the road and Harold came to a halt, wincing at the pain shooting through his ribs. 'Your mother might make out she's strong and can fight everyone's battles, but I reckon she'll be knocked sideways by this, and will find it hard to cope with the fallout.'

Hamish pursed his lips. 'You're right,' he muttered. 'My flaming sister can turn on the waterworks at the drop of a hat, and makes a bloody drama out of everything. I don't know how you put up with her, mate. You deserve a flaming medal.'

'That's as may be,' said Harold crisply, not wanting to discuss his moody, difficult wife with her brother. He ignored the pain in his ribs and began to walk again. 'Let's just hope we can find something in those papers which will protect your mother's honour and keep Wallangarra in the family. Did you bring the copy of the deeds with you?'

Hamish slapped the pocket of his long droving coat. 'In here,' he growled. 'Beryl pinned the flaming thing to the lining so I didn't bloody lose it.'

Harold didn't reply, but metaphorically took his hat off to Hamish's wife for knowing her husband so well. They reached Rum Lane and approached the front door, found it was open and went inside.

John Smithson looked ghastly, and Harold felt a twinge of remorse for dragging him away from his father's bedside. He made the introductions; the two men eyed each other warily and shook hands.

'How is Charles?'

'He was in the medical ward and asleep when I left him,' John replied, emerging from behind the reception desk. 'He's been heavily sedated, so my family and I will not be allowed to visit him until tomorrow.' He led the way into his father's office, took the key from Harold and opened the desk drawer.

Harold took possession of the thick envelope, longing to rip it open then and there to see what Christy had hidden away – but managed to restrain himself. 'Have you had any thoughts about the missing affidavit?'

John swept a weary hand over his furrowed brow. 'I've looked through everything in his desk and the filing cabinets and even went up to search through his rooms before I checked on the safety deposit box – but found nothing.' He handed over a thick brown envelope. 'While I was down there, I took the liberty of opening your box, Mr Ross, as I suspect you will have no need of it now.'

Harold couldn't quite look him in the eye as he took the envelope and stuffed it in the deep pocket of his drover's coat.

John picked up a folder from the desk and handed it to Hamish. 'I haven't had time to go through this, but it seems to contain his years of correspondence with your mother. I've added the telegraph she sent.'

Hamish opened the folder and read the telegraph, before looking at John in puzzlement. 'What does she mean by a Ballarat connection? The Brown woman lives in Adelaide, and, as far as we know, she was born and raised there.'

'Your mother met Dad in Ballarat over forty years ago,' said John wearily. 'It's the only connection I can make.' He ran a pale hand over his wan face, which was shadowed with worry and exhaustion. 'I'm sorry, but I need to get home to my family.'

Harold tucked the thick packet into his coat pocket alongside the envelope he'd brought from Bellerive, and warmly shook the man's hand. 'Thank you for everything, John,' he said fervently. 'Please give our regards to your father, and you have our sincere wishes for his swift recovery.'

'The doctor warned me it might take some time – he's an old man, and has given too much of himself to his clients and his work. He'll be coming to live with us when he's released from hospital.'

He opened the front door and handed Harold his card. 'If Christy wishes to see him on her return, she can contact me at this address.'

They shook hands again and went their separate ways at the end of Rum Lane.

'Seems like a nice enough bloke, even if he does have hands like a woman,' muttered Hamish. 'It's a shame about the old man, though, 'cos I reckon he knows as much as Ma and could have cleared this up instead of buggering about.'

Harold silently agreed with him. 'What worries me is the missing affidavit,' he replied instead. 'Charles was clearly very anxious to let me know about it, but he was too far gone to be able to tell me anything.'

'Well, it's got to be somewhere,' Hamish replied. 'Perhaps Baker's got it.'

'I was about to telephone him when you arrived.' He glanced at his new pocket watch. 'It's still early. I'll ring him now.'

As Hamish strode off to the stables to fetch his swag, Harold went into the hotel to order beer and sandwiches to be taken to his room, and then made a call to Melbourne. Baker took a long time to answer, and Harold was about to give up and ring his home when the receiver was picked up at the other end.

'Baker? It's me, Harold.'

'I'm sorry, Mr Ross, this is Mr Baker's clerk. He's had to visit a client in Echuca and will not be returning until tomorrow. Can I take a message?'

'Tell him to ring me the minute he gets in. It's urgent.' He disconnected the call and found Hamish standing beside him. 'I'm assuming you got the gist of that?' At Hamish's surly nod, he continued, 'Then let's get on and see what we find in those papers. It could be a long night.'

Hamish collected his key and followed Harold up the stairs to join him in his room. Dumping his swag in the corner, he slung his hat after it and pulled off his drover's coat. He scrabbled in the pocket, unpinned the deeds and threw them on the bed with the folder of correspondence.

'It looks like we've a fair bit of reading to do,' he muttered, eyeing the sheaf of papers Harold had taken from the large envelope to add to the things he'd found in Bellerive. 'How d'you want to go about this?'

'Why don't you make a start on the letters? They're more personal to your mother, and I wouldn't feel right about going through them.'

'You weren't so squeamish when it came to going through her safe and Dad's desk,' Hamish retorted. 'I want to see what Smithson's been hiding away.'

Harold was about to argue when the door opened and James strode in armed with a small keg of beer and a smart leather holdall, to be followed by the barmaid, who was carrying three glasses and a large serving platter heaped with sandwiches the thickness of doorsteps.

His gaze went immediately to the stack of paperwork on the bed. 'I see you finally persuaded Smithson to let you open the box,' he said, putting the keg on the table, his bag on the floor and taking off his hat and coat as the girl placed the sandwiches and glasses next to the beer. 'Have you read through it all yet?'

'We were just about to make a start. Glad you could make it,' said Harold.

'Where've you been?' growled Hamish.

'I was held up by a crisis at Yarrabinda. Clarice was rushed into hospital with a suspected miscarriage.' He tipped the barmaid and closed the door behind her, before collapsing into a nearby chair. 'It proved to be a false alarm, thank God, but she has to stay in until she's full-term. I didn't like leaving her, but she understands why, and, as her mother's close by, she's happy enough.'

'Well, you're here now,' said Hamish, impatient with domestic details he didn't find at all interesting. 'Let's get reading and see if we can get to the bottom of this mess. The sooner we sort it out, the sooner we can all go home.'

They helped themselves to the beer and sandwiches, found somewhere to sit and, having divided up the paperwork between them, began to read.

Silence fell as night closed in and documents were exchanged, exclaimed over and discussed – sometimes heatedly. By dawn, they knew enough of Christy's story to fill in many pieces of the puzzle. They sat staring at one another, their worst fears realised. The battle to retain Wallangarra and keep Christy's secret would be impossible unless that affidavit was found and proved to be the miracle they needed.

*

Aboard the SS Southern Cross

Christy had, for once, resorted to taking a sleeping powder, but her dreams had been vivid, disjointed and disturbing, and she'd woken at midnight in a tangle of sheets, her pillow damp with perspiration, her heart hammering.

There would be a vital piece of evidence missing once they opened that box, and she'd forgotten about it entirely in the initial shock of Charles's first telegraph and the ensuing trauma of facing her daughter and granddaughter. And that lapse of memory could prove fatal to the cause they were fighting.

She'd thrown off the bedclothes and got dressed, then hurried down to the purser's office and sent another telegraph to Baker and Charles, ordering them to work together to retrieve it.

Feeling a little easier, she'd returned to bed, but lay there wondering what on earth had possessed her to hide the affidavit away from the rest of the things she'd eventually put in Charles's deposit box. She had certainly not been of sound mind at the time it had been sworn; her life was in turmoil, and each day had become a struggle for survival. But as the years had gone on, she'd occasionally thought about moving it, and then deliberately put it out of her mind, never wanting to see it again or let her new life become tainted by the old one.

She must have dozed off, for, when she next opened her eyes, she discovered it was dawn. She lay there, her head feeling as if it was stuffed with cotton wool, her eyelids heavy as she watched the sky lighten and the sea turn from dark blue to turquoise. The day loomed before her and she knew she had to dredge deep to find the courage she'd need to face Anne and Kathryn. But face them she must, and she prayed silently that they would truly understand the awful situation she'd found herself in, and not think too badly of her.

She climbed out of bed and used the tiny bathroom before spending time on her face and doing her hair. She'd come to the decision that, if she looked better, she might feel more capable, and as it was quite chilly this morning, she selected a plain dress and draped her mother's shawl about her shoulders to boost her morale.

Her stewardess brought in her breakfast tray and Christy sat down at the table, determined to do the meal justice so she could face the day with a clear head.

As she ate the poached eggs and buttered toast, and drank the strong tea, she once again went over in her mind all the things she must tell them. The sequence of events was imprinted in her memory, and some of the scenes made her shiver, but Kathryn was right. This time, she must tell the unvarnished truth, leaving nothing out for fear of hurting anyone – nor glossing over things to show herself in a better light. It was her fault she'd involved her family in this mess, therefore it was up to her to explain fully what had happened to bring it about.

She finished her breakfast and took a second cup of tea out on to the deck. The wind was cool, with a hint of Australia's winter on its breath, despite the great ball of sun that was rising above the far horizon. She thought of the men back in Sydney who were, no doubt, working hard on her behalf, and could only pray that her latest telegraphs would arrive in time to help them.

Christy's thoughts were interrupted by the arrival of Kathryn and Anne, and she hurried in to greet them. She noted with deep concern that Kathryn was looking exhausted, and Anne's face was drawn and haggard, her eyes red-rimmed and her steps unsteady.

'Have you slept at all, dear?' she asked her granddaughter, as they helped a wilting Anne to a chair.

'Not much,' she admitted. 'Mother was very upset.'

'I couldn't sleep at all,' whined Anne. 'Everything kept going round in my head and at one point I thought I was going mad with all the worry.'

'Then it's time you pulled yourself together,' said Christy firmly. 'You're not alone in this, and making such a fuss isn't going to help anyone.'

Anne glared at her sullenly. 'It's all right for you,' she muttered. 'You don't suffer from your nerves.'

'And neither do you,' Christy retorted. 'But I suspect you've been getting on Kathryn's, so buck up, and stop feeling sorry for yourself.'

'I might have known I'd get no sympathy from you.' She sniffed into her handkerchief and glared balefully at her mother.

Christy ignored her. 'Kathryn, I hope you've had a good breakfast. It's always best to face a crisis on a full stomach.'

'Mother didn't feel like going down for breakfast, so I ordered something light to be brought to our room. But, to be honest, neither of us had much appetite.'

'I couldn't swallow a thing – let alone face the other passengers,' said Anne on a shudder. 'All this upset is making me quite ill.'

'Mother, please don't be so dramatic,' begged Kathryn rather sharply. 'I know this has come as a nasty shock, but it's affected us all, and you really aren't helping.'

Before Anne could reply, Christy said, 'You have asked me to tell you the reason behind this situation we've found ourselves in, so let's get on with it.'

She took a breath. 'You both know about the first couple of years my brothers and I spent in Hobart, so I will start at the point where Jamie and I arrived in Ballarat in search of Finlay, who'd left the year before to seek his fortune on the goldfields.'

Kathryn settled back on the chaise longue, and Anne kept her gaze on her lap as she dabbed at her eyes and gave pathetic little sighs.

Christy gathered her mother's shawl about her shoulders, her fingers buried in the fine old wool. 'I'd received a letter from Charles Smithson, who was an English lawyer recently arrived in Australia, telling me that Finlay had been badly injured as well as robbed, and needed help. But, by the time we got there, Finlay had left town and no one seemed to know or care where he'd gone.'

'Surely he must have had friends who would have looked out for him?' said Kathryn.

'Prospectors don't really have friends,' she replied. 'They have rivals, and although they would come together to fight for cheaper licences and a fair deal on their gold, they'd mostly spend their days alone, keeping their finds secret and jealously guarding their small plot.'

Christy decided they needed to know more about life on the diggings, so carried on, 'A man caught stealing would be judged by a kangaroo court and strung up from a tree within hours; fights broke out regularly, usually over the bar-girls or the Chinese diggers, who were increasing in vast numbers, and drunken brawls outside the pubs were commonplace. It was a hard-drinking, rough community and an unforgiving way of life back then, and very few women braved it, unless they were there to make money from the oldest profession.'

Kathryn's eyes widened. 'Goodness,' she breathed. 'You make it sound like the Wild West, but without the cowboys and Indians.'

'It was certainly wild,' she agreed, 'but in a strange way I felt at home there, and understood the urges that drove those men. Like them, I was spindrift – floating across the land in search of somewhere or something on which to settle – adrift from the ties that had bound me and free to wander at will. It was a heady feeling, that freedom, and I fully embraced it.'

'You make it sound as if you were nothing but a gypsy,' said Anne, with a sniff of disapproval.

Christy smiled. 'Maybe I was. The gypsy life suited me

then – and, although I'm content with my life now, I still enjoy seeing new places and having new experiences.'

She shifted in the chair, determined not to be sidetracked. 'You need to understand the mentality of someone who's been struck by gold fever,' she said. 'In the very early years, nuggets of gold could be picked up without any digging in places like Castlemaine, and this promise of untold wealth brought on the first great rush. Men became obsessed with finding a fortune in the silt of riverbanks and mudflats, or deep beneath the earth, where gold-bearing watercourses had been buried by centuries of silting and volcanic upheaval. But it's gruelling labour, in some of the harshest places on earth, and many soon realised that it was a foolish dream and went back home.

'But others would wander for hundreds of miles in search of it, a swag on their back, their mining equipment tied across their shoulders or the saddle of their horse. They'd spend their days digging and sifting and washing through the mud and shale, and if they were lucky, they might see the flash of gold in their pans. A few would strike it rich, but mostly it was just a nugget of a few ounces, which was soon spent on women, baccy and drink. But there was always the chance of finding the big one – and that's what kept them going.

'They abandoned any kind of civility, not caring to waste time in washing or shaving or cleaning their clothes. They forgot about their wives and children, the homes, families and jobs they'd left behind, and spent their lives wandering the most isolated places on earth in search of a dream that became more elusive with each passing year.'

'How sad,' murmured Kathryn. 'Is that what happened to Finlay?'

'He certainly caught the fever, and I suspect, like me, he felt at one with the wanderers, for every prospector I spoke to talked about the freedom of tramping the empty miles of the outback.' She took a sip of the tea, discovered it had gone cold and sour and rang the stewardess to bring some coffee.

'Did you ever find him?'

'He eventually found me,' she replied sadly. 'But it wasn't a happy reunion and he was clearly down on his luck. After a few hours, he'd disappeared again and that was the last I saw of him.'

'Perhaps he's still wandering out there,' said Kathryn. 'I hope he did find his gold in the end,' she added wistfully.

Christy doubted he was still alive, for Finlay had become a shell of the sturdy young man who'd left Hobart, and although he'd only been in his late twenties when she'd last seen him, he was shockingly unrecognisable when he'd turned up at Wallangarra.

His tangled beard had reached his waist, his boots were stuffed with paper and held together with twine, and his clothes were filthy rags that, when peeled off him, also lifted slivers of his ulcerated skin. His once-fiery hair had been bleached white by the sun, his eyes were faded and his face was as red and weathered as the ground beneath his feet. Christy blinked back the tears at the memory of how she'd begged him to stay so she could look after him, but the wanderlust had led him away again and he'd sneaked off during the night without even saying goodbye.

'He became like so many others,' she said, returning to the

present. 'Lost and destitute – but still driven by his dream. I just hope he found peace.'

The thoughtful silence was broken by the stewardess bringing their coffee; once she'd left the room, Kathryn poured it out and handed round the plates of biscuits and cake. 'I've seen some of the old lithographs of Ballarat and Bendigo and the stockade at Eureka,' she said, resuming her place on the chaise longue. 'They're in a collection at the state library. But what was it really like, Grandma?'

Christy's eyes became misty and, as she began to describe the scene, she was taken back to the past.

As the wagon rolled over the hardened earth of the main street, Charles pointed out the new buildings that were going up all through the town, and then they were heading into the emptiness of the broad, deeply red and green valley that was surrounded by rolling hills and laced with creeks and countless mining pits.

The sky was bleached of colour, the heat spreading shimmering waves across the dark red earth, making the few trees and the distant tents look as if they were standing in a great inland sea. The mournful cry of a solitary crow accompanied the jingle of harness and the creak of the wagon wheels, and high above them hovered a wedge-tailed eagle, intently searching for prey.

Christy was sweltering, despite the large black umbrella Charles had lent her, and she could feel the sweat gathering beneath her corset and running freely down her body. If she survived the day, it would be a miracle.

Charles seemed to notice her discomfort and handed her a leather water pouch. 'I would suggest you ask Mrs Harris at the Ballarat Hotel for some advice about your attire,' he said tactfully. 'She's sure to be able to find you something more suitable for the climate.'

'I can't afford to buy clothes,' she replied fretfully, embarrassed to be having this conversation with a man she'd only just met.

'I'm sure she'll lend you something,' he replied. 'Myrtle Harris is very good like that. Handy with the needle, too, and makes a good living out of making clothes for the girls at the Red Rooster Saloon.' He saw her frown. 'It's a bar that caters for a certain trade,' he explained, going red with embarrassment.

'We won't be here long enough to worry about clothes,' said Jamie. 'Once we've found Finlay, we're going back to Melbourne.'

Charles raised his eyebrows. 'Oh. But I thought you had work here – and of course it might be some time before we can discover where Finlay has gone.'

'It's good of you to let us stay at your place,' said Jamie, 'and I'm grateful for the work, but if Finlay can't be found, then me and my sister are going back to Melbourne.'

Christy had already noticed the opportunities here for making money, and had swiftly become entranced by the grandeur and wildness of the place. The thought of going back to a crowded, noisy Melbourne didn't enthral her. 'What if I don't want to go back there?' she challenged.

'Then I'll go on my own.' He folded his arms and returned her challenge with a steady gaze.

Christy experienced a flutter of panic at the thought of being left here on her own, and then decided to ignore his threat for now. He was still clearly in a bad mood and she didn't want to rouse him further by arguing. Thankfully, Charles seemed to realise it wouldn't be wise to say anything, and concentrated on steering the horse around the tree stumps and creeks and the deep pits that littered the enormous valley.

She looked out to the forest of tents that seemed to stretch for miles, and, as they drew nearer, she saw roughly built shacks, which served as shops or bars, and makeshift shelters made of bark and flattened kerosene cans dotted amongst them. Some shelters were simple domed affairs, made out of intertwined willow and weatherproofed with reeds, mud and bark – which, she learned later, were called 'humpies'.

There were tents formed from strips of tarpaulin stretched over a tree branch and tethered to the ground with wooden pegs and lengths of rope, while others had once been white and were rather grand. Everything was stained by the red dust that blew across the valley in swirls, and the leaves on the few eucalyptus trees that had survived shivered like silver coins in the hot breeze.

Christy realised that this city of tents was an industrious one, for men were panning in the rivers and creeks, or hauling muck up from the deep pits in great wooden boxes to be emptied into what Charles said were cradles, then sifted and washed. Nobody took any notice of them as the horse pulled them deeper into the camp, and she listened with interest as Charles explained about panning and sluice boxes and cradles.

He pointed across to a low rise. 'That's Bakery Hill,' he said. 'It's where the miners met, back in December 1854, to swear allegiance to the flag of the Southern Cross – and over there are the remains of the Eureka stockade, where they fought against the police and government troops. Those who weren't killed were arrested, and the ones who managed to escape had a price on their head – but their stand against an unfair justice system has become a beacon of hope for the working man. They stood up for the right to earn a living without being penalised by heavy licence fees or fines, and the trade union movement is now growing all across Australia.'

'You certainly know more about the history than I do,' she said.

'I made a point of reading all I could about Australia when I first arrived. I'll lend you my books, if you like. They are interesting.'

'What's that, over there?' she asked, pointing to what looked like an enormous wooden fortress.

'They're the remains of the old government camp. Some of the buildings are still being used by troopers because this place needs policing quite stringently. The latest problems are with the number of Chinese coming in, and they're getting edgy about having to pay a premium to prospect.'

He pulled on the reins and the horse came to a stop. 'Joe should be around here somewhere,' he said, helping her down.

She brushed the dust from her dress, discovered it was a waste of time and looked about her. Joseph O'Driscoll had set up camp in the shade of gum and coolibah trees. His home was a strip of canvas stretched between four poles, with sacking for walls and a strip of fly-net for a door, and his washing line was a length of rope stretched between the tree trunks. A rough-hewn wooden truckle bed, table and chair were his only furniture, and outside this makeshift dwelling was a ring of stones surrounding the ashes of a fire, upon which sat a billycan full of some dark liquid. On closer inspection, she saw dead flies and ants floating on the murky surface and shuddered.

As Charles wandered off to find Joseph and the flies buzzed annoyingly about their heads, Jamie kicked at the ashes and grunted. 'We were better off than this back on Skye,' he muttered. 'You'd have to be mad to live like this.'

'That's what the gold fever does to you, to be sure,' said the smiling man who was approaching them. 'And I'll be thanking you not to kick ash in me tea.'

Christy turned sharply at the sound of his lilting voice and was captured by a pair of dark blue, twinkling eyes. His hair was so black it glinted blue like a jay's wing in the bright sun as he took off his broad-brimmed hat and ran a handkerchief over his strong-boned face. His brows were as dark and thick as his eyelashes and beard, and his clothes, although worn and dirty, hung from his well-shaped body with a strange air of elegance.

'This is Joseph O'Driscoll,' said Charles, making the introductions.

'Ach, to be sure, there's no need to be formal,' he replied, shaking their hands. 'Joe will do. Would you be wanting some tea, Miss MacInnes? You look awful hot in that get-up.'

Christy nodded, unable to speak, for she couldn't tear her eyes from him as his grin revealed even white teeth and the suggestion of a dimple in his cheek.

''Tis bush tea: thick, black and strong, with a eucalyptus leaf and sugar to give it body,' he said, squatting down and raking through the ashes. He peered into the billycan and grimaced 'Though, I'm thinking there could be more bodies than necessary, but I can soon get them out.'

Christy shuddered at the thought of drinking that disgusting-looking brew, but was too polite and overawed to refuse his offer.

'Why don't you sit in the shade, Christy?' Charles took her arm and led her to the chair beneath the trees. 'You'll find it's a bit cooler here, and the flies shouldn't be so worrisome.'

Christy brushed away the flies that were constantly settling on her face and buzzing about her straw hat and black umbrella. She was so hot, she thought she'd begin to melt, and her clothes were soaked through, the corset chafing her skin. Yet, for all her discomfort, she had eyes only for Joe.

She sat in the shade and watched as he chatted to Jamie and Charles and set fresh kindling alight. He moved with the grace of a dancer, she noted, his long limbs perfectly in tune with his body as he busied himself at the fire and studiously ignored her.

She fidgeted in the chair, wanting to look into his eyes again and have the light of his smile shine on her – and yet she was confused by her feelings, for it hadn't been long since she'd been crying into her pillow for Peter Keller.

Deciding the heat had addled her brain, she set aside those disturbing stirrings and tried to concentrate on the reason they were here. 'I understand it was you who found my brother, Mr . . . er . . . Joe.'

'To be sure, I did, and 'twas a terrible shock, for he was lying down there all broken and bent. I'm only glad I found him before it was too late – he was awful injured.'

The thickly lashed eyes settled on her and his gaze seemed to penetrate to her very core. 'But we have a good doctor here and he put him back together again, and, to be sure, Myrtle Harris is a fine nurse, so she is.' He flashed a grin that did strange things to her insides and then turned back to the fire to stir the simmering tea with a length of twig and pick out the dead insects with a tin spoon.

'Do you have any idea where he could have gone?' she managed through a throat that had mysteriously tightened.

Joe sat back on his haunches and packed tobacco into his clay pipe. 'Well, now, 'tis my belief he could be anywhere,' he drawled, before striking a match on the flat heel of his boot and lighting the tobacco. He drew on the pipe and blew a stream of smoke into the air. 'There's gold to be found all over this wonderful country, and Finlay was determined to find his share.'

'But he had found his share,' retorted Christy. 'And it was stolen from him the day of his so-called accident.'

The blue eyes suddenly lost their twinkle and the dark brows met above the long, straight nose. 'Would you be questioning me about that, wee girl?' he asked softly.

'Not at all,' she said hastily. 'It's just a bit too convenient that his ladder should break and his gold should disappear while he's lying hurt at the bottom of the shaft.'

'Aye, I was thinking the same t'ing,' he replied with a solemn nod. 'Charles and I discussed it, but there's little trust in this place and, without any evidence, there's nothing we can do about it.'

'What happened to his claim? He would have paid the licence for it, and if it yielded gold, then it must be valuable.'

'He gave the licence to me,' he said. 'Charles was there when he handed it over. Finlay hadn't thought he'd make the night, you see.'

'But he did,' said Christy. 'So why didn't you give it back to him?'

'Ach, to be sure, the man was gone before I managed to get into town again. If he'd wanted it back, he knew where to find me. He was my mate and only had to ask.'

Christy frowned, for she knew her brother well enough to realise that he would never have given up on a shaft all the while it was yielding well. 'Have you since found more gold, Joe?' she asked tentatively.

'Aye, there's some down there, but no great amount.' He dug into his pocket and held up a small nugget to the sun, so that it glinted. 'Would you be after accepting this as a wee gift to welcome you to Ballarat, Miss MacInnes?'

She didn't know what to say, but before she could reply, he'd tossed it on to her lap. 'Thank you,' she stuttered. 'But you didn't have to – '

'Ach, to be sure, Finlay would have done the same.' He poured the viscous tea into tin mugs and handed them round. 'Be careful, now,' he warned as he leaned over her. ''Tis hot and you might scald your wee fingers.'

She blushed scarlet as he looked deeply into her eyes, and only released the breath she'd been holding when he turned away. Was he really talking about the tea, or was it a subtle warning that it wouldn't be wise to pry any further? Either way, she found he disturbed her, and she wasn't at all sure if she could trust him.

'I've asked everyone round here if they know anything,' he said to Charles, 'but you know what they're like – tight-lipped to a man, whether they know anything or not. If he was well enough to leave, then he could be miles away by now.'

'I did warn Christy that might be the case,' said Charles solemnly. He blew on the tea, took a tentative sip and scalded his lip. 'But he knows I wrote to his sister, so all we can hope is that he'll come back to see her.'

'Well, 'twould be a fine t'ing, but I'd not put a wager on it,' Joe muttered. 'Finlay made it plain he didn't want his family here.' He looked across at Christy. 'To be sure, I'm sorry, wee girl. But it's best to know the truth of t'ings.'

Christy wondered if she had been told the truth, but as Charles seemed to be backing him up, she supposed she had to believe him.

He turned to Jamie, who'd come back from wandering around the nearby tents. 'And what about you? D'ye fancy seeking the gold?'

Jamie shook his head and sat down on the ground to drink from the tin mug. 'It's not for me. I'm a carpenter and I'll make my fortune in Melbourne.'

Joe laughed and clapped a hand on Jamie's shoulder. 'Aye, 'tis a grand place, so it is – and there's plenty with money there. To be sure, I've seen the ladies in their fine clothes and jewellery – and the men in their carriages drawn by high-stepping thoroughbreds. The gold has made people richer than they ever could have imagined – and they can't spend their money quick enough.'

'Have you found gold?'

'To be sure, I have,' he whispered, 'but it's best not to talk too loud – these trees have ears.' He swallowed down the piping-hot tea and threw the dregs on to the fire, which made the flames hiss. 'I wish you well,' he said, 'but the day is wasting and I need to be getting back to me digging. Give Melbourne my regards, wee girl, and kiss a few of those lovely ladies for me, Jamie.'

Christy somehow managed not to blurt out that she'd be staying in Ballarat, and, having bobbed a curtsy, hurried after her brother and Charles to the wagon.

She emerged from the past and discovered that her coffee had gone cold and the others had eaten all the cake and biscuits. It was with some shock that she realised it was almost midday, so she rang the stewardess again and ordered luncheon to be served in her stateroom at one.

'Charles sounds very nice,' said Kathryn. 'You were lucky to have found a good friend you could trust. But Joe sounds a bit of a rogue, with all that Irish charm.'

'He certainly was,' she replied, 'and I still have that nugget of gold. You see, it didn't feel right to use it, as Finlay hadn't given it to me, so I have it tucked away in a box at home, with a couple of other mementoes of that time.' She thought about the hessian bag containing those thirty silver coins and made a concerted effort to set the memory of them aside for now.

'You clearly must have stayed, but what about Jamie?' Anne

asked. 'Did he really leave you there and go back to Melbourne?'

'He left eventually, but I made him help set up my business first.'

Anne regarded her suspiciously. 'And what was that? I do hope you're not going to tell us you became a bar girl – I really don't think I could bear hearing that.'

'Do give me some credit, Anne,' she replied crossly. 'Not that I bear any malice towards those girls – they worked hard and had to put up with the most terrible things to earn their money. And I admired the way they accepted what they had to do and just got on with it with the best of spirits.'

'Well, really,' gasped Anne.

'Yes, really,' she replied. 'In fact, I became great friends with all of them – especially a French girl called Nadine. She was only two years older than me, but her husband used to beat her, so she ran away, was taken in by Nellie Simpson and ended up working in her saloon bar, the Red Rooster.' She gave a sigh of regret. 'I really missed her when she was killed, for she was a good friend, with a wonderful sense of humour that would have me in stitches.'

'How did she die?' asked Kathryn.

'One of Madam Nellie's customers was a real brute, and she usually fixed him up with Big Sadie, who knew how to handle him. But Sadie had done a flit the previous night, and the other girls were busy, so Nadine had to take care of him. He ended up beating her to death.' Her voice broke. 'Poor Nadine, she'd escaped one brute only to be killed by another – and I still think about her with deep affection, even after all these years.'

'Good grief,' said Anne with a shudder. 'I cannot believe you were friendly with people like that.'

Christy shrugged. 'You make friends where you find them, and with so few women on the diggings, we were thrown together. The people weren't all bad. I soon learned to keep away from the ones that were, and with Charles and Joe watching over me, I felt safe enough.'

'So how did you make your fortune, Grandma?' urged an impatient Kathryn.

'From the first moment I went to the diggings, I was as drawn to the possibility of making my fortune as those miners were. But I had no intention of grubbing in the earth for my gold, or following the rumours of a rich reef out in the desert – I wanted to be paid in gold.' She smiled. 'I managed to persuade Jamie to stay on long enough to build me a shack, out on the edges of the Eureka fields, and to furnish it with the bare essentials. He paid my first year's licence fee with what he'd earned at the hotel, and I opened up a camp kitchen and laundry.'

'A laundry?' gasped Anne in horror.

Christy shrugged. 'It was an honest living and provided what was needed, and the men felt better with clean clothes and a decent meal in their stomachs.'

She smiled at the memory of that rough shack, where she'd lived in a back room with a sturdy bolt on the door and bars on the windows, and had spent her days working over a hot stove and vast tubs of boiling water that had to be heated over a fire outside. Washing lines were strung between the gum trees at the back, and when the hot winds blew – which they did frequently – there was always a mad rush to get everything in before it was covered in red dust.

When it was clear she couldn't cope with the mounting work on her own, she'd managed to persuade the young daughter of one of the bar girls to come in to do the ironing. It wasn't pleasant work in that awful heat, but it was better than earning a wage on her back, and when Christy had left Ballarat, she'd sold the business to her at a knock-down price. On her return, many years later, the shack had become a flourishing hotel, and the girl was a respectable matron, with four strapping sons and a husband who was an important member of the local council.

She blinked away the images. 'Charles came out to check up on me twice a week and Joe called in most evenings, but I was doing very well. The main currency was gold, and Madam Nellie advised me to buy scales to weigh the nuggets and a tiny pick to chip off the right amount, so I wouldn't be accused of cheating my customers – and, by the end of the first year, I had a very healthy bank balance.

'I used some of the money to pay someone to extend the shack to provide clean accommodation for those who didn't want to camp, and, for a shilling and nine pence a night, or half an ounce of gold, they got a clean bed, evening meal and breakfast.'

'Weren't you frightened of sharing your home with rough men?' asked Kathryn.

'I had a good bolt on my door and there were bars at the window. It felt a bit like a prison, to be honest, but on the whole the men were respectful, knowing that I wasn't a loose woman and that they'd be thrown out the minute they caused trouble – and, of course, Joe's regular presence was a good deterrent.'

'You fell in love with him, didn't you?' Kathryn regarded her evenly.

Christy nodded. 'He was easy to fall in love with – could charm the birds out of the trees, and had a way of looking after you that made you feel protected and special.' She gave a deep sigh. 'He could also tell wonderful stories about Ireland and make me laugh – and that made him hugely attractive to a lonely young girl who missed her family and was still getting over a youthful love affair.'

'I'm sorry, Grandma, but I have to ask. Was Joe my grandfather?'

Christy looked across at Anne before replying. 'Yes, he was – and I was besotted enough to think we'd spend the rest of our days together.'

'So, why didn't you?' Anne's voice was strained and there were high spots of colour on her cheeks.

'Joe had secrets, Anne,' she said softly. 'And those secrets were only revealed after it was too late for me to turn back the clock.'

As Anne was about to question her further, she raised her hand. 'Luncheon will be here in a minute, and the tale is too long and complicated to tell in a hurry. Besides, I need a rest – returning to the past is proving quite exhausting.'

20

Hamish and James had gone to their rooms to catch up on their sleep after the long, emotionally draining night of going through their mother's most private papers and discovering that, far from being helpful to their cause, they seemed to confirm Thomasina Brown's claims of kinship and the right to a share of Wallangarra.

Harold was sprawled across his bed, the double doors leading out on to the veranda thrown wide to get rid of the stink of pipe and cigar smoke and the pungent smell of spilled beer. There was a chill wind coming through the doors and the noise from the street below was making it impossible to sleep properly, but he was too tired and stiff to move, so he pulled up the blanket and buried his head beneath his pillow.

He was just dozing off again when he was startled by someone hammering on the bedroom door. 'Go away,' he shouted.

'You got a telephone call,' shouted the landlord.

'Righto. Coming.' Harold swore softly as he dragged himself

off the bed, pulled on his clothes and hurried out to the landing. Almost falling down the stairs in his rush, he ignored the landlord's knowing look and took the receiver. 'Hello. Who is this?'

'It's Baker. You asked me to ring as a matter of urgency.'

Harold took a moment to clear the fog of weariness and beer from his aching head. 'Do you know anything about an affidavit Christy might have left with you?'

'She's sworn several over the years. Which one are you referring to?'

Harold gripped the receiver. Baker could be dense at times. 'The one to do with the things we're working on at the moment,' he said through gritted teeth.

'I don't have anything to do with that time,' he replied through the static. 'It must be with Smithson. He was dealing with her affairs then.'

Harold quickly explained about Smithson's illness. 'He's out of the picture now, and his son isn't a solicitor and knows nothing. But it's vital, Baker. We have to find it.'

'Well, I don't have it, and it certainly wasn't among the papers in her safe when we were applying for probate. What's the significance of it? Surely you have enough to refute the claim now you've opened that security box?'

'What we found doesn't help our case at all,' Harold said carefully, all too aware that the landlord was pretending to sweep the front step as he listened in. 'In fact, it's the opposite. I have no idea what's in that affidavit, but Charles seemed to think it was very important.'

'I'm sorry, Harold, I wish I could help you, but I honestly don't think I can. I'll go through everything in her file, just to make sure, but don't hold your breath.' There was a pause and, when he spoke again, his tone was worried. 'I've had a telegraph from her asking me all sorts of questions, which I've had to answer. By now, she knows the who, the why and the when, and I can only hope she comes up with something that might help us.'

'I'll send a telegraph this morning to ask about the missing document. There should be time for her to reply before everything comes to a head.'

'Are her sons with you?'

'Yes.'

'So, when do you expect to be leaving Sydney? The hearing is in a week's time and we have to get to Adelaide before then.'

'I am aware of that,' said Harold tightly, 'but if we don't find that damned thing, we're doomed. Can't you persuade Brown's solicitors to give us more time?'

'Sorry, no. They know they've got us on the ropes, and won't budge.'

Harold gave a sharp sigh of frustration. 'Right. Then we'll just have to bluff it out, for, the way things stand, we're on the losing side. Look for that affidavit, Baker, and I'll send that telegraph.'

He disconnected the call and plodded back up the stairs to fetch his hat and coat. There was little point in waking the brothers, for he had nothing new to tell them.

Returning some time later from the telegraph office, he slumped down on the bed, overcome by a sense of failure. He'd let Christy down, and he could do no more. The only option open

to him now was to hide everything they'd uncovered and offer
the Brown woman enough money to silence and get rid of her –
and the thought made him feel sick.

*

Aboard the SS Southern Cross

Luncheon had been a desultory affair and the elaborate food had
mostly been left on the plates. They sat in silence as the stewardess brought in fresh coffee and cleared everything away.

Christy needed to stretch her legs, so she left them drinking
the coffee and went for a brisk walk, twice round the deck. She
was coming to the hardest part of her story, for the telling of it
would hurt her daughter and shatter any illusion she might have
had about the man who'd fathered her. She slowed and leaned
on the railings, staring out to sea, reluctant to go back into that
stateroom to face her.

Joseph O'Driscoll had stolen her heart with his winning ways,
his smile and his soft, lilting voice, but, in the end, he'd broken
her heart, and she'd paid a heavy price – one that was now to be
passed on to the next generation. She gave a deep sigh and headed
back the way she'd come. They would be in Melbourne within
days, and she could only pray that her telegraphs had arrived and
were being acted upon.

'Excuse me, madam, but this has just arrived for you.'

Startled from her thoughts, she took the telegraph from the
young officer and, with a muttered thanks, ripped it open. It was
from Baker, stating the bald facts of Thomasina Brown's claims

and the hearing due to take place two days after the ship had called into Adelaide. There was no mention of the affidavit, and she screwed up the telegraph in frustration. Surely he must have received her urgent instructions regarding it by now?

Instead of heading for her stateroom, she quickly went down to the purser's office to see if it was possible to telephone Baker. He was polite but firm: such a communication was not possible – so she sent off a terse telegraph instead, and, with a growing sense of panic, returned to her stateroom.

Anne and Kathryn were talking quietly as she entered, and they both looked up at her expectantly. Christy went straight to the bottle of brandy and poured a large measure, which she swallowed in two gulps.

'Good heavens,' breathed Anne. 'Whatever's the matter?'

Christy told them about the details in the telegraph. 'And, before you ask, I have never met Thomasina Brown, and have absolutely no idea how she's come to the conclusion that she has a right to claim against Wallangarra, but, if Baker does as I ask, he should be able to put an end to it.'

Christy plumped down in a chair and threw the crumpled telegraph on the table. 'I wish the man would hurry up and reply – all this uncertainty is putting me on edge,' she muttered.

'So,' murmured Kathryn, 'without that document, we'll have to attend the hearing and everything will become public knowledge.' She gave a deep sigh. 'This whole trip has been ruined, but I'm more concerned about how it's affected you and Mother, and I wish I could do something – anything – to help.'

'Bless you, darling; there's nothing anyone can do, and, as it was all my fault this mess arose in the first place, I only have myself to blame.'

She quickly explained why that particular document wasn't with the rest, and then poured a cup of strong black coffee to counteract the effects of the brandy. She needed a clear head to carry on with her woeful tale, and now it was more important than ever that her daughter and granddaughter knew every last detail, so they'd be prepared for what lay ahead.

Anne was close to tears again as Kathryn tightly held her hand. 'It's a nightmare,' she said tremulously. 'I can't bear to think what we might have to face when we get home.'

'Whatever it is, Mother, we'll face it together – as a family.'

Christy silently wished her daughter would pull herself together and stop whining, but she said nothing as she found her yet another clean handkerchief and settled down to tell them the next part of her story.

'The goldfields weren't all work and no play,' she began. 'There were dances and horse races and impromptu parties, as well as all the fun of going to listen to the travelling preachers and heckle them. How we got up the energy to dance after a long day's labour, I don't know. I suppose we had the energy and stamina of youth and needed to let off steam.

'Charles saw himself as my protector now Jamie had left and I was alone, and as the months rolled by, he began to visit more often, always with a little gift of sweetmeats, a ribbon for my hair or a feather for my Sunday bonnet.' She gave a wry smile. 'Joe didn't like it, of course; the two men were chalk and cheese, and merely tolerated one another because of me and their tenuous link with Finlay. I tried to ease the situation by insisting that Charles was my friend and he was just being thoughtful. Joe told me I was being naïve and that Charles was clearly trying to court me and steal me from under his nose. We had a terrific row about it.'

'But he was right, wasn't he?' said Kathryn. 'Charles wanted you for himself.'

Christy nodded. 'I knew that, and when it became obvious that there was a growing enmity between them, I had to face Charles and try to let him down as gently as possible. It was a hard thing to do, for he was such a lovely, kind man, who wore his heart on his sleeve, but I simply couldn't feel about him the way he wanted me to.'

Christy's hand was shaking and the coffee cup rattled against the saucer. 'He was bitterly hurt and told me that I was a fool to fall for a man like Joe. He even hinted that Joe was up to no good and could have been involved in Finlay's accident – or at least the theft of his gold. But I refused to believe him, thinking it was his disappointment making him so vicious, and told him to leave me and Joe alone – that we didn't need him spoiling everything.'

She felt the prick of tears at the memory of his doleful eyes and sad expression, and the way he'd left her with his shoulders drooping, his feet stumbling over the rough ground. 'I wanted to take back those harsh words when I saw how much I'd hurt him, and to assure him that I did care for him as a good and loyal friend and that I was sorry. But Joe came round the corner, swept me up in his arms in a kiss and, when I next looked, Charles had gone.'

Christy's voice broke and she hastily cleared her throat,

determined to get through this without breaking down. 'Charles avoided me after that and, within the month, he'd closed his office and left town. I learned much later that he'd gone to Adelaide – but it was the fact that he'd never even said goodbye that really hurt, and I suppose he did that deliberately to punish me for all the pain I'd caused him.'

'It felt so strange not to be able to confide in him, or enjoy his company, and so I turned more and more to Joe. And, as I look back now, I can see that was when things started to get out of control.'

Christy remembered that soft summer night a few weeks after Charles had left. The stars were so bright and numerous, it felt as if you could reach up and pluck them from the sky. There had been stars in her eyes, too, as she and Joe had danced to the lovely romantic music coming from the newly built house that had been raised that day. And when he'd slipped that cheap little ring on her finger and asked her to marry him, she'd thought her world was complete.

'Joe proposed shortly after Charles left, and I accepted. He gave me a ring he'd hammered out of a strip of tin, promising me that he'd buy me a proper one before our wedding, and he told me that he'd heard about a property going for a song out near Quilpie, where we could settle down and raise beef cattle along with our children.

'I hadn't thought about leaving Ballarat, or giving up my flour-ishing business, but the idea of starting somewhere new with him began to take hold and, as he talked about the adventurous life we'd have and the great investment it would be, I was slowly persuaded, and actually began to get really excited by the idea.'

Christy fell silent, remembering how he'd coaxed her into agreeing to sell her business, and how he'd shown her the gold he'd recently found, which would be his share of the cost of buying the cattle station and restocking the herd.

'I didn't know the first thing about raising cattle,' she said, 'but Joe assured me that he'd worked on a station before the gold rush and knew enough to get us started, and that we'd employ experienced men to help run the place. I'm ashamed to admit that I was too dazzled and in lust to think straight – let alone stop and give the consequences of doing such a thing proper consideration. So when he told me, some days later, that he'd sent a telegraph to the owners with an offer to buy, and they'd accepted, I was as excited as he was, and set about finalising the sale of my business.

'Joe was in a tearing hurry for us to get married and start our new lives on Wallangarra, so he arranged our wedding with one of the travelling preachers who'd just come into town.'

Anne raised her eyebrows. 'It strikes me he was in too much of a hurry, and that you were extremely foolish to let him force you into things so quickly.'

'I realise that now, but I had no one to advise me – and even if Charles had been there, I probably wouldn't have listened to him,' she said sadly.

'So you slept with him,' said Anne baldly. 'And, no doubt, he disappeared shortly afterwards.'

'I did sleep with him,' she replied, the colour rising in her face, 'but he didn't leave me, and we had a wedding ceremony.'

'You married him?' gasped Anne. 'But I thought . . . You said . . .'

'I know I did, and I wasn't lying, Anne. Just hear me out, dear, and you'll understand better.'

The stateroom faded and she was drawn back to the sights and sounds of the mining town.

It was a hot summer day and the preacher's tent had been erected on the outskirts of Ballarat. The mood in the town was happy, for it was rare to celebrate a wedding in a place where there were so few women, and it seemed to Christy that the whole population had turned out – even some of the Chinese.

Madam Nellie and her girls provided a horse and trap for her to arrive in, and decked it with paper flowers, tinkling bells and ribbons. Myrtle Harris had been an absolute magician to make her dress so quickly from a roll of buttery yellow muslin Christy had bought from a travelling salesman, and had lined it with white cotton to keep her modesty in the glaring sun.

Myrtle also dressed her hair, weaving ribbons and wild flowers through the curls before helping her to get ready for her big day. With a bouquet of wild kangaroo paw, red bottlebrush and pale pink kurrajong flowers, Christy nervously went out on to the boardwalk to the loud cheers of those who'd come to watch, and, after a short ride in the trap with Myrtle's husband, Fred, who was giving her away, she arrived at the vast tent, which had been decorated with bunting and Christmas tinsel.

'Are you sure about this, girlie?' Fred asked in his strong Cockney accent.

'Oh, yes,' she breathed. 'I've never been more sure of anything. I just wish Charles and my brothers were here.'

'I reckon they're missing out on a rare sight,' he said. 'You look lovely, darlin'; that Joe's a lucky bloke.'

As they stepped inside the enormous tent, Madam Nellie crashed a loud chord on the out-of-tune piano she'd had carted over from her saloon, and the packed congregation turned to look as Christy walked down the makeshift aisle between the many rows of wooden benches. She recognised the preacher, who was a regular visitor to the town – and was known to be a hellfire and damnation man, and one of Madam Nellie's best customers – but her eyes were only for Joe, who was standing tall and handsome in his borrowed suit, waiting for her by the table that was being used as an altar.

The preacher was clearly delighted to have such a captive audience and got quite carried away with his rousing sermon exhorting all to admit to being unworthy sinners who sup with the Devil in the sure knowledge that they'll burn in hell for eternity.

After a few minutes of this, Joe leaned forward. 'This is a wedding, my friend. Not the end of the world. Will you be toning it down and getting on with it?'

He toned it down and got on with it and, once they'd said their vows and kissed, quickly sent one of his acolytes round with a bucket to collect the offerings from his unusually large audience.

Christy and Joe signed the register and were given a fancy certificate to say they were now husband and wife. Madam Nellie fumbled her way through a jolly music-hall number as Joe led Christy back down the aisle to thunderous cheers and applause, and the moment they stepped outside, they were almost knocked flat by the stampede for the hotel, where the reception was being held. Weddings were a thirsty business, especially when the temperature soared to almost a hundred degrees, as it had done in that tent.

Christy laughed and clung to Joe, looking up at him, hardly daring to believe that someone so handsome and wonderful could possibly be her husband.

Joe kissed her lightly on the lips and swung her up into his arms. 'You're a beautiful bride,' he murmured against her cheek, 'and I'll be showing you off to every last person in this town.'

Christy felt so safe in his arms as he carried her down the main street to the shouts of congratulations and the raucous whistles and yells from some of the miners who'd already been well refreshed with the home-made grog they brewed in a secret still, hidden in the bush.

Joe carried her up the steps to the Ballarat Hotel veranda and carefully set her on her feet before he was carted off by his mates into the bar and Christy was surrounded by Nellie's girls, who chattered like rosella parakeets, excited by the wedding and relieved to have a rare day off.

Christy fell silent as she remembered how they'd enviously cooed over her dress and told her how lucky she was to get a man like Joe, and how she'd thought she glimpsed a familiar face in the great gathering on the boardwalk as the girls giggled and exchanged coarse jokes about her wedding night.

She'd stood on tiptoe, searching wildly through the shifting, rowdy mob for that dear face she'd thought she'd never see again, but when the gathering surged into the hotel in answer to the clanging tucker bell, there was no sign of him. It was with a profound sense of disappointment that she realised she'd been mistaken – and she'd also been very foolish to think he'd be here when he'd made it perfectly clear that he wanted nothing to do with her.

Christy blinked away the scene that was running through her head and realised her daughter and granddaughter were both looking perplexed. Not wanting to break the flow of her story, she didn't wait for them to ask the questions she knew they wanted answers to, and hurried on.

'We stayed the night in my old rooming house, which felt very strange now I was no longer in charge, and, after a good breakfast, we fetched the horses and loaded up Joe's wagon. It took us over a week to get to Quilpie, and almost another half day to reach the homestead at Wallangarra; having slept on the ground beneath a strip of canvas for all that time, I was longing for a hot bath and a decent bed to sleep in.'

'Was it the same then as it is now?' asked Anne.

'Far from it,' Christy replied flatly. 'The place was owned by an elderly couple who could no longer manage. The homestead was nothing more than a series of wooden shacks cobbled together within a wrap-around veranda that was so rotten it was all but falling down. The fly-screens were broken and useless, and the roof was rusty corrugated iron that hadn't been patched or replaced for years.'

She gave a sigh. 'They were including the furniture in the sale of the place, but that turned out to be riddled with termites and only fit for a bonfire. The cattle had been sold and the farm machinery had been left to rust and rot in the tumbledown sheds, and the windmill was so ancient it could barely draw up the water from the bore.'

'I'm amazed you went through with buying it,' said Kathryn.

'I very nearly didn't. In fact, Joe and I had a terrible argument about it as we rode over the property and saw how far it had been left to go wild, and how much work it would take to get it up and running again. And, don't forget, I knew absolutely nothing about farming, so I was being faced with an uphill struggle before I even began.'

'So, why did you buy it?' Anne asked.

'We had nowhere else to go and I didn't want to go back to the goldfields. I'd seen what it could do to men who got the fever, and I didn't want that for me and Joe – or the baby that I suspected I was already carrying.'

She glanced at Anne before she carried on. 'Joe haggled the price right down and persuaded the old couple that no one else would give them a better offer. I felt sorry for them, but knew we'd need every penny of our savings to put the place right, as well as restock it. They agreed in the end, and we went into Charleville to sign the papers.'

Christy found that her mouth was dry and her hand not quite steady as she poured some water into a glass. She took a moment to drink and get her thoughts in order.

'It was only after we'd both signed the papers that Joe confessed he didn't have quite as much money as he'd said, and suggested that I pay for the property and he would use the last of his savings on restocking the herd and buying the essentials we'd need to survive until we were up and running.'

She took a trembling breath. 'I was shocked by his confession, for I'd seen the gold he'd found, but he convinced me that he'd spent a great deal of it paying for our wedding and covering the expense of buying a wagon, spare horses and stores enough to see us through the first month. I was trapped in that office with signed deeds, a suspicious solicitor, two old people waiting to be paid and nowhere to run. So I went to the bank – escorted by the solicitor – and, after an interminable wait for the telegraph from their Eureka branch, handed over the money.'

'Did he do as he promised and buy cattle?'

'We had to make the house habitable first, and we spent every waking hour mending and building and clearing out the spiders, snakes and scorpions. We were lucky in that we had plenty of timber in the bushland that surrounded us, but the tools the old people had left behind were useless, so we had to buy new. Weevils infested our rice and flour, and our sugar was eaten by rats, ants and marauding wombats and possums. Our stores ran out, so we had to buy fresh, along with sturdy metal barrels to keep it all in, and then we discovered that the termites were eating away at the new posts beneath our house.

'Joe managed to use the metal from the discarded bits of machinery we found in the barn to make caps for the posts, but with the summer wet season came the mosquitoes and flies, so we had to buy new netting for the windows and doors, and fix proper guttering and downpipes to take the run-off away from the house to fill the water butts. By the time the windmill had been fixed and Anne was born, Joe's pot of money had run out and we were living off my savings.'

'But why didn't you just sell up and buy something smaller in town?' asked Kathryn. 'It sounds as if you were living hand to mouth – and, with a newborn baby to feed, you must have been frantic.'

'The place was still in no state to try and sell – and no one would have wanted it, anyway,' she replied. 'And, yes, we were frantic – me, because I now had Anne to look after, and Joe, because his dreams of making it as a rich cattleman had come to nothing.'

'What did you do?' asked Anne.

'I went into Charleville, got some advice from a neighbourly farmer and spent a large raft of my savings on some good breeding cattle from the stock pens. With the help of his drovers, we got them in the one field we'd managed to clear of poisonous weed, and the men quickly fixed up one of their spare windmills to draw water from the newly dug bore into the troughs.'

'It sounds like you took on the responsibility of the place. What was Joe doing whilst you were running everything?' asked Anne.

'The rains had made the grass grow thick and high, which was a magnet for the local kangaroo and wallaby population, so I got Joe to cut more wood and I bought strong wire netting so we could make a roo fence high enough to keep them out.'

She paused to consider how best to answer Anne's question. 'Joe had lost heart in the project and was constantly moody and complaining – even threatening to leave to follow the rumour of gold at Avoca, in Victoria. I think he was finding it too restricting in that small house, with an exhausted wife and crying baby, and had begun to yearn for the freedom of a single man and the excitement of looking for gold.'

'So, did he leave you stranded out there?' asked Anne fretfully.

'Not immediately,' she replied. 'Once the pasture was secure, my money was almost gone, and, without funds of his own, Joe could go nowhere. I copied the local Aborigine women by tying Anne to my back with a length of cloth, and I rode into town and got a job cooking at the pub, whilst Joe looked after the cattle.'

She grinned at their horrified expressions. 'It was a rough place and the work was hard, but I was used to that, and at least I met people, made friends and had a bit of life, as well as a few bob in my pocket.

'It was whilst I was working there that I persuaded the landlord to let me experiment with goat-meat stew – Wallangarra was still plagued by the darn things – and it proved to be such a success, I was doing regular round-ups. I butchered and skinned them, sold the meat to the pub and the skins to a tanner. The nannies produced good rich milk, so I kept two, with a tame billy, and Anne thrived. It was an acquired taste, I grant you, but you soon got used to it.'

'I still like it now,' Anne admitted, 'though it's quite hard to find, these days.'

'How long was it before you began to make something out of Wallangarra?'

'Well, Kathryn, we'd been on the place for eighteen months and our herd was expanding quite nicely when Joe announced that he'd had enough of living hand to mouth and wanted to go back to Ballarat. He made it plain that he didn't include me and Anne in his plans, and he wanted me to give him enough money to make the journey, promising he'd pay me back once he'd struck lucky.'

She took a trembling breath. 'I no longer believed a word he said, for he'd promised too many things that he'd never followed through – and I was still wearing that tin wedding ring, which cut into my finger. I knew that, once he left with that money, I'd probably never see him again.'

'It strikes me he wasn't much of a loss,' said Anne.

'He was my husband and, at the time, I thought I couldn't survive without him,' she replied softly, her thoughts turning to the last day he'd spent on Wallangarra.

It was midsummer, the heat shimmering over the bleached yellow grass, the water in the creeks slowly disappearing to nothing. The gum trees wilted and even the birds were silent, but for the occasional solitary cawing crow.

'I can't stay here any longer,' shouted Joe. 'I know you've got money hidden away – and, as my wife, you have no right to keep it from me.'

'I earned it,' she shouted back, a sobbing Anne perched on her hip. 'And I have your daughter to feed.'

'But I've already promised to pay you back,' he snapped. 'And there's gold out there, you silly bitch – enough to make us both richer than we could ever imagine. But I need a stake to get supplies.'

'Then you'll have to go out and bloody earn it,' she shouted back, over Anne's crying and the bleating of the goats. 'You already owe me for buying the house and stock and just about everything else we've lived on these past months – and don't think you can take the horse and wagon with you, because I need them to get about.'

'I'll take what I bloody want,' he ranted, slamming his fist on the kitchen table. 'You've no right to anything. I'm your husband, and you'll flaming well do as you're told.'

She was cowering from his raised fist, holding a screaming Anne on her hip, when the door was flung open. 'Touch her and I'll flatten you, yer mongrel.'

Christy and Joe froze as the two men strode into the room. 'Are you all right, Christy? He hasn't been beating you, has he?'

She looked up into their faces in disbelief and wonder, and then her knees buckled when she realised who had come to rescue her.

Christy returned to the present. 'I was overjoyed to see them, but by nightfall they'd brought my whole world tumbling down,' she said quietly. 'You see, they opened my eyes to the true nature of the man I'd been living with, and had him arrested.'

*

Sydney

Harold was sitting in the bar with Hamish and James when the telephone went in the hall. They tensed as the landlord went to answer it, hoping it was Baker and that he'd found that affidavit.

'It's a John Smithson for you, Harry, mate,' said the landlord. 'Sounds a bit agitated.'

Harold rushed to the telephone, the two brothers close at his heels. 'Hello, John. What is it?'

'I've been at the hospital all day and just went into the office to check everything was all right. My assistant gave me two telegraphs which had been delivered that morning for my father.'

Harold rolled his eyes in exasperation. 'Yes, yes, get on with it, John.'

'One was from your mother-in-law; the other one came from her lawyer, Baker. They both read pretty much the same, so I went straight back out to our bank and retrieved the letter she'd left with them.'

'What does it say?'

'I don't know. I haven't opened it.'

'Then open it, man, for goodness' sake,' barked Hamish, who was listening in.

'It specifically says it's not to be opened until her death, and I'm not authorised to do such a thing,' he said stiffly.

'Oh, for pity's sake,' snapped Hamish, grabbing the receiver from Harold. 'Where are you?'

'At the office.'

'Stay there,' he barked. 'We'll be with you in less than five minutes.'

He slammed the receiver down and ran out into the rain without his hat and coat, James and Harold trailing in his wake.

For a big man, he could move very quickly, and they had to run to keep up with him.

Light flooded out into Rum Lane from the open door and they charged in to find John waiting for them in the hall. His protest swiftly died as he took one look at Hamish's expression and meekly handed over both telegraphs and the unopened letter.

James and Harold read the terse telegraph from Christy and the more informed one from Baker as Hamish tore open the large envelope and drew out a letter and a sheet of thick parchment. The three of them huddled together to read it.

Hamish let out a yell and punched the air, James laughed and stamped his feet, and Harold grabbed hold of John and danced him up and down the corridor. 'She's done it,' he shouted at the startled man. 'Christy has proved beyond doubt that Thomasina Brown has no case.'

John was clearly shaken by the celebrations and the amount of noise Hamish was making. 'May I read that?' he asked, almost fearfully.

Hamish handed over the affidavit that had saved them all from disaster. 'Don't take too long about it,' he rumbled. 'We're wasting good drinking time.'

21

Aboard the SS Southern Cross

The night was closing in and Christy was exhausted, but she knew she couldn't leave the rest of her story untold, so, after another short walk along the deck, she returned a little more refreshed, only to find that two more telegraphs had been delivered during her absence.

She opened the one from Baker, which told her he'd read her will and realised the affidavit must be stored with her final letter at Smithson's company's bank, and that he had immediately informed the man of its importance and ordered him to collect it.

With a great sigh of relief, she opened the one from Harold. He and her sons now had the affidavit and would be leaving for Melbourne first thing in the morning. He sent love to them all, and hoped that Baker could now bring the case to an immediate close.

She handed the telegraphs over and began to pace. 'But it won't be over, will it?' she muttered. 'Not unless Thomasina Brown can be silenced.'

'I'm sure Baker will make sure she signs something to keep it out of the press,' said Anne. 'He must surely be aware of what damage she could do if she isn't muzzled.'

Christy gave a wan smile. 'You make her sound like a feral dog, but I suspect she's just an ordinary woman who truly thought she had a claim on Wallangarra.'

She fell silent, thought about what she'd said and came to a decision. 'I shall be leaving the boat in Adelaide,' she said firmly.

'Whatever for?' gasped Anne.

'Because, if she's who I think she is, then we need to talk.' She held up her hand to silence the protest. 'I'm going to send a telegraph back to Baker to warn him of my change of plans, and tell him to arrange a private meeting with Mrs Brown.'

'I think that would be most unwise,' said Anne. 'You could be opening yourself up to all sorts of trouble by doing that.'

'I don't think so,' she replied, and left the room.

She returned some time later, having ordered drinks and dinner to be brought to her stateroom, and once they were alone again, she raised her glass. 'Here's to Harold, Baker and Charles. My knights in shining armour.'

Kathryn giggled. 'I can't imagine old Baker as a knight, but Daddy's always been my hero, so I'll gladly drink to him.'

Anne sipped from the glass and then set it aside. 'You'd better finish the story if you're going ashore the day after tomorrow, and I want to know who those visitors were and why Joe was arrested.'

Christy savoured the lovely chilled wine and helped herself to one of the delicious little canapés that the maid had brought on a silver platter. It was ridiculous, really, she thought, as she munched on the sliver of smoked salmon and crisp, salty biscuit, that she was sitting here in the lap of luxury whilst, all those years ago, she'd been stony broke and desperate for enough money to feed herself and Anne.

'I thought I'd seen Charles amongst the crowd at our wedding reception, but, when I couldn't find him, I decided I must have made a mistake. What I didn't know was that, during his time in Adelaide, he'd uncovered some very unsavoury truths about Joe, and he'd come back to Ballarat to warn me to steer clear of him. But he arrived after the wedding ceremony and realised it was too late to do anything.'

'So what made him go all the way out to Quilpie to find you?' asked Kathryn.

'And what took him so long? You'd been gone from Ballarat for almost two years by the time he turned up,' said Anne crossly.

'Charles was not a quick decision-maker,' she said with a wry smile, 'as you no doubt realise by the length of time he took to send me that first telegraph. He had irrefutable proof that Joe was a no-good scoundrel, but he'd heard through Myrtle – who I'd stayed in touch with by letter – that I was expecting a baby. Consequently, he really didn't know what to do.'

'And what was this proof?' asked Anne.

'He'd discovered that Joe was already married and had a family in Adelaide, who he'd abandoned to go in search of gold.'

There was a stunned silence in which Christy drank some more wine and ate another canapé. 'His wife was struggling to keep their four children fed and clothed, and dear, soft-hearted Charles managed to get her a job as a housekeeper for a vineyard owner up in the Barossa, where she would have free accommodation and proper schooling for her youngsters as part of her wages.'

'Well, that was very good of him,' said Anne, 'but I really don't see why he should do such a thing.'

'He has a charitable heart, Anne, which is one of life's greatest blessings.'

'You said there were two visitors to Wallangarra that night,' said Kathryn. 'Was the other one Jamie?'

Christy shook her head. 'Jamie had made a very good life for himself in Melbourne, with a rapidly growing joinery business, and, although we wrote to one another occasionally, we had little in common and didn't see one another again until I moved to Yarrabinda with your grandfather.'

She paused, remembering the little brother who'd always been so angry at the unfair hand he'd been dealt throughout his childhood, but who'd managed to learn to use all that energy in hard work and a ferocious ambition to do well.

'He married a girl from Aberdeen, whose family had emigrated, but sadly she died during childbirth, and he remained single for the rest of his life. He'd built up a successful business and was regarded as one of the finest furniture makers in Australia when he passed away from a massive heart attack on his journey back from Yarrabinda. He'd come to deliver the desk as a belated wedding present, and although it's a bit old and battered now, it's a precious family heirloom.'

'What happened to his fortune?' asked Anne. 'I suppose you inherited it?'

'Actually, no; he left it to found the James MacInnes College for Apprentice Carpenters, and I happen to know that it is now an integral part of the Melbourne university, and considered to be one of the most prestigious colleges in Victoria.'

She took another sip and set down the glass. 'But I digress. Whilst Charles was in the Barossa, he met someone who was working as an assistant vintner, and who one day hoped to own his own place.'

She smiled softly. 'He was a young man with a dream, who'd never given up searching for the girl he'd fallen in love with and who'd been lost to him through his aunt's interference. He was the son of Bavarian migrants who'd escaped the vicious religious persecution and pogroms of his homeland to begin a new life in the vineyards of Australia, only to be killed during a terrible storm at sea. He was taken in by his father's brother and sister-in-law, and his name was Peter Keller.'

Kathryn gasped. 'It was Granddad! But how extraordinary!'

'I like to think it was fate that he and Charles met, and that Peter and I were meant to be together. I thought he'd seen me as someone to have fun with during the long summer holiday, and he thought I'd forgotten about him when I didn't answer his letters. But his aunt had hidden both sets of letters and had written to him saying that I had left the hotel and she didn't know where I'd gone. She told me he was engaged, and shortly after that I received the letter about Finlay's accident and really did leave.'

'I suppose Charles told Daddy about the mess you were in, which was why they both turned up at Wallangarra,' said Anne. 'That must have been quite a shock.'

'It certainly was, but not nearly as shocking as discovering that my husband was already married, and that the ceremony I'd gone through with him was a complete sham,' she replied flatly.

She took a deep, wavering breath. 'You see, Joe and the preacher were in cahoots, and he'd paid the man thirty pieces of Judas silver to conduct the service and provide a fake marriage certificate.' She watched the bubbles rising in the champagne glass. 'I still have those coins as a reminder of how easily I was duped – as well as that tin wedding ring.'

She gave a sigh, wondering if Harold had found them during his search, and what he might have made of them. 'It was Charles who'd gone straight to the preacher after the ceremony, and, for once in his life, he'd seen red, and punched the man on the nose. Having got his confession and made him sign it, he relieved him of the hessian bag of coins, and the preacher left town, never to be seen in the area again.

'As for Joe . . .' She gave a regretful smile. 'Charles and Peter had been to the police station before they arrived at Wallangarra, and it wasn't long before three constables came to arrest him. Charles and Peter insisted that, before he was thrown into prison, he must be taken to the courthouse in Charleville to swear an affidavit before the judge.

'Joe realised the game was up, for he admitted he'd married me under false pretences and had paid no money for Wallangarra, despite the deeds being in both our names. As he wasn't my husband, he had no right to claim any interest in the property. That affidavit is what has saved us from going to that hearing.'

'I'm finding it very hard to accept that O'Driscoll was such a wicked man,' said Anne with a shudder. 'I hope to goodness I haven't inherited any of his awful traits.'

'Of course you haven't,' Christy said, taking her hand. 'You're my daughter, the granddaughter of Anne and Angus MacInnes, and have the blood of the Vikings running through you. Besides, he was never a real father – Peter took on that role the moment he saw you.'

'He was a wonderful father,' said Anne tearfully, 'and I miss him so much.'

'We all do,' said Christy, 'but I firmly believe he hasn't really left us, but is watching over us until we join him. Make him proud, Anne, because he loved you very much and wanted you to have a happy, fulfilled life.'

Anne nodded and dabbed her nose with her handkerchief. She turned her reddened eyes to her mother. 'I suppose Joe went to prison because he was a bigamist. Well, it served him right. He was an absolute rotter, and I hope he had a very long sentence.'

Christy nodded and thereby told the only lie in the whole rotten story. Anne had enough to contend with, and Christy would never reveal to anyone that a witness had come forward in Ballarat and had made a sworn statement that had sent Joe to the gallows for the attempted murder of Finlay and the theft of his gold and his mine – a story corroborated later by Finlay himself when he'd turned up at Wallangarra that one time.

'So who exactly is Thomasina Brown?' asked Anne.

'She's Joe's granddaughter, and, before you ask, I have no idea how she must have come across those original deeds to Wallangarra.'

'Oh, Mum,' sighed Anne, 'I'm so very sorry for all the hurt I've caused you since finding that birth certificate. I understand now why you didn't want to tell me the truth about what happened all those years ago, and I admire you for the courage and strength that has seen you through everything. Can you forgive me?'

Christy opened her arms and held her daughter, relieved that finally they had healed the breach and could now be close again.

Christy slept soundly for the first time in too many nights, her dreams happy ones of the years she and Peter had been together. Christy had been wary, at first, that she was about to jump into the fire straight from the frying pan, but, as Peter moved into one of the outbuildings and helped her bring Wallangarra up to its full potential, she'd come to realise that he would never play her false, and that his enduring love would be a firm basis for their future together.

They had married a year after Joe had been arrested, and soon Anne had two small brothers. The only cloud on their horizon had come when Hamish was about five, for a young man had come looking for Joe, claiming to be his son and therefore entitled to a share of the cattle station. Peter had put him straight on the matter and he'd left, never to be seen again, but Christy had always wondered if Hamish had overheard the conversation on that hot summer's day, as he'd been on the back veranda – but, as he'd made no mention of it, she had ceased to worry.

Once Wallangarra could be run by a trusted manager, they'd then fulfilled Peter's dream by buying Yarrabinda, where they'd lived until James was experienced enough to take over. It had been clear from a very early age that Hamish was a born cattleman, so they'd handed over the reins of Wallangarra to him and retired to the house Peter had had built for Christy in Bellerive, where Peter could fulfil his other desire to breed first-class bloodstock. He'd kept every promise he'd ever made to her, and they'd been blissfully happy.

As the *Southern Cross* slowly drew into the quay in Adelaide, two days later, Christy stood next to Anne and Kathryn on the deck, searching amongst the uplifted faces down on the dock for Baker.

'That's Harold,' Anne gasped, pointing excitedly. 'And there's Hamish and James – and Baker too. It looks like we've got a real welcoming committee.'

The moment the gangway had been lowered, Harold raced up to sweep Anne off her feet and kiss her until she was breathless. 'I'm sorry I've been such a fool,' he said softly. 'Can we start again?'

'Oh, yes,' she replied tremulously. 'I do love you, Harold. Really, I do, and I can't thank you enough for all you've done these past weeks.' They kissed deeply and finally drew Kathryn within their close embrace – a family again, with a bright future ahead of them, the shadows of the past erased.

Christy witnessed all this with a loving smile and left them to it, going down the gangway to be immediately swamped by her sons. They were all she needed now, for they'd proved beyond doubt that she'd been forgiven her youthful sins and was once more at the very heart of her family.

EPILOGUE

Christy had insisted she meet Thomasina Brown on her own, and, as she finally left the private room the Adelaide solicitors had set aside for them, she shook her hand and smiled. 'Your grandfather was taken back to Eureka to stand trial, and was buried somewhere outside the miners' graveyard near the old goldfields, should you want to visit him.'

'After hearing what you went through with him, and the reason he was hanged, I don't think I'll bother.'

Thomasina's eyes were as blue as Joe's, her hair as black, and she was just shy of twenty-five. She had found a copy of the original marriage certificate and a copy of the original deeds of Wallangarra amongst the paperwork that had been sent to her grandmother after he'd been executed. Her grandmother hadn't opened the envelope, wanting to put the past where it belonged, for she'd remarried and needed to forget about the man who'd treated her and her children so badly, and on her death it had become lost within a trunk of things long forgotten in an attic – which was where Thomasina had found it.

'I'm sorry I caused you such trouble, Mrs Keller, and it's very generous of you to set up a trust fund for our two boys' schooling,' Thomasina said earnestly.

'It was the least I could do,' said Christy. 'After all, your mother was my daughter's half-sister, and I feel partly responsible for what your grandfather did all those years ago. And thank you for signing all those papers. I know I can trust you never to tell anyone about what has passed between us, but you know what lawyers are like – they need everything down in black and white.'

Thomasina nodded. 'I doubt we'll meet again, but it's been a pleasure meeting you.' She turned and ran down the steps, and was soon lost in the crowds on the pavement.

Christy smiled warmly at her handsome sons, who'd been waiting patiently in the vast reception hall. She linked arms with them. 'Harold and everyone get off all right?'

James nodded. 'Happy as two newly-weds now they've got your stateroom to themselves for the journey to Melbourne. Anne was positively skittish, which was most disconcerting, but I think Kathryn's just relieved to have them together again so she can enjoy the short trip to Melbourne with her friends.'

Christy laughed. 'I propose we have a very expensive lunch, with lots of champagne, so you can tell me exactly what's been happening while I've been away. And then you, Hamish, can hire me a carriage so I can come and visit my grandchildren. It's time this family saw one another more often, and I thought it might be fun if I took the boys camping in the bush.'

She looked up at her huge, red-headed son and giggled at his dour expression. 'You can come too, silly,' she teased. 'I know how you love a night in the bush, listening to my stories – and I have a great many to tell that might clear a few things up for you.'

'I don't know if I can trust you not to get up to mischief, so I suppose I'd better tag along,' he said, his eyes twinkling. He kissed the side of her head, thereby knocking her hat askew. 'You're a bonzer lady, Ma, and I'm proud to be your son, but can we just have a quiet life from now on?'

Christy giggled and hugged her boys to her. 'I'll try to behave, but I make no promises – there's still a lot of adventure in me, and I enjoy keeping you all on your toes.'

If you enjoyed Spindrift, *why not try Tamara's other novels . . .*

Echoes From Afar

**A powerful story of love and loss from the beloved
internationally bestselling author, Tamara McKinley.**

*So this is Paris, she thought in awe. Spread out before her beneath a
clear blue sky, it was like a precious gift after the smog and filth of
London. No wonder it was called the city of love . . .*

After a spiteful rumour ruins her career in London, Annabelle
Blake must travel to Paris to start afresh. There she makes the
acquaintance of Etienne and Henri – one a poet, the other a
painter – both charming, talented and handsome. They spend
their days flirting and drinking with the city's *artistes* and
Bohemians, and soon Annabelle too is swept up in the exotic and
exhilarating world of 1930s' Paris. But as ever more young people
are drawn to the fight against Fascism in Spain, Annabelle must
wake from the dream and confront the reality of war.

A lifetime later, gifted artist Eugenie Ashton falls in love with
Paris the moment she sets foot outside the *Gare de Lyon*. Like
her mother Annabelle before her, the artistic delights of the
city are a bright new world to her: but Eugenie will soon find
that in its shadows are hidden the secrets of her family's past.

If you enjoyed Spindrift, *why not try Tamara's other novels . . .*

Savannah Winds

A secret inheritance. A love that would last a lifetime.

When Fleur receives word of a surprise inheritance
from an aunt she never knew, it couldn't come at a
more opportune moment. Her relationship is crumbling,
and she's caught in the middle of a serious family rift.

Consulting her aunt's long-lost diary, Fleur sets out on a
voyage of historical discovery up the coast and through
the Gulf Country, to the isolated cattle ranch Savannah
Winds. But unbeknownst to Fleur, what she uncovers there
could have devastating repercussions for her own life.

Set between the 1930s and the modern day,
Savannah Winds is an exploration of family ties,
bitter rivalry and the strength of enduring love.

If you enjoyed Spindrift, *why not try Tamara's other novels . . .*

Firestorm

A tale of hardship, hidden identities and our shared struggle to survive.

Becky Jackson's family has been managing the hospital in far-flung Morgan's Reach for three generations. When Becky's husband is tragically lost at war, she and her young son Danny must leave the city and return to her birthplace to start over. But for all its charm, Morgan's Reach is a divided community, where blood is thicker than water and grudges run deep. So when a mysterious stranger appears outside the town and Danny begins to act strangely, it is not only Becky's newfound stability that's threatened.

And what of the fact that there's not been a drop of rain in over three years? The risk of wildfire looms large and the hospital is already pushed to breaking point. A single spark could level the area in minutes – burning away everything for which the town has worked so hard; exposing the secrets they've fought to keep so close . . .

If you enjoyed Spindrift, *why not try Tamara's other novels . . .*

Ocean Child

1920. Having disobeyed the wishes of her aristocratic
family, Lulu Pearson, a young and talented Tasmanian
sculptress, finds herself alone in London in the wake
of the Great War. The future is looking bright until,
on the eve of her first exhibition, Lulu learns she has
inherited a racing colt called Ocean Child from a
mysterious benefactor, and she must return to
her homeland to claim him.

Baffled by the news, Lulu boards a ship to Tasmania
to uncover the truth behind the strange bequest, but it
seems a welcome return is more than she can hope for.
Unknown to Lulu, more than a few fortunes ride on
Ocean Child's success – it seems everyone from her
estranged mother to the stable hands has a part to play,
and an interest in keeping the family secrets buried.